BY THE SAME AUTHOR

Equinox

THE
INHERITANCE

A NOVEL BY

Allan Seager

1948

SIMON AND SCHUSTER

NEW YORK

To my wife,

Barbara

THE
INHERITANCE

~PART ONE~

· I ·

IT IS HERE in a bank, a private bank in a small town. Public business is finished for the day. At the front door and the west windows the blinds are pulled down against the heat. The bookkeepers have gone. The tellers have gone, the good one home and the one who is unreliable to a saloon table with a seidel of beer and the afternoon paper. An old man with a long, brown, gleaming, bearded face, Alexander the porter, born a slave, brushes a narrow dune of oiled sand patiently across the wooden floor, retaining still a slave's pathetic easy grace of movement. (Yes, this is several years ago. No marble yet, all pine flooring, and in the barrier for the cashier and tellers and for the paneling halfway up the walls, the best mahogany, nicked, dusty, solid.) Miss Pugh in black glazed sleeve-guards meekly types the late letters. Touched with a wand of sunlight, the old president, Ancil Bailey, waits in his office at the back, tilted backward in his chair, snoring with his hands laced on his belly. There in the cage is Todd Phelps, the cashier, hot, irritated, counting gold.

To keep from showing how cheap he felt, Phelps pretended he was doing a trick, scandalous but delightful to perform, and he wanted the others to watch him. It was unlikely that Miss Pugh and Alexander had ever in their lives seen the careless slick facility of a professional gambler, a croupier, for instance, handling money. At any other time Phelps would have known this also but the annoyance and the sweat running in trickles down his legs made him forget they could hardly admire an imitation when they had never seen the original.

He was imitating a gambler adroitly, lifting a stack of coins from its mahogany slot and smacking it down on the marble slab in front of him,

[1]

sweeping the stack flat to count them, ten as usual, always ten, every day ten, deftly sliding the coins into a stack again and popping it back into the slot, all done slapdash for them but for him with fatigue, distaste, and disrespect. He wanted them to look up and take him for a gambler standing in his cage, and if Old Man Bailey woke up, he wanted him to spot the gambler too. It would be a monstrous profanity.

When the gold was all counted, he took a pen with a stub point, checked the withdrawal slips, and entered the total in coarse black figures on the balance sheet for the day. From a drawer beneath the marble slab he took a soft buckskin bag a foot deep with brass knobs on the ends of the drawstring and dumped the money into it. He went out of the cashier's cage and crossed the floor kicking and scattering a little of Alexander's oiled sand because he had played to a nigger who hadn't even watched him, and in the doorway of Old Man Bailey's office he paused and turned around to enlist their gaze a last time, a plump comedian with still another laugh up his sleeve. When he was sure of their attention, he shook the buckskin bag vigorously up and down. The gold pieces clinked. Old Man Bailey opened his eyes. Phelps, knowing the eyes old and badly focused, winked, grinned boldly, and entered the office.

The Old Man spread his arms wide and gave a loud shouting yawn with a bark at the end of it. He shook his head, blinked his eyes, and then leaned forward in his swivel chair, awake now, the president. "What do you want, Todd?"

Phelps swung the bag of gold onto the desk. "Here it is," he said. He did not smile. He waited, leaning on the corner of the desk with his elbow. Every afternoon he brought the gold into the president's office to be counted. It made no difference to the Old Man that it had been counted a few minutes before—he wanted to do it. He insisted on it. The counting was a pleasure and a spell.

Old Man Bailey allowed no vice-president in his bank. He had begun to lend money when he was twenty-six years old in the back end of a country store, and when he had come into town, fierce, suspicious in his one black suit, he was his whole bank. He tried to do it all, and it was not until he was fifty that he had taken in any stockholders and then only two. They had been farm boys from out Dover, his own township, and while he knew them too well to trust them, through his knowledge he could surmise almost exactly the ways through which they would try to cheat him. (He did not blame them for trying. It was natural. You don't sell a good cow just because she kicks once in a while.)

That noontime, as Todd Phelps had been going up the street to dinner, the stockholders, Cam Reynolds and Howard Sell, had stopped him to talk. Although their faces were different they looked alike or maybe he had just come to think they did because they were always together, guarding their mutual interest, big men reared back to hold their paunches up, with Masonic fobs on their gold watch chains. Todd could tell at once they had carefully waylaid him in the open street because they wanted to speak about the bank. As if they were buying a horse, they talked about everything in the world for the first ten minutes, Reynolds talking, Sell agreeing, about crops, his health, his family, the fishing at the lakes, and when he slyly excused himself and started to walk on, Reynolds came to the point. "Uh-say, Todd," he began. The Old Man was failing. A stroke might take him any time. There ought to be somebody to take over the work. They had been thinking Todd was the man. Reynolds paused here and both the stockholders stared at Phelps, who punctually expressed a modest pleased surprise. It was time he was made a vice-president, no use to publish it round just now, but he could consider it a fact. They all shook hands solemnly and parted.

Todd knew why they didn't want it published round—they were still afraid of the Old Man. Together they owned forty-nine per cent of the stock and they had an option, in longhand, to buy a controlling interest when the Old Man died. Until the death, they did not dare promote Todd openly. He was to be a vice-president sub rosa and after the funeral leap into the presidency. Reynolds and Sell knew nothing about banking. They stood in the shade on the Four Corners and sat in leather chairs at the Elks and talked sagely about the state of the country. He gave himself two years after he became president to take the bank away from them.

He could not understand why the Old Man wanted to count the money himself, and now when he was confronting this trivial ceremony, Phelps was able for the first time that afternoon to realize that he was the successor and to allow his ambition to settle within the four walls of the bank and enclose the money in the safe, the mortgages and notes on file and the furniture, even the desk he leaned against. He hated the Old Man for being old and tenacious.

Ancil Bailey knew he was old. He knew it and was anxious. The first surprise two or three years before, the discovery that his arms and legs, the mysterious contents of his trunk (he had seen only the innards of animals) were turning weak and unreliable, had worn off. He had accepted the damaged face he saw in the mirror, the ludicrous yellow eyeballs, the sagging lower lids rimmed with the brightest scarlet, the little purple veins that marbled his nose and cheeks, and the way the cheeks themselves had gone limp and hung below the jawbone. He had seen these things in others. He could say that he had expected them to happen, even the patch of bristle he forgot to shave, right side, left side, somewhere—it was always there; the tobacco stains in the creases beside his mouth; the crumbs of stale forgotten food that stuck to the edge of his lower lip. Everyone knew old men were untidy. The skin that covered his head was not valuable, not worth much trouble. He was a bank president. He took a bath every Saturday night. He was old and there ought to be a privilege to it somehow.

What no one had told him, and his resentment that no one had done him the courtesy of warning him made him truculent unexpectedly, was that you forgot what house you were living in when you got up at night and you bumped into the wall sometimes hunting for the door to go out back although there was a flush toilet right there in the bathroom. And when you swung your feet out of bed in the morning, awake and ready for the day, stood up, awake and ready to step off, you staggered, clutching at the bedpost like a fool or wound up halfway across the room hugging the chest of drawers as if it were a fat lady, at last slumping down on the bed again to wait until the floor tilted back and the furniture stopped palpitating to try to walk out of the bedroom, merely to begin a simple thing like walking, timidly, again. He could not forgive the friends he had outlived for their failure to inform him that a buzzing came into your head. Someone ought to have told him that at least. It was nearly the worst thing that happened, like a fly inside your skull—couldn't have crawled up your nostrils, of course. It whirred and buzzed and you had to stop talking (blow your nose then) or stop walking (light a cigar, puff slowly, no one notices) or, worst, stop remembering whatever it was.

He settled his pince-nez at an angle and began to undo the knot in the drawstring that Phelps had maliciously tied tight so as to postpone his pleasure. He plucked, pulled, wet his fingers, and pulled again. At last the knot gave and he opened the mouth of the sack.

Delicately he lifted the coins out one at a time. He saw his hands tremble a little and there was a light metallic scraping against the desk as he drew a coin slowly the eight inches from the mouth of the sack and piled it on top of another.

The first coin was always twenty-five bushels of wheat (one acre cut with a cradle, a clear hot day, and a jug sweating in the June grass under the elm); two coins more were a calf (the first little Jersey he had raised, on a bottle with a linen teat, a clean buff hide, and big innocent black-rimmed eyes); another coin was the ton of hay (clover—you could smell

[4]

it at night in bed, the year they had the wonderful catch of hay all over, the beehives down the fence row); the next coin was four fleeces of wool (he had cut eighteen pounds of wool off a Merino buck with a pair of hand shears in a contest at the Fair. "And I'm proud to give this ribbon to the best young sheep-shearer in Hamilton County," the judge had said.) He was slow with the counting. He liked a tall stack. He put twenty gold pieces in each one but it was hard to keep the stack exactly true and he bent sideways squinting, breathing heavily, and pushed each coin into the perpendicular, just a little push with his forefinger, and, still bent, he peeped up at Phelps, angry and impatient behind the afternoon's *Telegraph*. He grinned. It tickled him to keep a Phelps waiting. He coughed to stifle a giggle and went on telling over the days of his youth, staring at each coin as if it were the lens of a stereopticon through which a beautiful landscape is to be admired.

Hopefully at first and now profoundly because it had become a useful habit, a secret virtue that he practiced and did not dare examine because it would make no sense if he did, he believed that every single coin was a talisman which could keep him safe, which drew on strengths (hidden, past) but near by and available if only because he could remember them instantly. Death was a skeleton like the one that hung from a hook in Doc Andrews' office, except that Death could move, chase you, and at last catch up with you. (The Republican Party was a large gray elephant like Barnum's Jumbo. The Democratic Party was a jackass, thin and poor. Christmas was Santa Claus.) Death would come, his bones clicking, the breeze whistling through the dark empty sockets of his eyes and the nose-holes in his skull and if he found a strong man with so much life and strength piled on the desk in front of him, he might go away and return later, a lot later. He might feel ashamed, afraid, or unwilling to carry off a man who had seen the county grow and built the bank so well and—this was silly, peculiar—he might run and jump on the hook in Doc Andrews' closet.

The Old Man sighed, finished, and pulled the drawstring of the buckskin sack tight. Death, the donkey, and the elephant, these were the dolls of manhood, kept but seldom played with until the lime got into your bones and the buzzing came in your head. Old folks were childish, all right.

"All done?" Phelps said. He kept the newspaper in front of him as if he were reading.

"Todd, how old are you, thirty-three, thirty-four?" the Old Man asked.

Mildly startled, Phelps glanced down over the edge of the paper. In the bank, the Old Man rarely spoke of anything but the bank's affairs. "Thirty-four," Phelps said.

"Life's ahead of you. College graduate, wife, son, good job. Your life's ahead of you."

"It's nearly five o'clock," Phelps said. He said this and he kept the paper in front of him to satisfy his own defiance, and defiance was a concession he allowed himself to make to his anger.

"But you're getting fleshy, Todd. Ain't so trim round the waist as you were when you were doing that boxing in college. You'll go pretty near two hundred just's you stand, won't you?"

"Mm," Phelps answered, wondering where this would lead.

"Won't you?" Then the Old Man shouted. "Put down the god-damn paper and answer me!"

If the paper had been heavy, Phelps would have dropped it. This was the time of day when the Old Man whined, not shouted. "What?" he said stupidly.

"You know they used to keep a hammer under the Gibson House bar to break the glasses your father drank out of, don't you?"

Phelps had known how people had hated his father, but he had never been told this one fact. He said nothing and looked at the Old Man's eyes.

"A little ball-peen hammer. Every glass. Don't think you don't have to answer when I talk to you just because your name's Phelps."

The Old Man would be warmed all the evening recalling the hatred and astonishment Phelps was then trying to conceal. He had hated the father strenuously but he did not hate Todd Phelps. He was lonely and afraid and he wanted someone to talk to. He had a tomcat named Amos, nine years old, made of Jersey milk and fishheads, and he often spoke his thoughts to it, but there is something contemptuous about a cat. He did not like the game of Hearts up at the Elks; there was no privacy there and what he had to say did not impress men of his own age, the other old bankers, the factory owners and storekeepers, because they suffered a like fear, and if he talked to them about it he would get to bragging how fearful he was and that would not console him. He needed someone younger because he might be awed and if it had to be a young Phelps, he would tell his tale to him even if he had to cuss him into listening. "I said you'd weigh around two hundred just as you stand. That right, Todd?" he finished softly, kindly.

"I weigh a hundred and ninety-seven. It's too fat. My uncle Paul was too fat and he died of heart trouble. My mother thinks she's going to get it and die. I'll die of heart trouble. That's what you were going to

[6]

say, isn't it?" He could feel a drop of sweat slide, stop, swell, and slide down the middle of his back. If he could have thought of an insult in return, something piercing, something final, he would have shouted it at the Old Man, waiting to see the veins stand out on his forehead, for the one to break inside his skull, but his imagination did not work. He did not know him well enough, and, although it did not occur to him, the truth was he had been an employee paying an employee's formal deference too long to change his role, yet the absurd prophecy of his own death issuing from this rank and withering head gave him a certain confidence.

"You're right. I was going to say something like that, Todd. And then I was going to work it round where I could talk about my own death."

"What for?" His pride would not let him show it by lowering the paper but he was beginning to take an interest in the conversation. Perhaps the Old Man was going to make him a vice-president openly with a desk of his own and a brass nameplate.

"Why don't I just die and be done with it, huh?"

He took a deep breath. "Yes. Why don't you?"

"Well, I'll tell you." He tipped back in his chair and locked his hands behind his head. "You know I don't sleep much nights any more. Don't need it somehow and I always get up early. I like to hear the birds chirp and sing. Though I've always said if you had a door hinge that squeaked the same as a bird does, you'd oil it." He looked down at the desk, hunched himself toward it, and took one spotted hand in the other. "Funny how you talk, ain't it? I'm not telling you the truth, Todd. I haven't even come close to it. Oh, I like the birds well enough but what I mean is, I'm not having such a hell of a good time I hate to quit. Now that we're talking sassy to one another, I'll tell you: I'm afraid."

Phelps blew through his nostrils contemptuously. "Afraid to leave the gold?"

"No. I can leave all that." The Old Man did not look up.

"No, you can't. That's all that keeps you. You'd cram it into the coffin if you could."

To tell the truth was all right. It would soothe him when he really got started doing it but not all the truth, the Old Man decided. The darling childish play with the gold, how it lay the symbol of his life, its magic summoner, that he would not tell. "I'm not so old that I can't tell what I ought to feel. I ought to feel like breaking your neck and, time was, I'd have jumped right across this desk and done it. But now—well, I

[7]

don't feel that way. I don't care who you are as long as you'll stand there and listen, as long as you're not a cat nor a tree nor a wall with rose-flowered wallpaper. As long as you're just a man with ears." He could not quite bring himself to plead. He looked away from Todd's plump face and began to sharpen one forefinger with the other gently. "Hair'll grow out of your ears when you're as old as I am, Todd, great sprouts and curlicues."

"Get through. It's time to go home," Phelps commanded.

"You'll stay, Todd. Oh, you'll stay. It's too much fun to insult the boss, ain't that a fact? Always a pleasure to lash right out." He cackled a little and stopped.

Would he be able to tell? Could he put words to these vague intense disquiets he called his fear? If he could not, he would lie awake that night with the moon on his bed, hearing the house creak and settle and a dog howl somewhere. "I'm an old man. I've seen a lot. I've worked hard and I hate to think that when I die all that I've seen dies right along with me."

"The gold dies and your house falls down, huh?" Todd asked scornfully.

As if he were talking to a friend, the Old Man apologized. "In the ordinary way, you don't talk about this kind of thing, Todd. It don't come easy. Everybody knows your business in a town like this, but this isn't business. This is what you keep secret from people." He looked up and smiled. "And you want to know what it is? I'm keeping you standing here by hook and by crook and now you've stood this long you probably expect it's something, oh, startling. And all it is, I lie awake nights because I don't want to die. You think I ought to die and make room for you because I've lived my life and married off my daughters. That's true but it don't make it any easier to let go. I lie awake nights and as soon as my feet get warm, I begin to sweat. Runs right off me. It's the fear."

"You'll have a stroke and you'll lie there with one side of your face pulled down and one eye open and you won't move for six months. Then you'll die in the night sometime."

The Old Man agreed placidly. "Yes. That's how it'll be. In all probability, you're right."

"Alone, with only hired help in the house."

"I don't expect to die in South Park at the band concert, Todd. You're alone long before you die anyhow. No, I've been all over that. I know they'll lay me out on a marble slab and cut out my liver and lights and squirt me full of formaldehyde. And they'll pretty me up for the funeral with rouge and powder like an old totty at the racetrack. And later, sure enough, the worms will eat me all up. I wish you'd just listen, Todd. None of this frightens me."

Phelps picked up the afternoon paper and began to look through it.

The Old Man continued more quietly, as if he were relieved that he could speak without interruption now in a sort of privacy. Talking to a man with something in front of his face resembled something and as he spoke he tried to remember what it was. "As I say, I've seen it all change, this town and the county. I remember seeing the smoke standing up straight from the piles of walnut logs burning, whole trees burnt to get rid of them, just to get the land cleared. Walnut's worth fifteen, twenty dollars a thousand now." It was like a Catholic going to Father Ryan to confess. He had never thought of it before but it was not a bad idea. It made it easy to talk.

"Quite a while ago a fellow came and took a picture, one of the first photographs they ever took round here, and it shows Henry Hart and I guess Channing Whitney and some other fellows standing with them in the snow, and there are four dead deer they shot, lying on the ground in front of them. It was taken right up there on the corner where the post office stands now. There used to be deer in the woods then. Play hell finding any deer now."

He was about to begin again but it was hard to select anything from the pageantry of his life that slid past the eye of memory as quick as the films at the nickel show. It was all of it important and he could not tell it all. Phelps still kept the paper in front of his face. The old man began again, muttering softly.

"This is what I am afraid of. This is what I don't know and what nobody can tell me, Father Ryan, Dean Channer, or any of them. What becomes of all the changes I've seen? Where will it be kept? The post office stands where the deer lay spread out in front of the camera, but I can remember beech trees on that lot before they were cut down to make the open space for the deer to lie on and I can remember the pint of bourbon and the copy of the *Telegraph* they put in the cornerstone of the post office when it was building, but in my head the beech trees, the dead deer, the cornerstone, and the building are all there at once and there is something valuable in this. What becomes of it? Other old men remember, too, but not what I remember, not exactly. And when I die, all of this will be gone and only the post office will be left."

He looked up shyly at the newspaper spread wide, and continued to speak rapidly without emphasis like a man talking in his sleep. "And while I like to talk as if I were a living document of the past and worth something to this town because of it, with a kind of sneaky hope that the town might do something to preserve me alive in gratitude although I am still in my right mind and know very well that the town, singly or all together, could not hold up my death one minute, I know that what I am actually afraid of is this: what becomes of *me?* I am too old for religion now and I don't want to take it up because the clergy around here always seemed like pretty poor fish, although the one before Father Ryan did take complimentary tickets to the Sunday ball games and sat in his seat and hollered and ate peanuts, yet in the main I didn't like them and even if I would be willing to admit, in fact, I am quite willing to admit they know something that might help me now, I am too set in my ways to go to any one of them and ask. So I ask the foot of the bed, that damn wallpaper with the rose figure, and the thunder-mug Mrs. Vale sets out beside my shoes. I do my asking at night. You would not understand this because you are young and you sleep nights. You grab at your wife a couple of times and then you lie on your back and make a clatter, asking nothing until breakfast. But the night is a very peculiar time and conducive to thought and private conversation with yourself." He sighed. "I must stop talking *to* you instead of *before* you and see whether by asking my question once more I can make it any easier to accept what I already know is the answer."

Phelps rustled the newspaper. He had heard everything. He said, "I see Bryan has resigned from the Cabinet."

"And my question is this: What becomes of me? Where do I go when they have laid Ancil Bailey in Oakwood Cemetery? What happens? The answer is, of course, 'Nothing. Nowhere.' I feel as if I had been promised something and my fear is really anger, I suppose. I say, 'Is this all?' You'd laugh to hear me talking to myself at night. 'Is this all?' I say and I know I'll hear nothing for an answer. Then I begin to sweat to think that I, the real me, will be shut up in the coffin, because I am satisfied, I guess, that this is what will happen. But, as I say, I feel as if I had been promised something more."

The Old Man looked up at the newspaper Phelps was holding. He got to his feet and raised his voice a little, not much. "And now, God-damn you for a fat, hairy, lying son-of-a-bitch. Your mother had her feet over the dash of every buggy in the county, in every horse barn of every little country church every night except Sunday and Thursday prayer meeting. And God-damn you again for a sneaking, snaggle-toothed, stuck-up son-of-a-dog. Your father cheated every man he ever met, dirty little sand-in-the-sugar cheating, and he kept a smooth face because he thought nobody knew it. And never mind your sire and dam, God-damn you to hell for what you are, for being unkind to a lonely old man who only wanted a minute of your time."

Phelps lowered the paper a little and saw the Old Man clutch the edge of the desk to keep from staggering. The tears ran down into his stained mustache and he sniffed and snatched at them with one hand while he clung to the desk with the other.

"You go on like that, you'll die right here in the office," Phelps said.

"Go. Go on. Get out," the Old Man gasped. He sat down abruptly to wait until his head stopped buzzing. Out in the bank he heard Phelps shooting the bolts of the big safe, then a rattle of wooden hangers as Phelps hung up his alpaca coat, the bang of his heels across the floor of the bank, the door open and shut, and the diminishing sound of his heels on the sidewalk outside. The buzzing stopped. Only a few flies buzzed in the late sunlight. It was very hot. When he had rested a few minutes more, he would get up and go home. He could take a jug of ice water and a bottle of bourbon out into the grape arbor behind his house and sit there in an armchair until the housekeeper called him to supper. He would drink a little whisky and stroke Amos, the cat. The whisky would hurt him but he needed it.

Phelps was walking up the main street. He ignored the people, even the bank's clients, who waved at him from buggies and carriages. He forgot to stop at the cigar store for his copy of the *Telegraph* and his evening cigars. He felt in his knees a curious tingling and his whole body seemed light. He was very angry.

· II ·

THE STILL MAPLE TREES around him faded, and by drawing his eyelids together until they were nearly shut Walter Phelps contrived to make the shade cast by the trees brighten, the grass grow tinged with light and roll out before him in a wide plain. The stone, one of a dozen chunks of white-washed granite set to mark the boundary of his lawn, he stared at, humming, until he changed it into an image of a castle, towers, crenelations, moat, uplifted drawbridge, with the red, white, and black German pennons fluttering stiffly in the breeze they needed and he from his imagination had supplied.

[11]

Within the castle was, of course, the German Kaiser, his mustache up-lifted, his left breast crusted with decorations. On his head he wore a shining brass helmet with an eagle on top of it instead of a spike such as the common soldiers wore. Rolled tightly against the battlements (from a drawing in *Leslie's Weekly*) a 42-centimeter siege gun stood. Its muzzle pointed upward, nearly perpendicular. The tires of its two huge wheels had foot-long pads, perhaps of cork, tied to them to keep it from sinking down into marshy ground. In a neat semicircle around the gun, the gun-ners stood tense and erect, ready for the siege to begin. The Kaiser bent over a lever like the gear-shift lever on Father's automobile. He shoved the lever forward.

The Kaiser's gun did not fire. Slowly, as if they floated in water, the maple trees returned, green, to his vision. The castle vanished; the white-washed stone was a stone again, a boundary marker with ants crawling under it. It was hard to play alone in the heat and to carry the siege in his mind, the plain, the castle, the Kaiser and his soldiers, was too great an effort. He wanted someone real to play the Kaiser, someone alive who could suffer and be killed.

A black ant ran up a blade of grass six inches from his eyes. A little sun-light made it glitter like a jewel, the jet at his grandmother's throat. The ant was stopped at the tip of the grass blade. Delicately he pushed it off with a twig. The ant, confused, looked about for an escape somewhere among the litter of cut dead grass that lay about the roots of the green. He took the twig in a firmer grip and dug a little hole in the earth, an inch across, half an inch deep. A foot away he found the ant intelligently in flight through the jungle of dead grass, climbing over a stiff blade, pausing as if to look, skirting the shoulder of a small pebble, then run-ning briskly through a tiny open glade. He offered the tip of the twig. The ant examined it from both sides, made its mysterious decision, and climbed onto the twig. He moved the twig over the hole he had dug and shook the ant off into it. The ant ran around and around trying to get out but, each time it reached the edge of the pit, he pushed it gently down again. He was waiting, in the divine and terrible freedom of childhood, for something to occur to him to do with the ant.

The ant could be Eddie. Eddie had offended him by not appearing an hour ago to play. It was no excuse that Eddie's mother forced him to lie down on a bed with a pink silk counterpane and sleep for several hours each afternoon, and immediately Eddie was cramped inside this black enameled shell, given six legs, two pincers for a mouth, and set to hurry-ing in a circle. With the twig he flipped Eddie on his back at the bottom of the little pit. He could imagine Eddie's fury, heightened, because, as an ant, he had no way of expressing it. Wriggling furiously on his smooth back, reaching with each of his six legs for a purchase on one of the grains of earth, Eddie struggled. One spit would drown him. He spat, carefully aligning his head so that the drop would fall exactly on the ant. Through a large bubble in the drop of spittle he could see the ant's legs working desperately. He brushed some of the wetness away with the twig and pushed the ant to dry ground. He began to blow gently on it. He had forgotten Eddie. He had nothing against the ant, and since he had spent several minutes chasing it, digging the little hole for it, and teasing it as a character in one of his numberless dramas, he had become vaguely fond of it, if only because it had held his attention so long. He knelt on the ground blowing softly and the ant cleaned itself.

A screen door slammed. He looked up. Eddie, awake, was crossing the side porch of the house next door. His mother was beside him. She pressed both her hands lovingly on the part in his wet blond hair and let him go at last. Eddie did not hurry. He was dressed in a starched Russian blouse of blue twill buttoned up the side, a patent leather belt, long black stockings, and black shiny sandals. His face was clean but puffy with sleep. Eddie came down the steps and crossed the lawn slowly although he knew he was waited for.

He watched Eddie approach. He stood up with his hands on his hips and his feet apart, waiting silently for the sweat drying on his face and neck and the dirt on his hands to cow the other boy.

"My mother gave me a dime," Eddie began.

He was not to be bought off even if it was a hot day and a dime would mean an ice-cream cone apiece or a bottle of pop. "You've got to play the Kaiser."

"I want to play Lee. He's an American. You be Grant," Eddie said.

"That stone there is your castle and you're in it waiting for me to siege it," he said calmly, pointing to the stone.

"I don't want to be a German."

"You *are* a German so you might's well play one," he said.

"I am not."

"Your grandfather was a German. You said so yourself."

"He was a German. He was born in Berlin. But I'm not," Eddie said.

"Yes, you are."

Eddie knelt down, pushed him away from the little cannon coolly, and began to snap the plunger. "If I'm a German, you can't play with me. Your folks won't let you. So you better let me be an American."

"All right. There is your castle and I am the King of England coming with my army."

Eddie went over to the white stone and sat down behind it. He lifted his blouse and took from the elastic bellyband of his short trousers a sling-shot with a leather cradle. He looked around busily for pebbles in the grass.

"I've got an eighteen-pounder gun and a million soldiers with rifles. And seven Dukes," he added. "You haven't got anything but the castle and a god-damn old forty-two-centimeter siege gun."

Eddie stopped hunting in the lawn and the driveway for stones for his sling. He stood up. "Cut that out."

"Cut what out?" he asked needlessly.

"Swearing."

"What does she listen for all the time?" He looked up toward the windows of Eddie's house. There was a bank of three windows for the dining room and a single one for the parlor. The cream-colored shades were drawn exactly halfway down, like eyelids, and behind the screens, behind the stiff lace curtains, Eddie's mother sat, watching them at play. He resented her.

Eddie had pulled up the front of his blouse again and taken out a short pencil. He was looking for something to write on. At last he came across the grass, sat down, and wrote on the brass barrel of the little cannon. The metal did not take the writing clearly but when Eddie turned the cannon around so he could see, the words JESUS CHRIST were printed faintly on the barrel. "I don't care, see? It's her," Eddie said.

"Do you like her?" he asked.

Eddie moistened the eraser on his pencil with the end of his tongue and rubbed out the words on the cannon. "Once in a while. At night mostly is when I like her."

Walter jumped up and shouted in a military voice, "Get back!"

Eddie, recognizing that the game had begun, ran to fling himself behind the stone and heap up his pebbles, ready to shoot.

He lay prone with his cheek pressed against the trail and the plunger of his cannon, sighting along the barrel with one eye shut as if he were aiming. Hopefully he tried to summon the castle, to cover Eddie's neat hair with the magnificent imperial helmet, and to expand the tame little lawn into the rolling terrain of his private battlefield, but it did not work. A stealthy common sense prevented the unfolding of the vision. He knew that he and Eddie were two little boys playing in the yard between their houses in Athens, Michigan, U.S.A., Western Hemisphere, The World,

[14]

Space, as he had written in the front of his geography book. It was always the preparation for the play that was delightful. Then his plans were sumptuous; he could imagine anything. Dukes, castles, elephants, schooners, even airplanes (a man sitting between two ironing boards with the wheel of a baby buggy in his hands, Lincoln Beachey flying over the Fair Grounds) seemed ready for his command with a magical, frivolous ease, but the moment the voyage or battle should begin, his eye was forced to recognize the schooner as an ugly rowboat with a leak in it, a castle as a painted stone, and his Imperial Germanic Majesty as Eddie Burcham. Nothing ever happened as it should.

"I just had three regiments of Prussian Guards out scouting," Eddie called, "and as quick as they saw you they ran back to the castle. Now they're going over that ditch . . ."

"Moat," he called back automatically.

"And now they're crowding into the castle."

"Uh-huh," he said dully.

"Ready to start?"

"Shoot any time you want to." With disgust he watched Eddie select a pebble, place it in the leather cradle of his slingshot, and stretch the rubber bands to aim.

The pebble whistled past his ear. He picked up one of the black wooden cannon balls, let it roll lackadaisically into the muzzle, and released the spring plunger without even taking aim. The ball made a high arc and fell in the grass in front of the stone.

"Too short. Tip it up higher," Eddie called. He looked up over the stone with candid interest.

He loaded, elevated the muzzle, and fired carelessly again.

"That's all right now. You got the range. It lit right beside me."

He saw the Y of the slingshot rise slowly over the stone, and just as he heard the flat twang of the rubber bands, a pebble hit him hard in the forehead. He jumped up and ran across the lawn to the stone. He stopped. The game was over.

Eddie was sitting there giggling, looking up at him. "That's going to make an awful welt on your head. They'll ask you where you got that one."

His knees tingled and his heart felt swollen in his chest. Reluctantly he doubled up his fists. His father had told him there were occasions when he should fight, moments when everything looked the same as it had an instant before except for some word that had been said, some blow given, and then you must double up your fists, keeping the left one out in front, and attack the sayer or the striker to prove you had guts even though you resented nothing and what you wished most of all was to forget what had happened. Eddie was not a good shot with a slingshot. It was luck as much as anything that Eddie had hit him at all. He knew Eddie would not apologize, and if they fought, no matter who won, neither would speak to the other for a month and he would have no one to play with and the summer was short. Yet in his mind he could see a picture of his father, squatting before him, punching him softly with the boxing gloves, urging him to keep his left foot flat and his right heel lifted, pushing him backward laughing, and the gloves had a sour dead smell. "Stand up," he said hoarsely.

Eddie stopped smiling and a serious questioning look came over his face. He got to his feet, dangling the slingshot from one finger. "Yeah, what?"

"You want to fight?"

"Do *you* want to?"

He got down on his hands and knees and hunted in the grass until he found a twig. Taking a stand in front of Eddie, feeling as lonely and helpless as he had felt waking at night, he put the twig on his shoulder. "Knock it off."

Eddie brushed it off lightly.

The ceremony had committed him. Although he did not want to fight, his body fell into the stance with a child's limber ease, and as Eddie's arm was still descending from brushing the twig off his shoulder, he saw a patch of the Russian blouse unguarded, and he poked it carefully with a neat miniature straight left. Eddie staggered back. He followed and pushed his left lightly, so as not to hurt much, into Eddie's face. Two or three more times with the left and he would cross the right, as Father had shown him. That was always fun.

Suddenly Eddie, leaning backward, kicked out at him. His shin seemed to explode in pain like a firecracker. He dropped his arms and grabbed his leg and hopped around, sucking in his breath loudly. Eddie waited solemnly with his fists clenched.

"No fair," he said, trying his foot on the ground and taking a step or two.

"You started it. Take what you get," Eddie said grimly.

This was serious now. Limping a little, he approached Eddie, feet apart, his left stuck out. Eddie was the one who kicked, not the one he played with, and he meant to kill him with his fists. He had never watched anything being killed. Ants and flies did not count. Birds, dogs, and a brindle cat he had found dead. Killing was an act he had heard people speak of. It was severe, even terrible, and it ended with the bloat and stiffness he had hesitatingly touched in the cat, but how it was done he did not know, yet violence was part of it. He threw out his left fist hard and hit Eddie on the shoulder.

He fought steadily and expertly, watching out for Eddie's kicks, rushes, and round arm swings that were all he knew of fighting. Once Eddie caught him by the shirt and wrestled him to the ground. They rolled over into a bed of peonies. He felt Eddie's teeth coming together on his arm, and goaded by the pain, he jerked himself out from under and got up, waiting. Eddie, heaving great sobbing breaths out of his lungs, rested on one knee a moment, got up, and lunged at him again. He stepped aside nicely and crossed his right to Eddie's nose. Eddie was blinded with the pain and he stood swaying helplessly with ribbons of blood flowing from each nostril. He squealed "Oo-oo-oo" again and again. Coldly he tipped Eddie up until he was standing erect and held him there with his left hand. He hit him once on the chin with his right and Eddie staggered foolishly around shaking his head and going "Oo-oo-oo." Little drops of blood spattered his blouse and fell in the grass.

Now that Eddie was bleeding, he did not want to hit him again. He felt sorry for him and he thought he ought at least to wipe the blood off Eddie's face before they went on. He stood relaxed and ready, wondering if the next blow would kill Eddie or if it might take two or three more.

All at once he realized that Eddie's mother was screaming at them from the side porch. She was not dressed. She was wearing a gray satin robe although it was only five o'clock in the afternoon and she screamed steadily as if she were hurt.

While he was looking at her, Eddie hit him in the chest. Without thinking, he moved back and began to fight again. They clinched and tottered back and forth across the grass in the heat.

"Boys, boys!"

He was jerked backward and held by his shoulder. He looked up through the sweat and tears and he saw above him a red face with a mustache, smiling, and the heavy dark mass of torso in a blue summer suit, Eddie's father.

"You mustn't fight. No, you mustn't fight," Mr. Burcham said. Then he laughed. "It's too hot to fight." The screams from the porch had stopped but Eddie's mother kept pulling her handkerchief through one hand over and over, walking back and forth nervously. Eddie blew the breath through his nose in little snorts and licked the blood from his upper

[17]

lip. "It's all right, Clara," Mr. Burcham called in a rich, warm, silly voice. "They're not hurt. Just a scuffle."

Immediately, as if a signal had been given, the faces of the two boys relaxed into vacant masks to disguise themselves as children. The man, patting now, not clutching, stood towering between them giving a little lecture on genteel behavior—he was a lawyer—in bland jocular condescending phrases as if they were idiots, and they looked the same hopeless look at each other, unhearing. The man, seeing it, took it for shame, and fatuously believing they were sorry for what they had done, he started for the porch calling after him for Edward to follow.

Eddie glanced over his shoulder to make sure his father did not see him and swung his fist once more. Stiffly they began to fight again. A hoarse shriek from the porch warned Mr. Burcham. He turned, the affronted peacemaker, and walked toward them, heavy and angry. He jerked them apart again, cuffed Eddie's head, and sent him crying to the house. To the other boy, he said sternly, "You ought to be punished."

He could hear Eddie squalling and his mother twittering over him. In front of him Mr. Burcham soared like a steeple, telling him he ought to be punished. He was tongue-tied, like all children in trouble with adults. All he could feel was hatred, after the jawing and the patting, for Eddie's old man. He struck out, and to Burcham he seemed like a horrible toy as he led his small left fist past Burcham's side coat pocket in a deliberate feint and, almost leaving his feet, crossed his right to Burcham's paunch. The man grunted, shocked, hurt.

Then, gasping, he leaned over and slapped the boy.

"My father can lick you!" the boy shouted. His father, that is, the smooth face with the bumpy nose; the thick arms with the fur on them; the smell of tobacco and Ed Pinaud's Lilac Vegetal in the bathroom; and the armpit smell in bed on stormy nights when he was afraid of the lightning; the stubby fingers sliding the black hook into the pinkish worm; the noise of the furnace-shaking in winter and the scrape of the shovel against the cellar floor; the shotgun bang! and the poor bleeding quail, still and shining; the voice, rougher than other people's; and face, hands, smells, and sounds always *there* like the house, the newel post on the stairway, or the sky, blue or dark, protecting him. His father, then, Mr. Todd Phelps, could lick Mr. John Burcham.

"Sure he can."

And, turning at the voice, with a chill running down his back, he saw it was his father, home from work, come up in silence behind them on the grass.

And then it happened as he always remembered it, as if awe were a painted frame enclosing for the rest of his life the cloud of green trees with the black trunks hanging down from them, the smooth floor of sunlit grass, the blunt red-brick corner of the house next door with its clean-washed windows giving back the green again, the row of white rocks, and filling his whole eye from top lid to bottom, the huge shapes of the men blotting out treetops, bigger than life, there he saw his father lead his left hand over Burcham's shoulder, and, stepping in, hit him a terrible crack on the jaw. For a flash, Burcham hung limp on the end of his father's fist like washing on a line. Then he fell forward on his face, drew his leg up, straightened, and was quiet.

He could hardly breathe. His father had hit Eddie Burcham's father in the jaw and knocked him out (at his own feet, twitching) right in the side yard of his house. He looked around, expecting change—the trees to sway, his house to crack open, or to have it all put back unhappened as it was a moment before. When he saw Mr. Burcham raise his head with blood running out of his mouth, he ran, sobbing, after his father. And he noticed even through his tears that his father's coat was split a foot down the back.

· III ·

SHE HAD BEEN RESTING on the chaise longue when it happened. "Resting" was what the family called it because they believed that old people wanted rest instead of merely needing it, and by urging it on her day by day they had almost persuaded her that she liked these three hushed hours in her bedroom, and for the past eight years every afternoon at two o'clock she had sat down on this curious chair-bed (there were only two others in the town) all gilt and satin upholstery, and propped herself erect on round satin pillows without putting on a kimono, without removing her shoes, fully dressed in her black dress, and had tensely shut her eyes and waited for rest to come, dutifully, obediently subscribing to the family's hints that she was old, tired, fatigued, and there she would sit, twenty minutes, half an hour, with vivid enjoyment of this wasted time, this afternoon she could afford to waste, admiring behind the screen of her lowered eyelids this splendid, uncomfortable chair? bed? this new French device that held her up. A half hour was all she could stand. She began to fidget, to jerk her legs over the side, stand, and rush to the closet to count the row of black dresses on padded hangers or lift up one of her ten pairs of black shoes to see if the soles needed tapping or the heels were run over or to pry on her knees in the corners of the closet looking to see if one of the twenty moth balls had been rolled away by mice.

After these preliminary excursions, she sat down at her dressing table, never so much as glancing in the triple mirror. She would open the two japanned black tin boxes, each a foot long, with russet-colored pears painted on the lids, that stood before the mirror on the table-top incongruously and assertively occupying the space where another woman would have kept her cosmetics. The boxes were crammed with mementos and keepsakes, the symbols of what she believed were the gigantic events of her past. She would pick them out shrewdly and arrange them, a bone hairpin, a visiting card, a lump of beeswax, the withered stamen of a rose, aware that they were small and sorry in themselves yet she treasured them because, in a row, they made a calendar. Once the scheme for any given time was set, she would begin to rehearse, as one enacts his dreams in sleep with murmurs and sudden twitchings of the legs and arms, the scenes of passion and splendor that she owned, bobbing her head, flipping out her thin hands in adumbrated gestures, beginning to accuse or answer in a firm loud voice and letting the rest trail off unfinished in a mumble, sometimes staring straight ahead into the glass without seeing the performance. Or she would return again to the chaise longue dimly acknowledging this expensive gilt chair (or bed) a proper setting for the grandeur she had summoned by the juxtaposition of a yellowed newspaper clipping, a dry peach pit, and a wrought-iron nail.

Although her memory was extraordinary, she could not make it reach far enough to suit her. With some exasperation she had tried again and again to recall the earliest events of her life on the Vermont farm they had abandoned to come here, but nothing, disobediently, appeared. Her parents had told her that one Fourth of July she had been dandled and patted on the head by three old men who had fought the Hessians near Bennington. One of these old men had served under Washington. She yearned to remember him. It had taken place under an elm tree, before they made the speeches and shot off the cannon, an old, old man, a Mr. Breakenridge. Sometimes she made him clean-shaven; sometimes with a fringe of limp yellowish-white whiskers growing out of his neck around his jaw from ear to ear the way they wore them in those days, with his head bent toward her and his palm behind his ear. He had gone south after Ticonderoga and he had cheered the surrender at Yorktown. It was a link between her and The Father of Our Country. She had told of it hundreds of times, always employing the bearded Mr. Breakenridge with a wealth of false detail, but she could not actually remember it and consequently she tended to disparage General Washington.

Usually she suppressed the journey across York State. It was nothing to have ridden in a train, even one that burned wood, and she deplored what seemed to her the bad taste of her parents when they had taken a tame steamboat across Lake Erie. She would have preferred to have been brought by wagon around the lake shore where they might have suffered, seen bears, or slept in a hollow log like her uncle.

The beginning of her life for her—anything earlier was cheating and she knew it—the first recollection, the one with the longest tether, took place on the log stoop of an unpainted frame house that stood on the present site of the State Savings Bank. She was a little girl with a bucketful of garbage. Two Indians had come to get it. Once she had told this with some complacency because few people could remember any Indians in the county, and her usual listener, younger, silly (for it was silly, actually, to think those Indians exciting), seated in the gloom of the pink drawing room downstairs or on the porch that commanded, across the green lawn, a view of the main street lined with maples and further away the "paved district" with its tame and solid stores, would look at her as if she herself were exciting, as if she contained somehow both danger and adventure, and this was the best feeling of her life, to be looked at this way.

When she saw her grandson come out to play on the lawn beneath her window, the past stopped immediately as if a clock had struck. She got up off the chaise longue abruptly, cleared the table top, dumped her little baubles into the tin box, and shut the lid down with a snap. She pulled the chaise longue closer to the window, lay down upon it, and resting one elbow on the padded arm and her chin in her hand, in an attitude as graceful as a young girl's, she looked down intently upon the boy. He did not think her Indians so wonderful. He had been fed on pictures of the more flamboyant Sioux and Crows who painted their faces and wore, correctly, as she was made to feel, huge blowing war-bonnets, while her own savages were dirty shambling creatures only one of whom even wore mocassins. Telling herself that she did not, could not, she resented a little his unimpressionable calm.

Already in her box was the clipping from the *Telegraph* announcing his birth, and a lock of his baby hair, dull-red, tied with a narrow blue ribbon. She did not like him much, or rather, it never occurred to her to determine whether she liked, loved, or tolerated him. He was her grandson. Her blood was in him. He concerned her. Even though he was still a little boy,

[21]

he might do something rare, exciting, or magnificent and it behooved her to watch him lest that moment go by unsavored. Her whole family had remarked, one time or another, her avid bright black eyes watching them and an upstate cousin had once asked her if she had poor eyesight. No one understood what she was up to, and her grandson least of all. It puzzled him to look up on a wet day indoors when he was playing on the floor or looking at war pictures and find her standing silently in the doorway watching him. Although it happened that she never treated him unkindly, he avoided her. The cousin had said, "She looks at you as if you were making counterfeit money." But she did not know how she looked and she would not have cared if they had told her.

Ancil Bailey had not slandered her to her son. He had only told the truth nastily. As a young woman she had had many lovers. She had never denied it and Henry Phelps had known it when he married her. It was only a natural desire for privacy that had led them into the horse sheds of country churches on week-nights or down side roads to woodlots on summer nights, the livery horse tethered to an iron weight roped to his bridle cropping the grass, the tree-toads singing, and the sky overhead full of white stars. It had all been very beautiful, then and to remember, and sometimes, mornings in the bank, a rich old farmer in felt boots, overalls, and a dogskin coat would approach her to say, "How ye gittin' on, Em?" and she would peer at him a moment to seize for recognition the vestiges of the look that had attracted her so long ago, and she would grasp his hand and hold it while they talked, warm, animated, and still grateful.

Her grandson digs in the grass. (This is nothing.) The other boy comes. (Nothing added to nothing.) The game ends. They begin to fight. (And now, with the action, her lips part and she leans forward a little.) Then comes the man next door, the lawyer Burcham. (She begins to drum silently on her cheek with her fingers, and her other hand tweaks and smooths the folds of her skirt blindly.) Her grandson, the petty boxer, neatly hits Mr. Burcham. (She giggles once like a cough. An irritable scowl creases her forehead. Will this be all? It is not enough. If she could only call down and urge these three miniatures on toward something brighter, fiercer, or reach them with a finger and push them clashing together. There is more in this intrinsically. It cannot die now.) She sees her son, Todd, hurry across the lawn. He hits Burcham; Burcham falls. (With her hands clenched, she gives a long gasping sigh of pleasure. She relaxes then, slouched upright on the chaise longue, her feet making a V on the cushions like a doll's feet.) She is grateful because the scene played itself out properly for once, and she does not even watch the bleeding

Burcham drag one foot to a purchase, then the other, lurch up standing, and stagger into his house.

Suddenly she begins to think. She gets up and hurries across the room, her hand outstretched for the doorknob long before she reaches it. She jerks the door open, grazing her shoulder against it, stops in the dark hall at the top of the staircase, waiting for the outdoor light to go out of her eyes so she can see the steps, and, as the angles of the red carpet begin to be visible, she starts recklessly going down, bent at the waist, both hands holding up her skirt a little.

She knows where to find her son. Two years after Henry Phelps had died, after the will had been through probate and the money was then his, Todd had ordered the second pantry off the kitchen torn out and in its place he had installed a butcher's icebox as big as the one in Pete Spielman's market downtown. The shelves ran around three walls. On the top shelf were hundreds of bottles of beer, local, Milwaukee and St. Louis, and bottles of ale, porter, stout. On the next shelf were fancy canned goods—he sometimes woke in the middle of the night and liked to eat something hot. On the bottom shelf, as high as his navel, he ordered a ham kept, a cold roast of beef, a turkey, and two or three kinds of cheese brought up from the store in the warmer cellar. During the hunting season, wild duck and an occasional cold quail sat there also.

She rushed straight across the kitchen, ignoring the hired girl and the dinner steaming on the range. The heavy door of the butcher's icebox baffled her. The handle stuck tight in its slot and she never had the strength to pry it up. "Todd!" she called. "Todd! Let me in." She hammered on the thick door with the soft heels of her hands. There was no answer. She lifted her skirt and began to kick at the door. "Todd! Goldarn you. Let me in, Todd!"

He opened the door from the inside, let her in, and shut the door again.

"That darn handle. It always sticks," she said petulantly. There was not room enough for her to pace up and down but she kept rocking from side to side like a bear in a zoo, hugging herself, chafing her arms above the elbows and shivering with cold. "What did you hit him for, Todd? Will he sue, do you think? It's assault and battery, isn't it? He's a lawyer. Do you think he'll sue?"

Todd finished slicing off a wafer of Swiss cheese with a wire. He laid it flat on the cheese-board and cut the rind away neatly with the point of a paring knife.

"Todd!" she said sharply.

"Now, Mamma," he said, at last looking up at her.

[23]

"You hit him, Todd. You knocked him kicking. He was unconscious for a minute there, wasn't he? He fell over like a sack of wheat. Do you think he'll bring suit, Todd? He's got a case, hasn't he? What did you do it for?"

He had finished making a cheese sandwich. He bit into it and a blob of mustard swelled out between the bread slices and fell on the toe of his shoe. He started chewing and speaking, "I needed the exercise, jerking his head upward to catch a scrap of cheese about to fall out of his mouth.

"Todd! You're trying to fool me. That's not what you did it for. You don't just go up to a man and haul off and hit him for no reason. You didn't have any reason." She was motionless a moment, accusing him, her hands clasped in front of her.

He was calm. Hitting Burcham had made him remember that he was going to be vice-president of the bank, and in the main he was soothed by this. A trace of resentment against his mother remained with him because Old Man Bailey had insulted him through her. He was not angry but it made him patronize her. "You want a cheese sandwich, Mamma?"

Without altering her pose, leaning forward with the same intrinsic tension, waiting for his answer, she said, "No."

"You're god-damn right I had a reason. He hit Walter first."

"Yes. Sure. He was trying to stop Walter and Eddie fighting and Walter hit him in the stomach. I don't blame him for slapping him back."

"No man can hit a son of mine and get away with it."

"Well, I was just thinking. The case will come before Mark Tidwell, won't it? Won't Judge Tidwell try it? Well, if he does, why don't I go see him first? You know, talk to him. Mark knows me. Always has. I could just talk to him. Did you go out to Medina yesterday? You said you were going."

He was drinking cold beer out of the bottle, his head tilted back. He nodded his head shortly.

"Were there any wild strawberries along the road?"

"How would I know? The car kicks up too much dust."

"It's about time for them. Don't you remember last year we had them along about this time? Let me see," she put her hands to her lips and looked at the floor, "I could send Walter out."

Todd had found some fresh radishes in a glass of ice water and he was crunching them steadily, one after the other, paying no attention to her. All the time she had been talking, she had watched him eat, with a dull wonder lying under her talk why he should eat that way, finicky enough, never touching the least bit of fat meat, but demanding pounds, loaves, bowls, bunches, tureens of whatever it was, rising in the night to come to the icebox and eat. To her it had passed pleasure and become a vice. It would encourage heart trouble. All the Phelpses died of heart trouble. She did not try to interfere, partly because she knew she would be ignored, and partly because it was fascinating, as everything else with force and power was fascinating, especially in the family.

"I co send Walter out for strawberries," she repeated.

"What strawberries?"

"For Mark Tidwell. Then when your case comes up, he will remember the strawberries and go light," she said, rubbing her elbows.

He had found the salt. He was salting the radishes now. Tapping the shaker with his forefinger, he revolved a radish slowly, frosting it with salt. "Don't you go to see Judge Tidwell. Don't you send him any strawberries." He ate the radish and threw the green stem on the shelf.

"But why not, Todd? You'll lose sure as the world. He's a lawyer."

He stood looking upward with his fists on his hips. Another beer? Porter? Ale? Stout? He took down a bottle of stout. The rent in the back of his coat bulged and she noticed it for the first time.

"Why, you've torn your coat! How did you do that? Did you do that when you hit him? Here, take it off and I'll sew it up. That's one of your good suits. Take it off," she said.

He slipped out of his coat and she put it on at once and turned up the collar. He opened the bottle of stout and put his lip over the brownish foam that oozed out.

"You don't think he'll sue? Why not?" she asked. When he ate, his life was in his mouth. He did not want to talk and he did not seem to think. She knew this but she was anxious.

"No, Mamma, I don't think he'll sue why not." He belched, a long satisfactory eructation, tasting pleasantly of radishes. "And if he does, I don't give a good God-damn."

This was all she was going to get from him. "Oh," she said. "Well, let me out."

He opened the door and stood aside to let her pass.

"You ought not to stay in here these hot days. It'll give you rheumatism. That man up the street—what's his name?—he used to sit in the cellar on hot days and he . . ."

"You skidoo, Mamma." He gave her a little push and shut the door after her.

She walked through the kitchen with the torn coat over her shoulders. She heard the hired girl giggle but she did not take the coat off because

[25]

she still felt the chill of the icebox. She had the rest of her round to make to gauge the impact of the event on the family. She looked into the library. It was empty. She heard voices in the lavatory, and as she approached the door she distinguished the little boy's and his mother's. She opened the door without knocking.

The boy was standing patiently beside a washbowl of chocolate-colored marble while his mother combed his hair. He had a black eye, and he was paddling absently in the water in the bowl, fingering the soft floating red scabs that his mother had washed from his nose.

The mother said nothing.

"How you feel?" the grandmother said.

"All right," the boy answered. "They're going to put a piece of round steak on it." He winked his bad eye.

"What's it feel like to hit a grown man?" the grandmother asked.

The boy dropped his head. "All right," he murmured.

"There you go, son," his mother said. "You tell Daddy about the round steak." She opened the medicine cabinet, laid the comb in it, and shut the mirrored door.

In the doorway the boy stopped. "What you got on Father's coat for, Grandma?"

Surprised, she patted one sleeve and turned the collar down. She had forgotten she had put it on. "I'm going to mend it."

"He busted the back out when he hit Mr. Burcham," he said solemnly.

"It was wonderful, wasn't it, Walter?" the grandmother asked.

Shocked at the use of the word by a grownup, he was a little wary for fear it was a trap that his reply would spring and catch him somehow in punishment. He knew his grandmother was eccentric and sometimes sided with him against the rest for no reason he could see, yet he was still numbed by the afternoon's magnificence and he could not believe he was not culpable. This heroic surprise could be followed only by punishment. He looked at her smiling at him a moment, turned, and slammed the door behind him.

The mother was drawing one of her combs upward toward the topknot in her hair. In the mirror she saw the old woman behind her, holding up the coat to see how the sewing would have to be done. "What do you think will happen?"

"Nothing, Emily. Nothing's going to happen," the old woman said, glancing upward.

"I saw Dr. Stephenson go next door just now," the mother said, drawing out her combs and sliding them back in again. It was stealth. She was really staring at herself in the mirror, making a little private drama by asking herself, "Can such things happen in my life, time after time? Where is the girl who married him? Where, and her hopes?"

"Todd probably broke something when he hit him, I should think."

"It's terrible. It's just terrible," she said loudly in the way one makes a public announcement.

Suddenly she began to cry. She had been looking in the mirror at old Mrs. Phelps behind her, running the combs dreamily in and out of her hair. The tears sprang to her eyes. She seemed to notice them and then her face puckered and she bent to hide it in her hands.

Old Mrs. Phelps watched without comforting her. After a short wait, she said, "What's the matter, Emily? Why is it terrible? Todd says Mr. Burcham won't sue."

The young woman let down her hands in the midst of a sob, sucking the air in gasps through her mouth. The soft white skin of her face appeared red, swollen, and glistening in the electric light. "To do that in front of little boys. What will he think of his father?"

"He will remember it all his life. He will think his father is wonderful."

The young woman made a coarse angry sound of disagreement. She turned on the cold water faucet and wrung out a washcloth in the cold water. She began to dab at her cheeks and eyes.

"All little boys believe their fathers can lick anyone. But it never happens, not in these days. Except this once, this afternoon. Why, it's like something out of a fairy tale. Of course, he'll remember it," the old woman said.

She did not say this to console Todd's wife although it had the effect of consolation to reveal to her something of value in the brutality of the fight. It was very hard to be the wife of a Phelps. Encouragement and consolation would have been nice to have occasionally but nobody had helped her. And she had survived her husband. Emily would have to make her gestures of protest or submission unaided. She liked the younger woman; she would not advise her. She regaled her with anecdotes of her father-in-law and her husband which exposed plainly the kind of weaknesses in the Phelpses that a wife could use to her advantage, but these revelations were not put forth as such: they were only moments in the endless story of her own life and the old woman liked to talk. She would never openly side with the young wife in her struggle to determine where she should give in, where stand fast against her husband. She could pity her but if the old lady hoped for anything in her daughter-in-law it was some unexpected defiance of her son, something sharp and memorable.

[27]

The old woman went upstairs again to wait for the hired girl's call to supper. She took up her workbasket, and even in the dim late-afternoon light she threaded her needle at the first try. She had no sooner laid the coat out over her knees than she thrust the needle into it, laid it aside, and went to her dressing table. She opened the second of the black tin boxes. A heap of paper scraps began to move, uncurling themselves. A yellow pencil was held in a clip under the lid of the box. She drew it out, moistened it between her lips, and then, remembering she had nothing to write on, looked vaguely around the room. As she usually did, she went to a rack of papers and magazines beside her bed. She tore off a piece of the margin of a newspaper, blank, unprinted on, and placed it flat on the glass table-top. Again remembering, she tore the little strip into two halves.

Then, printing very small in block letters, she wrote, *Burcham will sue Todd.* On the other she wrote, *Walter will remember this all his life.* "This" was so vivid to her that she did not date the scrap of paper or otherwise specify. She put the two little pieces of paper in the box, snapped the lid down and took up her sewing, humming a popular song called "Too Much Mustard."

The scraps of paper in the box contained the future. She had collected mementos for many years before she realized that the past was meek and would come on call. It was the sloppy formless future that needed taking in hand. The very instant the idea had occurred to her, she had torn off the margin of a newspaper and written the date of her own death on it, impulsively, without computing chance or mischance, giving herself a hundred and one years of life merely because she wanted it, recognizing shrewdly the probability that she might attain these years because she had committed herself, knowing that if she became sick, she would cling to life more tenaciously than other old people because she could not bear to be wrong. The Bible said, threescore years and ten. People reached that age, healthy and vigorous. Then they heard or recalled that it was the allotted span. The tuck went out of them. They died. People should promise themselves more, that was all.

She was, of course, unscrupulous. In her prophecies, she was not recording only her wishes and desires; it was rather that, having once recorded them, she urgently wanted the events to happen as scheduled. If Burcham should show no signs of bringing suit, she was by long habit inured to nudging chance so far as to call on Mrs. Burcham some afternoon when her own daughter-in-law was at her sewing circle and the house was empty, to go stealthily across the side yard and present herself as the apologizer for the family and by insinuations overlaid by mock condolences implant the notion of a suit in Mrs. Burcham's mind; or if young Walter should not soon make some mention of his father's marvelous prowess, she would remind him of it without the least sense of inconsistency in herself, with, more, a swelling of triumph that she was guiding the very future itself.

She laid the coat across her knees and began to sew with fine neat rapid stitches, hurrying to finish before the hired girl called. She wanted to finish repairing the coat because Todd would not eat in his shirt sleeves even on a day as hot as this. He would hit a neighbor whom he would have to live beside maybe the rest of his life but, she chuckled, he had good manners. The inconsistency, plainly sprouting from his Phelps blood, delighted her. He saw only half of anything ever, and he would sit perspiring in his coat, dishing up the food with heavy courtesy (which *she* had taught him early), little Walter awed, as Dean Channer would be awed if a shining bearded patriarch done up in a bedsheet had appeared and delivered them just after he had said, "Good Lord, deliver us!," and Emily, bruised again by her husband's apathy before his own butcher's rage, still not a Phelps's wife, still struggling, flushed, hurt, silent but waiting a chance to protest. It would be a delightful meal.

"Grandma?"

She looked up. The boy stood in the doorway, waiting for permission to come in. "Yes, Walter?"

Swinging his shoulders like his father, he walked across the blue carpet until he stood in front of her. He was carrying a piece of brown wrapping paper. "Have you got a pencil, Grandma?"

"A pencil? Let me see. What do you want a pencil for?"

"To draw."

She stood up, looked in the litter on the mantel of the fireplace, lifting things, moving them, and finding nothing. She looked in the top drawer of her bureau, scratching like a hen in a midden of rings, lockets, cameos, brooches, and a candy box full of lumps of beeswax hoarded from the days when she did her own ironing, until she found a pencil stub. She would not give him her own, the one clipped to the lid of the tin box.

"Here," she said and took up her sewing again.

He unfolded the wrapping paper and laid it flat on the hardwood floor under the window where the light was best. She went on sewing up the tear with her fine neat stitches.

"What are you drawing?" she asked.

"A man," the boy said.

[29]

"What man?"

He did not answer and she did not ask again because she thought she knew. Her stitches did not change but a tingle ran down her curved tense back. He was a clever boy. He had made a statement that every boy made once, and he, like every other boy, had made it only in hope, his father could lick another man, and with no lapse of time, promptly as if it had been done at his own order, he had seen the blow and the blood (and for every other boy but him the statement stayed a wish, a hope, therefore a lie) and now he was properly on his knees elaborating it, drawing out the scene on paper so he would remember it all his life. And since she was his Grandma and the cleverness had to come from somewhere back beyond him, she was clever, too—she had foretold he would remember, and, like him, only beforehand, she had written it down. She smiled and bit her thread. The coat was done and she held it up before her and shook it to take out the wrinkles.

"Are you about done?" she asked.

"No."

Downstairs the hired girl called, "Supper!" in a shrill voice. The old woman stuck the needle in a piece of red flannel and put it in her sewing basket. She swung aside the portiere across the closet door and put the basket on a pile of old magazines lying on a chair.

"Are you ready to come to supper?" she asked.

The boy, patient on his knees, did not reply. She stood behind him and bent down a little. On the paper was the figure of a man in outline, finished apparently, but unrecognizable. The boy was drawing something else, a building, as she watched, a castle with crenelated towers that came only to the man's knees.

"Come on, Walter," she said.

The boy went right on drawing, paying no attention. She turned and crossed the room with the coat over her arm. She was halfway down the stairs when her curiosity got the better of her and she went back up to the room. Quietly but with no attempt to be quiet she crossed the room to the window and looked down over her grandson's shoulder again. The light was growing dim. Somewhere she heard a mourning dove. The cry had always made her feel old.

The castle was finished and a flag waved from its staff. The boy had drawn some kind of helmet on the man's head and as she watched he filled in an upturned mustache, a large heroic figure towering above the castle. It was the German Kaiser. Slowly on the left breast he began to draw an Iron Cross.

This time she tiptoed out. He had disappointed her. It was only fair and fitting that she leave him up there until his father came and punished him for being late to supper.

· IV ·

ToDD PHELPS and his family sat at a dinner table covered with stiff white damask. In the center was a little island of silver salt-cellars, pepper shakers, and pots of condiments intermingled with cut-glass cruets that stuck up like splinters of ice.

Todd bowed his head silently toward his mother and she passed him the cruet full of Worcestershire sauce. He drank a tablespoonful of it as he always did and applied himself to putting a sharper edge on the carving knife with a steel. As the knife rang against the steel, his wife shuddered and the old lady noticed it with satisfaction. She sat at the side of the table opposite her grandson and in order to watch both her son and his wife without appearing to do it, she had to dart her eyes from side to side busily. Todd held up the carving knife almost as if it were a sword and plucked the edge crossways with the ball of his thumb. It was sharp enough. He laid it down and his wife's eyes followed it. She was not thinking of any violence with the knife, rather the routine of the knife-sharpening and the gulp of Worcestershire which began dinner every night had connected itself with Todd's hitting Burcham and, possibly because she was warm, resentful, and somewhat confused by her intention to rebuke her husband within a very few minutes, she was afraid that Todd might come to hit people as regularly as he did these other loathsome things.

When the hired girl brought in a huge sirloin steak three inches thick, Todd rose with a touch of formality, a serious occasion, and carved the steak into long strips, divided them equally except for Walter's smaller share, asked solicitously who cared for gravy and who for butter, sat down again and began solemnly to eat. A silver dish of fresh asparagus was brought in, one of green peas, one of long buff baked potatoes, and a platter of sliced tomatoes. To fill the silence, old Mrs. Phelps complimented each in a dainty high tone that all the others, even her grandson, recognized as false. They all ate, not that they were all hungry. It was a habit imposed by Todd's example. He ate rapidly but carefully and the highlight on his forehead, a reflection from the light of the glass chandelier, grew brighter as it grew more moist. The day was divided for him by its

[31]

three meals and he remembered any event by linking it with the meal it happened nearest to. It had been after dinner he had been promoted vice-president; before supper, his pleasurable exertion against his neighbor. And here was supper itself blending with its sharp, hot, cool, peppery, buttery tastes these tributes to his strength. As he became sated and willing to talk about baseball, he began to think again a little and he watched his wife, who he could tell was on the boil about something, Burcham probably.

His son, eating mechanically, hardly tasting his food, took the silence, occasionally flawed, for reverence and his father's benign acceptance of it.

Old Mrs. Phelps waited, messing her food around on the plate. She remarked how hot it was because the weather in this house was a fatuous theme, irritating to both her son and daughter-in-law, but neither winced or spoke. Her son was calm, heavy, ruminative after a successful day and he could rise to no more than mischievousness when he looked at his wife and then he was merely ready to answer her if she spoke. She, who her young son thought was lost in worship because she kept staring at his father to refresh her bitterness, had reached a point of exhaustion that was becoming familiar. Was it worth while, was life long enough to live with a bear because he was well off and people envied her the cage, people who only saw him combed and proper, on his hind legs so to speak? To be able to think this so clearly made her feel strong but almost as soon as she had formed it in her mind, weakness filled it. There was no way to escape. If she had been able to brave the town's astonishment and disapproval, she could not divorce him because, in justice, there were times when he was not a bear and he had struck her only once or twice.

The room was quiet and the suppertime hush lay over the streets near by. For long moments the only sounds were the hired girl washing the tin dishes in the kitchen or the clack of a distant horse-trot on the pavement. To Walter, chewing his beefsteak, the silence was appropriate. What he had seen that afternoon demanded a severe, even irksome observance. There were a thousand questions he wanted to ask his father about his Muscle, his Boxing, Courage, Fame, and Life but he had not been brought up to be able to speak so intimately to his elders and he could tell that if he began to speak, awe would overcome him. It was enough to sit and stare covertly at his father, hardly tasting what was in his mouth, ignoring finally the big conical mound of homemade ice cream with strawberries over it, spooning it up mechanically, unenjoyed, almost unrecognized. "If this can happen—and it has happened, for I saw it—anything can happen," he was thinking. Suddenly there was more room for everything and the old rejected figures of giants, trolls, and ogres came into his memory, with Santa Claus and girlish silly fairies with wings of isinglass. He rejected them again almost at once but their return had given him confidence that there would be, somewhere, new gods equal in splendor.

With an ironic politeness to each other, a compliment paid to the ingenuity that had stifled a painful scene, the adults rose and left the table. Walter lingered. He went to the dining-room window and sat down by a luxuriant green fern that grew in a pot on a tabouret. He looked out across the lawn toward Eddie's house. After supper he usually went out to play with him until half-past eight. He no longer held any enmity and after what had happened to Mr. Burcham, he was more sympathetic than anything and he would have liked to know about Mr. Burcham's jaw, yet to go across the yard and give his customary whistle was impossible. The hired girl finished clearing the table, hardly noticing him, and she turned out the light. He sat in the darkness with his chin on his knees. With the light out, the rooms in the Burcham house appeared more clear.

He could see Old Man Burcham in the hallway grinding the wall telephone. Mrs. Burcham was pacing up and down the living room. He could see them through gaps in the lace curtains. When she turned she swung around quickly and her skirts flew out. She kept smelling of something, probably a vial of smelling salts. At last he descried Eddie sitting in a corner with a picture book in his lap and he identified just what Eddie was doing—he was keeping out of the way. It was the wise thing to do when *they* were upset. Try to say anything or do anything and you get your head taken off. Mr. Burcham threw out his free hand or doubled it into a fist as he talked. At last he slammed the receiver on the hook and went into the living room. The light was better there. The jaw was swollen but there was not a bloody bandage on it as he had half expected. After a few words, Mr. Burcham went out into the hall again, put on his hat, and left the house walking pretty fast. He seemed to have recovered disappointingly soon.

Mrs. Burcham made Eddie move over and she sat down in the same armchair. She kissed his temple and smoothed his hair with her hand. Eddie paid no attention. He went on stolidly turning the pages in his book, occasionally licking his thumb. Mrs. Burcham seemed to be talking all the time and there were probably tears in her eyes. This kept up a long time without any change and, as nothing seemed to be happening, Walter stood up, bent his arm to feel the muscle, and wandered into the library.

The rest of the family were all there. His father was seated in a big red leather armchair with a lamp standing at his shoulder, reading the afternoon paper again. In warm weather it was always somewhat damp in these high rooms and the chair was sticky and smelled of the tanyard, neither did it match the rest of the heavy Victorian furniture but his father had liked it, ordered it, and now defiantly sat in it. His mother was mending socks. His grandmother sat by the window with one of the lace curtains drawn back, waiting for the lights to go on downtown. The year before the Chamber of Commerce in a fit of civic enthusiasm had wheedled the Council into purchasing a dozen or so of electric-lighted archways to span the main street for two blocks. The lights would "provide the atmosphere of carnival and transform the shopping district into a veritable fairyland," and his grandmother waited nearly every night for the lights to go on to see if any of the bulbs had burned out. She thought the fairyland was silly.

When Walter came in, his mother looked up without smiling and neither of the others took notice of him. He traced the central design of the rug with his foot. It was always a mountain that he climbed with a little pickax and a rope around his waist until he reached the peak, then he slid down the other side on his Flexible Flyer, quick, snow in his face, a mile or more. He climbed again with his toe and slid down, climbed again and slid. Now was no time to speak to his father, and it occurred to him to play "Ogalala" on the phonograph. He began to wind it. His grandmother looked away from the window and said, "What are you going to do, play the phonograph?"

He nodded, fearing some objection. He was going to turn the horn around until it faced the corner. He would get into the corner and there he could hear the music plainly but it would not disturb anyone else. He took the horn by its fluted lip and started to turn it but it came unfastened at the small end and fell to the floor with a terrible clatter. He picked it up hastily and tried to screw it back on. He glanced once at his father who had not lifted his head but had raised his eyes, a far more ominous sign. He fumbled and rattled the big horn, waiting to be shouted at.

The doorbell rang.

His father nodded his head sideways and said, "Go to the door."

He went into the unlighted hall. It was dark outside but he could see a gigantic figure in silhouette against the screen. He turned the light switch. It was a policeman, Fatty Harper. His club hung at his belt and he was fanning himself with his helmet. At last Walter moved. He went slowly up to the screen door. It was hard for him to talk to a policeman. None had ever come to his house. "Hello," he said at last out of a dry mouth.

"Hello, son. Your dad to home?" The helmet stopped while he said this and then resumed its flight back and forth.

At first he had just been scared of seeing a cop at his own front door, a violation of a sanctuary, but when his father was mentioned, he thought his knees would give way, for it was then clear and as quickly clear as a blow on the head that Fatty Harper had come for his father. It seemed to him an hour or more that he stood there shocked before the word "arrest" occurred to him. He saw the neat indentation at the sides of Fatty's head where the sweatband of the helmet pressed, and the short curls that sprang up below it. He saw the rills of sweat on Fatty's cheeks, so full and red and menacing. He noted the little hump that concealed a chew of tobacco above Fatty's jaw. He saw Fatty's huge hand with a thumb that looked as big as his own wrist tucked into his belt, a monstrous hairy hand with fingers like long sausages. They said Fatty Harper weighed two hundred and seventy-five pounds. And he had come to arrest his father.

"Well, is he or ain't he?" the policeman said after this long time.

"He's here. I'll get him," he croaked out and turned and ran down the hall into the library.

"Dad!" he whispered. "It's Fatty Harper. He's . . ."

His father threw his paper crumpling down. "Fatty *Har*per?" He stood up and started for the hall. "Well, I'll be God-damned," and as he walked down the hall, Walter heard him say, "Why, that son-of-a-bitch . . ." and then, "Hello, Fatty."

"Who's Fatty Harper?" his grandmother said.

His mother knew. She stopped sewing and stared straight ahead of her, flushing.

"Shhh!" he said rudely for he wanted to overhear his father.

"Don't you shush me, you little imp. Who's Fatty Harper?" the old lady repeated.

His mother was frightened also. When she answered she sounded strangled and her chest heaved up and down. "He's a policeman," she said.

His grandmother jumped right up out of her chair. "A policeman!" she said delightedly.

His father came back into the room getting into his coat. He carried his Panama hat in one hand. He spoke directly to his wife. "Em, I've got to go downtown for a few minutes. I'll be right back."

His mother then did a very strange thing that worried the boy later because he did not think it could have meant all that it seemed to mean. She looked his father in the eye and said in a low voice that was only just audible, "It serves you right."

[35]

His father looked blankly at her a moment. His face set in a look of anger and he said, turning and leaving, "That God-damned Burcham got a warrant out for me."

Walter followed him down the hall expecting him to make some kind of farewell but his father began to talk to the policeman, even laugh with him, the door slammed, and they went off into the night. With a wild anger that they had allowed this to happen emerging from his fear and confusion, he wheeled and ran down the hall to reproach his mother and grandmother but he stopped at the library door. For the first time in his life, he realized that women were of no use in a situation like this and when it struck him just afterward that he, a little boy, was useless also, he sat quietly down on an ornamental chair in the hall.

If he had sent away for a blackjack instead of the itching powder, he could follow them, running noiselessly over the grass of the lawns, hiding behind the trunks of the trees beside the concrete walk and, at last over-taking them, he could leap like an Indian and clout Fatty Harper on the back of the neck below his helmet. He allowed himself to dally with this exploit a moment before he admitted that he could not reach the back of Fatty Harper's neck with a blackjack unless he stood on a chair, and the image of himself stumbling across the Maumee Street lawns lugging a kitchen chair destroyed his brief hope. He remembered the leather holster that swung from the last hook deep in the closet where his father kept his winter suits. A long heavy .45 revolver hung there. He had hardly been able to cock it when his father had let him. It was a little shameful to think that if he overtook his father and the policeman, he would have to hold the gun in both hands instead of gracefully drawing and aiming with one. He would have to get up close behind them to be sure of his shooting in the dark but, once he had pulled the trigger, "that gun'll blow a team of steers through a brick house," his father had said. Fatty Harper would lie dead, a vast window rimmed with blood torn out of his middle and some-where down the block would lie Fatty's insides like a chunk of raw beef. Again, however, a tired common sense reminded him that his father had told him *never* to touch the gun and he would not dare to disobey even to save him. A last discouragement occurred to him: no matter what he did to Fatty Harper, they would just send more policemen, by twos and threes, a streetful, Chief Carpenter himself superintending from horse-back as in the Decoration Day parades, clubs rising and falling, pistols shooting, and in the center of the maelstrom, his father fighting with mani-acal fury, punching, gouging, tripping, kicking, growing slowly larger than all the men who beset him, a gigantic shining figure stepping on ants.

The boy fell asleep in the chair in the hall.

His father found him there half an hour later when he came home from the police station. He picked him up and carried him into the library, where neither woman had missed him.

When he had gone with the policeman, his wife had not expected him to return that night. She expected the Law in some mysterious way to detain him. Now she was shrewd enough to recognize the expectation as a disguised hope, and this discovery startled her enough to keep her silent. His mother had already jumped up, crossed the room, and was standing before him, tense with her peculiar covetousness.

"Now, Todd, tell me all about it. What are people going to say?" she said as if she wished that they would say a lot.

Before he could reply, his wife had noticed her son in his arms, and had taken him firmly away from his father, and started to carry him, long and dangling as he was, upstairs to put him to bed.

"What happened, Todd?" his mother repeated, beginning to move around nervously.

"Obviously they turned me loose. On my own recognizance," he said, and bent to pick up the paper. His mother's avidity irritated him.

In the morning when he woke up Walter remembered nothing. He could hear old Kelly in the street calling "veg-et-ables" from his wagon and the sounds of the awaking house rose to him one at a time, pure and gentle in the silence. Sunlight lay across the foot of his bed. The whole day lay blank before him, a delicious space of leisure, the beginning of summer. Still at the verge of sleep, he began to make new schemes for play, projects, fresh journeys, new adventures for himself and Eddie. For some curious reason he could not make any picture of himself and Eddie together. There was something wrong. Eddie seemed reluctant to enter his mind. At last he remembered.

He ran for his father's and mother's bedroom and flung open the door. His mother was hooking a petticoat before the mirror.

"Where's Dad?" he shouted.

"Here," came his father's voice. Through the open door of the bathroom he saw his father, his face covered with lather, shaving. He lifted the strop and gave the razor a few strokes. "What's the trouble, son?"

He turned away blushing, already sure that what he had expected was a betrayal of faith in his father's omnipotence.

"He was asleep. He doesn't remember your coming home," his mother said.

[37]

"What's the matter, boy? You think your father spent the night in the hoosegow?" He ran some hot water over the razor and wiped it on a towel. There were flecks of lather at his nostrils and the tips of his ears. He walked out of the bathroom. "Thought they had the old man, didn't you, huh? Didn't you?" He started to poke his son sharply in the chest with his left hand. The boy backed away, bent over, fending him off with his two hands, giggling, glad that he was safe. The day could go on now.

The father stopped teasing him and went back into the bathroom to wash his face and apply the shaving lotion, talking. "No, sir, they couldn't keep *me*. Turned me loose on my own recognizance."

"But you've got to go to court this morning," his wife said.

The man frowned and straightened up.

Walter left the room immediately. He did not dare ask any questions. He had thought all the danger was past. In the darkness his father had somehow overcome the gigantic policeman, had come home safe, and everything was as it had been—but now it wasn't true. Danger had returned and it cut off the future. He could not think past it.

In the dining room breakfast was on the table. He was the first one downstairs. He ate his half grapefruit, a bowl of cornflakes, and drank his compulsory glass of milk and no one interrupted him. He went out on the side porch and sat down on the cold stone steps. He ran his shoe over the curved iron footscraper, thinking.

He knew nothing about trials. If his father had to go to court, he assumed the trial would take place in the courthouse, a vast building of red brick with a small gray dome and a worn flight of marble steps leading up to the front door. Beds of cannas and peonies colored the front lawn and now on warm days old men in suspenders sat chewing tobacco on the front steps. He had passed the building many times and thought it was familiar but he had never gone through the front door. He watched a drop of dew on a grass blade turn all colors in the sunlight and he ticked it off with his foot. Little yellow cabbage butterflies flickered over the purple lilies twenty feet away. Kelly had stopped his wagon piled high with all the colors of the vegetables. The sky was a high distant blue without any clouds, and none of these were any good to him the way they always were because of the trial in those dark, high-ceilinged rooms.

He could not go to his father and ask about torture or the dungeons that might run out under the lawn under the flower beds because he was not sure that those things were part of the true procedure, although some men had suffered them before and after trials in books he had read. If his father expected pain and a dark cell he would not demean himself by saying anything about it; and if he himself were entirely wrong, if this was not the way it would happen, his father would laugh at him, and there had been too many times he had laughed already. He did not want to look like a fool. There seemed to be very little he could do.

Behind him the screen door slammed, and he jumped at the sound. His father had come out of the house with the *Detroit Free Press* spread between his hands, reading the headlines. He felt his way down the steps with his feet.

"Father, are you going to the courthouse now?" he asked.

"No, the bank," his father said without lifting his head. Then he looked up. "It's not at the courthouse anyhow. It's at the City Hall."

"Can I come and see it?"

His father's head was down again. He was reading the paper. "No. It's nothing. You stay home where you belong."

He went out under the porte-cochère down the drive, and the boy watched him go, thinking how brave he was, how calm in the face of danger. When he reached the sidewalk, his father folded the paper and began to slap his thigh with it in time to the rhythm of his walk.

From his father's words, he assumed that the trial would be something special (or they would have held it properly at the courthouse). He could foresee the City Hall and the lawn around it crowded with a mass of silent people, all dressed in their best clothes as for an occasion of extreme importance, all of them talking about his father's guilt in low voices. He got up off the step and started for the City Hall. He did not ask permission to leave for he could see that his mother's permission in the midst of a catastrophe like this or a fire or shipwreck was a childish formality.

This was not like one of his common journeys downtown when he was sent on an errand or when he was merely looking for something to do. He did not scan the crotches of the trees for bird's nests. The brass studs, the ivory rings, and the ribbons in the manes of the horses pulling the sprinkling wagon did not seduce his attention. He barely glanced at two third-grade boys who were building a hut out of sticks and old carpets. When he passed the Central School where he was a pupil, he did not thumb his nose as he had done every time he passed since the vacation had begun. The house of Mr. Gilbert, the mailman, did not awake in him the echoes of his usual perplexity, a memory from his earlier childhood when he believed that mailmen walked their routes continually day and night so that it was ridiculous to think that any of them had so commonplace a thing as a house to live in.

It was only at the firehouse that he paused. He could not stifle the customary wild hope that the bell would ring as he was standing there, the big gray horses would gallop from their stalls to halt quivering with excitement underneath their suspended harness, a fireman would slide down the brass pole, that there would be hoarse shouts, a seizing of axes, and, most magnificent of all, that one of them would shout at him, "Come on, bud," and he could ride the hook-and-ladder openly through the streets of the town.

At the doorway he stopped and looked in. Back in the cool of the building, four firemen were playing rummy at the little table set beside the red hose-cart. They were not wearing their helmets. One of them scratched his chest and spat into a big brass spittoon. He could see the patient heads of the fire-horses looking out of the stalls at the back and the only sound was the slap of the cards and a knock of a hoof against the floor. He allowed himself to wait until he counted a hundred but nothing happened and he walked on.

He was approaching the City Hall. He was early. There was no crowd yet. It was a tall narrow brick building painted freshly a bright barn red with the doors and windows outlined in cream color. At one side of the roof towered a cream-colored wooden cupola with the town clock inside it. The police station occupied a room in the front of the building downstairs and through the window he could see Fatty Harper with his coat off and his feet on the desk, reading a paper. No one else was around.

He sat down on the curb under a tree in front of the library and tried to make a plan. He pulled out blades of grass one by one and piled them up. He had piled up quite a heap of them before he admitted finally that there was only one thing he could do: he had to cross the street, go into the City Hall and by asking or by instinct (which he hoped might help him) find the courtroom. He could not wait any longer because his father might come and find him.

Up the street he heard a loud banging noise approaching. Deliberately he kept his head down because he knew it was Carroll Smith, the president of the *other* bank, driving to work in his *Abbott-Detroit* with a straw sailor hat on the back of his head. The noise drew near and the automobile passed him spurting pebbles from under the tires. The boy stuck his head between his knees. He assumed that Carroll Smith would have learned all about the trial by the mysterious grapevine that all adults tapped to learn everything, and if he were recognized, Carroll Smith would laugh, or thumb his nose, or even stop the car and say something.

At last he stood up quite calmly and walked across the street intending to walk right into the City Hall but his heart was pounding with dread and excitement and he swerved. He went to the drinking fountain. By snapping the lever, he could make the water spurt up high, as high as the old girl's face. The old girl was a seated statue in marble of Aunt Laura Haviland, a Quaker woman who had helped establish the Underground Railway in Raisin Valley, and if the water shot up high enough and the wind was right, you could wet her face. As he reached out his hand, the waterspout became an omen. If he could wet the face of the statue, everything would turn out well. He snapped the lever. The water spurted up white but he had no luck—it reached as high as her head but the right puff of breeze was lacking. He stared at its rigid spinsterish calm—not a drop on it—but before dejection seized him he said to himself, "Three times," and tried it again. He missed. Angrily gritting his teeth, he did it the third time. Apparently he had missed again but he scrambled up and stood on the rim of the fountain, and peered over the old woman's face. It was freckled with bird droppings but at last on the edge of her Quaker bonnet something took the light. It was a drop of water. He climbed down and took a drink.

He walked across the lawn and entered the building. To look as if he knew where he was going, he walked quickly down the hall almost panting with fear but glancing from side to side. None of the offices he passed seemed solemn or dangerous enough. A man in a white summer suit approached and passed him without speaking. He reached the end of the hall and came back again. He took the left-hand staircase and climbed to the second floor.

There was another hall above the first but it was shorter and it led into an enormous dark room. Its double doors were standing open and as he stood between them he could tell this was the courtroom. He slipped inside and sat down in one of the folding chairs that filled most of the room in semicircular rows. There was a musty smell that stung his nose like pepper. No one had pulled up the window shades and the only light came from two stripes of dusty sunlight that came through the maple tree outside between the shade and the window casement. Facing him at the end of the room was a big low desk with a single chair behind it. The judge's seat. There was nothing else in the room besides the folding chairs and the judge's seat, no pictures on the brown walls, no carpet on the floor, no people. The emptiness increased his fear. It was like the frightful blank deserts of a dream.

He could not endure sitting there. He got up and went back into the hall. Just outside the courtroom doors he stood with his back against the wall to wait but this was very difficult because he began to imagine what the trial would be like and how his father might very soon come out of that awful room with his wrists bound and be taken away. He counted the cracks between the narrow pine floor boards. There were fifty-two cracks to the other wall. He counted them again, this time shutting one eye and counting with his finger to make it seem as if he had some business there so if anyone should think of questioning him he might be discouraged by his professional manner of counting and believe that he had been hired to do it, perhaps a helper to a carpenter who was going to lay a new floor. He was certain that someone in the upstairs offices had seen him pass and might come out any minute to ask what his business was. Desperately he caught hold of his wrist and held it tightly until his hand turned dark. That was how the handcuffs would feel.

He heard footsteps coming up the stairway. Black against the windows at the end of the hall he saw a straw hat with a flopping brim ascending, a big heavy man, but the light was bad and he could not see his face. After him the smooth knob of a police helmet was rising. He lurched away from the wall and walked briskly toward them, pretending a necessary errand, and turned abruptly into one of the offices. Passing them, he found that he had never seen the big man with the flopping hat or the policeman before.

A counter with a black metal wicket loomed in front of him. From a desk by the window an old thin man in his shirt sleeves got up and came toward him. He was wearing wrinkled black cloth sleeve-guards and his jaw moved from side to side.

"Well, sonny, what do you want?" he said.

He stood looking through the hole in the wicket. There were long bushy eyebrows. His breath smelled like a cellar with spearmint growing in it. There were the marks of a thick-toothed comb in the yellow-white hair. On the blotter stood a little pot full of BB shot with a wooden pen sticking in it. He heard footsteps creaking up the stairs outside, men's voices, none of them known.

"Huh? What's on your mind?"

"I wanted to come to see about a dog. If I have to pay a tax on him. He's a terrier and I want to know how much I have to pay in the tax," he rattled off breathlessly. Would this old man shout "Liar"?

"Hmm. Well, you come to the right shop," was all the old man said. He bent over and started to rummage under the counter. After a moment he straightened up and rubbed the small of his back, looking vacantly out of the window. Sighing, he bent again.

The boy heard some talk and some laughter that seemed to come from another office. There was a moment's silence and a long pompous mumble followed that broke into a spasm of clarity: ". . . on the 22nd day of June, A.D. 1915, at the City of Athens and in the County aforesaid, one *Todd Phelps* did commit an assault and battery upon one *Edward Burcham* contrary to the form of the Statute in such case made and provided. . . ."

The sound of his father's name read out jerked him toward the door but he came back, not daring to leave the old clerk. He saw him slap a book of narrow forms on the counter, dip the pen in the ink, try the point, and write something on the form. He heard a wagon bumping over the brick pavement outside and far away someone was lamely playing over and over a phrase of music on a fiddle.

A loud voice said, "You are charged as per the complaint with assault and battery. What is your plea?"

And his father said, "Oh, I'm guilty all right."

The old clerk said, "Terrier, you say? Describe him."

The boy could hardly stand still, much less answer.

The loud voice said, "One hundred dollars and costs." There was a loud whistle of surprise from somebody.

"Look here, young feller, you speak up. I ain't got all day."

"He's brown, I guess. He's not very big. I'm Walter Phelps. I gotta go." He ran out of the place and turned down the hall toward the courtroom. The doors were still open; the shades were down and the place was as empty as before. Reaching for comfort in his turmoil he tried to receive the voices as hallucinations but he heard loud talk behind him and he whirled around. Coming out of an office, a little office like the one he had been in, he saw Mr. Burcham, his face set and stern with the bump on the left side of his jaw. Mr. Burcham went down the stairs in a dignified manner. Then he saw Fatty Harper and the other policeman, two men he didn't know, and at last his father, who seemed to be laughing and joking. The policemen went downstairs one after the other. No handcuffs were visible.

He went up to his father. "Is this all?" he said.

"Well, for Christ's sake what are you doing down here? I thought I told you to stay home," his father said jovially.

"Is this all there is to it?"

"All there is to what?"

The other two men were watching him. "The trial," he said.

"By God, a hundred dollars is enough."

"I thought they were going to put you in prison."

The three men gave a roar of humiliating laughter. One of them said, "He could have given you ninety days, Todd."

"No," his father said. "Money'll fix anything, enough money will." Seriously, his father looked down. "That's all there is to it, son."

They all walked down the stairs and out into the heat of the day. To the boy, the lawn, the statue, and the curbstone in front of the library did not look quite the same: they were places where he had suffered.

The other two men left them at the corner, and, without thinking, Walter took his father's hand. His father stopped dead still at this childish trick. The boy looked up at him feeling the tears begin to scald his eyes and his throat grow tight. His father picked him up in his arms like a baby right in the open street. The shame of this made him cry and his father held him on one arm, saying again and again, "I'm all right, son. I'm all right."

When he stopped crying they walked on up the street toward the bank. They approached the Greek's. His business had not started for the day. The ceiling fans were not revolving and the Greek was mopping the tiled floor. His father stopped. "Gus, what's the biggest soda you ever made?"

"Alla soda big here, Mr. Phelp'," the Greek said.

"Here's a quarter. Give this boy the biggest one you ever made. Put it in a bucket if you have to. What flavor?"

"Chocolate," Walter said complacently. He had no surprise left.

"Come on, boy," the Greek said.

They went inside. It was cool and they sat at the marble counter beside the lamp with its shade of colored glass fruit. On the wall at the back was a colored poster depicting a battle where hideous Turks in baggy pants and scarlet fezzes were fleeing or writhing before the attack of Greeks who wore stiff white skirts and black pompons on the toes of their shoes. There were scimitars, flags, and blood. A wonderful scene, one he had always liked. His father told him candidly, as one man to another, all about the trial, using the words *warrant* and *arraignment* without explaining them and with his talk smoothing out all the fear and anxiety, filling in the dungeons and breaking up the handcuffs while in the middle of the morning, an extraordinary time to do it, Walter ate the biggest ice-cream soda the Greek had ever made.

⌐PART TWO⌐

· V ·

IN A BOARDINGHOUSE near the campus, Walter Phelps was preparing to lay out his dinner jacket and a new boiled shirt. He was standing up because his buttocks were sore and he blew his nose frequently because he had a bad cold. He sat down gingerly on a cardboard-bottomed chair and began to unwrap the dress shirt. He had an hour and a half to dress.

The old hand-twist bell on the front door downstairs gave its tinny chime. The landlady answered it, spoke a moment, and somebody started up the stairs.

"Right there, first one to your left," she called.

He heard a scraping and clinking against the banister outside as his visitor mounted.

There was a heavy panting outside his door, then someone knocked. He opened it and a flabby red-faced man with his overcoat wide open and his hat on the back of his head lunged past him and set a big suitcase in the middle of the floor.

"Domn these stairs," the man said. He sat down heavily on the narrow bed, fanning himself with his hat and gasping out a ripe sweet reek of whisky. He was about fifty-five years old. His eyebrows were black. His teeth were bad. His hair had the sculptured perfection usually seen in toupees but it was his own. He took a deep breath, pursed his livid purplish lips and blinked and spoke. "I just come from there. The clan's gathering. The street's full of cars and ye can hear 'em singing in the shower bath as ye come up the walk." He rammed his little finger into his ear, wiggled his hand vigorously, and looked at the end of his little finger.

"Was there a Packard sedan in front? That's our car. My father . . ."

"I disremember." He was leaning forward, carefully pulling a handkerchief inch by inch out of his tight hip pocket. Freed, he blew a loud horn note with it, sniffed, and put it back. "They's a dozen cars, maybe twenty. They'll be ready fer yez." He took a bottle out of his inside breast pocket and held it up to the light. It was half empty. He unscrewed the cap and rubbed his palm over the mouth of the bottle and held it out. "Here's something for yer sore arse." He laughed in a rich soft wheeze. "Yes, sir. That'll cure the welts on your behind. Cheer ye up. On the house."

Walter took the flask. This was no longer the permitted beer or the glass of port on Christmas. He raised the bottle a little too quickly to show a confidence that still eluded him. He took a large gulp, forcing it down fiery against his throat and palate, the saliva springing in his mouth as he handed it back, silent, still swallowing, with tears in his eyes.

"Cigarette?" the man asked in a cold dead voice, holding out a wrinkled pack.

He nodded and lit one, inhaling quickly, knowing he had failed to look good in this first test. "Whew! That must have just come off the boat."

"Look, sonny boy. When you get a free drink from a bootlegger, ye don't want to go just 'glug.' It's free. Ye want to go 'glug, glug, glug.' Like this." He tipped up the bottle and Walter could hear it chuckle like water in a pipe. "A-a-h!" he sighed. "It's a cold day out. How d'ye feel now, better?"

"Yes."

"It's a bloody shame, that's what it is, a bloody sobbing shame to feed this stuff to little milky boys like the both of yez. What's the other one's name? Burcham?"

"Eddie Burcham."

"Hm. Off a boat, ye said. Ye said this come off a boat? God love ye, this was made in a cellar on Grand River Avenue. Ye know Duke? Are ye big enough? Have the other boys told ye?"

"Sure, I've heard of him. He's one of the Purples, isn't he?"

"Duke is an Eyetalian gentleman and the hope of the Phelans is proud to work for him. But he ain't one of the Purples."

"You mean he's got his own mob?"

"A fat lot you'll pick up in the newspapers. 'Mob,' he says. Do I look like a mobster with nothing under me arm but long red hair and only a penknife in me pocket? No. He ain't got his own mob. He pays the Purples to look out for him."

"What do you mean, pays them? Is he the head man in Detroit?" The boy could not keep the awe out of his voice.

The bootlegger threw himself back on the bed over Walter's laid-out

[46]

clothes, waving both hands in front of him in mock panic. "I won't talk. Ye can't make me talk. Burn the ends of me fingers. Stand me up in a washtub full of concrete and toss me in the river, I won't talk!" he cried in falsetto. "Domn the newspapers," he said fiercely, sitting up. He pulled out the bottle and said, "Here, have another. Only take it slow this time. Ye don't have to show off before me. I know yer just a green boy."

Walter took a short drink; did not cough or weep; and thanked him.

He took another long pull and slid the bottle back into his pocket. He leaned forward affably, chafing his dirty hands. "No, I'll tell ye. The Duke's a small operator and he pays the Purples to let him alone. Every Thursday a lady comes with a basketful of washing. Duke pays her, and the Purples they fix the cops, ye see. Ye said 'boat,' and it was flattery in ye to say it because the Duke makes all of this in his cellar at night. He hires two men, absolute eternal teetotalers, the both of 'em, and all night long they mix the stuff in vats."

"What's in it?"

"One quarter true whisky and the rest is alcohol, water, and caramel flavoring like candy. And these poor sods mix and mix the whole night through and in the morning they're blind drunk from the fumes. Blind drunk and not a drop taken. When I was in India with the Oxford and Bucks, we used to put a sponge soaked with whisky under our arms on the long marches. Soaking, not swilling, done it and it was very comforting."

"What's the Oxford and Bucks, Mickey?" He felt that now he had gained the bootlegger's friendship, or if not friendship, his amiability, he could safely address him by his first name like the juniors and seniors, his regular customers.

"The Oxfordshire and Buckinghamshire Light Infantry. An uncle of mine, three or four layers back, commanded it once—Lord Phelan. The English like to have the Irish do their fighting for 'em." He put his hands on his knees and pushed himself upright. "W-e-l-l, what was it ye wanted, one or two?"

"I guess one is all I could stand, don't you think?" the boy said sheepishly.

"Ah, but tonight ye become a man, don't ye? Then maidenheads will come easy and whisky'll be like milk in yer gullet. I'll tell ye, you open the suitcase and get it out. It'll save me bending again."

Walter knelt down, unlatched the suitcase, and spread it open. It was full of quart bottles of whisky with old newspaper wadded between them. "Which are the six-dollar ones?"

"All of 'em. God love ye, they're all the same. We buy government stamps and labels by the pound from a printing house. Take any one ye fancy, only give me the six bucks."

He took out the bottle, set it on the floor, and shut up the suitcase. "You got change for a ten, Mickey?" He set the bottle on the bureau and took the lone bill from his wallet.

The bootlegger pulled out a roll of bills from his hip pocket. It was as thick as his arm, and even if the bills were all ones, there were several hundred dollars in it. He wet his forefinger on his tongue and flipped off four ones, laid the ten against the roll, and carefully counted out the ones on the bureau. "There you are. Now, let me see, after this week you'll be living at the house, won't ye?"

"If I get through all right tonight."

"You'll get through all right tonight. They all do. You want me to bring a bottle out for ye when I come Fridays?"

"Sure. Every Friday from now on."

"Good luck tonight, my boy." Mickey put out his hand and Walter shook it. He picked up the suitcase, put on his hat, and opened the door. He stopped and looked back grinning. "If they dip ye in boiling oil to-night, bite yer tongue but don't cry out."

Walter laughed. "I won't." He heard the bootlegger go down the stairs in the dark, knocking the suitcase against the walls and swearing.

He hefted the bottle of whisky and studied the label. He glanced at his wrist watch, gathered up his safety razor, a tube of shaving soap, the brush and a towel, and felt his way along the dark hall to the bathroom.

It was a dirty little bathroom with green walls. The hand-painted signs the landlady had put up scolded at him: *"Wipe out the bath-tub when you get done"* and over the washbowl, *"Don't let the hot water drip."*

He began to shave and it was not pride that made him or fuzz that he scraped off. At nineteen his face was covered with a wiry reddish stubble. He envied the flabby drunken man the India that was in his youth, the heat and sweat and pain of the long marches with the dust-devils whirling on the plains and the lieutenant's Waler sobbing in a canter, the cool of Simla and the colonel's daughters riding along the paths among the pine trees, and above all the battles won by the little screw-guns popping at the mud forts and the whine of the Pathans' Martini-Henry bullets past his ear. In his envy and admiration he did not stop to distinguish between his own memories of Kipling and what Mickey had told him because he was convinced that his own youth so far had been scant and empty; and if he had felt heat, it was only while mowing the lawn or fishing for bluegills on one of the little lakes in a white duck hat stuck full of fishhooks; if he had sweated, it was in the elaborate clumsy dance of a basketball game, the dribble, the pause (glancing), the feint, and the long shot—missed; and the only real pain he had suffered was during this past week and it was a silly pain that had no meaning. Naked, daubed with bright red paint, he had run up three flights of stairs from the faucet in the cellar of his fraternity house to a fire in the attic built of packing-case slats in a cast-iron washtub. He carried, when he started, a tablespoonful of water to throw on the fire but at every landing in the staircase stood an upper-classman with a long wooden paddle. As he rushed past, stumbling to keep the spoon balanced, the paddle would swat him on the buttocks and knock the water out of the spoon and he never did manage to carry any water to the attic and the fire at last burned itself out. And, fully dressed, he had been ordered to "assume the position," and he had bent obediently to clasp his ankles, and to put his head against a wall with a pillow between them so he wouldn't be knocked cold, and an upperclassman, having asked him a question he couldn't answer, would take a hop and a skip across the room. He could hear the whir of the paddle through the air and even the crack across his behind before he felt the pain. He did not think of the pain as torture. Why should the members of the fraternity want to tor-ture him, or college students one another, or Americans one another? And it did not occur to him not to endure it any more, just to pick up and walk out of the place and say "To hell with it" because nearly everyone he knew had been through it without complaining and he did not want to seem weak or cowardly.

The pain had been bad enough. He had been surprised once the past week to find himself trembling after they had let him alone at last and he had gone to bed, lying on his stomach, hearing the rattle of the taut bed-springs, really surprised that the tremor had come upon him as an after-math—he had not been forced to draw on any unusual resources to with-stand it, no unwitting cries or curses gasped out, but tonight the worst of all might happen. Perhaps, he had heard it, they saved the worst for the last. He had seen scars on other boys' forearms in the outline of Greek letters. They never said how the scars had been made. The general sup-position was nitrate of silver but there was always the possibility that they had been burned on with a red-hot branding iron. "Red-hot" maybe he could stand. White-hot, he doubted. He could see his forearm and clenched fist reflected pallidly in the glow of the white-hot branding iron, alone but watched by many in the darkness, and his stomach turned and he took a drink of cold water.

[49]

Tonight his father would be there, and his uncle Eri. Their faces firmly based on the white pedestals of their shirt fronts, they would stand somewhere in the darkness, watching and judging, and he supposed, no matter what was done to him, he would be able to grin while it was going on.

He stroked his chin and cheeks to see if they were smooth enough, picked up his shaving things, and went back down the corridor to his room.

He put the pillow on the edge of the bed, sat stiffly down on it, and tore the glazed laundry paper off his dress shirt. He looked his hands over carefully to see if they were dry enough and began the laborious job of inserting his studs and cuff links without marring the beautiful whiteness and stiffness of his shirt. He worked patiently, hearing his breath go in and out. Once he glanced up because, in the quiet, he missed the sound of water dripping from the eaves: he saw that it had begun the first snow of the year.

He did not hear Eddie come into the house. His bedroom door opened and Eddie was standing there brushing the damp snow off his hat. It was a black soft hat. Eddie wore a black overcoat, black hat, the correct attire for gents' evening wear. They were new clothes bought especially for the initiation and he could tell, before his glance reached Eddie's feet, why he had wheedled the money out of his mother. It was because his father was dead. Mr. Burcham had never belonged to a fraternity anyway, not even a law fraternity, and tonight after the ceremony was over, Eddie would have no father to pin the badge on for him. Some senior would have to do it, and he foresaw accurately that in this moment Eddie would feel forlorn, alone, not really belonging. To offset this, to make him somehow even with himself, Eddie had got the money and bought the new clothes so that he could have one little glow of superiority over him who was wearing his regular gray overcoat and brown hat, never mind how it looked.

"New black benny, huh?" he said to Eddie.

"Yes."

"What'd it set you back?"

"Sixty dollars. Guy Woolfolk's."

"Looks nice. The hat, though, no."

"Why not? You're supposed . . ."

"To wear a black skimmer with a tuxedo. I know. You look like a ginny waiter."

"I suppose you're going to wear that wilted tan fur number of yours." This was Eddie's triumph and he let him have it, the moment that was meant to pay for being fatherless.

"It'll keep the snow off my head. Want a short pour?"

Eddie saw the bottle on the dresser. "I thought you weren't going to start until afterward."

"Look at it. The seal's not broken. Mickey gave me a couple of snorts."

"Has Mickey been here?" At this they both knew that the triumph had been erased, and Walter felt ashamed that he had contrived the delicate negotiations that had made the famous Mickey Phelan come to the boardinghouse of a mere freshman. It would have been kinder not to have bought any whisky at all, to have drunk the good, the prewar, liquor that he knew his father and uncle would bring with them and offer him. Eddie, who had been pledged because his high-school grades were good but more because he had been vouched for by a Phelps, could never have prevailed over Mickey's stubbornness, and if Walter had intended that the balance of coups in their continual struggle for prestige should be for once equal, he recognized that it was heavier where it always was, on his side.

"Come and tie my tie, will you, Eddie?" he asked. He had got the shirt on and buttoned. The stiff collar was held only by the back stud. The ends flared out. He had never been able to tie a bow tie.

Eddie got up slowly and, crouching before him to get a straight look at the tie, scowling, his lips pursed, the only sound in the room the heavy breathing of the two of them, he folded, knotted, and drew until it was finished. "Now fluff out those ends."

"Much obliged. Did it hurt you to bend?"

"Sure it hurt me to bend. What do you think my tail's made of, sole leather?"

"You put anything on it?"

Eddie did not answer. He was straightening his own tie in the mirror, patting the white silk handkerchief meticulously into place in his breast pocket. He drew out a pocket comb and combed his hair. "You know?" he said finally.

"What?" Walter asked.

"They broke a paddle on me night before last."

"*Broke* one!"

"Yes. And Wiedemeyer picked up one of those folding chairs."

"Did he hit you with it?"

"No. They talked him out of it. But if he had, I'd have taken off the God-damn pin."

Eddie had seen Wiedemeyer pick up the folding chair after throwing down the broken paddle. He had seen an avidity in his eyes that made

Wiedemeyer seem strange to him. He had made his decision immediately but since that time he had worried about it and wondered why he had done it. It had seemed to him wrong that anyone should be hit with a folding chair outside of a fair fight, yet he had been personally afraid of injury, and fear was contemptible. Dimly and timidly he had begun to entertain suspicions that perhaps the whole occasion of initiation into a fraternity was not worth what he almost dared to call the brutality and indignity, not because he suffered them but rather because they were expressed by so many. Almost smothering these little doubts were the echoes of long conversations in high school about the value of belonging—the social prestige, the vague "good" it would do you after you got out of college, and the rare friendships that would automatically be formed by proximity.

It is difficult to criticize clothes in a country where clothes are worn, where your family and friends are all covered, you yourself have been brought up to wear them, and you have never heard of a place where people go naked. Eddie, however, had persevered. He had expressed iconoclastic notions. Among his friends he was a laughingstock. His mother wept over him and called him a cynic. Since there was no one among his relatives, friends, and teachers who would take him seriously, these irritations made him only the more stubborn. He had thrown out the statement to Walter, knowing it would shock him, because he could count on Walter's answer and he had learned that, once opposed, his doubts tended to become his opinions, and this was what he wanted. If he could not reason himself into the right position, he was sure he could be insulted into it.

Walter had never heard of anybody getting hit with a folding chair. It was too much to endure and if Wiedemeyer had hit him with a chair, his impulse would have been to break the chair over Wiedemeyer's head and take the consequences, but he would never have turned in his pin willingly and it annoyed him to hear Eddie pass any judgments on the fraternity as an institution, even glancing judgments. For him, it was part of the weather he would live in. When the weather was bad you took what shelter you could, but it was worse than wrong to question it. It was silly. Also he sniffed the stink of fear in Eddie's manner and, since fear was contemptible, he wanted to hurt him as a punishment. He said, unconsciously in his father's voice and his father's grunting words, "You couldn't take it, huh?"

Confirmed, convinced, Eddie said almost joyfully, "Why the hell should I?"

"I wouldn't give those guys the satisfaction."

"That's not the point. The point is the value of the whole shooting match. Is it a good thing to allow yourself to be the instigator and focal point of brutality like that?"

"What's this, Philosophy 31?"

"No. I mean it."

"You want to join, don't you? You want to become a brother," he said scornfully. During the week of initiation the probationers made fun of the fraternity. As soon as the ceremonies were finished and they were members, nearly all of them became almost religious partisans for it, defending it against all comers, making it look good as a man will try to make his wife look good.

"I'm not too damned sure."

"Well, you better get hot and make up your mind. You're going to be a member in good standing about an hour from now." He thought suddenly about his own fears. "What are you going to do when they bring out the branding iron?"

"I thought we didn't do that. Have you ever seen a brand on anyone's arm? Has your father got one?"

"It might have faded. They don't try to hit the bone."

"I'm not a steer."

"How do you know? You've never tried to find out yet. All you do with Clara is sit in the library and study."

"Don't evade the issue. I'm not an animal and I'm not going to be branded."

Through Walter's mind drifted a picture of the commotion such a refusal would cause. The lights would be flashed on. Grown men in dinner jackets with white hair and mustaches would gather in clumps to talk excitedly. The members of the active chapter, startled and inept, would stare and shift from foot to foot. Eddie would be led slinking out in disgrace with nowhere to go but the Campus Lunch, and the neglected branding iron would fade slowly from white to red, then duller, duller, and out, a grayish black.

"You know what people would say," he said slowly.

"Sure. I'd be yellow. They could also say that I was the first guy that ever turned them down."

Walter was not ready with anything to reply. He slipped on his waistcoat of black figured silk and took a stance with his feet wide apart before the mirror on the bureau, thrusting the stiff edges of his dress shirt under the lapels of his waistcoat and studiously correcting the set of his tie. As he looked in the glass, he was trying without knowing it to mold his own features until they had the expression, the solidity, the age and experience of his father's. Eddie lay across the bed with his head propped against the wall and his feet dangling to the floor, not watching him.

To Eddie's apprehension, there was a little rind of pleasure. He was glad he had got to college. He was glad he had been pledged to this fraternity because it was a sign that he was acceptable to the kind of people who had money, and, although he did not like them, he assumed that he liked money and he could partly forgive them because of the houses they lived in and the cars they drove. He was in the predicament of many small-town boys who have grown up beneath the same trees, walked and run past the same houses, entered the same stores, still young enough so that everyone they know seems to have stayed the same age, and, for them, whatever they want is elsewhere because it must be strange to justify the passion with which they desire it, and there is no strangeness they can see under these old trees or inside these somber houses or the familiar stores. They feel themselves to be different and they are timid about proclaiming this because they are not certain where they are special or unique, yet the conviction is strong. Unless they inherit money, have a real talent for making it, unless they become some kind of athletic hero, or unless a war sweeps them up and they go, fight, have luck, and return, no one in the town admires them and they have few ties that bind them to it. This makes them sullen and dubious of the local gods and their parents do not know what will become of them.

Eddie was marking time, he thought, waiting to escape, awaiting, even counting on some sudden event to thrust him out of the dullness and stupidity that beset him to some glorious pinnacle where, abruptly rich, famous, full of confidence, he would begin to live.

To go to college, forty miles away from the house he was born in, was not escape; it was withdrawal, slow, but better than nothing. The fraternity, he suspected, was not so romantic a brotherhood as they made it sound. The old members who came back to get drunk at football games were bankers, lawyers, factory owners, like Walter's father, men who passed their lives day by day monotonously in stuffy offices. When he was asked to join, he accepted because, in his loneliness and secrecy, he was too diffident to turn down what seemed to everyone a kind of honor. It had pleased his mother, also, that he had taken a step upward socially and she increased his monthly allowance. And he could not yet, although he intended to soon, defy the adults, stupid and hidebound, who congratulated him on the street when he came home weekends. It seemed to him that he had conceded something, had tarnished his deepest convictions when he had joined the fraternity at all and it would be an affront for them now to make him use a courage he had reserved for greater, more distant adventures, before more noble spectators. The fraternity could be at best a superficial allegiance; he had decided that earlier in the week. If they hurt him, he would turn in his pin and walk out. Yet, in his anticipation, there was a tingle of pleasure—he had never in his life stood in a group of men who were all in evening dress.

Walter, if he thought about it at all, foresaw his life somewhat in the way Europeans do, without the hideous rigidity with which their young men must project the future, yet planned and not by him. His great-grandfather had been one of the three men whose clay-daubed log houses had started the town, at the edge of the river, and who at the end of his life had moved up the street and built in brick the core of the house the family now lived in, and dying left a mill and stock in the new bank. His watch still ticked, a vast flat silver biscuit, in Todd Phelps's pocket. His grandfather had owned the bank and the mill but he had sold them both too cheaply, "pissed them away" he had heard his father say. And now his father owned the bank again, merged with another, parts of three factories, and two farms outright. These were his roots, the ones he recognized. Since he was nourished by them, a part of them, they were too tough for him to pull up and it had not entered his mind to try. Oh, he would roam. There would be for him also adventures, the braveries elsewhere to accomplish, but they were merely ornaments. He would come home and read the *Telegraph* when it came and make sandwiches to eat with a bottle of beer out of his father's icebox. (He liked the icebox particularly.) And since his grandfather had been one of the founding members of the original chapter in the old house on Madison Street, he had always assumed that he would join the fraternity, endure what had to be endured, and later enjoy the fruits of his endurance in the same inevitable way that the Phelpses were buried in the same plot in the cemetery, shaded by the same ash trees his great-grandfather had planted. If he had qualms about his ability to stand the pain, they worried him because he might disgrace his father or his uncle by crying out or his grandfather, who, he assumed without believing at all in ghosts, would be somehow present, vague, numinous, and disapproving.

Although he and Eddie had grown up together, they did not know each other very well. Like most young Americans who are intimate, they talked about their hopes instead of their beliefs and in fierce pride showed themselves, often ludicrously, as they wished they could be, not as they were.

They had a good deal of unregarded knowledge of each other's actions but it made no part of the picture they held of one another. Walter had a shocked intimation that the fraternity did not mean as much to Eddie as it did to him, because his father was dead and had not been a member anyway. This lack could not be enough to make Eddie threaten to walk out on the last ceremonies—that, he thought, must be pure idiotic bravado. He really did not think it possible for any man to live at the university alone, outside a fraternity, with any but a sense of deprivation. If someone had told him that the whole fraternal institution might be silly or at best an expensive boardinghouse, he would have called him crazy. To keep Eddie from this rash foolishness he did a rare thing: he became candid.

He was settling the handkerchief in his breast pocket with great care so that he would not have to look at Eddie after he spoke. "Eddie?"

Eddie did not move his sprawled-out body but he twisted his head, grinding his hair against the wallpaper. "Yeah?"

Two corners of the handkerchief had to show. It was very important. "Don't walk out on it," he said in a low voice, his head down.

"Why the hell not?"

The coarse, almost belligerent tone scared away the candor. He became reasonable. He lit a cigarette. "Well, you'll lose a lot."

Eddie looked straight ahead at the door again. "I can't lose what I haven't got."

"You know what I mean. We're almost in and if you quit now . . ."

"What do I lose? Go ahead, tell me what I lose."

Irritated by Eddie's patience, he said, "You'll be alone. You won't have any friends."

"There are five or six thousand guys on this campus. They speak English."

"I mean, you won't have the right sort of friends."

A calm smile awakened on Eddie's face. "All right. I won't have the right sort of friends. What else?"

"You don't need to be so damned tough."

"I'm not being tough, Walter. I'm just lying here asking you what I stand to lose."

"You like women. . . ."

"There are three or four thousand babes in this town. They speak English too. Some are even good-looking."

"Co-eds," Walter said in contempt.

"It's just in the fraternity we aren't supposed to date co-eds." He sat

[56]

up, saw that the bosom of his shirt was bent, and reached up under his waistcoat and pulled it down. "What you mean is, bud, I won't get to go to those debutante parties in Detroit. I won't meet money."

This was too clear-sighted for Walter. He had taken it for granted that co-eds were stupid. There was a song they sang at the fraternity:

> *"The co-ed leads a sloppy life, sloppy life.*
> *She eats potatoes with her knife, with her knife,*
> *And once a year she takes a scru-u-ub*
> *And leaves a ring around the tub, the dirty thing."*

Although he had known three or four clean girls in high school who had come to the university and made better grades than he had, he believed the song. Also he had taken it for granted that the Detroit debutantes were more beautiful, more polished and charming since they had been turned out by Eastern schools, certainly better dressed than his high-school friends, and if, in the long future, he were to marry, it would naturally be among these rich girls that he would seek a wife.

All members of the right fraternities met money. It was one of the services the organization could unobtrusively render, something that one knew all and said nothing about, a perquisite, and if anyone, well brought up, suffered any faint disgust at the inhumanity of such dealing, he stifled and forgot it. It was bad taste in Eddie to blat it out with open scorn. After the confidences, the long evenings they had spent lying on the grass and talking of their futures, and the beautiful women as unreal as succubi they would find and possess, Walter had believed they both thought alike about women, but Eddie was making him seem to be a fool with his quiet reasonable answers, and feeling chilled by this strange train of opinion, recoiling from it as a betrayal because Eddie had worked it all out secretly, he thought maybe their friendship was decaying, maybe something had happened to it. He was sitting bent over on the cardboard-bottomed chair with his elbows on his knees, working his hands and looking at the floor. He blushed with embarrassment and did not look up when he spoke, "I sort of hoped we'd go through together."

Eddie was still staring at the door panel. "Well, I'm all dressed," he said before he caught the intention of Walter's remark.

"No. I mean, we've grown up together and . . ." He stopped. It was genuine emotion. This kindness, this concern had never appeared in the friendship before.

At first Eddie had a flicker of amusement that one of the tough coarse

Phelpses should make this kind of appeal to him. He was old enough to see Walter as one of his family line instead of a single person. But the amusement did not last long enough to color his reply. He was touched and he knew he would have to respond to Walter's emotion with kindness, but it struck him as a sinister trait in himself that he should know all this in a flash, and for the first time since they had known each other he chose the less brutal manner of reply. "I know. I hope we go through together, too."

"I don't think they're going to brand us," Walter began confidently. "I never heard it for sure."

"Well, if they don't, all right."

"If they do, what?"

Eddie knew what he would do. He would walk out. He respected not so much their long friendship as this strange moment of emotion when it would be unfair to be ruthless and reasonable. "I don't know," he said. "Wait till it comes time."

Walter accepted this as a victory for his own argument—Eddie's bravado had waned. "It's a quarter to seven. I'll go call a cab." He started for the door and stopped. "Have a drink," he said, nodding toward the bottle on the dresser, the first time he had ever been able to be casual about liquor.

"I thought you were going to wait until afterward," Eddie said again, pushing himself up off the bed.

"Help yourself," Walter said. Eddie heard him banging down the stairs to the telephone in the hall.

He took up the bottle and looked at it. The cork was driven in flush with the top of the bottle. Eddie took a Scout knife out of his trousers pocket, with a big blade, a corkscrew, a leather punch, and a short screw driver attached. Before his death his father had given it to him for completing his first ten merit badges and he knew he ought to feel ashamed of himself for opening a whisky bottle with the corkscrew. He waited a moment, looking at the knife in his palm, but he did not feel anything. He pulled the corkscrew out at a right angle to the handle, inserted the point in the cork, and twisted it. He took out a handkerchief and wrapped it around the stag handle of the knife as he had seen drinkers do at the fraternity. He stuck the bottle between his knees and gave a hard pull. The cork slid out so easily that he nearly sat down. He lifted the bottle to his lips and took it down again. He set it on the dresser beside him and lit a cigarette. He was in a hurry now because he could hear Walter talking to the cab company on the phone. He lifted the bottle again and swallowed twice. He could feel and hear an abrupt purling retching in his throat. He swallowed convulsively several times and gasped for breath. He had the cigarette safely in his mouth when Walter came back into the room and he was leaning nonchalantly against the dresser.

"They'll be here in a couple of minutes," Walter said. "How'd it go? Any good?"

"It's OK," Eddie said huskily.

"Taste anything like you thought it would?"

"It tastes like hell."

"Well, I think I'll have a snort before we go," Walter said with a legitimate rakish ease. He took the bottle from the dresser, lifted it once and said, "Here's how."

Eddie said, "Go ahead."

Walter drank, coughed, and shuddered. He held the bottle out and looked at it. "By God, this is going to have to do something for me if I'm going to keep drinking it."

"Well, we're started now."

Just then they heard the cab sound its horn in the street outside.

· VI ·

UNDER THE BIG bare maple trees, Eri Phelps stood on the curb in front of his house. Although it was only a little after three in the afternoon, he was wearing a black derby hat, and a dinner jacket muffled in an English topcoat with long full skirts. He took out a silver cigarette case, opened it, and stared into it scowling and moving his lips. He put the case back in his side pocket, and, flouncing up the skirts of his topcoat, he reached into his hip pocket and drew out a long monogrammed silver flask holding a quart (his tailor sewed special pockets in all his trousers). He unscrewed the hinged cap, tipped the flask to catch the weak winter light, and blinking one eye, he peeped in to be sure it was full. He was already a little bit drunk.

Todd Phelps was also in a tuxedo but all he wore over it was an old spotted trench coat and his hat was a gray fedora with a crazy brim. He was behind the wheel of his Packard limousine and he was nearly lying on his right side so he could look up and watch his brother's last preparations. He said, "Get in," and Eri got in. If it had been a man exactly like Eri but not his brother, he would have said, "Get in, you lazy bastard."

He drove sedately to the edge of town and at the limits he jammed down the accelerator until they were making seventy miles an hour. He liked to drive fast. They did not talk much. Todd never had much to say to his brother, and Eri, looking as if he were propped in the seat, took a little drink every ten minutes neatly and silently.

Like many men who have learned to drive when they were past thirty years old, Todd sat hunched up over the wheel like Barney Oldfield. To any farmer he passed he looked alert and the robust pose made the car seem to be going faster than it was. He was now a competent, even an expert driver but he could not relax. Some memory of the first elation (and fear) that speed had given him kept him rigid. He gave the necessary minimum of attention to traffic and curves in the road. He made a few lightning appraisals of farms they passed. Once he stopped at the foot of a long hill and stuck out his hand toward Eri, who put the flask in it. Todd took one long drink, returned the flask without thanks, and started driving seventy miles an hour again.

If he knows the road, everybody must do something while he is driving because it is so dull. If he is not playing games passing other cars or talking to someone, he must let his mind fiddle with something. Todd took up the long stern fantasy that distinguished him, the secret occupation that everything else he did provided the time for. He could retire into it adeptly, look you square in the face, nod, smile, talk, and still pursue it, no more seeing you than if he had grown special eyelids, invisible but opaque.

If you had asked him what he was thinking about and he thought you worth an honest answer, he would have said he was thinking about money. He would not have said any more. He was not articulate in this because it was one of his talents to have learned that few people had his peculiar ability and he had never talked about it to anyone, yet he thought in images like a poet, and he did his thinking in little free precious stretches: when he was driving somewhere; at night when he lay down before he slept; in the mornings shaving; and while he was talking to half the bank's customers, the stupid half. It was a grim precise dream about money, he thought, and without it he would have died.

The money was not pretty pieces of paper, green and yellow, with little silk threads stamped into it. It was not specie, nor was it the perhaps expected mental furniture of a banker, the notes and mortgages and contracts, the stocks and bonds. And it was not any such equation that appeared to his vision like a slogan on a billboard lighted at night: MONEY IS POWER.

Musicians often have musical sons. Todd's father, Henry, had given his life to the accumulation of money; Levi, Henry's father, was devoted to it, liked to rub it and smell it and surreptitiously to hold a gold piece in his mouth like a plug of tobacco, a saver, not a maker; and Todd's great-grandfather, Mark, a poor York State farmer, never had any money to speak of but he trembled with hatred when anyone passed his place in a double buggy with matched horses or toward a man wearing a diamond in a claw ring or toward any rich man. Maybe one of the strains of Todd's inheritance was a memory of these attitudes, to be born already refined, even learned, so that there were steps in his thinking he did not have to take because Grandpa or someone earlier had already done it. For Todd thought about money in a way no Phelps ever did.

He did not contemplate the things money would buy. To take it for a medium of exchange demeaned it. That was Old Man Bailey's error and, to Todd's fastidious mind, an error of taste.

Since he was too arrogant to conceive that he would ever lack money, the behavior of his banking colleagues was hardly less tiresome. To them money was something to get like coal in the cellar with winter coming on. He could deal with them without open scorn because they manipulated the symbols of their trade smoothly enough and a financial abstraction is more pleasing to the intellect than a load of hogs, squealing and stinking. The trouble with them, they conducted their affairs as if the symbols were real, as if the word "asset" were as tangible as one of the hogs, or "credit" as sure a bridge into the future as the signs of the winter they feared. Their demeanor gave them away, however. It made Todd chuckle to watch them. They held themselves with the solemnity of priests, and exacted little homages from the community because somewhere inside them, perhaps in their spines, they knew their vocation was a ritual of worship, what they talked was a theology, and what moved them was a faith. They believed what they did was to assist the inevitable while Todd, with a cynicism that irritated them, damned the whole financial structure as arbitrary, sanctified by mere time.

Todd was a little more adult than anyone around him because he had passed beyond his contemporaries' fascination with abstractions and gone on (or returned) to the contemplation of men. For his own purposes, of course. It gave him no pleasure to watch a stock ticker (and he worked only for his own pleasure, an artist) because GM 50.87 stood for some pieces of paper in a broker's office that were earnests for 5000 crisp shares of stock and the 5000 shares might be the equivalents of some lathes or dies in a factory, a long improbable train of promises. It was at this point

[61]

or earlier that the imagination of his colleagues petered out. Todd went further. It was the man who ran the lathe or the manager of the division who interested him. Todd wanted to know why he wanted money so he could take it away from him, not that the money was specially valuable but for the pleasure in the taking away.

Banking provided the opportunity. Men came in person to ask for loans and Todd liked to study them. He might have been as happy in the law or medicine but his father had been a banker. Todd had a professional rough affability. Nearly everyone in the county knew him and he had cultivated a memory for faces. When some poor forty-acre farmer approached him haltingly to borrow $100 for feed because an early frost had hit his corn, the chances were that Todd knew his little place, remembered the patch of low ground that would in the natural course of things be touched early by the frost, and he would lend the $100, a routine matter.

If some young clerk asked for enough to pay for a third baby and offered a mortgage on some little back-street house, Todd would have heard somewhere that the clerk had already been turned down for a raise in salary because he was not bright enough or willing enough, and Todd, complacently prescient, would write out the mortgage knowing perfectly well that finally the bank would take the house because the young man's uttermost efforts would never bring him enough money to get clear, and Todd, shaking hands, patting him on the shoulder, would watch him leave impassively, thinking, "Now why doesn't he know that?"

The prescience tickled his self-conceit, that and keeping everlasting tabs on people to watch his foresight confirm itself, but it was the more complex situations that stimulated him. One day he would happen to follow a man's wife down the street, perhaps a pretty wife, and with the usual sharp glances he would discover a new thickening around the thighs and hips, and, passing her, touching his hat, and smiling in her face good morning, he would detect the puffing of the second chin perhaps with a tinge of personal regret. Six months later he would hear of the husband's antics with a blonde chicken on a business trip to Akron or Fort Wayne. There was never any hurry; there were half a dozen such little troubles ripening that he could bring to crisis. Soon the business trips might come oftener or a handsome widow come to town (the widows were rare). At this point there remained only to choose the moment, and it was the choice that took the finesse, the delicacy. Perhaps he might overhear word of a family quarrel, a little sign to show the full maturity of the situation. Then Todd would approach him tactfully and offer a loan, leaning back in the chair watching the husband struggle with the weights of habitual devotion, his reputation, the children, the dejection turning in him because he was going gray and there was hardly any time, and the greater, the heaviest weight of his eagerness for the new woman whoever she was. It was all business, of course. Security was demanded and Todd never gave a hint that he knew what was going on. If the man turned down the offer, Todd was not sorry; if he took it, Todd did not jump up and crack his heels. Either way he had learned something, enjoyed himself, and perhaps made the bank some money. The bank was a school and Todd was nearly a philosopher. He knew intuitively that credit was merely a name for some man's hope, and if he used credit, it was as a tool to examine the man and what the man thought the future could bring him. All this was done without any good will whatever.

Although he was contemptuous of his clients because he could see through them so often, bringing all the elements of their lives to focus on their desire for money, he did not, any more than did his father, suspect that he was doing anything wrong, anything that had a moral color to it at all, nor could he quite recognize in their subservience their hatred.

Eri had drunk himself pale by the time they reached the fraternity house. Todd watched him as he got out of the car without stumbling and decided that he was good for five or six hours yet. Eri stood beside the car waiting, swaying a little. Todd got out. The light rain had turned to snow. Todd stood there a moment looking at the Packard, slapping his pigskin gloves together, watching the snowflakes light on the car's ridged hood, melt, and disappear. It was the gesture of the old-time automobilist, his pride in his car. "Well, we made her," he said. They went up the front walk under the bare trees into the house. It was a big Elizabethan place erected only the year before by enthusiastic Detroit millionaires. The bridge chairs cost forty-eight dollars apiece.

They put their hats on a shelf in the cloakroom among a heap of tennis rackets in presses, odd golf clubs, and packages of returned laundry. The cloakroom opened into a lavatory in tile and marble. It was empty. Eri filled the silver flask from a bottle of whisky and Todd washed his hands, looking carefully at his fat face in the mirror above the washbowls, pulling down his jowl, raising his lips and sucking at his teeth.

Neither of the brothers spoke and Todd wondered briefly why Eri had come at all. He was a bachelor who had all his hair. He could come and go as he pleased. He could take a drink whenever he wanted it. He could go to see a woman any time. He had no acknowledged son. Todd did not think it likely that stag drinking with fraternity brothers all in established professions would hold Eri for a whole evening, but, remembering his position, he did not want to display the envy his question would reveal so he said nothing.

As he passed by his overcoat in the cloakroom he took a new bottle of Scotch out of a pocket. In deference to the house rules of the fraternity (which allowed no drinking within its doors), he thrust the bottle under his dinner jacket where he could hold it in place with his arm. They went out of the cloakroom into a large hallway, nodded curtly to two or three boys, members of the active chapter, and immediately climbed the tiled stairs to the second floor.

They entered a long corridor on which about ten doors opened. Todd walked down the corridor until he found one that was closed. He opened it without hesitation. Inside the room a naked youth was shaking talcum powder into his armpits before a washbowl mirror. He looked into the mirror to see behind him.

"Hi, Mr. Phelps. It's going to start in about an hour," he said.

"Is, eh? Where's an empty room?" Todd said.

"Next door. Pete's father's sick. He had to go home yesterday," the boy said.

Todd and Eri went into the next room and shut the door after them. It was the living room of a two-room suite. A study table with a wooden electric lamp in the center and green blotting pads speckled with ink blotches stood next to the wall. Two battered wicker armchairs with padded seats stood in corners. A small bookcase ran along one wall filled with textbooks, leather notebooks, a few novels, and some detective stories. Tacked to the wall was a Coles Phillips hosiery ad, a photograph of the Taj Mahal, and an oblong blue felt pennant which bore the words THE HILL.

Todd set his bottle of whisky on the table. He went into the bedroom and found the occupant's toothbrush glass, spotted and dirty. He poured himself four fingers of whisky and looked toward Eri, who was leaning on both hands against the wall inspecting the hosiery ad. "Mud in your eye," he said perfunctorily and drank it all.

He sat down in the chair by the desk and threw one fat thigh over the arm. This was what they had come for, to get drunk and to see their friends. They were now settled and ready to receive. Although Todd knew that many of his classmates in the fraternity were richer than he, presidents of bigger banks, trust companies, or loan and title companies, or corporation lawyers or factory managers, he would not deign to go wandering up and down the hall looking for them.

"Well, here we are," Eri said. He had sat down with the open flask cradled in his hands. "What time's it start?"

"About an hour."

"Did you ever sleep with that girl that lived out by the Arboretum?" Eri asked seriously.

Todd laughed in two abrupt barks and gave no other answer. Eri was good and drunk, already, and it gave Todd a calm feeling of superiority over the other families of his town that the Phelpses could afford Eri. Eri fooled a little with local and state politics but he had never worked, never been employed. He did not hunt or fish. He lived in his own house. He got up late in the morning and read the *Free Press* in bed until his houseman called him to breakfast. Later he stopped in at the bank for a few minutes and went on up to the City Club, where he played bridge until lunch and after lunch until three. Then he began to drink for the rest of the day, which he ended wherever it suited his fancy, in Detroit, Chicago, or in his own house, a small decorous brick house on one of the best streets in town, alone or accompanied. Todd admired the stamina it took to lead such a life of pleasure and such simple unvaried pleasures, liquor and women. Eri was sharp enough about his investments, kept them up, and showed a little profit every year but they did not take much of his time. The politics he could work while he was drinking and most of his energies were directed toward amusing himself in what the Reverend Channer had once publicly called "a round of open debauchery." It did not occur to him that Eri was stupid—he was too proud even to make the inquiry.

Todd was startled and a little flattered when Eri asked him about the timid girl, a classical student with a genuine taste for the Horatian Epistles, whom he had seduced in his freshman year at law school. It showed him that Eri was maudlinly entertaining the past, their years in the university together, and he approved of this sentimentality. He liked to have his brother the custodian of virtues he scorned or was not inclined to.

"What made you think about her?" he asked.

"I always liked her looks," Eri said dreamily. "Nice figure." He flipped back the cap on top of his flask, took a little drink, and put it gently back in his lap. "I wonder what became of her."

"What difference does it make?" Todd asked, startled.

"It doesn't make any. No, it doesn't make any difference to me. Not any difference to anybody except her. I was just wondering, that's all," Eri said.

"She was a silly little bitch," Todd said in a warm reminiscent tone. He was getting ready to make Eri a gift, the whole story.

"She wasn't so pretty for nice but she was hell for stuff," Eri said, giggling, and Todd recognized it as a phrase Eri must have recently picked up, probably from a girl, and a young one. Eri yawned. "You remember the night I was initiated?"

"No."

Eri leaned forward beseechingly. "You remember. I couldn't find my studs." He was searching Todd's face, certain that the memory would begin with some relaxing of the cheeks or flicker of the eyelid. "I COULDN'T FIND MY STUDS," he bawled, not that he thought Todd was deaf or because he was irritated. It was the sudden despair of the very drunk.

"No," Todd said.

"Well, I wonder how *he's* feeling. I remember how I was feeling." He sat up and nodded his head coyly, smirking. "I was scared."

"Who's *he?*"

"Walter, you damned fool. Your son. The child of your bowels."

The occasion had seemed to him so much one for his private enjoyment and he had looked forward to it so hard for a week or more that Todd was ashamed when Eri made him think of his son for the first time. He said, "Oh," and then, "Oh, he'll be all right."

"He'll be getting a girl out by the Arboretum along about next year," Eri said.

"He'll be in hell with his back broke, too," Todd said savagely. He did not intend to allow his son any liberties he had taken himself. Walter was the only young Phelps and he wanted him to come into the money with a good reputation.

Eri snorted contemptuously and had to wipe his nose just afterward.

"Well, he will, by God."

"Any son of mine . . . ," Eri began in a stern mocking tone. "You try and stop him."

"It's all right if he wants to take a couple of drinks. I don't mind that but you let him start playing around with women and I'll break him in two."

Eri yawned again. "Yes. I expect you will."

Todd did not want to talk about his son. A good reputation was a business asset, and one of the few things Todd knew he was afraid of was the way his son might turn out, foolish, spendthrift, or weak. Although he had watched him carefully, he had not yet been able to ascertain Walter's attitude toward money, and of course, he had to expect any one of the obvious ones since he did not know his son.

He poured himself another drink in the toothbrush glass, a bigger one.

He leaned back in his chair until the back touched the wall and threw one leg on the study table. He was just lifting his glass to drink when the door opened and a young man in a dinner jacket looked in. He had yellowish hair and he wore horn-rimmed glasses. He seemed to be embarrassed at once.

"I'm sorry, fellows. I'm on the House Committee. Kind of watch that drinking, will you?"

It made Todd sore to be called "fellows." He drank his drink and made a loud "A-a-h!" after it. Eri said nonchalantly, "We always watch our drinking, bud."

"Well, will you do that?" the young man said with fake deferential joyousness. "There's going to be some of the *fratres in facultate* over here tonight, you know, Psychie Wallace and like that, and we don't want to get in bad."

"Are you trying to bum a drink or what?" Todd said.

"Never touch the stuff," the boy said facetiously.

"Well, then," Todd said.

The boy turned red and shut the door. It was flung open at once so hard it hit the wall by a man in a derby hat and Chesterfield overcoat. He had a package under his arm wrapped in newspaper.

"Hello, you Phelps bastards. Hello, you drumheads. Hello, you . . ."

"You what?" Todd said sourly.

The man laid the package on the table and patted it with exaggerated gentleness. He tossed his hat and coat on a chair. His face was very youthful with firm pink cheeks but his hair was nearly white. His nails had been manicured and covered with a transparent polish that caught the light almost as if he were wearing rings. He stuck out his hand to Eri, bending toward him so far that it was hard to tell whether he was bowing or merely keeping Eri from rising. "Eri," he said politely and shook his hand. He turned to Todd, said, "Todd," and shook his hand. "Delighted to see you. Have you been here long? How're the family?"

"Save it, Andy. We're not customers."

"How long you been here?" Andy asked.

"All afternoon."

"You . . .," Eri began. He stopped and looked out of the window. They waited. At last he took a deep breath, swung his head around to look at Andy, and said, "Just get out from Detroit, Andy?"

"Yes, and I had a hell of a time. I couldn't get any liquor. I usually buy my stuff there on John R., the Clover Club. I was having a big go-round

[67]

with the Dodge boys this afternoon and I couldn't get away until quarter to four. I stopped by for some liquor but Louie said he just had a phone call and the cops were on the way and for me to get the hell out quick before the cops got there." He had opened the package and thrown the newspaper in the wastebasket. Two bottles of whisky stood on the table. "Got a corkscrew, Todd? No, wait a minute. I'll bet the glue's still wet on these." He took one of the bottles by the neck and smacked the bottom with the heel of his hand. The cork flew out and some of the whisky slopped out on the floor.

"Just smack it. J-u-s-t smackit," Eri muttered admiringly.

Andy picked up the cork and examined it under the light. "Just what I said. See? Glue's still wet on it." He held out the cork to show it glistening under the light.

"The Dodge boys wouldn't want you to drink stuff like that, Andy," Todd said mildly.

"Where'd you get it? You must've got it somewhere. The cops didn't catch you, did they?" Eri said in a spurt of vivacity apparently made to test his coherence.

"It was a place under a brownstone house. It was just a bar and he sold me this rotgut for seven bucks and I had a couple over the counter and here I am. What you boys been doing lately?"

"Why, I've been mortgaging a few farms, letting out a little here, taking in a little there," Todd said. "You going to drink any of that, Andy, or you just going to keep it and be friends with it?"

Andy looked at the bottle with a wry face. "Come on. We'll burn some of it and see." He took the bottle into the bedroom. Todd followed. He poured a little whisky on the white enamel edge of the washbowl and held a lighted match over it. It took fire. Bending down and squinting one eye, he watched the flame.

"Is that blue or ain't it?" he asked.

"It's got some yellow in it but not enough to matter. It won't kill you," Todd said.

Scowling, Andy held the bottle up to the light. A yellow reflection mantled his face. He tipped up the bottle and took a big swallow. The tears rose in his eyes. He held his breath for three seconds and blew it out. "Jee-*zuss*," he gasped. "Tastes like red pepper and broken glass."

Todd slapped him on the back. They went back into the bedroom and sat down again. Andy stood the bottle on the table in front of him and said in a voice of awe, "You send a young man out, you get an old man back, drinking that stuff." He resumed in a normal firm businesslike voice, indicating that the formalities of greeting and reunion had been accomplished. "You got any Chrysler, Todd?"

Todd pursed his lips and shook his head.

"What's the matter? Who handles your account, Pierce?"

"Don't anybody handle my account."

"You caught the close before you left, didn't you?"

"Yes. Broke a hundred today," Todd said.

"Then what do you mean you haven't got any Chrysler? Are you nuts? Is that true, Eri? Hasn't Todd got any Chrysler?"

Eri, sitting contemplatively with one hand supporting his jaw, opened his eyes and said politely, "I don't believe he has."

"Well, now I'll tell you what I heard today. I won't say who told me but it's straight and it's hot. What was the close today, a hundred and what?"

"One and a half."

"Chrysler had a board meeting yesterday in New York. My informant talked to one of the directors. The stock is going to five hundred and . . ."

"What have they got, a derrick?" Todd asked contemptuously.

"And . . ."

"A lot of god-damn moonshine if you ask me."

"Listen, Todd. And when it gets to five hundred, they're going to split it three for one and they confidently expect it to go to five hundred again," Andy finished triumphantly.

Todd took a cigar out of his breast pocket, bit away the end and spat it out on the floor. "Now I'll tell you something, Andy." He put the cigar in his mouth and held a lighted match to the end of it, sucking and puffing. "If you fellows go on playing around in this market, you're going to lose your shirts." He blew a big ring of smoke and smiled complacently.

"I'm going to pick up money when I find it in the street. Aren't you in the market at all?"

"I run a bank, not a bucket shop," Todd said. He was enjoying himself. To tell Andy Campbell, the secretary of a big Detroit trust company, that he was going to lose his shirt made it all the more pleasant.

Tender for the prestige of his firm, Andy said coldly, "We are putting a good many of our clients into stocks we have investigated."

"Sure you are. I'll bet you are," Todd said grinning.

"We've made them a lot of money."

"Sure you have."

"What the hell are you grinning like a Chessy cat for? Say, you don't know something, do you?" he finished anxiously.

"After twenty years in the banking business? Not much." Todd looked at the end of the cigar he was holding and pushed off the ash with his little finger. "But I do know this. This ain't a real boom."

"I just bought a new car out of it. It's a real car."

"And I know what credit is and I know what credit is not," Todd said pontifically.

"Production's up all over the country," Andy said. Todd worried him and he forgot that Todd always worried him.

"Up but not up enough to account for all this hoo-raw. No, this boom is purely a psychological phenomenon, all in people's minds, that's all it is."

"Oh, horse-shit," Andy said bitterly.

Todd bowed his head and held out his open hands in a gesture of false acceptance. "All right. All right."

"No, but damn it, Todd. Here's the country in the most prosperous condition in its history . . ."

"Won't last. Won't last. Somebody will start teetering and get scared and then, whammo!"

Eri was lying on his side in the wicker chair with his knees drawn up and his flask in his lap. He spoke with great precision. His eyes were shut. "I am playing the stock market and I am making money."

"But all your money's not in it," Todd said. "You're dragging some anyway."

"Certainly. Take some, leave some," Eri said.

"Sure. Your name's Phelps but most of these people . . ."

The door opened and the member of the House Committee said, "They're starting, fellows." He looked at the liquor on the table disapprovingly. Downstairs they could hear singing.

"W-e-l-l-l," Todd yawned. He stood up and stretched.

"Let's leave the bottles here. We can come back later," Andy said.

"Somebody'll steal 'em," Todd protested.

"That's the idea. I want to see the one that steals mine."

Todd grabbed Eri by the arm and pulled him up to his feet.

Andy was sympathetic. "Is he all right?"

Erie straightened up. His eyes were still closed. He said reproachfully, "Why, Andrew. I heard every word you said. More, too. 'Once more, ye brothers, come once more,' " he sang, staggering toward the door with his eyes closed. He bumped into a chair. "Open eyes," he murmured.

When they got downstairs to the smoking room, they found a line of men and boys, each with his hands on the shoulders of the one in front, singing and swaying in step, moving slowly downstairs to the chapter room in the basement.

The two boys paid their taxi in the driveway beside the fraternity house. They walked through the snow to an areaway with a flight of steps that led down to a cellar door. Walter raised his hand to knock on the door, changed his mind, and offered his hand to Eddie. "Good luck," he said. "Don't give in." Eddie said nothing. It was dark and the darkness would excuse his silence.

Walter gave a complicated series of knocks on the door with his knuckles. There was one knock in reply. The door opened. They were seized and blindfolded by three members dressed in gowns and hoods of black cambric like costumes in amateur theatricals. It was dark in the cellar and no one spoke. When the bandages were tied around their eyes and their hats and coats taken away from them, they were led down one of the cellar corridors. Walter tried to remember where they were going but he became confused and gave it up.

They were stopped. Whoever was leading them took his hands away and left them standing there alone. Walter could hear footsteps going away and the creak of a door hinge. After a minute he said quietly, "Eddie?"

"Shhh!" someone said.

Walter stood erect like a soldier at attention. His conduct now would contribute if only a little to the total mass approval required for him to become a member. He was sure after this last test he would be entrusted with some secrets. No one had ever said much about them but he expected knowledge of them to help him in some way. He had heard that the Skull and Bones Society at New Haven was one of the richest corporations in the state of Connecticut and if you were a member you could get a job selling bonds in any house in Wall Street. He assumed that the secrets of his fraternity, since it was a national organization with chapters in all the best colleges and universities, would have better secrets than Skull and Bones, which existed only at Yale. The arch in his back made him tired but he did not relax and he wondered about the secrets.

Ten feet away from him, on the other side of some laundry tubs, Eddie shifted from one foot to the other nervously. He was very tired from the exertions of the week before, the mock initiation. His buttocks hurt him and he rubbed them from time to time. Reaching out, he touched the edge of a laundry tub. He moved over so he could lean against it but someone watching him grabbed him by the arm and jerked him away from the tub.

Eddie shifted his feet, rubbed and kneaded his muscles. He went over in his mind the speech he would make if they tried to brand him with a red-hot iron. He wanted to compose something that would make them feel the pride he had in himself and force them to be ashamed. The first thing that came into his head was "Stop, unhand me," but he knew this was from some novel he had read a long time ago and it was comically pompous. Everything he thought of seemed pompous or an appeal for pity.

After twenty minutes standing in the cellar, the two boys heard one of the fraternity songs through the walls and floor of the house. They knew the last dangerous ceremonies had begun. Eddie rubbed his hands together. He found they were sweating and he swore under his breath. He was fighting against a childish yearning, a strain that drew his throat tight, for someone to come in, switching on the lights and saying jovially, "That's all, boys. It's all over. You can go home." And it was home he wanted to go to, not his boardinghouse. He was able to recognize this clearly as the last beckoning of his childhood and he swore all the harder. When Walter heard the song, he drew himself even more erect, although there was an ache under his shoulder blades.

At last two young men in dinner jackets came into the laundry room, tightened their blindfolds, and shoved them stumbling down a corridor of the cellar past the furnace room. They stopped in a little hallway in front of a polished oak door ornamented with hammered strap-iron hinges. Bolts were shot and a long chain rattled. The door creaked open and they were pushed ahead.

They were on a tile floor and they could tell the room was full because little sounds made no echo. They were posted in a semicircle around a small table. Eddie sniffed sharply two or three times but he could not smell any fire where they might be heating the irons. At last the blindfolds were taken off. The room was perfectly dark and they could see nothing at all.

Abruptly a song began. Eighty male voices sang loudly. It was not a song the initiates had ever heard before and the few phrases they could make out sounded ominous. After three or four verses it stopped short. Someone blew his nose.

A figure in a glazed black gown and hood took a black cloth off a plaque lying on the table. Glowing brightly with a greenish light was a bird in bas-relief. A bass voice at the end of the room chanted solemnly: "This is the bird of Wisdom. This is the attendant of Zeus. This is our bird, the raven."

The whole room shouted, "BE YE WISE!"

The initiates jumped and twitched at the shout. The figure in the hood put the black cloth over the plaque, and laid the plaque on the floor beneath the table. He removed a cloth from a second plaque. On it was merely a glowing circle about a foot in diameter.

The bass voice began again, "This is the circle of Truth. Truth is endless. Truth is symmetry. Truth is beauty."

The room shouted again, "BE YE TRUE!"

Walter surmised that these were the secrets and he knew they would never be any help to him. He could hardly tell what he had expected, perhaps a sesame that would admit him to the best society everywhere, or a password to give to rich men, or some spell or charm that would help him with women, something real and powerful at least, not this simple stuff he had heard all his life. It was something like Sunday school or a present by an old aunt, yet even as he was thinking this way, he tried to push his mind toward something else, and, since he had counted on so much, it was easy for the tension of this expectation to find something else to satisfy it. With a tinge of shame he told himself that the words were beautiful, that the bass voice was solemn, that the ritual gave him a mystic feeling. He remembered that his father and uncle were somewhere in the darkness looking at him. They had heard the same words, his grandfather also. A President of the United States had heard them, sixteen governors of states, a Justice of the Supreme Court, bishops, generals, corporation presidents, big lawyers, mining engineers in the Urals (he had read about them in the fraternity magazine); chemists working for coffee plantations in Brazil; oil men in Arabia. He constructed his own little aura of reverence and entered into it.

There was now a third plaque for them to look at. It was a skull and crossbones. As soon as it was revealed, all the men in the room made a circle around the initiates. Eddie could see their stiff shirt fronts gleam dimly in the pallid light.

The bass voice, still coming from the back of the room, chanted: "These are the bones of Death. These we carry. These we lay down. Death awaits the man who is false to his trust."

There was a tremendous shout, "BE YE FAITHFUL!"

Eddie was not impressed. It reminded him of Hotspur's "deal of skimble-skamble stuff." All the members had come crowding around to watch and he could smell the fumes of whisky. The time must have nearly come for them to bring out the branding irons. He could feel the trickle of sweat run down his spine. He had composed the speech he would make and he was almost eager to see the brazier, bright and smoking, carried in.

[73]

The bass voice, a little tired, began again, "Hear ye the words of God as set down by the Apostle Paul: *'We beseech you, brethren, to be at peace among yourselves. And we exhort you, brethren, admonish the disorderly, encourage the faint-hearted, support the weak, be long-suffering toward all. See that none render unto any one evil for evil; but always follow after that which is good, one toward another and toward all.'* "

A youthful tenor voice, Freddie Tolburn's, a senior, said, "We humbly ask that the following pledges be received in our fellowship:

> Foster Carroll Briggs
> Edward Robert Burcham
> Spencer Ellis
> Herman Fenstermacher
> Walter Todd Phelps
> William Henry Potts
> George Withers Radford
> Ashton John Wood, the third
> Philip Ott Ziegler."

Cheering and handclapping began. The electric lights were switched on. The new members stood grinning and blinking at the sudden brightness. Walter looked around at the crowd until he saw his father and uncle, smiled and bobbed his head at them. Morose and shocked, Eddie ran his finger around inside of his collar and stared at the floor. Their ceremonies were all over and he had not had a chance to say anything.

Carl Bachman, a rich junior from Toledo, to whom he never spoke because he envied him his clothes, ran up to Eddie, grabbed at his hand, and shook it. "God, Eddie, I'm glad you're in. It's really fine to have you, boy," he said in a choked, sentimental voice. Astonished, Eddie looked him all over to see if he was drunk but he moved on and began saying the same thing to someone else.

Todd Phelps stood fishing in his waistcoat pockets. He felt in his side pockets. At last out of his hip pocket he brought a small white cardboard box. He opened it and took out a gold fraternity pin ornamented with pearls. There was a fancy kind of safety catch that held the pin-point and he had to put on his glasses to see to get it open. With the pin in his hand he swayed through the crowd looking for his son. Walter saw him coming.

"Well, boy, you made it. Nice work," he said. He gave his son the secret handshake of the fraternity, and stooping, he fastened the pin to Walter's waistcoat. "There you are, full-fledged, like your dad and your grandpa."

There was a lump in Walter's throat and he was afraid to speak. His uncle, almost dead drunk, shook hands with him silently and patted him on the shoulder. Walter thought he was overcome with emotion. Near him there was a father with tears shining on his face embracing his son. "I will always remember this moment," Walter thought, exalted.

Eddie had his hand shaken by several alumni whom he did not know and by most of the active chapter. He was watching Walter pulse the muscles in his jaw when a pale little senior, Emery Valentine, shook hands with a perfunctory pressure and said breathlessly, "Say, Eddie, I'm awfully sorry. I was supposed to be your sponsor and I had the pin in my pocket all the time but I just forgot all about it. I'm terribly sorry." Emery was the only Phi Bete in the house and Eddie supposed they had made him his sponsor because he himself got good grades. Emery bent over, squinting through his glasses, and pricked his finger once or twice but at last he had the pin fastened on Eddie's waistcoat. It was all over. He was a member. And he thought gloomily, "What am I doing here?"

· VII ·

THE CHAIRMAN of the House Committee stood by the fireplace rubbing his horn-rimmed spectacles with a silk handkerchief and trying to think what to do. The alumni guests were making him angry. They had all come up from the chapter room laughing and talking to gather in little clumps in the smoking room. The Chairman had to admit that it was a fine-looking gathering like something in a movie or a story, all these men in tuxedos (only one or two in business suits) silhouetted against the walnut paneling of the smoking room, lolling in the red leather chairs. It looked rich and high-class and he was proud to be a member of such a group.

He wished, though, they had more respect for the fraternity. If they had, they wouldn't drink in the chapter house. It was, in a way, a profanation. Some of them were passing flasks around and tipping them up, and others were walking around openly with water glasses they had pinched from the dining room full of whisky. This was strictly against the house rules and they all knew it. As Chairman he ought to walk up to every brother who was drinking and just tell him, "You're not supposed to drink in the house. That'll cost you five bucks fine." But he did not dare. He knew they would laugh at him.

All he did was to move nervously from one group to another, saying in a monotonous whining voice, "Say, watch that drinking, fellows." At last, embarrassed and ashamed of his own cowardice, the Chairman went up to his own room, took off his collar and tie. He opened a textbook of abnormal psychology and tried to study.

Walter and Eddie came up the stairs from the chapter room together. Walter said, "Are you going to get drunk?"

"What for?" Eddie said.

They had reached the top of the steps and Walter was just beginning to encourage him when a friend of his father's, a disheveled old man whose shirt bosom was sticking out of his waistcoat, seized his hand and began to pump it up and down and shout. He saw Eddie's back in the crowd. By the time he had received the old man's full congratulations, Eddie was gone.

Walter went to stand at the edge of the crowd in the smoking room. Carefully he put his left hand in his trousers pocket so his forearm would hold the front of his coat open. The fraternity pin was thus exposed. Occasionally he would touch it surreptitiously with his right hand as if it needed straightening. When one of the alumni came up to offer him congratulations or a drink, Walter bowed, bending a little from the waist with the pleasant feeling that the formality of his bow and the informality of the situation of his hand, stuck in his pocket, showed that he had ease, savoir-faire, made him a true clubman. He felt a little sorry for the other initiates, most of whom sat in a row on the window seat, giggling and punching each other like boys. He did not take any of the drinks offered him—he was waiting for his father to give him one, now that he was a member and a man, but he did not go upstairs to look for his father right away. He seemed to feel himself growing. He stood there with a faint smile on his face, ready to prove his equality by speaking to anyone who looked at him, and quietly savoring the height of his new estate.

What he really wanted to do, what he could hardly restrain himself from doing, was to run around, pointing at the pin of gold and pearls, hollering, "Look, I made it. I'm in. I'm a man now." As he stood there sneering at the shy ones and condemning the initiates who were already drunk, who had even got drunk before the ceremony, he congratulated himself soberly on his correct behavior. He was very happy.

He saw his uncle Eri pushing sideways through the crowd. His eyes were half closed and his face was pallid. He took him by the sleeve. "Congratulations, Walter," he said clearly, pausing after each word.

"You're not going now?" Walter asked him.

"Call cab." He straightened himself abruptly and opened his eyes wide.

"I'm going to call a cab. Tell Todd. Be down at the Station. Tell Todd pick up there." He straightened himself again and essayed a loose friendly smile. "Congratulations, Walter." He turned with almost a jerk and edged away.

Eri was going to the State Police Station downtown. It was part of his political activity to be friendly with state coppers. He made it a point to call on the Colonel whenever he was in the state capitol. He subscribed generously to police benefits and bought tickets to all their parties. He liked to hang around the stations and listen to the calls over the radio. There was always someone to talk to there and with the leather puttees and the guns there was an atmosphere that stimulated him as it had in the army.

Walter went upstairs to look for his father. He found him in the same room he had appropriated when he arrived. Layers of bluish smoke shifted slowly around. His father had taken off his tuxedo. He was leaning back in one of the wicker chairs in his shirt sleeves. There were several bottles of whisky on the study table, a bowl of ice cubes, and bottles of soda water and ginger ale. Three men were in the room besides his father, men he could dominate, who showed him an embarrassed respect because he would say anything unpleasant that came into his head without thinking if it would injure his reputation as a businessman or whether, insulted by it, some man might want to hit him. Walter did not know any of them. One was plump. One was thin and bald. One had an artificial hand in a black kid glove. They were all drunk and, except his father, hunched over in their chairs, each with a glass in one hand and a cigar in the other— even the man with the false hand had a cigar jammed between the stiff fingers. No one looked at Walter as he stepped inside the room and closed the door.

He waited standing flat against the wall and listened. They were talking about women now. As husbands they had to talk about the women of their youth. The man with the kidskin hand was telling a story while the others blew smoke rings or looked at the ash on the end of their cigars, impatient for him to end so they could begin. The tale dragged on to a silent audience. All laughed perfunctorily at the finish and the bald man and the fat man both said at once: "That's like the time I . . ."

Todd Phelps, with the bottle tilted, cut them off. "Drink? Drink?" he said.

When he saw his father making the drinks Walter took a step away from the wall diffidently and said, "Hi, Father." He waited to see if his father would offer him the whisky bottle; he did not expect a glass.

Todd, pouring out three fingers of whisky with his head cocked on one side, glanced up over his forearm with a scowl. His face softened a little. He said, "Hello, boy." He set the bottle down, picked up a cube of ice and threw it into the glass, filled the glass with soda, and handed it to the fat man.

All the time he had been growing up, his father had promised him. At Thanksgivings, Christmases, or Saturday nights when men came in to play poker on the dining-room table, when, in his first long pants or later carrying his first watch, Walter would hang around awkwardly, greeting the guests, lighting their cigars, as if manhood was something he could inhale like tobacco smoke, Todd Phelps had said fifty times if he said it once, "As soon's you wear the badge, boy. As soon as you wear the badge, I'll hand you your first whisky."

Walter moved back against the wall with his hands behind him.

"Tell about the widow out on Geddes, Todd," the bald man said deferentially.

Todd rolled his cigar around in his mouth blandly, took it out, looked at the wet end, and glanced up, smiling. "Do you remember her?"

"Sure. I heard about that trick when I was a freshman," the bald man said.

The other two men urged him on because they were afraid of him and wished to flatter him. Later, the next day perhaps, they would be ashamed of this and they would confuse the fear they felt now with the shame they felt then and, in an effort to rid themselves of it, they would berate Todd and call him a fool, but now they were alert, nervous, and anxious to placate him although he was not doing anything in particular. They were afraid of some violence they could not match or escape. Walter, standing by the wall, could see their eagerness to please. It was what he always suffered or worshiped in his father, the intimation, almost the smell of violence, only, if he called it anything, it was heroism.

"It didn't happen to me," Todd began. "It happened to Raynor Watkins. Remember Raynor Watkins?"

"Didn't he play baseball? He made a letter, didn't he?" the man with the black hand asked.

"Played third base," Todd said. "Well, Raynor was always after a piece. Always rooting around. Never got much, I don't think, but he was always trying. I come up to him one day and I say, 'Raynor, you're a lucky man.' 'Yeah?' he says, all excited. 'Yes, sir,' I says. 'There's a little girl lives out on Geddes Avenue.' 'Yeah?' he says. 'Lives out there with her sister. And this girl's seen you somewhere. Playing ball maybe, anyhow she's seen you and she thinks you're just about right.' 'She does?' he says. 'Well, how do I get at her?' Now Raynor had confidence with women. He was tall, rangy, and he looked pretty good in his baseball suit. . . ."

"He got a try-out with the Tigers once, didn't he?" the bald man said.

"I believe he did," Todd said brusquely to rebuke the interruption. Then he changed into his story-telling tone again. "So I says to him, 'Raynor, I think it can be arranged. Yes, I think it can be. You just leave it to your Uncle Dudley. I know her sister.' 'Whatcha gonna do?' he says. 'Well, now, there may be an obstacle. For you, I mean. I don't know how you stand,' I says. 'What you mean? What obstacle?' he says, wagging all over like a terrier pup. 'She's married,' I says. 'Oh,' he says and you never in your life saw anybody so downcast. 'But,' I says, 'her husband's on the road. Don't get home except weekends and I was thinking, oh, say, along about next Wednesday night if you and me were to make up a basket of beer and sandwiches and take it up to her house, we might all have a pleasant evening.' Raynor was no fool. He says, 'Uh-huh,' and runs his tongue over his lips. 'Uh-huh. What's her husband's territory?' 'Why, I don't know's I ever heard him say. He works for Lee and Cady out of Detroit.' He looked at the ground a minute and says, 'Fine. Let's do it.'

"The next Wednesday night, Raynor and me put on our high collars and we go down to Louis Ziemer's saloon and get him to put up a regular feast. Raynor was paying. Money no object. There were ham sandwiches and cold beef sandwiches, Swiss cheese and Limburger sandwiches, and there was a dish full of radishes and a bottle of pickles and a bottle of olives, as nice a Dutch lunch as you ever saw, imported Bismarck herring, too. We got a case of Stroh's and we hired a rig and we out to the place on Geddes Avenue. Well, we get out of the rig, and I says to him, 'There's the house right there,' and I go round and get the beer out of the back and set it on the carriage block and I take the basket in one hand and all the time he's standing there staring at the house as if she was buck naked in the window. I give him a nudge and say, 'Come on. She's waiting.' So we open the gate and start up the brick walk and we hadn't any more'n rung the bell when we hear someone running around the house and a man's voice hollers out, 'After my wife, are you?'" Todd started to giggle, puffing himself up in jerks like a tire inflated with a hand pump. "Well, *huh*, Raynor turned, *huh, huh,* and he ran like a whitehead. I had to shout after him, 'It's her husband' to make him even hear it, *huh, huh.* Out the front gate, the horse started to rare, and down he went Geddes Avenue and Raynor right with him." Here Todd burst into loud laughter. "Oh, my God, I thought I'd die. Gil Seeley came around the house and the girls came out and we stood there watching after him, oh, my God, how he ran."

Todd laughed again until the water ran out of his eyes.

As his father subsided, Walter Phelps against the wall put a sly expression on his face, a man's expression, rolled his eyes coyly, and said, "I knew a girl once . . ."

That was as far as he got. The four heads swung and lifted toward him as if he had turned them. His father's fat cheeks dropped and his eyebrows lowered. He said to his son, "Get out of here, you God-damned ape."

His face immediately red and tingling, Walter Phelps fumbled with the doorknob and awkwardly kicked the door almost out of his hand. Just outside the room, he remembered himself. He reached back and shut the door quietly. With a light precise step as if he knew exactly where he was going, he passed down the corridor past the shut doors, hearing the laughter and the drunken singing behind them. He met no one on the stairs. A few of the sober initiates were talking to some of the older alumni in the smoking room. He went through the hall, the darkened dining room and kitchen, and out on the back porch. It was still snowing heavily.

His bottle of whisky was standing in a corner of the porch. He picked it up. There was a little hat of snow on the cork and some on the shoulders. He blew it away and took out the cork. He took a big drink, too big, for he had hardly put the bottle away from his lips and begun to swallow the mouthful of liquor when he choked and swallowed down again against the loud purling of bile and whisky that had risen in his gullet.

He waited a little, feeling the big damp snowflakes touch his face, and then he tried it again, a smaller drink, more slowly. He waited again and drank again. He bent down and scooped up a handful of fresh clean snow and crammed it in his mouth. Holding the bottle by the neck, he went back into the house. At the end of the dining room he stopped. He set the bottle on the floor against the baseboard just inside the door.

He went up the length of the broad hallway and into the smoking room. The lights were out and the room looked empty. The party was dead—everybody had gone home or upstairs. The radio was playing. It stood in a corner and he went over to it. Sitting far down in a red leather chair almost on the back of his neck he saw a boy. In the faint light from the radio dial he could tell who it was, Fuzzy Wilmot, the sixteen-year-old freshman, just initiated like himself. They called him Fuzzy because he had not begun to shave and his cheeks were covered with a soft blond down.

In a high false voice he had never used before, he said, "Why, Fuzzy, aren't you in bed yet?"

The boy had not heard him approach. He looked up, pleased. "No. My dad's upstairs. I was waiting for him."

"You certainly picked a nice spot, Fuzz. Comfortable chair, radio music, warm. . . . Mind if I sit down?"

A little surprised at this formality, Fuzzy answered politely, "Why, no, Walter. Glad to have you."

Walter sat down, put one ankle on his other knee and folded his hands against his breast with his elbows on the arms of the chair. Something Fuzzy had already said, although he had not said much, fitted like a puzzle-piece into some intention, some aim he had which was itself not clear because he was repeating over and over to himself the sharp answers he might have made to his father, the answers he ought to have made, the ones he had now a right to make, and these obscured the plan or aim. When he remembered his whisky, standing by the door of the dining room, he could see a little of the direction he would take with Fuzzy. There was a direction but he was not yet sure why he wanted to take it.

"That's a wonderful ritual we have, isn't it?" Fuzzy said.

"Yeah. It gets you," Walter said piously. He got up. "Say, excuse me a minute, Fuzzy."

He went to the dining room for the whisky and brought back a water glass from the sideboard with it.

"I was just going to have a little snort and I thought you might join me." Fuzzy was a smart little prep-school boy. Sheltered, they said, timid and mannerly, and Walter was adopting a politeness to match Fuzzy's.

"Are you going to drink it right here?" Fuzzy asked, his eyes actually growing wide in surprise. "It's against house rules, isn't it?"

"What the hell, Fuzz, what the hell? We've just been initiated. What's five dollars?" He thrust the open bottle over. "After you," he said.

"I—I don't believe I want any right now," Fuzzy said.

"What, not even tonight?" he asked, making his tone incredulous.

"I don't drink."

"You just mean you never have. You don't mean you don't want to."

"I never thought about it much. I promised my dad."

"What did you do, swear up and down?"

"No. He just said one day he'd give me five thousand dollars if I didn't smoke, drink, nor chew till I was twenty-one."

[81]

"Why doesn't he want you to?"

"I don't know. He said it wasn't a good idea. This bootleg stuff."

"But he drinks."

"Yeah. I know."

"I saw him upstairs drinking this bootleg stuff, just necking it back." This was not true. He did not know Fuzzy's father.

"I know. He drank when he was in college, too. I've heard him tell about it."

"Sure he did."

Fuzzy sat up straight in his chair and looked at Walter instead of the little light on the radio. "And there's nights he doesn't get home from the office until eight or nine o'clock. He starts out from the Fisher Building at five and he's with somebody maybe or he goes there to find somebody. Anyhow there's a speak in an old house near there and he gets in there and drinks and stays and stays."

"And your mother raises hell when he does get home."

Embarrassed, Fuzzy said, "Yes."

Walter glanced down over the arm of the leather chair at the water glass he had brought from the dining room. It was important to stay with Fuzzy every minute. He got up, talking all the while in a matter-of-fact tone, opened the latch of the mullioned window, rimmed now with snow. He began to scoop up handfuls of snow from the slanting sill and put them into the glass. When it was filled with a grayish melting slush, he took the whisky and poured some into the glass. He had been saying, ". . . of course, this is one of the basic questions of our education, Fuzzy. At what age do we become socially mature? You're physiologically mature now. You could be father to a kid, I mean. Now anybody'd think that when you go to college, you're pretty nearly a man. My father was. Your father was. They did the things men do. Get the idea now, Fuzzy, I'm not saying you want to get stewed. It's a question of whether you got the right to get stewed or not, see? You don't need the five grand, do you? Your old man's got lots of money." And in an earnest tone, like a man handing out a free sample, he said, "Here, see what you think of this. A snow highball." He offered the glass to Fuzzy.

The boy took it automatically, sipped a little, and said nothing. Walter sat back in his chair watching. The argument was one he had heard a professor use and he had tried it on Fuzzy because Fuzzy studied hard all the time and the argument would make them intellectuals together.

"That's some of Mickey Phelan's. Not bad, is it?" Walter asked.

Fuzzy shook his head and took a large swallow. "Aren't you going to drink any?"

"I'll take mine straight," Walter said. He tipped up the bottle and managed two swallows, held them down without coughing or choking, and exhaled smiling like a man who has done a difficult trick.

In emulation Fuzzy gulped the rest of his drink down and shuddered involuntarily.

"Can you feel it in your stomach? Warm?" Walter asked.

"Yeah. When will it hit me?"

Already sophisticated, Walter kept back his laughter and said, "It takes more than one. This stuff's got a lot of poot, though."

Fuzzy could hardly believe there was no more to drinking than this. He had seen drunks. He had admired their wit and recklessness and fervor. He was now disappointed that his one drink had not brought him these gifts.

"God, Walter, I wouldn't want my mother to hear about this," he said. It was the first time he had ever used "God" in conversation.

Walter was back at the window scooping up snow off the ledge and putting it into the glass. He looked back over his shoulder. "How will she hear about it?"

"She might."

"She won't hear if you don't tell her. Your father won't say anything about it. He won't dare."

"No."

"Here," he handed him another drink.

"We'll have a toast," Walter said. He thought he could impose this much formality on the moment without Fuzzy catching him at it. "We'll drink to your mother."

He lifted the bottle. Fuzzy lifted the glass, saying, "God bless you, Mother." They drank. Fuzzy kept swallowing desperately until the glass was empty.

"Now don't rush it, Fuzz. It'll come. It'll come," he said.

They sat there for an hour, drinking and inevitably talking about girls. Walter took smaller and smaller sips of whisky to make it last so he could give the younger boy more. At last the pretense of a gentlemen's conversation in their club broke all to pieces because Fuzzy began to get very drunk and he could no longer make the effort to judge the legs and breasts of the girls they saw on the campus or guess how big a fight they would put up if you got them alone in the back seat of a car or what you could do to make them quit fighting and give in. He began thinking of his mother and his childhood home in Port Huron, of his innocent boyhood waving at the long lake boats sliding past in the St. Clair River. His upper lip stiffened. The tears came into his eyes and rolled down his cheeks, and at last he was sobbing. He took the glass that Walter offered and gulped it down and was sick all over the starched crumpled bosom of his shirt, very quickly, before Walter had time to lurch out of his chair to hold his head, which he would have gladly done. He lay there with his head sagged over on one side until Walter, having opened a third window for the snow on the sill, gave him another drink, lifting his head solicitously. The first swallow came up again with a jerking retch, and Walter drew aside, but the rest of it stayed down. Fuzzy lay sprawled in his chair with his chin propped on his chest and his breath bubbling through his nose, groaning. Walter stood looking down at him, swaying a little.

He was just going to let himself fall into his own chair to wait when he heard loud talk and laughter on the stairway. As if he had planned it a long time before, he opened a window, deftly climbed over the sill, and stepped down into a foot of snow. He pulled up the collar of his tuxedo and hid himself. He could look in but not be seen.

Giggling, laughing, and staggering, the bald man, the fat man, and the man with the kidskin hand came into the smoking room. They switched on all the overhead lights. The bald man finished a joke and pounded the fat man ecstatically on the back, laughing himself into a fit of coughing. The man with the false hand solemnly picked up a newspaper and held it wide, swaying a little back and forth, trying to focus his eyes on the print. Someone noticed the sound of the radio and the fat man started toward it. He discovered Fuzzy, limp, snoring, covered with vomit. Cunningly the fat man turned around and approached the spread newspaper, tiptoeing on the sides of his feet. He tapped the newspaper with his finger as if he were knocking lightly at a door. The man with the false hand paid no attention. The fat man got out an automatic lighter, thumbed it twice, and, with the little flame, he lit the outer sheet of the newspaper. The flame mounted the fold slowly.

Suddenly the whole newspaper flared up. The man with the kidskin hand stood there for an instant shocked, with fire instead of paper between his upraised hands. He dropped the burning tag-ends of the paper and stamped out the ashes on the carpet, swearing loudly, pale with surprise. The fat man kept trying to take him by the arm and he kept jerking his elbow away. The fat man pointed and the other man looked.

He went over to Fuzzy's chair with his hands on his hips and his feet wide apart. Even through the window, Walter could hear him shout, "Well, for Christ's sake!" With his good hand, he grabbed Fuzzy by the lapels and hauled him up standing. He held him there batting at his head and face with the flat of the kidskin hand, except that it was not quite flat. It remained a little curved although it was flexible enough to flatten with the impact of his slaps.

Fuzzy woke up slowly and his head stopped wagging to and fro as his father hit him. He fell sidewards against the radio and held up one arm to defend himself. His father stopped hitting him but every now and then Walter could hear a word of his steady cursing. Fuzzy shook his head, yawned, blinked, and feebly brushed at the puke on his shirt as if he still did not know what had happened. His father had the whisky bottle, holding it in front of him, tapping it with his leather fingers. Fuzzy yawned again and shook his head.

The bald man and the fat man stood ten feet away, choking and gurgling to keep from laughing. At last they could hold it no longer and they went "HA-HA-HA-HA!" rocking back and forth. The fat man would point to Fuzzy and start to explain. A high falsetto screech would burst from his mouth and he would bend over with both hands on his knees while the bald man leaned weakly against him, patting him on the shoulder.

Fuzzy's father set the bottle down on the window seat and gave his son a shove that sent him weaving and stumbling to the middle of the room. He walked slowly out of the room ahead of his father, who followed him, quite sober now, with his face set against the laughter of his friends. The last Walter saw of Fuzzy he was digging at his eye with his fist and yawning like a little boy. His father marched behind him swearing and giving his son a push every few steps.

The giggling fat man ran teetering to the radio with little mincing steps and picked up the bottle of whisky. There was about an inch of it left in the bottle. The bald man joined him and they had a drink. When it was empty, the fat man flipped the bottle backward over his shoulder and it broke on the flagstones in front of the fireplace. They each put an arm around the other's shoulders and staggered out of the smoking room singing.

As soon as they had gone, Walter climbed back through the window into the smoking room. He stamped the packed snow from his dress shoes and brushed it from his shoulders. He felt calmer now. He lit a cigarette and sat down in one of the red leather chairs in front of the windows. He kept his feet off the window seat so that anyone looking into the room from the doorway would not see him. He waited for several minutes, smoking, and listening abstractedly to the weather reports that were coming in over the radio.

He heard footsteps clacking on the tile stairway. There were breathless snorts and titters and he heard scraps of conversation from the fat man and the bald man, "Maybe you *weren't* his age when you started. Maybe you *were* older. . . ."

"Like father, like son. What the hell. . . ."

"But we never put *you* to bed with your clothes on. . . ."

Walter heard at last the voice of the man with the kidskin hand, cold, furious, sober, "You shut your god-damned mouths."

There was a howl of laughter. He heard the front door of the house open and slam shut. He saw the three dim figures go down the front walk and find their car. It was still snowing, softly, silently, the big flakes dropping through the windless air.

When they drove away, Walter went upstairs. He felt the liquor in him as a sort of burning hunger but he was no longer very drunk. As he passed the doorway of the second floor corridor he could hear loud talk and laughter from some of the rooms and a thick stale smell of tobacco smoke hung around the doorway. He went on up the stairs to the third floor and found Fuzzy's room. The sitting room was as neat as if the porter had just left it. In the bedroom one bed was empty—Fuzzy's roommate had not come in yet—and in the bed nearest the windows Fuzzy lay. The windows were wide open, two of them, and a little snow had dropped in on the comforter. He brushed it off and shut the windows a little. Fuzzy had the covers drawn up to his face. He was lying on his back snoring heavily. Walter pulled the covers down and saw he was still dressed.

Beginning with his necktie and being careful of the puke-smelling sticky shirt and waistcoat, Walter undressed him down to his underwear, pulling him around like a doll, arms flabby, head flopping. He laid him back down, covered him up, and tiptoed out, shutting the bedroom door gently. He piled the filthy clothes in the center of the sitting-room floor.

He went to find his father. He opened that door cautiously. The room was dark. He switched on the light. At the click of the switch, his father's head lifted a little and then lay back. He was sitting in one of the wicker chairs. His plump legs were wide apart and they had taken his shoes off and undone his tie and collar. His head lay back almost at right angles to his body, supported by the back of the chair, and he was making a heavy stertorous gargling noise, with his mouth wide open. The debris of the

[86]

party lay on the study table, empty whisky and soda bottles, puddles of melting ice, cigar butts and ashes, and a jagged broken water glass.

Walter stood over his father, watching him, unconsciously breathing when he breathed. He cleared his throat and spat in his father's face.

Dimly Todd Phelps seemed to know what had been done to him. He felt the splat of the spittle. He rubbed his fist against his glistening nose, opened his eyes, opened his hand, and lurched forward out of his chair, swinging his fists.

As if he had swallowed something too big for his throat, Walter felt the fear in him and stepped back quickly and clumsily as if he faced a giant, a little boy in a grove or forest of green leaves, awe-struck, adoring, and terrified, a hero coming at him and he with nothing. Then he looked at his father, a middle-aged fat man, growing bald, blinking, swaying, twitching his clenched fists, and swearing in a hoarse muffled voice. Walter put the flat of his hand on his father's chest and shoved him back into the chair. It was easy. He flopped down like a dummy, already asleep, his head cocked on one side and a foolish smile on his face.

Shock at his own daring held him still a moment. Then he reached down, took his father's wrist, pulled it over his own shoulder, and leaned into the load. The old man was not so heavy as he had expected. He got him to his feet with his arm around his own neck. He said loudly, "Come on, Father. Go to bed now." He eased him into the bedroom, undressed him, and put him to bed.

In the morning when he woke up he found his father half dressed, shaving before the mirror with a borrowed razor. He himself had a pounding headache and he was a little afraid to show himself awake for fear his father would remember the night before. But as he himself remembered it, he got a little confidence. He threw back the covers and got up.

Cheerfully his father said, "Hi, boy. I guess the old man got a snootful last night."

"So did I," Walter said.

His father turned around and looked at him. "You did?" He turned back to the washbowl, shaking the razor under a stream of hot water. "Well, it's about time, maybe."

~PART THREE~

· VIII ·

WALTER PHELPS lifted the telephone receiver and put it to his ear. It was a hot steamy day and the receiver was damp. He leaned against the wall chewing a match stick and staring out from the darkness of the hallway through the library window at the startling moist green of the sweet-cherry tree in the side yard.

"Number, please?"

"Eight-two, M," Walter said quietly.

He lifted the match stick from his lips and stuck it behind his ear. The whirring of the ring broke and a woman answered, "Yes?"

"May I speak to Emily?" he said, tenor, through his nose. He was disguising his voice, a habit he had acquired in reading detective stories, and he did not want his father to hear him anyway.

"Hello, Emily?" he said. "All right to pick you up at eight tonight?"

"Why, I guess so. Is everything all fixed?"

"I've still got to get the car."

"Oh," she said, dubious.

"I think I can get it. See you at eight." He hung up with some pleasure starting in his mind.

He stuck up his right foot and took off his shoe, then his left, and with his shoes in his hand he tiptoed through the hall into the library. He set the shoes on the floor. He put a hand on each arm of the overstuffed red-leather armchair and lowered himself quietly down to its seat, watching his father all the while.

Todd Phelps lay on the sofa across the room with his head on a round rose-satin pillow. A copy of the *Chicago Tribune* had slipped from his face to the floor. An open book, *La Reine Pédauque,* lay balanced face down on his belly. There was a big crystal ashtray on the floor beside the couch. In one corner of the ashtray lay half a cigar, still lighted, with an inch and a half of ash on it. A ribbon of blue smoke rose straight up and dispersed in curls and feathers.

Walter stretched his neck to get a better sight of the ash on the cigar. Usually his father's naps lasted half an hour, give or take a few minutes. The length of the ash indicated he was about halfway through.

There was a mahogany rack of magazines beside his chair. Walter did not take one out for fear a leaf might crackle and wake his father. He rubbed the side of the rack to see the oily path his thumb made on the humid wood. He surveyed the nails of his hand, clean, narrow, with puffs of flesh on either side. Hanging on the wall above Todd Phelps was a painting of a quail, a ring-necked pheasant, and a mallard duck, hung heads down from a clean steel chain that ran to the margin of the canvas and continued inexplicably in a bas-relief of silvered wood on the frame. He had shot duck and pheasant but never quail. He had eaten all three. A loose dim memory of the woodeny sound of pheasants' wings as one took off in a morning field of stripped cornstalks, the bird rising whip-whip-whip, coasting, rising again, his own lead and shot and the silly maladroit tumble of the bird shifted slowly, changed, and faded until he found he had been staring at the picture so hard that he had begun to see the pattern of veins in his own retinae.

His father began to snore, a rattling suck of air, then a silken exhale. His fat hands were interlaced under the book. The book went up and down. The thought struck Walter that he might sleep longer than half an hour since he was not going back to the bank that afternoon. There was nothing to do but wait. He did not dare wake him.

If he could not get the car, he would have to call Emily again and suggest they spend the evening at her house. If her family went out, the two of them could drink a little, carefully. Her front porch was hidden with wistaria vines and no one could see them from the street. Maybe he could get her to take off her brassière this time. Then the next time or at worst the time later, he ought to be able to get her into bed. With his eyes half closed he warmed the possibility in his mind, and, as it cooled, he cautiously figured up his chances again: she was good neck but she never became passionate. Also, there were a lot of guys hanging around town this summer. None of them could get jobs and they could be with her daytimes while he was working in the bank. Somebody, he could not think who, might already be "in there" with Emily. He could not imagine a girl having two actual lovers simultaneously, and if someone else were already high man, he took for granted his own immediate proud withdrawal as soon as he discovered it. He winced to think of the money for liquor, gasoline, and cigarettes he had spent on her. Once he had sent her a dozen American Beauty roses and the gesture had made a nice effect. He had a certain investment in her which he hoped to be able to protect until it yielded a return.

As he lay there somnolent, he knew all this was foolishness. He had never yet gone to bed with any girl, and he was privately ashamed. He was growing restless because he was ashamed, a mounting irritation different and more intense than the mere doglike itch for something he had heard about but did not really know that seized him every now and then. He was tired of being mysterious, winking and whistling softly before the queries of other young men, never saying anything because there was not yet anything to say. He was disgusted with his silences when women were being talked about, sober pauses staged to imply that he was protecting some girl's name, too chivalrous to speak out, a real gent.

When he was a freshman in the university, watching and listening to the heroic upperclassmen, the kind of computation he made and the rigidly defined tactics he practiced now had seemed insanely intricate but he had learned them patiently through his college years, and now he believed these arid posturings to be the only effective means of making love without also making a fool of one's self, and of course if a lover had to be a fool, he would keep alone.

He had begun passionately. One beautiful moonlit evening in his eighteenth year, the girl standing pale by a honeysuckle vine (that had been the last little nudge, the scent of the honeysuckle), he had dropped on his knees without the least self-consciousness, clasped her around the waist and murmured, "I love you. I love you." As he hung there, both of them silent, a genuine tremor running through him at the thought of the beauty he had spoken and how greatly it must have moved her, he had perceived a jiggling under her tulle skirt. When he peeped down, he saw the silver toe of her shoe tapping. She was keeping the beat of the music playing in the gymnasium, and when, still on his knees, he looked up at her, he saw she had her handkerchief pressed to her mouth to keep in her shaking laughter. He had stood up, dusted the knees of his trousers, and walked off. Then or later, it did not occur to him that there might be anything wrong with him; he just had not done it right. There was something to learn. He had learned it now. He was afraid of his old naïve ardor. He had gotten cagey.

Beads of sweat had formed on his father's bald head, sliding, joining, and running into his eyes. A fly walked slowly down his nose. With a sigh, he reached up to fan it away. In a moment the sweat in his eyes would sting and wake him up. Walter got ready to raise himself out of the chair. As his weight shifted, one of the coiled springs in the upholstery caught and made a loud twang.

Todd Phelps opened his eyes and began to dig at them with his fists. Walter crossed noiselessly over to the sofa and when his father had stopped blinking, he began in a soft conciliatory voice, "Father, may I have the car this evening?"

As if tormented past endurance, his father snarled, "Why, God-damn you . . . ," and he flung himself over on his side with his face to the back of the couch.

Without regarding any noise he made now, Walter walked over to his chair, sat down with a lurch, and put on his shoes. On his way through the hall he lifted his coat off a peg on the clothes-tree and laid it over his arm. Maliciously he let the screen door slam behind him. He clattered down the steps of the side porch, felt the heat of the afternoon sun, and slowly walked under the sweet-cherry tree out the gravel driveway.

The sun was hot enough to make him notice the street and he crossed it to get to the shady side. He lived only two blocks from downtown. The farmers' cars were parked on both sides of the street, some with a sack of feed on the front bumper, others with the windows rolled down full of sweaty little children with dirty faces. He passed the two churches, the Methodist in red brick on his right, and the Episcopal where his father was warden on his left. There the maple trees ended and he walked out into the sun past the post office, the small hotel, the movie, the other bank (not his father's), the gas company and two blocks more of stores until he came to the *Telegraph* building. He did not have much hope that Eddie Burcham would lend him his car but he was going to ask him anyway. He would go as high as two dollars.

The *Telegraph* was the only daily paper in the county. The big Goss press stood on show behind a plate-glass window being readied for the afternoon run by a couple of printers in denim aprons and the crowns of old felt hats on their heads like caps. Just inside the door lay a meteorite two or three feet high with the side cut off and the surface polished like marble to show the veins of yellow metal in it. Digby, the editor, collected them.

Walter nodded to the switchboard girl and went up the stairs to the editorial room to find Eddie.

In his junior year at college Eddie had gone into Detroit to ask the editor of the *Detroit News* about journalism as a career. He had cleansed his mouth with Listerine and worn a hard collar. Secretly he had hoped to impress the great man so deeply with his earnestness and knowledge that he would offer him a job on the spot. The editor asked him where he was from. When Eddie told him, he said, "Stay right where you are, son. Except maybe Bill White, Digby's got the best small-town paper in the country and a small-town paper's where you learn the newspaper business." Disappointed of the miracle yet proud he came from a town where lived a famous man, Eddie had asked Digby for a job, and in spite of the depression, Digby had given him one. For over a year Eddie had been writing obituaries, occasionally a courthouse item, and learning slowly what to say and what to suppress in the little paragraphs of the "News in Brief."

Walter found him in his shirt sleeves slouched down in a chair before a typewriter with a pencil in his mouth. A felt hat was tilted low over his eyes. He chewed the pencil slowly and stared at the sheet of paper in the typewriter. Seeing him busy and knowing that Eddie would cuss him with a hitherto impermissible fervor if he disturbed him, Walter sat down at a long table and began to look over the morning's Detroit papers, waiting. Except for Eddie and Barry Sickles, the managing editor alone in his cubicle, the office was empty. It was nearly time to go to press. After a few minutes he saw Eddie come to life, jerk the story out of the machine, and begin it again.

In ten minutes the story was done. He took it into Sickles' office. Sickles nodded his head and Eddie went downstairs to get it set up. He came back, sat down in his chair, and heaved a foot up on the table. He had not yet looked at Walter. He turned now with a cool businesslike air and said, "Hi."

"Hot. What's the official weather?"

"Ninety-ninety. Ninety, heat. Ninety, humidity."

"I put on a clean shirt this noon."

"Always look nice for the bank's customers. Get ahead."

Walter gave a hissing snort.

Eddie slid his foot off the table and sat up straight. "What's a fact?" he asked earnestly.

"A fact?"

"Yes. What's a fact?"

"Oh, my God. It's too hot," he said, yawning again. Eddie's face did not change its look of serious inquiry, and Walter, responding, assumed a false bland patience. "Look, bud," he said as to a child, "I work in a bank. I know what a dollar is. You work here. You know what a fact is. Let's leave it at that. Shall we? Huh?"

Impatiently Eddie said, "Come on. Live right. You gotta think once in a while. What's a fact?"

"Little trouble with the word? Barry jump on you about that story? What *is* the story?"

"Runaway. A farmer. His team got a burr under their tails or something. Ran off the road, hit a tree, busted his wagon, and broke his back."

"That's tough. Times like these."

"He'll have to go on the county."

"Will the county take him?"

"Have to, I guess." Eddie put his feet up on the table. "Now what would you have seen if you had been there? A couple of old glueys rare up and run into the tree. You'd have seen the wagon tip into it and break. You'd have seen Charley Leavis wrenched around somehow. Now is that the fact? What would the average man see if he was there?"

"Thanks, pal. It's too hot to reply."

"Or is this part of the fact—that the important thing to Charley Leavis is not so much that his back's broke or his wagon's a wreck but that he hasn't got the money to pay for it? He's in the hospital. I went up to see him this morning. I had a hell of a time getting him to say anything about what happened. All he wanted to talk about was 'Where am I gonna git the money to stay here?' Mortgaged up to the eyes. Corn ready to cultivate. So I asked him"—Eddie looked over his shoulder carelessly toward Sickles' office—"if he cared if I said he was on the rocks and he said, 'Hell, no. I am, ain't I? Everybody knows it.'"

"Did you say in the story he was broke?"

Eddie shook his head. "But you can see that's the important fact to him and it's the important fact to the county because the county'll have to pay for it. But we can't print it. We're a family newspaper," Eddie finished scornfully. He got up and went to the water cooler to get a drink.

Unwilling to listen more, uninterested in the obscure ethical point Eddie was making, Walter yawned again and brought up the subject he had come to discuss. "What you doing tonight?"

"I'm going out to the lake. I'm going out to the lake as soon as I leave here and I'm going to get in it," Eddie said.

Eddie and his mother had a cottage at Sand Lake, seventeen miles away. Eddie spent some of his evenings there, driving out after the paper was put to bed and driving back in the morning. Other evenings he spent reading in their house in town, where all except the bedroom furniture was shrouded in dust covers for the summer while Mrs. Burcham, Eddie's mother, sat lonesome on the porch of the cottage until it got too dark to crochet.

"Water'll be like soup," Walter said.

"It won't be ninety, that's a cinch. What's the matter, looking for transportation tonight?"

Walter knew that Eddie with exasperating shrewdness could probably reconstruct the little scene of his father's denial of the car. It was bad enough to have to ask favors but it was worse to have the reasons for the asking known. "Oh, we may stay in town," he said. He could not wheedle or offer the two dollars.

Sickles, the managing editor, approached them sipping from a paper cup of ice water. He was a tall pale man with a mustache. They said he was a Harvard man, a rarity this far west. He was waiting for a copy of the day's paper. As soon as he had checked it over, he would go home and read to his wife. There was something wrong with her, nobody knew just what, but Sickles read to her every afternoon. He talked almost as if he were reading.

"I was happy to hear your acknowledgment of the paper's status, Eddie. It is indeed a family bladder." He sipped. "Hello, Walter. How's your father?"

"OK."

"And you know what comes out of bladders," Eddie said coarsely.

"*Bladder* in this sense is from the German, *blätter*, pages or leaves, hence a newspaper. There is a *Lustige Blätter* published in Berlin," Sickles said pleasantly without condescension. "You must learn the language. You have lived in a town full of Germans all your life and you don't know that." He turned half formally to Walter. "Eddie is young, therefore obdurate. He thinks we should print all the news."

"I think we should print the truth," Eddie said with a touch of self-righteousness as if he were sure he had the advantage.

"Oh, so do I. But never all of it. This is an old argument, Walter."

"Why not?" Eddie persisted.

"Because the nature of truth is unfortunately such that most families would feel themselves disgraced if we did print it."

"Or is it the nature of the families?"

"I am not a Platonist. Surely you must see they are interchangeable. Charley Leavis has a brother in Tecumseh who is worth at least ten thousand dollars and he would be mortified, he might even sue us, if we said Charley was broke, fact though it is. He would think it a reflection on the Leavis name."

"Why the hell doesn't he help Charley out then?"

"That is irrelevant."

Walter stood up and stretched. "I've got to be getting back to the bank."

One of the phones on the table rang. Sickles picked it up. He stood leaning against the table with his legs crossed, holding the mouthpiece in a V of his first and middle fingers, his head cocked on one side and the receiver against his ear.

"Yes. Sickles speaking. Oh? . . . Really? . . . When? . . . Oh . . . Why, his son's right here now." Eddie and Walter looked up toward the phone. They could hear the distant whine of the speaker from where they sat. "Yes. On US 112 by Larzalere's Corners. . . . Yes, I have that. . . . Just a minute, I'll ask him. Hold it a minute." Sickles let the mouthpiece down a little. His face was grave. "Walter, your father and mother just hit a telephone pole out on 112." He stopped, waiting.

"Yes?"

"This will be a shock. They think they were killed instantly. They're bringing them in in the ambulance now. Do you want them to go to Kingsley's or Rowe's?"

"Kingsley's. We always have them, I guess," Walter said.

Sickles moved the mouthpiece up. "The Kingsley Funeral Home," he said. "Yes. Thanks." He hung up the receiver and set the phone back on the desk softly as if a bang would matter.

"Take it easy, kid," Eddie said, patting his shoulder. Outside the event, he felt protective and older.

"Why, I'm all right," Walter said wonderingly. He had always heard that news like this did something to you but it had not. He was all right. "What did they say?"

"Your father and mother were in the Packard going west on 112. There was a little thundershower out there and the man in the car coming toward them said they hit the wet pavement and the rear end began to swing back and forth across the road. He said he could see your father wrestling the wheel as they passed. The man looked behind and all of a sudden the car just dove into the telephone pole. It broke the pole off." His voice changed a little. "That's tough, Walter. That's awfully tough."

Walter ran his tongue over his lips. "They said both of them?"

Sickles nodded. "There wasn't any doubt, they said."

"Well, I . . . ," he began. He gave a heavy sigh. "I guess I'd better get on up to Kingsley's. No use hanging around here, is there?"

"Have you your car, Eddie?" Sickles asked.

Eddie said, "Sure. I'll take him."

"I'll take him. Your key in the car?"

"Yes."

Speaking a little more loudly as if to a child or a deaf person, Sickles took Walter's arm, saying, "Come on, Walter. We'll go up to Kingsley's."

At the head of the stairs, Sickles turned around and came back to Eddie, who was watching them leave. "The reason I wanted you to stay, Eddie— look up the obit on Todd Phelps. I think there's a picture. We can't get it in till Monday now."

Eddie brightened a little. "OK," he said, glancing briefly at Sickles and back at Walter. His own father had died. The house had been empty for a while and that had been his grief. Probably Walter's was different. He wondered what he was feeling.

Walter was standing looking down the stairs waiting for Sickles, as if he could not go down until Sickles was with him. The steps each had round brass corners and a rubber mat across the wood. Sickles took his arm again and they walked down.

Sickles drove very slowly and Walter sitting beside him began to assume almost deliberately a solemn distant manner because he knew it was expected of him. He himself seemed scattered. No sincere behavior suggested itself and it was necessary to "behave" somehow at this, at such a time. The manner came as a relief. He did not speak to Sickles. He did not nod or wave to people in the street who spoke to him. Without any pleasure, he could see they were surprised at his rudeness but he knew they would forgive him when they learned of his parents' death. They would remember they had seen him riding with Sickles and they would say with something of pride in having been closer to the talked-of event than other people, "I saw him just after it happened. He was riding with Barry Sickles."

The car stopped in front of a big white house with a broad porch running around it, set back from the street under three oak trees, the funeral home.

"Are you going to get out, Walter?" Sickles said gently.

"Oh. Yes. Sure," he said and opened the door.

They were met on the front porch by the undertaker, Fred Kingsley, a grave handsome man with white hair. He inclined his body supitly toward them without smiling or speaking.

Walter remembered to take his coat off his arm and put it on. As he did it, he asked himself, "Why? They won't know," but he knew Mr. Kingsley would expect him to, and irritated that he was conforming to these unspoken expectations, he said a little loudly, "I want to see my father and mother."

Kingsley bowed again, murmuring, "They were just brought in. It was a severe accident. Are you quite sure you want . . ." He left the question hanging.

"Yes," Walter said.

"Follow me, please."

The bodies were in the cellar in a cool little room that looked like a veterinary's operating room. His father and mother lay side by side on slabs, covered with sheets.

He walked over to the slabs and stood beside them, looking down at the humps and folds of the sheets as if that was all there was to see. "I'll just leave you for a minute," the undertaker said as if business called him elsewhere. He tiptoed out and drew the door shut.

Walter was again annoyed by the deference, the intimation that he was "bereaved," or "stricken." The sentimental ceremony Kingsley wished to construct was not one he intended to observe. Nothing mystical was going to happen. He merely wanted to see how badly they were hurt. Without hesitation, he reached down and took the top of the sheet, and as he did it he had in his mind a picture of Larzalere's Corners, the pavement wet and shining, and from the memory of past speed he was trying to feel the last sickening dive at the telephone pole so that he might calculate the number of wounds and gashes when, his hand pulling the sheet down steadily, he saw his father's face.

There was no blood on it. The bald skull was not crushed. There were no gashes anywhere. The skin was pallid and the eyes were not quite closed. Walter thought that his appearance was quite good luck somehow, and, at the same time, he had an impulse to say "Father!" aloud.

He said it. "Father!"

He pulled the sheet down further, nodding his head sagely as if he now found what he had expected. Just below his chest his father's shirt was soaked with blood. He jerked the sheet down and it fell to the floor. The deep print of the steering wheel still showed on his belly. Where there should have been the proud well-tended mound of flesh, it had been shoved, pressed, ground flat, and his father's chest rose high above his middle as it must have done when he was young. The impact had driven

[98]

the wheel into him and left that mark. It had mashed him inward until the blood rushed out. On the back of his right hand was a long clean grayish gash with bright red lips. Two streaks of dried blood ran around his palm. He could not imagine how the crash had felt. Perhaps it had happened too quickly for any pain. He stared again at the sodden shirt and trousers and the queer thin waist, unnaturally wide. He poked his father's belly. The flesh gave a little, not cold. He decided there must have been one last big burst of pain, like a flame, and he died with it.

Painstakingly, as if he were anxious to show that he had been brought up to be neat, Walter picked up the sheet from the floor, shook it out in front of him fussily, and laid it over his father again.

He stepped forward between the slabs and drew the sheet down with almost a flourish from his mother's body.

Her throat was cut to the bone and her chin was lifted as if to display it. The colors, still brilliant but drying gummily, reminded him immediately of chickens he had seen the maid drawing and cutting up on Sundays in the kitchen. He stooped down to look closely at her face. The eyes were tightly shut—it must have been her last act, to shut them tightly. Her cheeks were drawn up full and her lips with them, showing her teeth in a grin of terror. He had never seen his mother look like that and as he was staring at her, feeling the smooth edge of the slab under his fingers, he began to speak aloud in a low voice, very quickly, "This is my mother. This is my mother's body." After his surprise at hearing his own voice, he knew that his speaking was a performance he was putting on, trying to arouse an emotion that was suitable to the occasion, but he kept on. "My mother was always kind to me." As he tried to remember examples of her kindness, none came, but it was true. "My mother tried her best to make me a good man. I owe her a great deal. And I don't know whether I ever fulfilled any of her hopes for me, whether I had time to, because she was too timid ever to tell me what they were and it was my father's son I was. If I think of the life she had with him, it was not much of a life. I always acknowledged and made allowance in my treatment of her, something in my mother I knew nothing about, a fierceness, a sort of honor or justness, something like that which she concealed and never let out, and watching the Packard make that last dash at the telephone pole, maybe she had time to be disappointed once more. If she had been counting on showing that pride or fierceness just once in her life to my father or to anyone else that mattered, perhaps to me, she knew that the chance was sliding away from her, sixty-five miles an hour. I can't tell what it will be like to be without her. She never told me what I ought to do except little things like cleaning my nails, no big advice, no damned helping me. I will never see my mother any more." As he said that, he stopped. His nose and palate prickled. His tongue felt thick and he knew the tears were warm in his eyes and running down his cheeks, and he also knew that it was his last words that had done it. They were like the words of "My Darling Nellie Gray" that his mother had sung to him in the big rocking chair looking out the window on the snow when he was little. It had seemed to him the saddest song he ever heard and it had always made him cry.

He gave a loud sniff, pulled his sweat-soaked handkerchief from his pocket, and started to wipe his face. He stopped. It did not matter to him whether Kingsley or Sickles said that he had been crying. Why should he try to hide it? He stuffed the handkerchief into his pocket and looked down again at his mother's hideous face, expecting some pang to take him, waiting to do her at least this honor, an answer that might surprise her if she were anywhere to see it to the question that must have glared in the last brightness of her mind, "Is this all?" But still he felt nothing. He covered her face and left the room quickly, almost briskly.

Standing in the doorway at the end of the hall above, he saw Kingsley and Sickles break off the conversation. Kingsley approached him gravely with the soft precise step of his trade.

"Thank you, Mr. Kingsley," Walter said.

The undertaker fell in step beside him, a processional kind of pace that slowed him down. "There are some questions," he murmured.

"I want the funeral to be here," Walter said, to forestall him.

"I thought perhaps your house would . . ."

"No. Here. The pallbearers will be the directors of the bank," he said crisply as if he had thought it all over.

"And for your mother?"

Curious. He had thought of only one funeral. "There must be six?"

"That is right," Kingsley said in the vulgar phrase that was beginning to become popular because telephone girls were instructed to use it.

"Red Comstock. Alton Park. Channing Whitney. Burke Johnson." He paused. "Zeke Burnham. And Joe Bonfiglio."

Kingsley had taken out a leather notebook and was copying the names rapidly in pencil. At the last name he looked up, his heavy face showing a servile mild surprise. He was about to speak when Sickles, leaning against the doorjamb, said, "I'll wait in the car, Walter." He went out the door, shutting it quietly, and Walter saw him strike a match on one of the big concrete flower pots that stood at the bottom of the low baluster of the porch steps. He turned back to the undertaker. "What were you going to say?"

"Joe Bonfiglio, the Italian?" Kingsley asked imperturbably.

"Yes."

"I'm sorry, but are you sure you . . ."

"My mother traded there for twenty years. She used to talk to him. She liked him."

Kingsley nodded and wrote the name down. He snapped the notebook shut and as he was putting it and the pencil away in his pocket, he said, "Mr. Phelps was a member of the Athens Commandery. They will undoubtedly call me. They will call us both. Do you . . ."

"I don't want them," Walter said. He had a memory of a group of businessmen with feathered admirals' hats cocked at all angles on their heads and with drawn swords at the carry, each man looking to the right to dress the rank straight, the rank still crooked, many out of step, straggling up Main Street, embarrassed in the glare of other people's eyes. "No. Tell them not."

"Very well," Kingsley said primly as if he were noting it down to remember against Walter. "There is one more thing." He turned to a side table that stood beneath a mirror in the hall. He took from it Todd Phelps's wallet, his watch and chain, and Elizabeth Phelps's black leather purse. "I think you ought to have these."

The watch was his grandfather's, thick and silver, with the familiar Roman numerals on its face. It was supported by a thick gold chain and at the other end were carelessly attached as counterweights a Distinguished Service Cross and a Croix de Guerre without their ribbons and three gold medals his father had won boxing in college. Walter held it up to his ear to listen. It ticked. He pursed his lips slightly in satisfaction and slipped the watch into his side coat pocket.

When Kingsley handed him the wallet, a smooth narrow envelope of brown calfskin, Walter opened it without thinking and counted the money. There were five new twenty-dollar bills, a five, and three ones. Todd Phelps carried nothing else in his wallet but money, no cards, no memoranda, no credit cards, no photos. It did not occur to Walter to feel rich. He was merely keeping the money for his father until, he still assumed, it would be asked for. He stuck his mother's flat purse under his arm without opening it, said, "Thanks very much," to Kingsley and opened the door.

Kingsley said, "Will two o'clock Monday be suitable?"

[101]

He stopped in the doorway with his hand on the knob of the screen door. "That's all right," he said. He crossed the porch, went down the walk across the terraced lawn, and got into Eddie's car beside Sickles.

"I'd like to go up to the house," he said. His parents were dead. That was the only fact yet. He was unable to mourn them and a guilt for that oppressed him. Perhaps grief would strike him at the funeral.

· IX ·

WALTER CLIMBED the wide stairs. He heard more and more plainly a Sousa march, beating softly, the oom-pah muted but persistent. His grandmother was where he thought she would be, lying on the bed in her room with the blinds half drawn and a bedside radio turned down. There was no use knocking. He opened the door. She was lying on her back with her knees drawn up, fully dressed in a black dress, her head and shoulders borne up by a heap of the little embroidered pillows she thought so lovely, pink, baby-blue, a bright frog-green with flower buds worked in satin at the centers surrounded by circles of protruding cheap lace. One of her feet wagged up and down in time to the music and she lay with her bony old hands folded upon an open magazine that was spread across her chest, immobile, smiling with her head thrown back like a man who is about to blow a smoke ring.

"Grandma!" he said loudly.

She did not change or answer.

"Grandma!" he said, stepping toward her.

She saw him and switched off the radio without moving her body. "Yes, Walter. What do you want?"

"Mother and father were killed this afternoon."

She lurched sharply upright, nimbly crossing her legs under her skirt. He could see her black eyes shine in the dim light. "How did it happen?"

He told her the story of the accident as briefly as Sickles had told it to him. She swung her legs over the edge of the bed, stood up, and left the room in her quick hobbling gait, saying over her shoulder, "Don't go 'way. I'll be right back. I want to hear all about it. . . ." Her speech faded and at once she began calling to the maid from the top of the stairs. "Clara? Oo-hoo, Clara! Oh," she said as the maid evidently appeared. "I want to tell you to set just two places tonight. Mr. and Mrs. Phelps were killed this afternoon in an auto wreck . . ."

The maid interrupted with her regrets and his grandmother rushed on,

". . . out on a hundred and twelve near TIPTON, WAS IT?" she called to him.

"Yes," he called back.

"Out near Tipton. They were going fast and the pavement was wet and they began to slip and they hit a telephone pole. Instantly, they were both killed instantly. So there'll just be the two of us. Isn't that terrible?"

The maid replied and his grandmother hurried back into the room and sat down on the edge of the bed. "Sit here, Walter, where I can see you." He sat down on the chaise longue.

"Now I want you to tell me all about it. I always said your father drove too fast but he never paid any, *where* near Tipton?"

"Right at Larzalere's Corners, they said."

"Oh, you mean right near the Tipton *road*. Yes, I know where that is. Well, you see, your mother went over to Maud Roberts' for a minute after dinner and she came back about, oh, I guess a quarter past one, she wasn't gone very long, and your father said, 'If we're going, let's get started. . . .' "

"Where were they going?" Walter asked.

"How do I know? He never tells me where he's going. So Elizabeth changed her clothes. That dress just came back from the cleaner's and it isn't even paid for . . . ," and on she went stitching up the end of the tale she held, quick, bright, and eager, chafing her hands until he could hear the clicking of her rings. He had known from the first in the kind of off-hand conviction that makes you accept the weight of your clothes without thinking that she would find the deaths chiefly fascinating. She would not grieve although she would make the proper mows when the time came and she would seem by her gabble actually to approve these deaths, her son's and her daughter-in-law's, as if she had forgotten them already, not how they looked or what they wore or what they said or what they paid, but whatever filaments of affection bound them to her. She was telling over and over again how they got ready to go away in the car. He followed her with difficulty but, as he listened, a suspicion began to expand in his attention and at last he was sure that his grandmother had not loved her son, Todd. This endless verification she was performing contained all the signs. She had not evaded what he had always thought was the mother's natural affection. She had not liked or tolerated him. Least of all had she hated him.

Now he was looking at her rigidly, a cigarette burning in his hand, and he could not imagine what his father's triumphs had meant to her when he strode into the house, jovial, calling for drinks, kissing his wife, and whirling his limber old mother around the room in waltz steps; or the sullen defeats when he himself had hidden upstairs and could hear his father's obscenities in every room in the house, what exactly was the tincture of her approbation or censure, or whether she had not cared, not been involved one way or the other. Whatever it was that had started these spasms of flittering birdlike movement, what was reflected in these bright quick eyes was something he could not understand now. He had discovered his grandmother. At least he had discovered his grandmother lacking. Once he had thought it was clear love that had inspired this ceaseless absorption and the energy. Now he was finding that she ran on other fuel.

He interrupted her, pushing himself erect from the low chaise longue with a hand on each knee. "It's nearly dinner-time."

She was up at once, stooping before the mirror of her dressing table, patting and tucking. "I'm coming right away."

He waited at the top of the stairs to give her his arm. She always tried to go down them too fast. She was eighty-four years old and a fall would break her hip.

At the door of the library he left her.

"What are you going to do?" she asked.

"I'm going to get a bottle of beer."

"Out of the icebox? Your father will . . ." She stopped and grinned. "I forgot. Bring me one, too, will you?"

"Are you sure you want one, Grandma?"

"Oh, I drink beer. Used to, anyway. I always liked beer. Now you just bring two when you come."

Walter went into the kitchen. When the maid saw what he was going to do, she raised her head and watched him. He went into the icebox and got two bottles of cold beer and a big slice of Swiss cheese. He was chewing the cheese when he came out. He opened the beer, took one glass from the cupboard, and capped his grandmother's bottle with it.

He poured out a glassful of the beer and handed it to his grandmother. She set the bottle on the rug beside the sofa and lay down on it full length beneath the picture of the duck, the pheasant, and the quail.

The old woman plunged her lips into the foam and swallowed three times. She had a mustache of foam which she wiped away with her handkerchief. "My, beer's good," she said in a hearty voice, looking at the cool beaded glass in her hand. She leaned on her arm toward him, giving him her intent look. "I don't think we ought to have the funeral tomorrow, do *you?* It's too soon."

Walter took another bite of the slab of cheese. He shook his head and swallowed. "Monday."

"Did you talk to Fred Kingsley?"

"Yes. Monday at two."

As if they were planning a party, just the two of them, she hunched her shoulders forward, saying, "Now who will we get for the pallbearers?"

Walter told her the names he had given the undertaker. When he said, "Bonfiglio," she said, "Joe Bonfiglio? Why—why——" She seemed flabbergasted. She took a swallow of beer, and then, composed, with a conspiratorial smile, she said, "I see what you mean. But he won't know."

"Who won't know?"

"Todd. Your father."

"I don't care if he knows or not. Joe was Mother's friend. I picked him because of her. He used to talk about Italy to her. She always wanted to go there. . . ." As he went on explaining and justifying his choice, his authentic reasons for it became clear: he had picked the Italian to help carry his mother's body partly, it was true, because she had always liked him but mainly to annoy his father, an act that would be, he thought, still genuinely annoying but done somehow with impunity. His father might curse him but he could not get at him now. He was disappointed that a tribute to his mother turned out to be a defiance of his father.

"Now let's see, there'll be the bank, and the Chain Company, and the Tool and Die, and the Elks, and the Commandery, my, the Commandery always do beautifully. They sent a whole blanket of roses to your grandfather's funeral. And the City Club probably. I wonder if the Country Club, Walter, do you think the Country Club will send flowers?" she asked.

"I don't know."

"Umm . . . who else?"

"A lot of people, I suppose."

"Oh, I don't mean individuals. Certainly there'll be dozens of single bouquets and pieces and like that. Your father was a prominent man. No, I mean clubs and corporations, *groups* of some kind. Wasn't he president of the State Bankers Association one year?"

"Three years ago."

"There. That's what I mean. Something like that."

"But what the hell difference does it make, Grandma?"

She was absorbed in some picture. She was looking straight at him, pulling one hand through the other like a glove. She did not seem to see him although she said tartly, "I hope you're not going to start out the

[105]

way he did, swearing all over the place. But Dean Channer's getting so feeble and if it's going to be as hot as this . . . ," she went on in a dreamy childlike voice. "Is Watson's flower store open tonight? You never know, with this depression whether . . ."

"Yes."

"I was just wondering. Do you suppose the Bishop would come? Of course we couldn't get Channer to recommend him. That would be going over his own head. Couldn't you go to church tomorrow and see the other wardens, Walter? After all, you're Todd's son and I should think that would carry some weight."

The maid called them in to dinner.

A five-pound sirloin steak reposed on a silver platter, broiled black, in its own gravy. Covered silver dishes contained the potatoes and the vegetables. The yellow leaves of a head of lettuce lay in a silver-mounted wooden bowl and a silver boat of Roquefort cheese dressing stood beside it. Walter's place had not been set at the head of the table, he noticed, and, as he drew out his grandmother's chair, the maid, standing beside the table, said in an anxious wail, "That steak was all we had in the house except the chickens for tomorrow. I know it's big but he wouldn't ever let you cut into them and . . ."

"That's all right, Clara," Walter said.

He sliced the steak, and with the slices on his grandmother's plate he put French fried potatoes and new peas. Walter poured out a dessert-spoonful of Worcestershire sauce and took it neat, as he had learned from his father. The sweat broke out on his forehead. He was beginning to eat the last meal his father had ordered and it did not occur to him that it was a heavy meal for the kind of weather they were having.

For ten minutes neither he nor his grandmother spoke. Like all the Phelpses, they did not allow conversation to interfere until after their hunger had been smothered and they were eating only for the fun of it.

"I'll have some more peas, Walter," she said, "And you might just give me another little piece of steak. Not much. Just a smidgen."

Walter cut her two large slices of steak, gave her some more potatoes and a spoonful of peas, while she, in apparent abstraction, ate her salad.

"There. That's fine," she said. "Walter, what are you going to do?"

"Do? What do you mean?"

"Well, I suspect there's quite a lot of money here. Your father was well off, wasn't he? He never told me anything about his finances but I always surmised he'd done pretty well. I wouldn't be surprised," she said archly, "if you're going to be a pretty wealthy young man."

"I don't know," Walter said. He had not given his father's money much thought, but now that it had been mentioned, the inevitability seemed pleasant that he would have it, all of it. His grandmother had money of her own.

"Half a million, would you say?"

"I don't know. I doubt it," Walter said.

"Well, there'll be three or four hundred thousand anyway even after it gets through probate. Of course, if I were in your place, at *your* age, I'd just sell everything, lock, stock, and barrel, and get the money, and put it into a safe-deposit box so I'd have the cash. You can't tell what's going to happen. The country's going to the dogs, the way it looks."

"The country'll be all right in another ninety days," Walter said with his father's voice.

"I doubt it myself. Anyway, that's just an old woman's idea." She leaned forward on her elbows over the empty plate. "You're young. What're you going to do?"

There were many idle young men, some of them college graduates like himself. Now, in the summer, they lived in an idleness of stagnation, not the busy idleness of amusement at their families' cottages at the lakes, driving their mothers on errands, swimming three times a day, and making cautious visits to the beer joints on allowances of three dollars a week. It would be worse in the winter and for poor guys it was worse now.

"Keep on at the bank," he said.

His grandmother had the set expression that marks a hostess when she is feeling for the electric button under the rug. There was silence. At last they heard the buzzer in the kitchen, and his grandmother changed the subject while the maid removed the plates and brought in the coffee and dessert, huge slices of apple pie covered with vanilla ice cream.

"Have you seen the car, the Packard, Walter?" she asked.

"No. Barry Sickles said the were bringing it in this afternoon."

"It'll be nice to have your own car."

"Look, Grandma, they were going sixty-five miles an hour when they hit that post. The car's junk."

"Oh," she said vaguely, "I thought maybe they could fix it. They fix everything nowadays." She was waiting on the maid and as soon as she was gone, she leaned forward again. "You know what I would do if I were you and had all this money? I'd sell the house first. . . ."

"Where would *you* live?" he asked.

"Good Lord, all I need is some beans and some rafters. An old party like me can live anywhere, doesn't make a bit of difference. No, do you know what I'd do? Sell the house, sell out everything, stocks, bonds, furniture, everything. And I'd go abroad."

"Where?"

"Why, anywhere. France, England, Germany, Italy."

"What have they got over there? Dad always said the French were as dirty as pigs."

"What on earth's difference does that make?" She looked down at her plate. "Eat your ice cream. It's running all over." They ate dutifully with calm pleasure in silence for a moment.

Then she leaned toward him again, her palm pressed against her face, gazing at the crystal chandelier vacantly, her whole perch surprisingly expressing not the grace but the ephemeral awkwardness of a young girl. "Or China? Why not China? No Phelps has ever been there. Or, good heavens, Russia or India or South America."

Walter lit a cigarette and moved his coffee in front of him. She amused him and if there was any link between the sinister lack of affection for her son that he had discovered a little while before and the source of his amusement in her, he did not discern it. "Why are you so set on my going away?"

Fiercely, as if she were defending an obvious principle of rectitude, she threw out her hands and said, "Why, there's nothing *here*. A little town like this? What is there?" She drew her cheeks down comically and wagged her head from side to side. "Same thing, day after day. Anyhow the Phelpses have worked it all over. We know all about it. We own most of it—me and your father and Eri. Say, did you call Eri?"

"He's in Detroit. He was in the bank this morning. Coming home to-night, he said."

Forgetting Eri, she rushed on. "There's nothing here. Get out. Have some fun. Adventures. You could go to the Paris Opera House, or to Rome to see the ruins, or that Isle of Capri they talk about. Why don't you go to Europe? I would if I were you."

"No," he said. It did not seem to him a place he would want to visit now even if he could reach it successfully. There were difficulties. He did not know the languages except Caesar's Latin and a little useless college French. He could see himself on a station platform, harried, sweating, impatient, trying to get his bags away from a porter, or being over-charged in restaurants, dirty French restaurants. What would be the ad-ventures in such surroundings? What could they be?

As he was thinking, his eye fell on the severe silver coffeepot resting on a little silver plate with a gadroon border. With a little start, he accepted

[108]

them; now he could call these his. Why should he hightail it all over Europe when he could live here in this comfort, envied because he had a job, secure in the complacent certitude that if adventures were necessary to his happiness he could easily arrange them since he knew all the chances to be taken? Now that it had come to be a matter for his decision, only that, a toss of a coin, he could say to himself for the first time in his life, "This is my home," and appreciate what he said.

"No. I'm going to stay here in the bank," he said, looking at her, knowing that she would think him faithful to his father's work.

"You know what you're doing, I suppose," she said, shaking her head to disclaim all responsibility. "But a bank . . . ," she said scornfully. "Sitting in a cage all day long. I never could see it."

"There's money in it."

"But you're the generation that ought to spend the money. You know what they say, 'Shirt sleeves to shirt sleeves in three generations,' Well, you're the third generation."

"Uncle Eri's spending it."

"Pooh! All Eri does is skulk around looking for widow-women and discontented schoolteachers. I wanted you to be the one to get *out* of this town."

"No. I think I'll keep the house and stay right here."

"Well . . . ," she said in a voice of warning. Then briskly, "Are you through? Let's go in the other room."

They went into the library. The maid had put the afternoon *Telegraph* on the table under the lamp. The old woman seized it and pored over the first page.

"That's funny. There's nothing here about your father."

"It'll be in Monday," he said.

"Oh, that's right. Say, if I were you I'd go put on a dark suit." She was looking up and down the inside pages.

"What for?"

"Why, there'll be all kinds of people coming in here tonight as soon as they hear about the accident."

"I think I'll take a walk. I don't want to see them."

He wanted to escape the dreary condolences of the family friends. They would be insincere and he would have to pull a long face to make his answers. He was not old enough to comprehend that if the speeches were set and awkwardly given, some of the impulses were kind.

The sun had set but its light was not gone. He walked slowly along the hot sidewalks under the maple trees. A few men in shirt sleeves sprinkled their little lawns. Women sat in their porch swings reading the evening paper, and here and there groups of children played violently in the heat. One or two of the men he passed called to him, "Sorry to hear about your father and mother," and he called, "Thank you," in reply. Out of the corner of his eye he could see the women on the porches look at him as he passed, and, if the porches were close to the street, he could sometimes hear them say just after he had gone by, "There goes that Walter Phelps. His father and mother . . ." The news seemed to be all over town. He felt himself conspicuous. He rarely took an evening walk, to walk along slowly as if he were out for the air, and he was embarrassed because people might think he wanted to be alone in his sorrow.

He saw no light in Emily's house but he could hear the slow rhythmical squeaking of the porch swing and he went up the steps. He found her alone, lying in the swing, reading a magazine in the dim light. She sat up.

"Hello, Emily," he said. He was somehow ashamed that he was in a position to receive her sympathy yet he wanted it.

"You're early. What's the matter, couldn't you get the car?" she said. It was plain that she had not heard of the deaths. She seemed cold and hard anyway.

"The car's wrecked," he said. He was stirred with the desire to string out the story, to give a dramatic presentation and at the same time he knew it was cheap to want to.

"Oh, God," she said in disgust. "I wanted to go to Island Lake to-night."

They knew each other well enough for her to be so far candid and there was nothing unusual in her disgust, yet it made him a little angry, as if since nearly everyone else seemed to know, she ought to have known about his father and mother, and treat him with the respect he deserved as a bereaved son. Paradoxically—it was becoming clearer now—he wanted the respect from her as a personal tribute although he was sure he was suffering no grief. And—it was odd—he wanted to chuck the whole thing, forget her, and go somewhere else. But now that he was there sitting in the ornamental green iron chair, looking across the glass-topped table with the plants growing beneath, conscious that she was pretty, his eyes shamefacedly peeping at her bare brown calves, he wanted to humiliate her and exact the tribute.

"Well, I'm sorry," he said humbly. "We'll have to stay here."

"Where's Eddie? Couldn't we go with him?"

"Eddie's gone out to his cottage."

"Well, who could we call? You know everybody. Think of somebody we could call." She stood up and stretched, arching herself, with her hands locked under the mass of hair at the back of her neck. "I've been sitting around here all day." She flapped her hands as if she were sweeping him off the porch. "Go on. Call up. Call up. Get somebody."

He did not move. He said, "Maybe I don't want to go to Island Lake tonight."

"Oh, come on, Walter. Please," she coaxed.

"I don't want to go to Island Lake tonight."

"Why not?"

He stood up, his face sullen. "My father and mother were killed in a wreck this afternoon, that's why." He walked off the porch slowly, almost sedately, hearing her call after him that she didn't know, she wouldn't have asked, she was sorry. He kept going.

It had grown quite dark. The street lights were lit and as he came up the street toward his house he was sure he saw his grandmother cross under the light in her brisk limping gait, a woman in a dark dress with her upper body humped over as if she were clenching it around her clasped hands. He doubted that it was she because she had not gone out at night alone since he could remember.

A few minutes later he entered his house and he went upstairs at once to his grandmother's room. He knocked. She said, "Walter? Come in."

She was sitting at her dressing table fully dressed. The side lights were lit and one of the black japanned boxes was open. She was dreamily unfolding and unrolling the spills of paper that bulged from it.

"It's funny," she said without looking up.

"What?"

She turned around to face him. "You know, I haven't one thing about Todd and Elizabeth's accident. I've looked and looked."

"Why should you have?"

"Oh, you can make all the fun of me you want to but there hasn't been one single family event, hardly, that I didn't have written right down on these pieces of paper." She stirred them sourly with one finger as if, whether she had written it or not, there should have been a prophecy of the accident discovered there.

"Do you think you're psychic?" Walter asked.

"Psychic?" She glanced up sharply with a puzzled scowl. "Oh, you mean a medium," she said smiling. "My Lord, no. With one of those glass balls? What do you take me for? No, I just think when people have a blood tie, you *know* somehow. Haven't you heard of women waking up out of a sound sleep in the middle of the night and *knowing* their children have spoken their name and the next day getting a telegram saying that they're dead?"

"Yes. I've heard about it."

"Well, then," she said as if she were vindicated.

"Did you wake up out of a sound sleep this afternoon?"

"I wasn't asleep."

"Have any premonitions or anything?"

"No, I didn't. I don't claim to have the second sight or anything like it but I could show you some pretty startling things on these pieces of paper. I haven't missed much, I can tell you."

"Show me," he said.

With an odd gesture like a miser protecting his gold, or a little girl her dolls, she raked the box and the tags of paper toward her in her two arms, staring at him over her shoulder. "No such thing. These are private." Seeing they were not threatened, she relaxed. "I want you to promise me one thing, Walter."

"What's that?"

"When I go, I want you to put these in the fire, box and all, without your looking at them, or anybody else. Now promise me."

He began to grin and he stood there so long without answering that his grandmother said, "You darned kid."

He said, "I promise. How much longer do you think you'll be spared?"

"It ain't a question of that," she said huffily. "I just want the satisfaction of knowing that my private effects are not going to be molested."

"Grandma, I'll burn 'em all up."

"Well, see that you do. Now you skidoo out of here. I'm going to bed." She began to take the bone hairpins out of her hair.

At the door Walter asked, "Did anyone come to pay their respects?"

She turned around again. "You know that's the strangest thing. I sat down there in the library the longest time and no one came, not one solitary person. Now you'd think with a prominent man like your father, or some of your mother's friends, someone would come to call, wouldn't you?"

"Maybe they haven't heard yet." He knew this was unlikely. "Nobody, huh?"

"Not a single soul. Don't you think that's peculiar?"

"There'll be somebody tomorrow. Good night."

"There better be. Good night, Walter."

He shut the door and went down the corridor to his own bedroom. He had untied his necktie when he noticed the electric clock on the bureau.

[112]

It was only twenty minutes past nine. It seemed too early to go to bed, especially on a Saturday night.

Two doors away, across the corridor, was his father's room. He opened the door quietly and switched on the light. At one side was a big brass bed with knobs at the corners. It had a special hair mattress and his father would never have the bed moved and he had stubbornly defended it when the house had been decorated again. It was one of Walter's earliest memories, going in to kiss his father good night as a little boy, and his father lurching down from his mound of pillows, his face in the shadow from the light of the reading lamp attached to the bed behind his head, a book open in his hand, and the crusts of a plate of sandwiches slipping over the bedclothes. Walter switched off the overhead light and turned on the reading lamp over the bed. The room took on its familiar, its correct aspect.

Straight ahead of him, blocking one of the long windows, was a roll-top desk; beside it, a bookcase, a ratty old-fashioned walnut thing, with leaded glass doors that were always kept locked. There were curtains behind the glass of the doors and he had never known what was in the bookcase. Even with a small boy's ingenuity he had never, lurking, found it open or caught a glance of the shape of the key. On the walls were two prints of paintings by Frederick Remington of cowboys and Indians. He had never been able to take any pleasure in Western movies because the heroes, even William S. Hart, seemed to have such bland childlike faces compared to these rough, these first authentic men. He had always liked to look in his father's bureau at the piles of white shirts. He opened the doors and pulled out the trays. In the corners and the aisles lay the customary little bags of lavender, the sweet smell rising, and, he reflected, the shirts would fit him now. If he wanted to, he could move them into his own room. He picked up one of them, a heavy silk, rubbed it between his thumb and finger and laid it down again. He shut up the bureau.

He went over to the desk and threw up the top. He sat down with a businesslike air and began to open the little drawers. In the first were receipted bills. They did not interest him. Another drawer in the tier rattled with bullets for his father's .45 automatic which he knew he would find in the top one of the bigger drawers by his right knee. His father said he kept it there because of burglars, but Walter knew he liked to have it close by where he could handle it. Another drawer contained a broken pair of spectacles, stubs of pencils, an elk's tooth set in gold as a watch charm, a pearl-handled pocketknife with all blades broken, and other useless litter. Another drawer was crammed with checkbooks and their stubs. Was this all? Could he discover nothing else? It was too early to go to bed, and, he had had to remind himself not to go on tiptoe—his father would not be shouting up the stairs for him to get the hell out of his room. He had nevertheless a sneaky feeling as if he were prying into something he should not see. He pulled out the last drawer. It was full of all the discarded keys of the family, undoubtedly keys to the cottage at the lake, with its cupboards; keys to hunting lodges his father had rented for a season and forgotten to return; hotel keys with brass tags; old iron keys maybe to unlock the doors of the carriage house that was now their garage; plain Yale keys.

He remembered the bookcase and he pawed the little heap over until he found two or three keys that would possibly fit its lock. He got up and tried them. They would go in. They would turn part way but they would not unlock it. He tried four in all without any success. He gave the last key in the lock a jerk. The doors did not open but the latches at the top were sprung. By pulling back and forth he finally slipped the bolt and the doors opened. A photograph fell to the floor. He picked it up. It was a tintype of his father and Eri, taken when they were boys, both in high buttoned boots and striped stockings, with two serious tinted pudgy faces watching the birdie. He tossed it over on the desk, thinking that he would give it to his grandmother. She would recall the occasion.

The bookcase was full of books but the light was dim and he could not see the titles. He went over to the bed and raised the green glass shade and tiptoed back to the bookcase. He was excited, not at what he expected to find but at his breaking in, and he could feel his heart pounding. The first book he picked out was *The Dialogues of Luisa Sigeia*. The name meant nothing and the title seemed dull. Then he saw beneath a title the name *de Sade*. He pulled out the *Juliette* and the *Justine*, followed by a magnificent illustrated edition of the sonnets of Aretino. With the books in his hands, he seemed to retain almost a memory of having suspected their existence in the house, impossible as it was. There was nothing else in the world his father would have put a lock on in his own house, except money, and a lock meant a curious deference to the principles of his wife and his mother—the effort to explain the presence of these books would have made him furious and he had shrewdly balked the need to. Well worn, in all kinds of bindings, were Cleaveland's *Fanny Hill,* Frank Harris's *My Life and Loves,* a *Kama Sudra,* and two thick volumes in German with a good many pictures, *Die Erotische Kunst.* Walter pulled out half a dozen of them, some plainly bound, without titles, and took them over to the desk. They were books of erotic photographs, the

[114]

women furiously coy, the men solemn with handlebar mustaches, wearing socks and garters. He would have been agitated by them a month before but now, here, in front of him, his father's, they made him a little sick. This sort of thing was maybe all right for young guys, he thought, but for men his father's age it was wrong.

He remembered him, night after night, in pajamas, dressing gown, and slippers, trudging up the stairs with a bottle of beer in one hand and a plate of sandwiches balanced on the other, curt, sarcastic, taciturn— and only people who were *right* could afford that manner, Walter thought —stopping to kiss his wife perfunctorily good night and plodding on into his bedroom to lie there, "reading," as the women always said. "Your father reads a lot." His father among his books.

Walter put the books back and shut the doors as tightly as the broken locks would let him. If he had come for information, he had found it, and if he didn't like what he had found, it would teach him to keep his hands off other people's keys. And yet—he stood in the middle of the room. The night was very still. No air stirred to rustle the leaves beyond the window. He could hear the sounds of the traffic downtown but they were distant and everything near by seemed wrapped in softness and in silence —and yet, whether he had ever found it out or not, the fact had been there and if his father had lived, some of its taint would have revealed itself someday he believed, but known, encountered, it was daubing and shrinking the image he held of his father. And, as he turned off the light, he remembered the undertaker's room that afternoon it seemed to have taken a very small sheet to cover him. Hadn't he heard that somewhere? Didn't all corpses look smaller than life size? As he passed down the dark corridor, he believed that his father was now at last dead.

Standing in her doorway in the dark, and he jumped in surprise to find her there, his grandmother said, "Walter, don't wander around this way. Go to bed, sonny."

"Thanks, Grandma," he said and went to his room.

· X ·

The funeral of Todd and Elizabeth Phelps was undoubtedly the "largest" the town had ever seen. There had been thunder the night before but the day turned out hot and clear with strands of heavy summer haze piled up against the woodlots in the country and the grass damp under the maples in town. Walter dressed himself in a blue suit, too thick for the weather, a black tie, and passed the morning in a rocking chair in the library on the shady side of the house, rocking back and forth, reading snatches from the morning papers, and catching himself staring vacantly out over the lawn.

His grandmother had strengthened herself for the occasion with two nips of cherry brandy she kept privately on a shelf in her closet. She had put on a new black dress she had been saving, a flat black hat from whose brim depended a heavy crepe veil bound with an inch-wide satin ribbon. Around her throat she had hooked a black velvet band on which she pinned a white cameo. She had eluded Walter all the morning, taking breakfast from a tray in her bedroom, and when it came time, she had hired a taxi and gone alone to the funeral.

She refused to sit in the place reserved for the "family" and had gone to the back of the largest room. It was there that Walter found her at the end of a long row, her chair flat against the wall, a black morocco Bible-and-prayer book in her black silk hands, erect as ever in the heavy moist heat, with a palm-leaf fan supplied by the management untouched on her lap.

Walter sat down beside her. He saw his uncle Eri, ushered by Fred Kingsley, come in through a side door and take a seat in the "family" room. He nudged his grandmother lightly but she did not look around. He noticed her lips moving. He doubted prayer. He feared that she might have taken sick, not from grief but excitement, and grown mildly delirious. He watched her surreptitiously and at last he nearly laughed out loud. The old woman was counting the house. All through the long Episcopal service, her veil swung from side to side like a little skirt as she craned her neck in the effort not to miss anyone.

When it was over, neither one of them went forward to view the remains. Walter helped his grandmother into the undertaker's car with the little purple flags at the fenders. As they began their slow progress through the town to the cemetery, the first thing he said to her was, "How many were there?" Eri, seated pale, drunk, and apparently torn by a genuine sorrow, clucked in reproof but she was not at all abashed. She said, "I made it two hundred and twenty-three inside but of course I don't know how many stood on the porch."

"Was it the biggest?"

"Far and away. The biggest they ever had in this town before was Major Cole's and there were only a hundred and eighty-odd at his."

"I'm glad," he said, holding his face blank.

"It's nice. I like a big funeral," she said complacently.

[116]

"Oh, my God," Eri bayed in disgust.

"You shut up, Eri," she said sharply. He had never been so impressive as her elder son because she thought she could trace everything of herself and his father that had made him up and there was no unknown residue to surprise her.

At the graveside the old trembling minister, the Reverend Dr. Channer, threw a handful of sand on the coffins so smoothly and mechanically descending, feebly crying, "Ashes to ashes. Dust to dust," with the sweat pouring down the long slope of his bald head and his surplice dank around him. Walter saw the tears pouring from his grandmother's eyes. She was biting her lips. Her arms were pressed stiffly against her sides and she was opening and closing her hands spasmodically. Were her mother's memories overwhelming her or was this merely the suitable gesture performed with an impregnable tact?

After the burial when all the cars were starting and he had taken his grandmother's thin arm while she pecked in her purse for a handkerchief, he had seen Kingsley, the undertaker, lingering somberly. Was he expected to compliment him on the arrangements? He wanted to get away but the old woman was snuffling into her handkerchief and he was forced to stand there nodding at the people, who passed by him to their waiting cars, in response to their sad embarrassed smiles. At last the undertaker approached him slowly, courteously grave and diffident. "Perhaps you would like to have these?" he said. He offered Walter a pack of little white cards and Walter, irritated by the delay, was about to say, "What the hell for?" when he saw that they were the cards that had been attached to the flowers. The copper-lined coffins were shut. They were resting on the bottom of the grave. The prayers had been duly said and he could see the old rector lying back exhausted in the front seat of someone's car, mopping his face and fanning himself with a palm-leaf fan snitched from the funeral home. The gravediggers had already begun to fill the grave but the ritual was unfinished. There was still more to do. He would have to spend a whole day writing "Thank you." He stuffed the cards into his pocket and assisted his grandmother into the waiting limousine. As they drove away, he could see the undertaker winding things up with a last suave bow to nobody in particular.

That night before he went to bed he was hanging up his dark suit and he noticed the sag from the weight of the cards in the side pocket. He pulled them out and laid them on the bureau. Impelled by a slight curiosity, he stood there in his undershirt beginning to go through the cards to learn who valued their friendship or association with his parents

enough to regret its end with their bouquets. He was pleased to find one
from Eddie and his mother. He had not gone through many when he
noticed that the name "Mrs. Winthrop Phelps" had turned up three
times. He thumbed over the whole pack carefully. His grandmother had
sent nine floral pieces. And she had not once said, "Did you ever *see* so
many flowers?" There was that much grace in her at least.

The morning after the funeral he turned up at the bank promptly to go
to work. The stenographers and the other tellers raised their heads to
look as he walked through to his own cage. He changed into the gray
alpaca jacket and went to the vault to get the day's cash. He was just beginning to set it up when Vernon Barker, the second vice-president,
pulled back the door and stepped in. His face and his bald spot were
bright red from sunburn and the lenses of his gray horn-rimmed spectacles
were so thick that his eyes when he looked straight at you were like
marbles, and if he turned his head they disappeared. He was smart and a
little suspicious of everyone. "Walter," he said.

"Morning, Vern," Walter said.

"We won't need you for a couple days," he said, taking off his glasses
with one hand and pinching at his eyelids with the other.

"Oh, I don't mind working." It occurred to him he was being done a
favor. "It's nice of you, Vern, but . . ."

"Sure thing, Walter. The shock and all." He pursed his lips and screwed
one eye shut as if he were giving a hot tip on the races. "Tell you what
you do." He patted Walter's arm. "You just lay off a couple days. Take
it easy. Do you good. Right?"

"I haven't got anything to do. I might as well work."

"You're going to have a lot of stuff to wind up there. Lot of figuring to
do. I'd get on it if I were you. Go see Horse Egan." He patted Walter's
arm again, winked, and walked out.

He had expected to see Horse Egan, or rather, the little he had thought
of it, he had half expected Horse Egan to come to see him, in the evening after business hours, carrying a black leather portfolio, a visit framed
in his anticipation by the accounts he had read in novels of the minis-
trations of a family solicitor. Not that Horse was a family solicitor—he
saw a few doors down the street the entrance to the stairway where, to the
left on the wall, there was a black sign with gilt letters, *Wood & Egan,
Att'ys-at-Law*. He went up the worn marble steps to the second floor.
The door was held open for a breath of air by a wooden wedge.

It was an old-fashioned law office, lined with shelves full of reports and statutes back to the time of Horse's father and beyond. Two big steel engravings hung on one wall, Lincoln and Governor Lewis Cass.

At the far end of the office silhouetted against the brightness of the window was Lide Carter talking to the stenographer. Lide was old but how old he could not tell because her flesh seemed firm and she painted her face so heavily you could not see the wrinkles. She always wore jewelry—this time it was a heavy necklace of oval red stones flaunted as rubies—and feather boas in season. She was grave and businesslike and she would have been picked out for a madam anywhere in the civilized world. She drew back, folding her hands decently in the recesses of her lap and closing her mouth with an air of delicate affront when Walter came up to the stenographer's desk and asked if Mr. Egan was in.

He could see Horse at his desk through the crack in the half-open door but the girl said, "Just a minute. I'll see."

She returned and said, "Mr. Egan will see you now."

In his private office Horse had brought things up to date. There was a bold Van Gogh print of flag lilies on the wall behind his head. Opposite him where he could see it and perhaps refresh himself (and in a ray of sunlight that slipped past the drawn shade Walter could see there was no dust on the frame) a large photograph of one of the University of Michigan football teams and in the front row, next to Yost, sat Horse, stiff, solemn, transfixed by fame, with a football in his lap, an All-American tackle. Horse was crouched behind a "period" walnut desk on which reposed a folder full of papers which he was studying.

He was six feet, two inches tall and now, sagged and torpid, he weighed two hundred and thirty pounds. Coming, as it had, before the radio and the movies could have exploited it properly, his fame had been spread only by the newspapers and his name had never been truly a household word except in the county where he lived, yet, comparatively minor as it was, it had sobered him. He was too intelligent to have been impressed by the gaping of small boys. It was rather the handshakes and the backslaps given him by older men, some of them strangers, that had changed him, and the growing intimation that his name was praised and his dim pictures looked at by people he had never seen, upstate, in Ohio, Chicago, and perhaps, who knew, on the Eastern seaboard. Most men, even athletes to whom the crowd is a confused roaring mass, feel they are anonymous, free to move, unwatched. When his last football season was over, he had been troubled by the avid glances, the stares and the recognition people gave him wherever he went. A stupid youth would have imposed on his fame but it only made Horse ambitious; he was not articulate enough to say to himself, "I owe these people a continuing spectacle, my success. I can't let them down."

He entered law school, where his weight sank to a hundred and eighty his first year. He learned table manners, gave up taking whores around to saloons, and drank only among trusted friends. Slowly, year after year, he constructed an appearance and a manner which Walter now confronted. He was a good lawyer and in hot weather, in this small town, he wore shirts that required cufflinks.

He lifted his smooth face, a little raw from his morning shave. He stood up and said in a heavy baritone, "Hello, Walter," with his hand stuck out. They shook hands and Horse indicated a chair with a supple gesture. "I didn't get a chance to speak to you—yesterday." He gave the word its sad homage. "It's tough. I'll miss your father a lot. It's very tough," he repeated in a low voice, looking down at the desk.

Walter said nothing.

"Well," Horse dismissed the grief with a loud sigh that changed into a firm businesslike smile. "I'm glad you came in, Walter. I wanted to go over these things with you."

"Yes." He had to say something.

"There was no will." Horse said this hesitantly. There was in it a latent inquiry.

"He wasn't old. He wasn't ready to die."

Horse looked down at the folder. "No. He was a young man." He looked up again. "Todd always kept a list of his holdings with me, you know. He gave me a monthly statement and I recorded any changes. Good idea. Comes in handy now."

There was only one reason for his visit. There was no use waiting. Walter asked, "How much is there?"

"Let's see. Here's the stock. Here's the bonds. And here's the mortgages." He shoved the three sheets of paper across the desk, one at a time.

Walter picked up the lists and looked them over. They did not mean much for all the talk he had heard about securities.

"You'll notice the dates," Horse said quietly.

There was a date opposite each stock entry. "What do they mean?"

"Date of purchase." Horse stood up, put his hands in his pockets, and began to walk stiff-legged up and down the rug. "Let's see, Walter, you got out of Ann Arbor when? Two years ago, right?"

"That's right."

"Lit School."

"Yes."

"Ah, what was your major?"

"Business Ad."

"Uh-*huh*."

"Why? What about it?"

Horse could not help succumbing at times to the stagy gesture. All natural movements he had suppressed years ago. Any he made now he had learned, and courtroom practice had given them a floridity he did not always suspect. He had one elbow couched in his other hand. He was stroking his chin, his brows drawn, his eyes turned up. Walter recognized it as a plastic cliché of puzzled thought.

"Business Ad, eh? I was just thinking," he explained redundantly. He turned quickly and leaned over his desk on his widespread hairy hands. "Just what are your plans, son? What are you going to do?"

A little wearily because he wanted the money with no palaver, no good advice, Walter said, "I'm going to stay on at the bank."

Horse straightened up. "That's fine. That's fine. I'm glad to hear you say that." He began to pace the rug again. "Going to keep the house? Your grandmother going to be with you?"

"I think so."

"Big house for two people, don't you think? Hell of a place to heat in the winter. *Must* be."

"I like it. I've always lived there."

"Sure. Sure." He stopped and poured himself a drink of water from a bright nickel carafe on his desk. He corked it up again, wiped his mouth, patted his brow with his handkerchief and tucked it back into his breast pocket with barely a glance, saying in a relaxed voice, an aside, so to speak, "God-damn, it's hot, isn't it?" He sat down and shot his cuffs, moved the folder aside, and looked straight at Walter's eyes. "Walter, you must prepare yourself for a shock."

He had been watching the details of Horse's performance dully but this came out clear. "How do you mean?"

"Your dad was not so well off as you may have thought."

Walter sat leaning forward in his chair, waiting.

"He was a heavy and, I may say, a constant speculator in the market," Horse said solemnly.

"Who, the old man?" Walter said loudly, rushing on as Horse nodded. "Why, he was always cussing people for getting into the market. Everybody that came in the bank. What do you mean he was a speculator?"

"He lost his shirt."

"I don't believe it," Walter said, but Horse's phrase was an echo with justice in it somehow.

"He's short every god-damn one of those stocks, every single god-damn one. And 'way short."

Walter looked at Horse. "When anybody dies, you keep finding out things," he said. He felt the heat in the office, seeping in through the bricks in the wall, bouncing up from the pavement below. The soft flapping of the electric fan seemed idiotic and with the same, no more, intensity of apprehension it seemed worse than idiotic that this fat sweet-smelling man should wield, as a routine piece of business, this iconoclastic power. He had reached back into his father's life and made a fool out of him. "Well, Horse. Show me. Let's have it."

It took over an hour. The little folder on Horse's desk contained only the results. There were drawers full of brokerage receipts, letters, adding-machine slips with penciled notations attached, ledgers and notebooks to be gone through. Horse took off his coat and put it on a hanger and his nice white shirt was at last soaked through.

"Now do you see? If you sell the stock now, sell the bonds, and if you can get the bank to take those mortgages off your hands at, say, twenty cents on the dollar, sell the house, the furniture, and the cottage at the lake, you ought to come out of it with a thousand dollars maybe. You got many bills outstanding?"

"The funeral. And then there's the grocery. . . ."

"Oh, yeah, that's small stuff." He brightened. "I don't see, Walter, why you shouldn't come out of it with a few hundred to spare, cash money. You're young. Good education. You've got a job. What the hell?"

"Yes." He dragged it out doubtfully. "I could hold those stocks, couldn't I?"

"If you can stave off those Detroit boys."

"If I could, then what?"

"Depends."

"On what?"

"On what you think of the United States of America. 'It's going to be over in six months.' They've been saying that every six months for the last four years. The only trouble is, it's not over. Now I'm not the man to say those stocks'll *never* be worth anything but I got a hunch you'll have a long gray beard before they are. I'll tell you, Walter, if this Roosevelt doesn't begin to hump himself and say something besides 'My frans,' we're going to have red socialism in this country and you can use all your stocks and bonds to light fires with. I mean it." Horse's face showed awe.

"Better sell them, then."

"Sure. I would. Get out clean. Then you're not living on hope every day. You ought to see some of the people that come in here. Why, you see 'em every day at the bank. They can't believe it yet. They hang on and on. Every morning they get up hoping, hoping, hoping, Jesus God, how they hope that, come night, they'll go to bed rich the way they were. The way they thought they were. The dumb clucks."

Walter stood up. "Much obliged, Horse. I'll see you when?"

"You want to come down here seven o'clock tomorrow night? We might be able to get everything decided then."

"OK."

"Sure thing, Walter." He patted him on the shoulder. "I like the way you're taking it, boy." He took Walter's hand and had begun the squeeze when he dropped it suddenly. "Oh, say, have you got the key to the safe-deposit box?"

"Yes."

"Have you opened it yet?"

"No."

"You understand, Walter, it's none of my business. Not one damn bit, but I think we better go open it. You can't tell what you might find. I doubt if your dad was the man to stuff it with new twenty-dollar bills but you never know."

"If you want to go up to the bank now, we can open it."

"BEULAH! Get me Tommy Haight," Horse shouted. "We've got to have him with us. He has to deliver the assets to probate."

Walter knew that. Tommy Haight was the City Treasurer.

They met him in the bank. He had been City Treasurer thirty-four years. He wore a floppy Panama hat with dirt ground into the weft, a spotted cream-colored summer suit, and brown vici-kid shoes with hard nicked toes. As soon as he saw Horse and Walter, he began to complain about the heat and how they had forced him to come out in it.

"You need warming up, Tommy. Besides it'll be cool downstairs," Horse said.

The three men went into the vault and down the narrow steel stairway to the room lined with safe-deposit boxes. Walter had been in the room dozens of times with the bank's clients. He knew where his father's box was. It was No. 100. He searched his pockets for the key. He did not even wonder what was in the box. It seemed to him that he was a spectator to all this: the other two men were running things and what they did could barely touch him. He knew that he ought to feel that his life was changing, maybe it was, but it was not he who was making the change and all he could do was to watch. He opened the box. Tommy Haight snapped at him as he was about to lift out a packet of letters, "Don't touch it!"

Walter stared at the fierce old man but he did not think he was fierce or funny or bossy or anything, not even when Horse winked at him over Tommy's shoulder. All he wanted to know was why he shouldn't touch the letters.

"That's *my* job," Haight said. "I've got to make a *list* of all this stuff."

Horse leaned over his shoulder as he pawed through the box. It was not stuffed with money. The contents seemed to be letters mostly, packets held with thick rubber bands.

"Could I look at some of those letters, Tommy?"

"Is it against the law?" Horse said jocosely.

Tommy straightened up and looked at Horse and then at Walter. "I suppose you've had sciatica. I suppose you know what it is to have to lie on a hot-water bottle all night long without a wink of sleep. I suppose you'd like to be hauled out on a long walk when every step you take feels like a red-hot wire."

Walter said the first thing that struck him. He said it mildly, "It's your job, isn't it, Tommy?"

"Go ahead, take 'em," the Treasurer said, shoving a bundle of the letters at Walter. "Don't look to me like there was anything worth listing in there anyway."

While the old man was making a list of the contents in a little notebook, Walter looked over the letters. The first batch were in his father's hand. They were letters he had written his wife from France during the war. There were also the citations for his medals. Walter did not need to read these. He could understand why his father had kept them.

The second packet contained letters from different people. Walter unfolded the top one. It was written in pencil on ruled tablet paper, the kind he had used in grade school. It began, *Dear Mr. Phelps, I want you to have my thanks for the advice you have gave me covering the last twenty-two years. I own my place free and clear now and I wouldn't have been able to cut it if it hadn't been for you.* Walter glanced at the signature. Some farmer. He didn't know him. He opened another letter on blue note-paper in blue ink. The hand looked feminine. There was no place or date. *Dear Todd, You know how deep Bert was in this. If it hadn't been for that two thousand dollars, we'd have just had to quit and left town, that's all.* It was signed *Irma.* He examined two or three others. They were all letters of gratitude. It was natural that he keep these also.

[124]

He began to read the letters in the third bundle. The first one was type-written. It began, *Dear Sir, I do not know what you conceive the purpose of the banking business to be but when I come to you offering the very best security* . . . The last sentence read, *I hope it will please you to learn that I have started bankruptcy proceedings because of your refusal.* The next letter had no heading or salutation. In a heavy soft-lead pencil scrawl it said, *You are a god-damn sonofabitching bastard and if I ever catch you in Hillsdale, I'm going to take a two-by-four and beat your head in.* Walter read all of these. It was cool in the vault and he could hear his own breathing. He glanced up once. The other men were waiting for him, Horse chewing on a hangnail and old Haight rubbing his hand over his hip and down his right thigh. Every letter in this set was a reproach or an insult. He was puzzled.

Horse was tapping some papers against his hand. "Done?" he said.

Tommy Haight said, "Well, what'd you find? Letters, huh?"

"I just want to show you these, Walter. Then we won't bother you any more, Tom," Horse said.

Walter recognized the stock certificates of the tool-and-die company that was the big factory of the town.

"See what they are?"

"Yes."

"Count 'em."

Walter counted the number of shares. He gave them back to Horse, who put them in the box again. "All right, Tommy. Walter can keep the letters, can't he? They're personal effects."

"Can if he wants to."

"I don't want them. Lock 'em up," Walter said.

Tommy snapped the box shut. He tossed the key up once and put it in his pocket. "I keep this," he said as if he expected an objection.

"All right, Tommy. Thanks for coming down," Horse said.

"Oh, it's my job," the old man said sarcastically. He limped out of the vault and they could hear his uneven step on the steel stairs.

"Todd never voted for him and he knows it," Horse said. "Well, what do you think now?"

"Are they worth anything?"

"Yes. They're the only ones that are."

"How much?"

"Now this just shows you how little you know a man. I knew Todd had this stock. I thought he did, anyway. I knew when he bought it but for some reason he never put it on any of the lists he gave me and I didn't actually know whether he sold it or not." Horse was leaning against the wall of boxes, his feet crossed, pulling his plump lower lip. He was being thoughtful. "Your dad was a damn smart poker player."

"How much are they worth?"

"I wouldn't sell 'em, Walter. I don't think you'll have to. And it wouldn't surprise me." Horse narrowed his eyes. Shrewdness. "No, sir, it wouldn't surprise me a damn bit if that stock would give you a little income. Not much now but later."

Walter suspected that Horse was also a stockholder in the tool-and-die company, probably a large one. He would not want a big block of stock to go into the open market just then, the way prices were, and very likely he lacked the cash to buy it himself. He did not have any impulse to say this. Other people were running things. Let them. "All right. I'll keep them. If there's enough left so I can."

Horse looked at a wrist watch. "Good boy. See you tomorrow night." Horse hurried out and ran up the stairs two at a time with surprising lightness. Walter followed him.

Above the door of the bank hanging out over the sidewalk was a big round clock. It was 11:25, Naval Observatory Time. It was an odd time of day to be free on the street. He was hungry but if he went home for lunch he would have to tell his grandmother and he did not want to talk about it until he got over this strange passive feeling. If he stood where he was, people passing would stop and say things to him. He had already missed a couple of acquaintances by pretending to set his grandfather's big silver watch.

The City Club had its rooms above the jewelry store a few doors up the street. He had often eaten there and they had put it on his father's bill. He could impose once more on his father's membership but the bill would come to him. It was always cool up there.

On the way up the stairs he heard the sharp woodeny click of a miscued billiard ball and after it a burst of laughter in two or three voices. He did not want to accept any more condolences from his father's friends. He turned straight into the dining rooms. He was early and he was able to get a table by himself in a little anteroom that joined the main restaurant. It was where the orchestra sat on the night of the yearly dance. He had the breeze from a broad-bladed ceiling fan all to himself and it seemed possible that he might not have to speak to anyone.

He had just picked up the menu when the steward, Harry Usher, came softly up to his table. Harry was the first colored man he had ever known. Everyone said he was smart but Walter had never seen his intelligence at work until this moment. He put a lump of ice in the water glass and filled it with water. As Walter looked up and said, "Hello, Harry," he said only, "Hot morning, Walter."

On the menu were the usual club steak and Lake Superior whitefish, and a cold plate with potato salad. The steak and the fish cost a dollar; the cold plate, fifty cents. Any time in his life before he would have ordered the steak, partly because he liked steak but also—he had learned it this morning—because it was an assertion of caste. "Too hot for steak, Harry. Bring me the cold plate and iced coffee." It was his first economy since he was five years old and his father had given him a five-dollar bill in a boy's size pigskin billfold to teach him the value of money.

Harry brought in the cold plate and the coffee, set them down, and went away again in courteous silence. Walter began to eat.

The billiard game in the other room had ended. The players were coming in to lunch, a wrangle of loud talk and laughter, and the scraping of chairs.

Then Walter picked up one speech. "Well, *I* heard he didn't leave a goddamn cent." It was Reese Curtis, the real-estate man.

"Oh, he must have done better than that," someone said.

"That's not what I heard. He died broke," Curtis persisted. "You ought to know, Horse. Did he or didn't he?"

"Did he or didn't he what?" Horse said.

"Gentlemen, this is what you call the ethics of the law. It's good advertising, Horse, but you don't have to act so dumb," Curtis said.

Walter heard a high, old man's voice, Ferry Culver's, the retired furniture man's. "If Todd did die broke, he was the first Phelps that ever did. They may spend it but they always let some stick to their fingers. I remember old Henry . . ."

The next voice was Paul Iverson's of the electric bell factory, interrupting, "How would Todd Phelps die broke? Christ, he inherited half a million, didn't he, Ferry?"

"That's what they said. That's what they always said. Your father'd have known, Horace. He handled it."

Exultant, glad to reveal, glad to claim credit for revealing, Curtis said, "This is what I heard. I heard it over a year ago and I heard it again this morning. He played the market. . . ."

A burst of voices denied it.

More loudly Curtis went on. "You heard me. He was up to his ears and he lost every cent he had. If it wasn't true, Horse would have said so. Go ahead, Horse, call me a liar."

"He was the guy that was always saying . . ."

A tenor mockery of his father's snarl, "Stay out of the market, you god-damn cabbagehead."

"Well, it was good advice," old Culver piped.

"I always liked the way he gave it, too," Iverson sneered. "The son-of-a-bitch, always cussing everybody to his face."

"I never liked him," Curtis said.

"If you boys didn't like Todd, you should have known his father," Culver said, using the rotten lever of his age. "Now Todd was just rough, *coarse,* you might say. But Henry was nasty. He had an eye like a pearl button and when he looked at you, you could feel the dirt under your fingernails. That was when they started calling that bank The Ice House." Old man Culver chuckled. "Rough as he was, I never heard none of you question a word he said when he used to set up here noons. . . ."

"I was afraid of him, frankly."

"So was I."

"I don't mind saying so. You weren't, Horse. You're so damned big, but when he'd start in on me I'd shut up. I was afraid if I crossed him he'd hit me, so I'd just sit there and grin and take it."

"He did hit Abel Wilcox."

"When?"

"Up here about ten years ago. Knocked him right through the candy case. Abel said something Todd didn't like and he hit him. Just once. Harry had a hell of a time sweeping up."

"No, Todd wasn't like his father. I heard John Bachman stand in Henry Phelps's bank right in front of all the tellers and depositors and everybody and call him every name in the book. Oh, God, it was terrible, the things he said to Henry. On and on and on. All the women skedaddled and John was standing there pounding his fist on that mahogany counter and when he got winded and run down, Henry just smiled and says, 'And now, Mr. Bachman, you still owe me six hundred dollars.' Never fazed him a bit. He didn't care what they called him as long's they paid."

"I don't think Todd cared what they paid him as long as he could cuss them. I wonder he got anybody to do business with him at all."

"Why, no you don't either wonder," Culver said. "You know why we did business with him."

"Why?"

"Because he was smart. Because what he said was true. We'd all be a damn sight better off if we'd followed it."

[128]

"So would he," Curtis said, and then in a tone of wonder, "Say, you don't suppose he . . ."

Horse Egan cut him off, "Careful, Reese."

"The hell with it, Horse. I'll say what I please."

". . . if he committed suicide, huh? Just picked out that pole and hit it." There was some agreement, murmured.

But Ferry Culver said, "I doubt that. He liked money but not that much. Not enough for him to make away with himself. Not like a good many round here."

It was necessary before he stood up, before he did anything (and anything was bloody, with the table upset and chair legs broken), it was very necessary, Walter thought, to discount what they said. He knew them all. None of them had to work very hard because it was a small town and the pace was slow. They could afford to take two or three hours for lunch, and after the steaks and the Lake Superior whitefish they could play long drowsy games of bridge and rummy and what were they to do above the knives and forks and the bright green felt, shut up? They were bound to talk and on a hot day with their stomachs full, praise was dull. Sitting there too proud to sleep, their paunches chafing their thighs, they could find the faults of any man because they had the time. They could scan them, pick at them, and hash them over, excreting their little daily jets of poison. Here, at two o'clock in the afternoon, Jesus was a man who sassed his mother.

His forehead still felt prickly, though, and the fan did not cool him off. He was thinking that they might have Harry remove the cloth and play their game of rummy right there when they finished lunch, and, if they did, how was he going to get out of the dining room? They would see him go . . . and if you are afraid they will see you, you must be afraid they are right about your father.

His old man since his death had turned into a stranger. By leaving the key to his bookcase he had turned himself, and by these men this morning he had been turned, changed, damaged until Walter could hardly trust his memories of him. They had not said he was crooked. They had not said he was lazy. Drink and women they had let alone but, then, they hadn't seen his library. They had admitted he had guts of a kind. And they had dug up Grandpa Henry. What was there to say? A man with a rough tongue, born of a hated father, honest enough, worked hard, who met with a big muscle everything that came in his way. Walter tried to make this sound well, a good epitaph, a soldier's maybe, but the trouble was, and he knew it as he said it to himself, it did not come near summing up his father.

As a banker, he had lost the first thing he was expected to keep, his own money. That made him, of course, a fool. And what kind of guts were they? If it were true—and Reese Curtis's implying it would make it true for him forever—that he had driven his car into the telephone pole to kill himself, he must have been afraid to face these very men, a fool, at noontime over the steaks and whitefish. There was not much left to admire but there was more to it than only to admire, he discovered sitting there in the alcove fiddling with a spoon. He was son to never-mind-what-kind-of-father. He could not deny him.

He picked up the check and went out through the restaurant without hesitation, nodding with a grin at the men playing rummy around the table.

⌐PART FOUR⌐

· XI ·

CLETUS HOLLAND was sitting in the living room of his house on the blue overstuffed couch. A bridge table with a particolored oilcloth cover stood in front of him littered with papers. It was one of the first warm days in April and he sat in his undershirt with the front door open, waiting for his wife to finish primping in the bathroom upstairs. While he waited, he had set up the bridge table to make a start at writing up his orders.

He was in what some people considered a curious business, the selling of egg-case fillers. Except when he was talking to the trade, he found that nearly everybody laughed at the filler business, supposing it to be an uncouth and rustic occupation without, however, knowing exactly what egg-case fillers were. They would hint that egg-cases were filled with eggs, hence an egg-case filler was only a politer name for an egg and some twerps would carry on the pretense that Cletus was a chicken farmer every time he saw them for weeks. He insulted them amiably in return, secure in the knowledge that no one would take him for a chicken farmer. He took a modest pride in dressing a little better than his friends even in times like these.

He always wore a blue serge suit, a white shirt with a semi-stiff collar attached, the best wrinkle-proof ties in blue or red, tan Florsheim oxfords which he cleaned and polished once a week with a special kit while rubbing them up every morning he was away from home with his discarded dirty socks. He always paid five dollars for his hats and crushed them conservatively. He owned two handkerchiefs special for his breast pocket, a wine-red and a smoke-blue, one to wear while the other was at the wash and he asked his wife to starch them just a little so they would stick out fresh and perky all the week long. Even on Saturdays when he had been out on the road all week and the car was dusty, to see him climb out and shut, not slam, the door and walk sedately up his front steps with his neat split-leather portfolio in one hand, he thought you would think he was an executive.

Cletus warmly solicited all questions about the nature and purpose of egg-case fillers and he answered them with a voluble bewildered awe as if he could not understand how the human mind had conceived such a wonderful device. The warmth and the awe were not quite genuine. They were symbols of gratitude for his salesman's job, not that he didn't believe he was doing a good job for the company. He had averaged forty-eight dollars a week commissions for the last twelve months. That meant business, he would say, and that's what the company had the factory for. He was not exactly grateful to the company when he thought of his wife's brother on the WPA and the dozens of fellows, high-school graduates, who were on relief, or some of their own friends whose savings had run out, the man lying around the house all day unshaven, reading yesterday's paper, listening to the radio, and beginning to eat popcorn and milk three nights a week, laughingly at first as if it were the kind of Sunday or holiday on which you ate popcorn, then grumbling, and at last refusing. It had nothing to do with the beneficence of God. No, this warm thankfulness was his luck, and sometimes driving alone down a hot road with the heat waves trembling up from the tar with a big elm tree sliding toward him, he would almost cry, and then he would begin to sing "Melancholy Baby."

Cletus could hear the water drained from the bathtub running down through the pipes in the walls and, bent over his order blanks, he whistled softly thinking of his wife naked and how pleasant her plump little haunches would look in her blue silk dress. Then for a moment he had to figure freight equalization with Evansville, Indiana, on a big order and he gave his whole attention to his multiplication. The product gotten, he relaxed his mind to the anticipation of his own bath, the fresh linen, and the sober look of competence his face would assume when he was dressed for the evening. He contemplated with pleasure, writing all the time, the jokes that he and Carl Swenson would make over the bottles of beer and the game of casino, and how he could sneak a glance at Eula Swenson's legs when the game broke up and they settled down merely to drink and talk. He was very happy, although he did not know it, his bungalow nearly paid for, $316 in the bank, with a pretty wife, and the picture sharpened his near-by pity for his friends in poverty.

He heard someone come up on the porch. The doorbell rang. Since he was in his own home, he was not embarrassed to be found in his undershirt and he called out, "Come on in."

When he saw it was Walter Phelps, he was startled. He stood up and automatically shook hands as he would have with a customer.

He and Walter had been in high school together and they had been graduated in the same class. An effort to overcome his surprise could have presumed on the area of their common memories, the class jokes, the football victories, and the antique jibes at the teachers. High school had been the time when he was Walter's equal, even his superior, since he had played guard on the basketball team while Walter, in spite of his size, had imperturbably avoided athletics and nobody had dared sneer because it was known he was a boxer like his father.

Confusing him and obstructing a proper tone for his welcome was the knowledge (although it was an axiom of his life he often just kept from speech that he was as good as any man) he was only little Cletus Holland, born in a street full of houses all alike, and Walter was a Phelps, one of the old families who carried with him, as in the white silk shirt he was wearing, a mysterious superiority.

Yet Walter, they said, was poor now and that father of his had committed suicide. Why should he stand in sudden sweat saying the polite false phrases he gave to customers just because Walter Phelps had come in his front door? All these questions, this fear and humility passed through his mind while he stood, half up and half down, with the bridge table catching him across the thighs. How did people learn to act? Undecided, he lifted the bridge table away from himself, mumbling, "Sit down. I'll get a bottle of beer."

Halfway out to the kitchen he made a decision. The rug, the diningroom suite, the green glass dish on the sideboard with the shriveled orange in it, all were his, all paid for. Why should he cringe? Sly, he went into the kitchen, opened the door of the icebox so that Walter could hear the click. On the bottom shelf lay half a dozen bottles of Stroh's beer. He smiled at his cleverness and shut the door loudly. He came into the living room and said with a sullenness he could not help, "I forgot. I haven't any beer."

"That's all right, Clete. We'll live just as long." Walter leaned back in the rocking chair and looked around the crowded little room. "Nice place you got here. The filler business must be looking up."

As if it had come up through the floor, Cletus saw for the first time leaning against the rocker of Walter's chair a split-leather portfolio, black, like his own. He glanced at the table to see if he had left his against the rocking chair, but his portfolio lay open and bulging there. They said Walter was selling insurance. He must be careful.

"They don't raise enough hens around here, Walt. If they'd just raise some more chickens, why, I could do real well. But you know how it is, these farmers. They keep a coupla hogs, run a few sheep. They won't put the time on hens. They're just a side line."

"Sure, but a good man can get out the business. And you're getting it out, Clete."

"Ah, go on, Walter," he said, warily pretending shyness, pleased even with a compliment he knew was bogus. He had paid that kind of compliment himself.

"Don't tell me. I heard Frank Thayer say you were writing more business than anyone they had out."

"Oh, I do what I can but it ain't much. Expenses eat me up—drive a hundred miles to sell a couple of cases. You sure get to see the country but that don't buy groceries. Say, Walter, I didn't get to see you last year after your mother and father got killed. I was sorry to hear it."

Walter said, "Yes. It was a shock."

"Yeah, it must have been, losing both at once that way. I lost my mother when I was little. I don't hardly remember anything about her, and Dad, of course, he's still going."

"Where is your father now?" Walter asked perfunctorily.

"He's weigh-master out at the mill at Addison." Cletus was embarrassed to bring this out because a job weighing cattle feed was only a jump ahead of farming itself, and he was determined he would never slip back onto the land his family had come from. He was willing to embarrass himself, however, to put off Walter's inevitable question, the moment when he would get down to business.

"Weigh-master? My God, is there enough work for a man just weighing out there?"

"Well, he does the weighing and, you know, sort of keeps an eye on things. It pays his board. Dad's seventy-seven."

"I'm glad to hear he's got work. A lot of people haven't."

"Aren't you right."

"Clete, I'm not going to beat around the bush with you and take up your time. Because I can see you're busy." Walter rocked forward in his chair and leaned on the arms. "I came up here tonight to discuss your insurance program with you."

Cletus drew back at the word "insurance" and looked up sharply at the word that followed it. "Program?" he said. "Good God, Walt, I haven't got any program. I haven't got any insurance at all."

"Well, then, how about some?" Walter said jovially. He reached down deftly and had the portfolio open on his lap in an instant. "Let me see," he said, thumbing over his rate book. "How old are you? You can't be over twenty-five."

"I was twenty-five last month." Cletus felt himself sinking into a helpless civility. He was acquiescent because he did not know how to stop Walter without shouting at him. For him insurance was one of the signs of the rank he hoped to reach someday if farmers kept more hens. If it had any real advantages, he did not think of them. When he could wear fifty-dollar suits and drive a Buick instead of a Ford, he would take out insurance. Now he could foresee that he would answer all the questions and the answers would inevitably lead him almost to the edge of acceptance.

"Twenty-five, eh?" Walter said warmly as if it were a splendid age, the peak of manhood. His finger stopped and went sidewise. Holding his place, he flopped some pages over, and looked again. "You're strong as an ox, Clete. You won't have any trouble with the doctor. You've never had a serious illness in your life, have you?"

Reluctantly, now lying slack against the pillows of the couch, he said, "Well, flu. And I had measles and chicken pox and once I had scarlatina. It's the name for a light case of scarlet fever."

"Kid's diseases," Walter said contemptuously. He looked up almost sternly from his notebook. "You know, Clete, you're married. You've got your home and you've got a good steady job. The only way you could lose it is for the hens to all die and there's not a chance of that. . . ."

Cletus reached to the table and feebly turned up the cover of a Department of Agriculture pamphlet on diseases of the hen. "A lot of things go wrong with hens. You wouldn't hardly believe it."

"Yes, but you know what I mean. In spite of this depression, you've made your way through to a certain solidity and you've done it all by yourself. Just through hard work. You've got a right to feel pretty darned proud of yourself, Clete."

Cletus turned his hand over and looked at the palm. "Uh-huh. I've done what I could."

"And any day now you're going to have a kid. Your wife, ah, Lorene, she wants one, doesn't she? I'll bet she does."

"Yes. We want a family." He realized that he had been following his wife's movements upstairs, the scrape of a drawer, the rasp and clack of the heels of her shoes, a closet door shutting. She would be coming down in a minute, ready to go, and she would find him in a plight he could not master. It was getting dark outside.

"And the community needs a family like yours, Clete. You want to give your kids every advantage, college and a good start, don't you? And you want Lorene to have a feeling of security. What the hell, Clete, we don't live forever. We're liable to get knocked off in the street any day. You drive a car—well, you see what I mean."

Here he had been all set, home in his own house, working a little and whistling while he did it, beer in the icebox, money in the bank, himself anticipating a good warm bath and a pleasant evening among friends. Now he felt himself trapped. The image of himself that he kept in such delicate poise before his wife, the masterful man, succeeding in much, about to be successful, was tipping, falling, smashing.

Cletus pushed himself forward and stood up. "I can't afford it, Walter," he said.

"You can't afford not to, Clete," Walter said.

"I haven't got the money."

"You haven't got a measly seventy cents a week?"

"No, I haven't got a measly seventy cents a week. I don't want any insurance."

Walter stood up also and looking slyly sidewise, smiling, he said, "You god-damn flathead, I never said you did, did I? I'm just trying to sell it to you, that's all."

They stood looking at each other. The electric icebox in the kitchen began to hum. Kids were playing hopscotch across the street and shouting. A compact was shut upstairs, making a light metallic snap.

At last Cletus said quietly, "It was that kind of talk lost you your job at the bank, wasn't it?"

"That's right, Cletus. I couldn't stand the idiots. They used to come and line up in front of me every day. Good night, Cletus," Walter said. "Say 'hello' to Lorene." He picked up his hat and the black portfolio and started for the door. He stopped and turned around. "I guess I ought to tell you, Clete. I didn't mean you were an idiot. You're a nice guy." He walked out the door and down the street.

Now in the early evening it was a children's street, the offspring of the men who worked in the factories farther up the Hill and owned these neat little houses shaded by soft maples smaller than the ones downtown because they had been planted later. Walter moved in a riot of games and dances, scorned as an intruder, invited to run or hide or jump, and jump-

[136]

ing just in time to miss straddling a small boy on a scooter. He retrieved a baseball, and waited upon command to hold a small girl's doll while she did up its didies. The early stars were out. A few forsythia bushes in bloom made patches of light against the houses. He passed a Lutheran church, and a grocery store jammed with housewives. It was downhill and easy going. He seemed to be lighthearted.

As he walked down the Hill, the houses he passed were larger, most of them owned by clerks and foremen. The cars parked in front of them were still chiefly Fords and Chevvies but there was an occasional Buick or De Soto. A block or two before Broad Street he reached the demesnes of the people who ran the town or thought they did, wooden houses with big screened porches, brick houses with small entries hooded with heavy wooden scroll-work. The maple trees were thicker in bole. There was shrubbery in the front yards and beds of flowers in back beside the garages. There were hardly any children.

He approached one house he knew. It was small and neat, white clapboard, with green shutters and a white picket fence around the yard. The lights were on and he could see Bill Reynolds and his wife sitting in the living room. They were people a little older than his father and he had known them all his life. Mrs. Reynolds had once had a colored cook he called "Twenty-three Skidoo" because she had always driven him out of the Reynolds kitchen when he stopped in for cookies. Although it was quite a warm night, they still had the furnace going probably, because Bill was sitting in his shirt sleeves reading the paper and Mrs. Reynolds had her back to him and he couldn't see what she was doing.

He had seen them sitting that way dozens of times when he had passed the house in the evening. He stood by the gate, fingering the latch, trying to think of some excuse to go in. They would be surprised if he knocked at the door and they found him standing there. It had been years since he had walked into their house merely to call on them. When they saw the portfolio in his hand, Bill would think he had come to sell him more insurance and this least betrayal would make them both awkward. He really did not want to talk to Bill or Mrs. Reynolds either. Not very much, anyway. It was just that they looked nice and comfortable sitting there and maybe he would be nice and comfortable if he could join them. He could ask to use their phone but who was there to call up? Eddie was in the hospital, and he did not want to call any girls because they had not finished revising their estimates of him.

There was one girl, Dorothy Wickham, whose family had settled in town at the beginning of the year. He had sat in the same booth with her

[137]

once at Bonfiglio's. She had been with somebody else but she had seemed cordial. She had never known him except as Walter Phelps with the portfolio, a guy who didn't have a car.

He lifted the latch of the gate and went in. He raised the brass knocker on the door and let it fall. Inside they would both be looking up and Mrs. Reynolds would be saying, "Was that somebody at the door?" They were the age when nobody came to see them much. He banged the knocker again. The door opened and Bill Reynolds stood there with the newspaper in one hand.

"Hello, Bill," Walter said.

"Why, hello, Walter. Come on in."

Walter stepped over the sill, saying quickly to allay their suspicions about the portfolio, "Hello, Mrs. Reynolds. I wonder if I could use your phone a second."

"Why, sure, Walter. You know where it is," she said.

As Walter went into a dark hallway, Reynolds called after him, "What are you trying to do, locate a prospect?"

"That's right," Walter said. He had to ask Information for the Wickham number because it was not yet in the phone book. Waiting, he could hear Reynolds talking about him faintly. "Hello, is Dorothy—oh, hello, Dorothy, this is Walter Phelps."

She remembered him. She asked how he was.

"Are you engaged this evening?" he said with deliberate nicety of phrase in order to make a good first impression.

She was. She was ready to leave the house. She was sorry.

Walter decided to quit selling insurance. The decision had been growing at the back of his mind ever since he left Cletus Holland's. The children in the street had helped it. In the time it took him to draw breath to answer her regret, he made the decision. Freedom went with it. He asked, "May I see you tomorrow morning?"

"Tomorrow *morning*."

"Yes. About ten-thirty, say?"

"Why, yes. I think so."

"I'll see you then." He hung up and went back into the living room.

"Right on the job, huh?" Reynolds said. "If you can't get 'em tonight, get 'em tomorrow morning."

"Why, Bill Reynolds," his wife said.

Facetiously Reynolds said, "Man comes in and uses my phone, I've got a right to hear what he says, haven't I, Walter? Just trying to nail a prospect anyway, weren't you?"

"I know, but the idea . . . ," Mrs. Reynolds complained. She had their old snuffling Boston bulldog on her lap. She was patting and talking to him. She had raised a son and two daughters.

"It wasn't a prospect. It was a girl," Walter said.

"Girl's a prospect, ain't she?" He burst into loud "ho-ho's."

"Isn't he the limit?" Mrs. Reynolds said.

"I was just trying to line up a date for tonight," Walter said.

"I know. Wine, women, and song," Reynolds said.

"Say, get Walter a bottle of beer. Oh, it's all gone, isn't it? He drank it all up yesterday, no, Thursday. We ought to get some more, Bill. Shouldn't we, honey? Shouldn't we, shouldn't we, shouldn't we?" she finished to the bulldog.

"I'll pick up some tomorrow. Sit down, Walter. How's the insurance business? Writing much?" Reynolds said.

It was a pretty living room. There was a wood fire laid in the fireplace and it struck highlights on the furniture. The armchairs and the couch were covered with bright chintz and on the table was a bowl of fresh flowers. Bill Reynolds sent them to his wife every day and when he had been poor, just starting out, they said he had picked dogtooth violets and mayflowers along the railroad tracks to bring to her. The dark red Oriental rug showed wear and the hearth was covered with a gray film of ashes. It was a comfortable place but, as he had expected, Walter could not share the comfort or take part in the legend that went with the flowers.

"Not much," Walter said.

"I know. It's terrible. Nobody has any money nowadays. Why, you've got a flea. Bill, Tiny's got fleas," she said, parting the hair on the dog's flank with her fingers.

"I'll dust him off tomorrow."

"Who was the girl, Walter?" Mrs. Reynolds said, looking up from her task.

"Dorothy Wickham. She's new around here."

"Wickham? I don't think I know them," she said. Walter could perceive the change in her tone. It was not dismissal. It was the echo of the old families' footsteps as they closed their ranks a little tighter until they had scrutinized the newcomer.

"Sure. He's up at the bell factory. Say, *there's* a fellow you might hit, Walter."

"Is she pretty?" Mrs. Reynolds asked coyly.

"She's tall. She has reddish hair," Walter said.

Reynolds clucked loudly, the way you start a horse. "Gimme a red-head every time."

"Pooh. You wouldn't know what to do with one. Hold *still*, Tiny. This is the first time he's had fleas in four years, isn't it, Bill?"

It was the kind of empty question that could be ignored. Reynolds leaned forward, pointing the stem of his pipe at Walter. "You know, Walter, this is just the time to make hay in your business. You take a lot of families—they never thought of insurance as necessary. Never could see it as something you could borrow on. Along comes this depression and they're stuck. Don't know where to turn. Now you come along and if you can put up any sort of spiel at all, you can sell 'em. What's that ad they used to run? It showed the palm of a hand with three pennies in it? That's what I mean. They may be poorer than Job's turkey but they can still pony up three cents a day, and before you know it they can make a loan, and they got protection, too. See what I mean?"

Walter could see now that one of the reasons he had decided to quit the insurance business while he was talking on the phone was to tell Bill Reynolds about it. He wanted to shock him. "I'm through selling insurance, Bill," Walter said.

The shock appeared. Mrs. Reynolds, automatically recognizing her husband's expression, withdrew from the conversation and quietly searched the bulldog's skin for fleas.

"What for?" Reynolds said coldly.

Walter had intended to say only that he had got sick of it but he resented the presumption and he decided to argue, to be stubborn, to make Bill sore. He himself could go on the WPA like many others. "I don't like the idea of insurance."

"Why not?"

"I don't like peddling lottery tickets."

"What do you mean?"

"I don't like betting on my own death. The company bets you the face of the policy you won't die until you've paid up. You bet the company you will die. Horse racing is more fun. You live to see the finish." Walter grinned.

Reynolds, too, had hated Todd Phelps. He knew what a small town is, and how, if you live in one, you must pretend to be friendly with people you dislike because there are few chances for new friendships. You all cling together like passengers on a ship, or, rather, like a crew who must work together and take their amusements together and cannot get off the ship. Reynolds was decent enough and he had made efforts to discover something he could like in Todd Phelps so that the abrasions of their inevitable meetings would be softened; then, after ten years, not to like but something merely to tolerate. He had not found it. He had never said he was glad Todd Phelps had been killed because he was superstitious about such candor. And now that he was being opposed foolishly and, he was shrewd enough to perceive, a little maliciously by a Phelps, he let out the anger he had saved for the father on the son. "You're a damned fool, Walter. . . ."

"Nice language," Mrs. Reynolds muttered.

Out of no deference to his wife, merely for what she had said, he finished weakly, "Just as you're getting your clientele worked up, you quit."

"That's right. I quit."

With sullen mildness, Reynolds looked at the floor and said, "You know what you're doing. I don't." He rummaged in his pockets for his tobacco pouch.

"Now you're really sore. You think, 'He sassed people at the bank until they fired him. He went into selling insurance and was just getting started. Now he runs it down and quits.' You don't think I'm safe. You've had me in your house and I'm really turning out to be a stranger."

Reynolds had filled his pipe. He brushed the loose grains of tobacco off his thighs with both hands. The people he knew did not use this kind of frankness. It caught him unprepared. It seemed a little unfair. He said almost shamefaced, "I didn't say anything like that at all."

"I didn't say you did. You're just thinking it. I've turned into somebody else. Maybe I'd better go," Walter said all in one tone of voice.

"What? What did you say?" Reynolds asked, jerking his head up.

"I've got to be going," Walter said.

As a reflex they both began to protest his departure without admitting they would be glad to see him go. "What you want to go now for? You've hardly been here ten minutes."

Walter left, however. It was dark by this time. The calm of supper-time was over. The street was filled with cars, and people to make up the Saturday night crowd were heading downtown. As he walked along he wondered why he had not called Dorothy Wickham before. He remembered the vague chill in Mrs. Reynolds' voice as she spoke of the Wickhams. He discovered that he also had been waiting, with the assured leisure of a scion of an old family, for the Wickhams to prove themselves socially, to get themselves accepted although, if he had been asked, he would have said that pretty girls had no social distinctions. It amused him. He recalled her profile against the shining wood of Bonfiglio's booth, and it seemed even funnier that he had soaked in such primness without knowing it, especially since he was on the way to becoming an outcast. Insults make outcasts and he had certainly insulted Bill Reynolds.

As he walked through the streets toward the hotel, he did not appear to be looking for anything. It did not occur to him to permit himself to seem to look. Yet he stared as long as he could without turning his head at the young girls he passed who responded giggling to the spring warmth in the air; at the young men in their footless wandering, some seedy, some seedy and fierce, some sullen, others slack and discouraged; at the red necks of the farmers walking with deliberate muscular awe of the hard pavements. He had never been lonely, at least not long enough to make him begin the search for something to do, and if he hoped that someone would stop him and ask him to go someplace, anywhere, and do something, anything, the hope lay secret in his readiness to answer. Adventures were accessible. To deflect himself from the path of his inevitable bedroom, fourth floor front, he would have only to wink at one of the girls or take the arm of a passing youth and say, "Hey, bud, want a beer?" and the adventure would unravel from that notch. He paused on the front step of the hotel as if to give the crowd of people one more chance. They passed. No one spoke to him. He went in.

The lobby was nearly empty and it had the useless look of a furniture display in a store window. An old man and an old woman, everlasting guests, sat facing each other with open eyes and hands spread on the chair arms, without speech. The ceiling lights were dark but over the cigar counter a shaded bulb gave down on the silver head of the night clerk. Walter was about to pass him, saying "Good night, Bert," when he looked up.

"Got something for you," the clerk said.

Walter stopped and laid his portfolio on the showcase. "What?" he said.

The clerk reached down with decrepit energy and tossed up on the counter a block of plain unfinished wood, put together in segments.

"What is it?"

"Can you work it?" the clerk asked, leaning on his elbows and stroking his forearms with satisfaction. He wore a large ruby ring in a claw setting, pink satin sleeveholders, and his upper plate clicked when he talked.

"No. I can't work tricks," Walter said.

"Go on. Give it a try. It's clever, by Jesus."

"You work it."

"Go on. You're a sharp one. Try it."

"What happens when I work it?"

"Try and take it apart."

"Show me."

The clerk craftily laid his round dirty hands over the block of wood so that his thumbs did not show, and by pushing them, panting falsely, and contorting his face, he made a click and a rattle and shoved a dime and a quarter out of the block of wood.

"You wouldn't have thought that money was in there, would you?"

"I sure as hell wouldn't," he said, jovial and sarcastic. "You must be hard up for something to do, Bert."

The clerk looked up at him and growled, "A-a-h."

Walter started for the elevator. Bert called to him and he turned around. "Sell you this for a quarter. Sell it to you and show you how to work it."

"What do I want with it?"

"Help you sell insurance. Amuse the customers."

"Help who sell insurance?"

"You."

"I don't sell insurance."

"A-a-h, go on upstairs," the clerk said.

Walter stepped into the cage of the elevator and pressed the Number 4 button. He rose with grave unsteadiness, the doors parted, and he walked out into the dim corridor. There was one red light over the door to the fire escape. He took from his hip pocket a key with a plastic tag and opened the door to his room.

It was a corner room with four windows, one open with the heavy net curtain furling and unfurling slowly, letting in the noise of traffic from the street below. He snapped on the light. Bed: hotel, three-quarter, with a brown institutional blanket just failing of a neat fold at the foot; desk with a row of books on top; spindly desk chair; and a light table, once in someone's home perhaps, bought at auction, with a marble top to hold without stain the drummers' drinks, and curving legs of insane grace; a brown shabby armchair crouching in its stink. He had not been able to do much to the room even in ten months. He had planked a little bookcase against the wall and a small radio-phonograph sat on a low table—he liked opera.

He opened the door of the closet and tossed the portfolio on the floor. He sat down in the armchair and switched on the radio to let it warm up. While he waited he took off his shoes and set them carefully beside the chair. He took off his necktie and opened the top of his shirt. From an

[143]

upper pocket of his vest he took a five-cent cigar, the same brand as his father's, peeled off the cellophane, bit off the end and spat it into the cellophane, wadded up the whole and tried to toss it out the window as the curtains parted in the light night airs. He missed. Out of the lower right-hand pocket of his vest, he took the big silver watch with the medals on its chain, wound it, and laid it on top of the radio. He put on a record of the Quartet from *Rigoletto,* lit the cigar, and settled back.

He listened but not attentively. He let the music fly past him and it awakened images and memories as water brings out the color of dry stones. He did not ponder over the girl or specially regret his visit to Cletus Holland's or to the Reynoldses'—that one had already shaped itself in his mind as a rejection. They had rejected him but it did not worry him. He heard the rich voices and he was restless. Pieces and fragments of other, fuller Saturday nights floated vaguely through his mind, nights when he had at least done something. He remembered suddenly what he had expected of all those evenings and how this bright expectancy had kept him at the telephone or sent him places in his car until he had found companions. Now the ash on his cigar was an inch long and he was sitting alone, in his sock feet, in the bedroom of a dingy small-town hotel, unready, unprepared. It was then he understood that he had already had his evening's miracle, peculiarly suitable to himself as he was, failing, deficient, the trick with the block of wood.

· XII ·

THE NEXT DAY was Sunday and it rained. He lay up all day and read the papers. He went downstairs to the hotel restaurant for his meals and in the afternoon he wrote a letter to Eddie Burcham, who was sick, but most of the day he lay on the bed reading the Sunday papers and smoking cigars. He was depressed. To be idle, then, when so many were out of work, frightened him a little because he could no longer retreat into the special immunity his family had once supplied. To defy his fear would smother it but to make his defiance real he would have to say it out to someone. While it stayed private inside him, it was no more than a sharp wish. As soon as he told someone it would become a contract whose terms he would have to fulfill, so he waited for Monday, when he would see the girl, staring at his beard in the mirror, reading the classified ads, and shining his shoes. Although he did not know what kind of girl she was at all, stupid or intelligent, and he was attracted to her only by her eyes, her hair, and the way she curved up and down, he knew he was going to do something in front of her that would cheer him up. He tried to go to sleep early to make the night pass but he lay awake counting all the fair-weather friends in the town who like the Reynoldses had rejected him. There had been many such rejections in the ten months since his father's death. The rain struck the windows of his room in gusts. He lay in the darkness with his eyes open and he seemed to see passing before them the cool strange smiles of all the people he had grown up with and taken for granted. It was late before he was tired enough to shut his eyes and resume his lost friendships.

On Monday the sun shone. He left the hotel at a quarter past ten. The rain had washed everything down. The streets looked clean. Where the downtown buildings ended and the homes began, he could see the trees were now full green; the foliage had grown overnight. Spring was the only morning season in his mind. Summer, fall, and winter were for the afternoon. When he spoke to people on the street, he wondered what they would say if they knew he had quit a job just because he felt like it. He glanced at himself in store windows approvingly.

When he approached her house, he saw the windows were blank. The curtains had been taken down and old Adolph Kiser, the handy man, was standing on a ladder washing the outside panes. Her mother was doing the spring house-cleaning. For a moment he feared she might not be able to come with him because she would be helping her mother but the fear subsided at once. New people who lived in a house on State Street could not afford to admit that their daughter had to help with the house-cleaning.

He rang the doorbell. She came to the door. She was as pretty as he remembered her. She wore a light green dress. She asked him to come in.

"Let's sit out here," he said.

The house did not have a front porch. The porch was at the side, glassed in, with palms and ferns at the windows. Before the door were three brick steps that rose to a little platform.

"You mean, on the steps?" she said.

"Sure. Why not? It's a beautiful day."

She opened the screen door and came out. He sat down and she sat beside him with her feet close together on the steps below. He lighted her a cigarette.

There was a silence. She did not know what to expect from a stranger who called in the morning and asked her to sit on the front steps where nobody ever sat, and he always found it hard to begin talking to a new girl. He did not want to look foolish. His pride would not let him flatter.

[145]

He knew this as if it were a secret and he could watch the ineptness left him by his own decision and the girl's polite efforts with silent hilarity.

"What are we going to do?" she asked finally.

He said, "We're going for a walk."

She stood up and started down the front walk to the main sidewalk. He followed, not knowing which way he would turn, right or left. She turned right, and a step or two behind her, he followed. He had recently come to believe he could make things interesting for a girl who had given him her time but he thought he might have trusted his ingenuity too far. There was really nothing for a man and a girl to do, afoot, at ten-thirty on a Monday morning in a town like this. He could take her downtown and buy her a chocolate soda and she would think he was an idiot. She was not headed toward town anyway. Five blocks away was the open country. He walked beside her, speechless, trying to think of something.

"Why did you want to see me?" she asked.

Did she mean, why, if you can offer no better entertainment than a good long walk, or was she coquettishly offering him the opening for a flattering answer? He believed it was the first—girls expected entertainment and they expected to be carried to it in a car, usually at night—but he tried the second answer as well as he could allow himself. He wished he could have said coolly, "Because you're so beautiful." It was true enough but he couldn't say anything so bald. Instead, hoping she would pick out the right inferences and think it suave, he said, "I thought it was about time. I waited too long. I should have called you before. You remember that time in Bonfiglio's. . . ." He trailed off, trying to chatter to see if he could toss out some interesting statement.

"I thought maybe you wanted to sell me some life insurance."

This was luck. Immediately he began to create the figure he wanted her to recognize as Walter Phelps. "Oh, I don't sell insurance any more."

"No?" she said simply. At this time it was not tactful to ask why anyone left a job.

"No. I quit."

"What are you doing now?"

"Being poor, I guess." He was not asking for sympathy. He wanted her to see a man with other riches.

She looked at him to see if he was joking, because nobody wanted to be poor then when it was a sign of luck or peculiar agility to be well off. His face was calm and he was looking straight ahead of him and she did not know what to think. Maybe he was joking. Maybe he had money after all. He was a stranger.

[146]

For some reason he noticed her hand as she swung it forward with her step. It was slender, muscular, and, though he never looked at women's hands especially, well shaped. He kept glancing down at it as he walked.

She had been talking and he had barely listened. Something about the WPA, many nice fellows on it in the town where she had lived before. She was softening it for him, titivating it, making it a fine place as if for a visit. It was courteous of her.

"When it comes time, I'll get my shovel. Not yet, though. How do you like this town?"

"I like it very much."

"I don't own anything here."

"What do you mean?"

"You may speak freely. I'm your friend."

"I like it very much."

"What do you like about it?"

She told him she liked the people; she liked the maple trees; there were some lovely old homes; she liked the Country Club. It was a very nice town. She was polite but she obviously did not trust him yet.

"Name me some people you like. Name three."

She named three. They were not young men.

"Now name some of the trees you like."

"You sound so sour and it's such a nice day."

That showed she was a stranger. No girl born in the town would have said "such" a nice day. It would have seemed an affectation. Suddenly he knew where he was taking her.

It was a place he had been told to stay away from as a boy and he had visited it at all seasons. Some low flats lay beside the river, rising in some spots to farmland, sinking in others to spongy marsh grass, full of cat-tails. He and Eddie had gone there in the early spring for pussy willows; in the late spring, at this time, for flowers which they had to throw away before reaching home so their parents would not know where they had been. In the summer they swam, a little fearfully, in the river. It was dangerous, with holes forty feet deep, and it had "claimed" the lives of half a dozen boys. In the fall they gathered walnuts from a few old trees and built huts out of withes and dead grass as headquarters for the wars they were fighting. When the farmers tried to burn off the dead marsh grass, they had pretended it was a forest fire and had slapped away at it with their coats whole afternoons. Once in the middle of the winter they had gone down beside the river, shivering, moody, discouraged by the cold weather. As they stood on the bank of the half-frozen water, they remem-

[147]

bered the Civil War battle of Stone River. They knew nothing about its tactics or what time of year it had been fought but they had at least a river and in two minutes Eddie had slid and clambered out (at the head of his troops) to a spit of ice thrust out into the river, waving his sword. The ice broke and led Eddie down to his armpits into the cold water. He had laid down flat on the unbroken ice, reached Eddie a stick, hauled him in and hurried him home, whacking him to keep him running. Eddie's mother had stood at the head of the stairs wailing, "Edward!" at the sight of him with his clothes frozen stiff. He had not been down to the river flats for over ten years.

Now that he knew where he was going he quickened his step. "Do you like flowers?" he asked.

"All but gardenias."

"We're going to pick some."

They had to go down a concrete highway at the edge of town, cross a bridge, and leave the highway by a steep path that took them down to the edge of the river. Crossing the bridge, he said, "How about your shoes?" They both looked down. They were white pumps with brown trim.

"What about them?" she asked.

"They may get dirty."

"I can clean them."

He went first, slipping and bracing himself, holding her by the hand. He did not realize he had been holding it until they reached the end of the path and were standing at the edge of the river where it flowed under the bridge. Her hand had acquired some quality of aloofness because of its beauty and he was startled that he had violated it so casually.

The river was not much. Clear once, it had been polluted to a dirty brown. It was sluggish. Floating sticks and refuse soon gathered little beards of green slime. The bridge was made of stone with two graceful arches and he wanted her to look at it.

"My great-grandfather worked on this bridge," he said.

"It's nice," she said politely, perfunctorily.

He felt a little pang of distaste for the mere politeness of her answer. He wanted her to like the place he was taking her to. They walked down a path by the edge of the water. Weeping willows with new leaves of fresh and shining green threw their branches over the stream in long exquisite curves. He noticed this and the nervous mobility of the branches in the light warm wind, the changing patterns of color as the leaves quivered in and out of the sun or each other's shade, and the modulations of the green when the leaves threw up their grayish undersides. He would have liked to have said candidly, "Aren't they beautiful?" but he did not wish to seem to be the proprietor of the beauties or to display the sensitivity of a nature-lover which might make him appear soft in her eyes. Severe and quiet, he led her along the path beneath the willows. He was looking for the mouth of a little creek that joined the river somewhere near.

The creek was clear. It ran along the edge of a cow pasture. Willows leaned over it, only these had been polled. It made them look ancient like the trees of a fairy tale. They turned and walked along the creekbank in deep grass. Suddenly a cow mooed loudly. It had been standing in a clump of high rushes and they had not seen it. He glanced at her to see if she were frightened. She did not seem to be. He walked ahead, gave the cow a tremendous boot in the rump and it went away bellowing at a heavy splashing gallop.

"There should be forget-me-nots along here," he said, looking down. They had been walking over them, half hidden in the grass, myriads of little blue flowers bright as enamel against the green. She knelt down and began to pick them. He walked farther on and found buttercups, mint, and a few old purple violets, late blooms, with long stems above the mud where they grew. He reached out once and pulled a vine of water-cress out of the creek. He went back to her.

"When you get enough, there's a nice place to sit up here a ways," he said.

They both began to pick and he watched her covertly. The sun had come up hot. The light breezes stirred her hair. Her bare arms were as lovely as her hands, and as he watched her arm move out, bright in the sun, the underside in a green shadow, bend, and take the flower to her lap, over and over, he became fascinated. He stopped picking. He wanted to reach out and stroke her arm but the longer he sat there staring, talking occasionally, the more he became conscious that the scene was a cliché, conventionally romantic like something in a movie. He stood up, stretched, and yawned loudly, something the hero never did, yet doing it, exorcising what might have been a spell, he felt cheap. In a few minutes she had enough flowers.

"Come up this way," he said.

Six feet away from the slanting creekbank at the height of the pasture were two hummocks with a dip between them. Once the pasture had been plowed. These hummocks had been the ends of furrows and were now sodded over with grass. It was a rude chair with two arms.

"A throne for you," he said, giving his voice a sarcastic tone.

She smiled. "It is, isn't it?" She sat down and began to sort and arrange her bouquet.

He sat beside her and leaned on one elbow, chewing a mint leaf. He found a blue pebble and tossed it into the creek where it splashed with a little chug sound. An oriole flitting about in the tree across the bank caught his eye. He touched her arm and pointed until she saw it also. It was very still. He could hear the creek flowing over its stones. A gentle breeze was passing through the lithe willow branches above their heads and he could hear it and the slight interior sound of his teeth against each other as he chewed the mint. Spangled with shadows from the moving leaves, she was breaking stems for an even length, pinching off brown leaves, and throwing the faded pinkish forget-me-nots away. He thought her hands were wonderful, the full curve of her forearm, and the horn of her elbow. He wanted to tell her but he did not.

The cow had been silly. He wished instead for a man to come. He did not know any longer who owned the land they were sitting on but it might be a farmer, big and dirty, who hated trespassers. He might come down the creekbank and start to cuss them out. Then he himself would rise slowly, almost uncoiling so threatening would this slowness be, civilly request him to stop, and when he went on, pop him. A left hook to the belly. Farmers never knew how to fight. Hardly had his little vision faded from his mind when the ruthless acknowledgment of its childishness followed it, but now instead of enduring his self-reproach and accepting it as the normal echo of his actions, he wanted to stifle it and let himself be pushed into something, some bravery, some romantic foolishness by a force he had already vitiated because he had recognized it.

He looked up and down the creekbank. It was almost an unendurable irritation to see nothing fine to do, nothing big. Some special radiance of power and excellence shimmered about him. He got to his feet awkwardly, in a hurry. She looked up.

Standing in front of her, he bent down, nervously expecting her to dodge, and kissed her. When he began to kiss her neck, she threw one arm almost casually over her shoulder. He fell to his knees, still thinking, "God, you must look funny," and wrapped his arms around her waist. He went on kissing her throat with his eyes shut, trying to feel himself lost and good, and at last, in the perfume she wore, the softness of her skin and the warmth, losing himself. At last she pushed him away.

He stood up again, shaking his head, coming out of darkness, staring at her.

"It's a beautiful day, isn't it?" she said.

"Does it make any difference to you who I am?" he said fiercely.

"Not now."

"I haven't got any money. I haven't got any friends. I haven't got any job."

"Does it make any difference today?"

Talking had killed everything. He could feel himself blushing and he knew he was ashamed.

"Let's go," he said brusquely.

She gathered up the flowers, shook them, and clasped them into a bunch. She stood up, settled her dress inside its belt, and passed in front of him to go down the creekbank.

When they reached the edge of the river, she stopped and looked back at him. "Thank you, Walter," she said.

He could hardly look at her. He knew what she was fishing for—she wanted him to tell her he loved her. There was a reddish mark like a bruise on the side of her neck where he had kissed her. She went ahead of him and began to climb the steep path up to the edge of the road. He looked behind him once, back at the little aisle of willows over the creek. It had been a long time since he had been there. The place was unfamiliar. It was ridiculous to have brought her down there.

To kiss her had been a mistake. It had not been the way to express the exaltation he had been feeling, or, at least, he did not kiss women when he was moved by exaltation. It was not the way one treated women, going down on one's knees, eyes shut, squeezing them and nuzzling in the necks. Everybody would laugh like hell if they knew. He had simply forgotten himself but it made him obscurely sad, even while he was angry at the sadness, that it should be wrong to forget one's self.

She was ahead of him, climbing, pulling herself up by grasping bunches of grass. Below her, he could see up under her skirt. She had nice legs. He reached up adroitly above the top of her stocking and pinched her on the thigh. She stopped and looked down at him, surprised and angry, and he gave a loud snorting laugh.

· XIII ·

THE DIAGNOSIS, coming as it had, abruptly, surprised him. He was chagrined that he had not recognized the symptoms himself since he had been taught them at school. There had been, there still was the cough that had "hung on" until he had got used to it and did not think of it. He felt a certain complacency when his mother called it a spring cold as if the label were almost a cure. He had lost weight. He could tell because his trousers kept slipping down. On warm spring days he wore only a coat over his shirt and, thinking his winter suspenders would look funny, he used a belt to hold up his trousers. As he grew thinner, the belt came to rest on his hip bones, drooping in a curve below his navel. His shirt pooched open in the front and he was always hitching up his trousers with one hand but this, too, became habitual and he ignored it. It puzzled him to wake in the morning with his pajamas wet with sweat and a big damp spot on the pillowcase where his face had rested but he was soothed when one of the other reporters wrote an editorial called "Spring Tonic" about the old-fashioned uses of sulphur and molasses to clear out the winter's accumulation of impurities in the blood. It was a humorous little piece but the mention of the winter's impurities seemed to make some vague connection in his mind with the night sweats and if anyone had asked him about them, Eddie would have said facetiously, in the manner of the editorial, that he needed some sulphur and molasses. Without giving his full attention to any one of his symptoms, never regarding them as symptoms at all because they gave him no pain, he gave himself serially these dim comforting assurances and when Doc Stephenson said, "Eddie, you've got tuberculosis," he felt cheap, hoodwinked, as he did when someone did card tricks and palmed the cards right in front of him with his sleeves rolled up.

The next morning after the shock of the diagnosis, his mother's tears and hand-wringing and his chagrin, he lay comfortably in bed, speculating about this betrayal by his body. How was it that such decay could slip up on you without your knowing it? Yesterday he had been a reporter on a daily paper. Today he was what they called a "lunger," full of bugs.

He made an effort to pull himself together, to be honest and realistic: he had a mortal disease. He might die from it—his mother was half dead already; she had been on the phone making local and long-distance calls all the morning to his uncles and cousins. He would do what the doctors told him but it might kill him anyway in spite of all his earnest compliance. However, it would be interesting to watch the progress of the case, he thought.

A part of his education had been devoted to teaching him that he, Edward Burcham, did not initiate action; he responded, like a bear in a cage, when he was poked with a stick. He had also learned that what colored and conditioned his responses were his memories of events that had pleased or frightened him long ago, as a child, and the growth and persistence of these clusters of memory gave to his thinking its form, its emphases, and its tension. He was, he thought, mainly supine, and after someone had poked him, his reactions were governed by remote control.

All this had seemed eminently plausible. He had taken notes as fast as he could with his fountain pen in a large black leather notebook in all his psychology classes. Pride made him consider himself an intellectual because he came from a town where it was not yet the accepted thing for young men to go to college. The mind was the seat of his being, and, as the mind became the scene, not the originator, of his intellectual life, he did not really expect his mind to serve him. Thus there did not seem to be anything he could do, any decision he could make that would help him fight the disease beyond obeying the doctor, so he lay comfortably in his bed, even a little pleased at the change in his routine, willing to be extremely attentive to all the details of his "cure," fast in the knowledge that its efficacy was in other hands. He would watch. (Yet who was this "he" who would watch? He was not quite well enough educated or sincerely enough of an intellectual to ask. He was merely doing the best he could with the learning he had been taught.) It would be almost like a journey, a vacation trip somewhere. He would look at everything closely so he could remember it. It seemed to promise to be a valuable experience. He had no fear.

For instance, he would have a ride in an ambulance. Doc Stephenson had said that the local hospital was not so well equipped for the treatment of tuberculosis as the university hospital in Ann Arbor, forty miles away. He had never ridden in an ambulance. He could remember the albino Arabian horses with the bright pink eyes that had pulled the Kingsley ambulance through the streets when he was a little boy, a splendid medallion of staring eyes, flying manes and tails. He had chased them once out South Main Street, terror in the clanging of their bell. He had arrived in time, a wonderful moment, to see a tramp, who had been hit by a train, lying peacefully on the cinders. No one had covered him yet. There was no spatter of blood but one thigh had been scraped and there to Eddie's eyes lay the vast blue shiny wound. He stood there, sobbing with breathlessness, awed that such violence could happen to a man, glad that he had scampered fast enough to see it but troubled by it as he walked slowly homeward. Now whenever an automobile ambulance went past and he could see the sheeted figure of the sick or injured person through the window, the same trouble returned, not fear that it would happen to him but awe that it could happen at all. And now he would be the sheeted man, and it seemed proper to him that he should lean out of the ambulance somehow and apologize to the people in the street who saw him pass, "Please don't worry. This is nothing. I'm all right."

When they brought the stretcher into his bedroom, he wanted to walk down. It was silly to be carried. Yesterday he had walked home from the office. But the doctor said, "Get on it. You won't be walking for a long, long time."

"How long?" he asked at once. His mother began to cry again.

"That'll depend on the X-ray."

The trip to Ann Arbor began well. It was a warm bright day. He saw one or two people he knew and waved to them through the window, at once proud to attract the attention and embarrassed that it should be necessary. His mother tried to make him keep his hands flat on his chest. She urged him not to smoke. She nervously reviewed the histories of other members of the family who had been ill. Most of the illnesses had ended in death. Moving his eyes from the rushing spring countryside to his mother's face, he noticed that she was taking it for granted that he would also die. It amused him but he said nothing.

As he began to pay some attention to her instead of letting her words drift over him, it turned out that she was somewhat affronted that his particular disease should be tuberculosis. It was cancer that ran in the family, and rightly to assume his place in the family tradition he should have had a cancer although he was, she would admit, a little young for it. It was almost, he took from her aggrieved tone, as if he had chosen tuberculosis, a strange and unfamiliar malady, in defiance of her deepest expectancies. The shock of this defiance, out of schedule as it obviously was, upset not only her long-composed plans for his life but also the anticipated manner of his death which she had scarcely counted on living to see.

She did not know what you did for TB patients, she said, forgetting that her care would not be necessary. She had never even seen one. She did not know how they acted. If he were to grow worse, how would she know? What would be the signs? If he had a "spell," then what? Was he comfortable right now, at this moment? He seemed to be, she said, pulling at the blanket and smoothing it, but there was no way of knowing, he had always been so secretive.

They must have taken him out of the ambulance and through the hospital corridors very gently for he woke only because an orderly was tapping him on the shoulder, speaking to him in a low voice, "Come on, wake up. You're here. Come on, wake up."

Eddie opened his eyes. A strange face. A man with red hair and a white coat. Then he recognized the hospital smell and he heard his mother's voice jingling on to the doctor. He climbed off the wheeled stretcher into the high hospital bed. As soon as he stretched out between the fresh sheets, he knew that the trip had tired him. He seemed to be much sicker today than he was yesterday. He shut his eyes.

He heard the doctor explaining to his mother: this room would be temporary. He understood that she wished a two-bed semiprivate room instead of a four-bed ward. He could not tell her how long her son would be ill until he had made a further examination. Yes, it would certainly be longer than a month. It was quite likely that he would be in bed for six months; that was the period they recommended even with light cases. It might be preposterous but if she wanted her son returned to her healthy, it would be better for her to agree. No, there was no particular medicine she could buy that would hasten the cure. She could sit by his bedside now, today, for an hour or two if she wished but not every day. Because it was often a good idea, they had found, to keep patients separated from their families. Why? Because complete rest was an absolute essential, and sometimes there were strains of various kinds in the life of a family, hidden antagonisms that would be lightened if the patient could forget about them for a while, not that he meant necessarily to imply . . . On the whole, tuberculosis was quite as deadly as cancer, yes, especially among young people her son's age. She had misinterpreted him; he did not mean to be pessimistic. It was only that he did not want to keep anything from her. There was no sense in raising false hopes—it would take several weeks to obtain any real knowledge of her son's disease and his ability to combat it. He might have a very high resistance; on the other hand, he might not. No, he would certainly not advise her to take him home from the hospital within a month. No home offered the facilities of a hospital. He was quite sure she would be willing to nurse him faithfully but she was not a trained nurse, was she? She would find that a bedfast patient was a good deal of trouble. Custards, tarts, and little cakes would be acceptable although there was really no need of them. A dietician did nothing else but plan menus for the TB patients. It was no trouble at all, Mrs. Burcham, the treatment of tuberculosis was largely a matter of education. If there were ever any further questions . . .

"Edward!" he heard her say in a hoarse whisper.

He opened his eyes. "What?"

"How do you feel now?"

"Sleepy."

"Is there anything you want? Is there anything I can get you?"

"I'd like a cigarette."

"Oh, you don't want to smoke now. Doctor, he can't smoke with all this trouble in his lungs, can he?"

The doctor stepped up to the bed. He was a tall, vigorous man, bald on top with a fringe of light hair. His movements were firmly defined and clear, as if he exercised a lot. The light on his glasses hid his eyes. There was a name stenciled on his breast pocket but the white coat had been laundered so many times it was blurred. He did not answer Mrs. Burcham. He took a package of Luckies out of his vest pocket and offered Eddie one and held the match.

"Why, I should think with lung trouble the very first thing you would forbid him would be cigarettes," Mrs. Burcham said.

The doctor watched Eddie inhale. "Does it irritate your throat?" he asked. "Do you want to cough?"

"No. I don't think so," Eddie said.

"You can smoke, then. Ring for the orderly. He'll get you some." The doctor turned to Mrs. Burcham. "We let them smoke if they don't cough from it. The smoke turns the lungs black but we haven't been able to find that it harms them if it doesn't make them cough."

"What do you mean, turns them black?" Eddie asked.

"Your lungs are as black as coal tar, iridescent. They shine. So do mine. So does anyone's that smokes."

"It's the nicotine," Mrs. Burcham said with contempt.

"No. It's carbon, Mrs. Burcham. . . ." He would have said more but she interrupted him.

"Well, I'm sure I don't know anything about it. I'm going now, Edward. There doesn't seem to be anything I can do to help," she said petulantly as if Eddie should be ashamed not to be helpless. "I've asked them to hold the ambulance for me. I can ride back with them. . . ."

"That's a good idea," Eddie said.

"Well, with all these hospital bills and everything I thought I'd better try to save money. . . ."

She took one last formal look at him, drawing herself up, staring as if her weak blue eyes were the lens of a camera, seeking a permanent image. Eddie saw her do this, fearing that she would return to his bedside the next day, yet sensing that she was taking a farewell look. It was not that she was convinced he would die in the night although she admitted it as a possibility. It was rather that she wanted him to notice her scrutiny. She wanted him to think she believed she was seeing him living for the last time. She wanted him to feel that he had injured her—suddenly ill and of a strange disease, unfamilial and unfamiliar, a gross, even almost a deliberate and certainly unkind intrusion into the placid sadness of her life. He knew her well enough to know that even in her agitation she did not blame him directly. At worst he was perhaps the willing instrument of forces, powers, spirits beyond himself, the ones who had wrecked her life—"wrecked" was the word she used, the ones who had taken away her husband in his prime and left her alone.

He said soothingly, "I'll get well quick, Mother. Don't worry."

"Don't worry?" The tears ran out of her eyes and forlornly leading the movement of her body with her head, she turned and left the room with a handkerchief at her nose.

Impassively the doctor watched her go. He turned to Eddie. "You go ahead and take a nap. I'll come back later." He picked up a push button attached to a cord. "If you want anything, push this."

Eddie lay back and went to sleep very quickly. When he woke up the light in the room had faded a little and he judged it was after five o'clock. There were three men in the room with him, one in a bed beside him six feet away, the other two facing him across the room. With the snobbery of a newcomer, he insisted on the great difference between himself and them. From their pallor, they were old-timers, hence decayed, weak, with less manhood than he who only yesterday had walked freely in the streets in the bright air. He pushed back in his mind the fact that they all had the disease and let the equally undeniable fact that his disease was newer occupy his thought. It was newer, fresher, better in the way a new hat was better, a new car, anything new was superior.

This made him reticent. He had a dim impatient hope that they would acknowledge him as superior and speak first to welcome him. Perhaps, although the room was clean, it received no sun directly and seemed gray and colorless like their faces, they would, they even ought to ask him about the world he had just come from, which seemed greater and more splendid every minute he lay there. He waited, taking them in with deliberately offhand glances.

The two across the room were talking between themselves. The one beside him, the only thin one, a dark silhouette against the light from the window, coughed every few minutes and spat into a kidney-shaped dish he took from his side table. None of them spoke to him although he surmised that they too were watching him. At last he decided to say, "Nice day!" in a loud voice and see what came of it when he heard the noise that had awakened him, a clatter of dishes in the corridor.

Almost at once a nurse came in with a wooden tray with short legs on it. She laid it across Eddie's stomach. On it were a basin of water, a piece

[157]

of used soap, a clean washcloth, and a towel. She was a pleasant girl with dead-black hair. Her starched white cap rose to a conical peak. It made her look like a figure from a book for children, a pretty sprite or brownie.

"Time to wash up for supper," she said. She went out immediately and brought in trays for the other men. Eddie washed his hands and face.

At five-thirty, the ward helpers brought in supper. It was creamed chicken on toast, mashed potatoes, string beans, what Eddie identified as a female salad—cottage cheese and mayonnaise on lettuce—stewed peaches and cake, a little green pot of coffee, and a glass of milk. It tasted good. It was very good food. He ate all of it, pleasantly surprised that any institution could supply such a meal. Without thinking, he asked spontaneously, "Do they feed you this good every day?"

The man facing him looked up. He was young and he seemed to be an Italian or a Greek. "This is like it is every day. You can call it good if you want to." Then Eddie noticed that each of them had left half his supper and the man beside him had tasted nothing except a little milk.

He saw Eddie looking his way. He turned his full face to Eddie. It was gaunt, with cheeks sagging heavily away from white shiny cheekbones. "You get tired of the food. I drink this because it feels good in my throat kind of." He pointed to the glass of milk and Eddie stared at his hand. It was big, long and broad, with heavy knuckle bones and thick dirty nails but it was as white as the milk itself and so thin that it was like a drawing of the skeleton of a hand. Black hairs stood out harshly against the pale skin.

"How long you guys been here?" Eddie asked, and as soon as he said it, he saw a joking look pass between the Italian and the boy beside him.

"Oh, we ain't been *here* but a little while. We was down in the old building. They're tearing that down so they moved us up here just a month or so ago," the man beside him said hoarsely. He stopped and cleared his throat as if he hoped that would be all that was necessary. Suddenly he grabbed for the dish on the side table and spat into it.

"And how long were we in the old building, you want to know, huh?" the Italian said. "Well, I'm there two years and three months on a Bradford frame."

"What's a Bradford . . ."

"I'm just going to tell you. It's a frame made out of inch or inch and a half pipe. It's eighteen inches wide, about, and it's canvas between the pipes, and there's a hole in the canvas for 'em to wipe your ass and another hole for the abscess to dreen. The first month or so, they tie you on."

"What for?" Eddie asked.

"So you won't roll off," the Italian said and, turning, winked at the man in the bed beside him as if he would say that all Eddie's questions had been foreseen and were being asked on schedule. "You try lying on something eighteen inches wide all the god-damn time, never getting off. They have to tie you on at first. You wiggle. Your back itches or you get a strain or something."

"But they quit tying you on after the first month?" Eddie asked.

The Italian clasped his hands above his head like a prize fighter and grinned at the blond man in the bed beside his. "Yeah. They untie you. You quit moving. You just lie there. They turn you over once or twice a day so you can get your back rubbed."

"They rub your back?"

"Sure. You'll git your back rubbed. Everybody gits their back rubbed."

"Why?"

The Italian and the blond boy said in unison, "Bedsores."

"Have you got an abscess on your back?" Eddie asked.

"I got spine TB. There's always an abscess if it's bad." The Italian jerked his head sideways. "He's got a foot off. Show him your foot, Carl. Foot off and a kidney out." By that time the blond boy had uncovered his leg and was holding it up, a thin wasted stump, ending above the ankle in a pursed brownish purplish scar. He held it up a moment, clutching his thigh with both hands, grinning, and then lay back and covered it again.

"We're old-timers. I was on the frame three years. Carl, he ain't never been on a frame."

"No, but I been here three years same as you."

"When do you think you'll get out?" Eddie asked.

They glanced at each other again, mocking him. Eddie burst out, "What the hell's so funny? I just asked when you thought you'd be well."

They laughed out loud. When they stopped, Carl, the blond one, said, "All you new guys, the first thing they ask is, 'When we gonna get out?' Every new guy. Every time."

"You'll forget that stuff after a while," the Italian said condescendingly.

"It takes a long time to get well and you don't make it sometimes even then," Carl said.

"You mean you lie on a frame of pipe for three years and . . ."

"Hell, there was a fellow named McBride was on a frame five years and on Christmas Eve night—he was on the frame three years then——"

"Four," Carl said.

"All right, four. And this Christmas Eve night, the nurse left a bottle of rubbing alcohol on the table and McBride, he jumps up off the frame and grabs the rubbing alcohol and starts drinking it. Pretty soon the nurse comes back in and McBride grabs her and shoves her against the wall and he's got her skirts all up and everything and she's screaming and the orderly comes in and gets McBride back on the frame. They don't think about the rubbing alcohol. They just think he's nuts from being on the frame, Christmas and all. And McBride's got the bottle under the covers with him. So when they go out and the joint quiets down, he goes on drinking it until it's gone. Pretty soon he sees another nurse go down the corridor and he jumps up again. He ain't walked in four years, remember. And he gets hold of her and is just hauling *her* skirts up when he hears the supervisor and the interns and the orderlies, the whole god-damn staff coming after him. So what does he do? He cuts down the corridor into his room, throws open the window and jumps out into a snowbank, by God. The old building's only one story and he jumps right out bare-ass into this snowbank. . . ."

"Did it kill him?" Eddie asked.

"Well, they catch him and when Walters gets here—he's the doctor then—Walters is laughing so hard he can't hardly tend to McBride. They give him a lot of hot blankets and coffee and stuff and McBride gets a beautiful case of pneumonia."

"With empyema, too," Carl said.

"And he's sicker than a dog for three months but he doesn't die and Walters said he was a son-of-a-bitch if he could see that it hurt him at all."

"Where is he now?" Eddie asked.

"Aw, he went to his sister's as soon's he got off the frame. He got pneumonia again and it got him, but Walters said, 'That fella will never die of tuberculosis.' "

"Do many people die here?" Eddie said, seeing that talk of death did not abash them.

Smiling, the blond boy answered, "You listen tonight about ten o'clock or so. Right above this room is the room they bring 'em to when they're just about ready. You can hear the oxygen tanks. It sounds like somebody laughing steady all the time, chuckle, chuckle, chuckle. Don't it sound like laughing, Tony?"

The Italian pointed at the man in the bed beside Eddie who was then coughing again into the crescent dish. He said, so quietly Eddie hardly caught it, "He'll be up there tonight or tomorrow sure as hell."

"Who is he?"

[160]

"He was a lumberjack up north."

"Six foot three and two hundred pounds," the lumberjack said. He began in a loud voice that trailed off into hoarseness and ended in a cough. Eddie was embarrassed. He was sure the man had been listening. It was getting dark outside and they had all switched on the lamps at the heads of their beds. Eddie could see the lumberjack's face, loose, lined, terribly emaciated, with a week's stubble glistening as it caught the light. He was lifting his chin, swallowing like a chicken drinking, and it was clear he intended to go on speaking when he could. They waited.

At last he said in a whistling murmur, "Six foot three, two hundred pounds and look at me now."

"How much, Mike?" the Italian asked.

"A hundred and sixteen the last time they done it. When? When was it they weighed us?"

"A week ago Wednesday," Carl said.

The lumberjack held his hands out in front of him and looked at them, turning them from back to front. "Eighty-four pounds gone in a year. I . . ." He coughed hard three times and began to gag. In the pool of light from the lamp Eddie saw what he had not seen before. It was blood, bright red blood the lumberjack was coughing up. The little crescent dish was nearly full of it.

"What did you used to do?" the Italian asked.

Eddie turned away from the lumberjack. "I worked on a paper."

"What doing? Reporter?"

"Yeah."

"What paper?"

"*Athens Daily Telegraph.*"

"You make your home there?" Carl asked in a formal phrase.

"Yes. I've lived there all my life."

"What does a reporter do?" Carl asked.

"Get stinking. All they do is run around with good-looking broads and get stinking. I know. I saw a movie," the Italian said.

Eddie winked at the Italian and said seriously, "Oh, if there's anything big, a fire, or an accident or some big shot come to town, you go and look at it or talk to him and then go back to the office and write it up. Or you hang around the City Hall or the Courthouse. A lot of news comes in by phone. People phone it in. They'll do anything to get their names in the paper."

"You use a pencil in this writing or you use a pen?" Carl asked.

"Typewriter!" the Italian shouted. "Ain't you ever been to a movie?

Lee Tracy—bing, bing, bing!" The Italian drummed on the coverlet with his two forefingers. "Ain't you ever seen Lee Tracy play a reporter?"

"No," Carl said. "I never been to a movie."

"Jesus, *I* been to a movie," Mike said. He got it all out before he began to cough. While he reached for the dish, he held up his other hand as a signal that he intended to go on talking. They waited, watching him cough and spit, cough and spit. They could see it would be some time before he would be able to talk so they continued.

"You mean I been laying beside you three years and you ain't never been to a movie? What's the matter with you? You eat, don't you? You sleep. You'll take a drink. How come no movies?"

"I don't know. I just never thought I'd like 'em, I guess," Carl said.

"Christ, you ain't human," the Italian said.

"I don't have to go to 'em if I don't want to, do I?" Carl asked. He was not truculent. He just thought the Italian was funny.

"Hey, you—what's your name?"

"Burcham, Eddie Burcham."

"Now, look, Eddie, is this guy nuts or ain't he? Never been to a movie. All them broads. Jean Harlow. You mean you ain't never seen Jean Harlow?"

Mike had been lying back resting, still panting from the effort of coughing. He heaved himself up on his elbows and began in a hoarse whisper. "Jeeze Christ, I been in the woods most of my life but I been to movies. I used to go . . ." He started to cough again. He was determined to speak. He shook his head again and again, coughing. Some blood ran out of his mouth and dripped on the sheet. He kept shaking his head with his lips shut. At last with his eyes staring and his hands clutching the sheet, as if his message were of high importance, he said in a faint soft whisper, "I used to go all the time," and as he opened his mouth to speak, as he was speaking, the blood ran out all the time.

"Oh, for Christ's sake, Mike. Hurry up and die," the Italian said.

Unoffended, Mike grinned, red mouth, pink teeth, and a scarlet shining chin.

· XIV ·

WALTER HAD NOT expected anyone to send him a thousand dollars. It had come to him in a letter one morning about eleven when he was on his way to the hotel coffee shop for breakfast, shaven but still yawning. As he passed the desk, the day clerk threw the letter on the cigar counter. "You got some mail, Walter." It was a long envelope with the name and address of the tool-and-die company on the corner, the company his father had helped to found. He slapped it against his thigh as he walked into the coffee shop. He ordered coffee and orange juice and then he opened the letter.

He saw the perforated edge of the buff-colored check sticking out of the folded letter. He pulled it out, looked at it, saw that it was made out to Walter Phelps for one thousand dollars, and with a natural haste he opened the letter and read it. The tool-and-die company, after lying dormant for four or five years, had decided to pay a dividend of fifty cents a share. With ponderous jubilance, the company through its first vice-president stated that there was every indication that such payments would be continued quarterly.

He folded the check and put it into his wallet. He crumpled the letter and tossed it into a wastebasket behind the counter. He began to drink his orange juice.

A quarter of a year was ninety days. Three hundred and thirty-three dollars a month. He had seen them yesterday in front of the courthouse, twenty-six men tapping old bricks in two and laying them carefully in patterns over what had been the strip of lawn between the sidewalk and the curb. Bob Fowler, college graduate, took busses and thumbed rides all over the state asking citizens about the history of their towns—what is the oldest building? Where is the biggest tree? Can I see the oldest headstones in the cemetery? Win Traphagen, who had been making a hundred dollars a week in a Detroit architect's office when he was two years out of college, now designed privies. This was the WPA. He had not precisely feared that he would have to go on the WPA. He had not been able to imagine himself doing such niggling work but he could see himself drifting into it when the time came. He would not have borrowed money. He would not have gone to beg from his uncle or his grandmother. He would not have made any conscious decision whatever. He would have altered, slipped, melted into a man with a shovel in his hand. That was the way things seemed to happen now. Nothing was sharp or crisp.

He finished his coffee and paid the waitress. He made a feeble joke with her and passed the time of day. She was not pretty. She had a birthmark, a pinkish purple splotch all down her neck. She had developed a giggle as a protection. His joke and the answering giggle made the first indulgence of his leisure. (He thought of it as leisure. He was not a man out of work any longer. He could afford to be idle.) His faint anxiety fell away and he accepted the weight of the fact that he had an income to live on.

[163]

He walked solidly, heavily, out of the coffee shop and bought a *Free Press* and half a dozen cigars at the cigar stand. There ought to be someone to tell. Eddie would do but he was gone. He wanted to tell someone but the day clerk was not the man. The day clerk wore gaudy striped silk shirts with white soft collars and initials embroidered on the left breast. He was a horse-player who laid his bets by telephone to Toledo. At the moment he was daintily filing his nails. Walter surmised that if he told him, he would get only the huskily given name of some dog in the fifth at Aqueduct or Belmont or wherever the hell they were running, the name given with a plea, no congratulations. He glanced around the lobby at the old men and rocking women, as if he might, for their gasps, make a lightning revelation of this wealth, jump up and crack his heels, and teeter gaily out. They read and dozed and one of them snored gently. He took the elevator up to his room.

The maid had finished and the room was clean. He threw the *Free Press* on the bed and sat down in the armchair by the window. Who was there to tell who would tell him in reply that the money was a fine thing and think so?

Women were rapacious. He had learned this, he was sure, by observation. Therefore he would not telephone Dorothy Wickham to ask her out for wining and dining. (He had not called her in a week. As nearly as he could gauge it, the pinch on the thigh would have left resentment and this would have faded with the bruise into perplexity by now.) It would be shrewder, he thought, to let her discover his wealth. By now she would have heard all the gossip and she would know him for poor. Later, standing beside him while he paid for something, she would see the little sheaf of new clean twenty-dollar bills in his wallet and it would be a stimulating sight. She would, although he was sure she thought well of him now, think better. Later for old Dorothy, then.

He could write to Eddie Burcham or he could take the bus to Ann Arbor and visit him but writing was work and it would take a long hot bus ride to construct Eddie's reluctant astonishment, for he would be sure to refuse it as long as he could, or, worse, tell him he ought to get a job, money or no money. And Eddie was sick. He was down as a fallen horse was down. Walter had no fear of tuberculosis, since, like many people, he could not admit that malignity resided in something invisible. He feared rather the prone person, sick or asleep, changed somehow, abnormal.

He would buy a second-hand car. That would be a celebratory act. Buy it cash down, no turn-in. He took out his wallet to see if he still had his driver's license. It was there between a frayed receipted bill, six months old, for two neckties he had bought in Detroit, and a greasy calling card that bore in flowing script the name *Sir George Chrystal*. He had forgotten the man and where he had met him but he had kept the card because he believed the man to be a nobleman. The card was proof that he (here on this distant summer plain) was linked however weakly to ermine, castles, coronets with strawberry leaves and the strong old mysterious foreign life of the English.

The driver's license had two years to run. He could undoubtedly get a second-hand Dodge or Plymouth at the Kerr Motor Sales down the street. Walk in, close the deal, drive it away—that was the way to do it. Pete Kerr would tell around that he had paid cash and all the people who thought him poor would see him in the car and it would puzzle them.

He bought a three-year-old Plymouth coupé in ten minutes and he wheedled Pete Kerr out of a tankful of gas and six quarts of oil after they had settled the price. He wrote a check for four hundred and twenty-five dollars and drove the car carefully out of the place. It was noon and there were few people on the streets because they had all gone home to dinner yet he drove the new car slowly the length of Maumee Street from the Wabash depot at the east end of town to the city limits at the west. He thought many must have seen him as he drove past their houses, lolling at the wheel with one elbow sticking out the window.

As he drove through the town a second time, he thought of something else to do as a celebration, something that would be a kindness, a pleasant surprise. He would ask Cletus Holland and his wife out to dinner. It would dazzle them.

There are two kinds of people in a small town, those who shut the doors and pull down all the window shades to keep the heat out, and those who leave all the doors and windows open to catch any stray breeze. Mrs. Holland left the doors open. Walter rapped on the screen. After a minute he saw her head peek around a corner at the end of the hall inside the house. She came into the hall and walked slowly toward the front door, nervously touching her hair. She was wearing a spotted gingham dress and shapeless soft-soled kidskin slippers.

He called, "Hi, Lorene," as soon as he saw her.

"Hello. . . ." She waited and then decided on his first name, "Walter. Cletus isn't home."

"No. I didn't think he was. I can talk to you just as well."

Peering deliberately up and down the street, she opened the door and came out on the porch where anybody could see them, see her talking innocently and talking only with a man not her husband. "Ah . . . what was it you wanted?" she asked wretchedly. "Clete can't afford any insurance, Walter. Don't come here and talk him into it, please don't, Walter. Because you can. He'll buy if you keep at him long enough. He . . ."

"Look, I don't give a damn whether Clete wants any insurance or not. I just wanted to ask you and Clete to come out to dinner with me tonight."

"Dinner?" Her face remained worried, closed, suspicious.

"Sure. We could go out to Hoffman's at Wampler's Lake or somewhere."

"That would be real nice," she said automatically, looking straight ahead of her over the porch railing. She turned and stared at him. "Is this some trick?"

Although he could not fully understand why he wanted to take them to dinner, unable to assay the patronizing swagger he was making, he was aware of the sources of her anxiety and he wanted to laugh because he was threatening nothing that she had. She was a good wife. With her face washed, her hair combed, and her lipstick on, she was even pretty.

"Do you want to go to dinner?"

"Why, sure. . . ." She scraped her toe back and forth over a hole in the coco-matting rug on the floor.

"Then come on. I'm not trying to sell you anything," he said. "I'll pick you up at six."

"That's awful nice of you, Walter." She looked up and smiled. "We'll be ready about six."

"I'll call up and order some big steaks."

Now at ease, standing erect and graceful, the vision of the evening secure, she said formally, "I'm sure we'll enjoy it."

Walter skipped down the steps, and, as he was starting his car, he waved at her standing on the porch.

At five-thirty he bathed and dressed. At six he stopped his car in front of Cletus Holland's. Cletus was sitting on the front porch with his feet crossed on the railing reading the evening paper. He had put on his blue suit and a white shirt, all dressed up for the party.

As Walter came up the walk, he rose from his chair and shook hands, saying with what Walter took to be his salesman's cordiality, "Hi, Walter, come on, set indoors. It's cooler."

They went into the little living room with the overstuffed chairs and they each sat down in one. "Lorene'll be down in a minute," Cletus said. "Cigarette?" He offered Walter an open silver case, probably a Christmas present from the little woman, Walter thought.

They lit their cigarettes and drew on them exhaling similar little clouds of gray smoke. There was a pause. Cletus was goggling at his hands in his lap and Walter did not notice the embarrassed pose because he was looking around the room. The furniture did not seem hideous to him or the room overcrowded. He was not seeing it in that way. It was a home, not a hotel room. In the words of popular ballads, it was a little nest where two people lived who loved each other. It was a safe familiar place, perhaps the one safe familiar place. He did not put any of this into words. It was rather a string of impressions, the dent in the arm of the sofa where Cletus's head had lain, the housewifely care shown by the cheap little lace antimacassars on the chair backs, the relaxation of his own neck and shoulder muscles. He looked at Cletus with envy and he was just about to tell him how lucky he was when Cletus pulled himself erect in his chair and began firmly, "Walter . . ." Then he stopped.

"Yeah?" Walter said.

"It's nice of you to want to take us out to dinner but I want to tell you it's no soap." This was not the glib salesman's manner. It was embarrassingly meek and sincere.

"What's no soap, Clete? You mean you can't go?"

It seemed to make Cletus feel better to stare at his hands and rub and knead them. "I've just been thinking since you came. I know what you're after and it's no soap."

"Forget it. I'm not trying to sell you insurance," Walter said, grinning at his timidity.

"No, I know you're not," Cletus said quietly. If he had not been such a little man, it would have sounded ominous.

Now, because he had no clear reason for wanting to take the Hollands out to dinner, Walter had nothing much to say. He was lonely. He wanted to celebrate the arrival of his new money but other people would have served as well for guests. He was condescending, almost doing a charity. To him charity was often stimulated by guilt of some kind. It was a petty expiation, yet the guilt he did not know how to acknowledge was evaporating since he had come into their house. He was beginning almost to respect Cletus, to entertain little fleeting schemes to badger him out of his shyness and make friends with him because he had made such a fine little place to live. He said, "I just bought a new car today and I wanted to try it out and, hell, we haven't seen each other in a long time and I thought some steaks would taste good."

"We been right here, Walter."

"What do you mean?"

"You say you ain't seen us in a long time. We ain't hard to find. We been right here in town every minute practically."

"Yeah, I know, but . . ." He slowed down, let the sentence peter out. He could not honestly say he had been busy.

Cletus stood up and Walter got the sudden impression from a stiffness, an arrogance of posture that he was being brave. "So when I was coming down the stairs, I figured out why you were asking us out to dinner all of a sudden this way and I want to tell you that me and Lorene love each other and you can get out and pull this somewheres else."

"You mean you think I . . ." He began to laugh in loud choking snorts but he stopped abruptly. The sound of his own words made him angry. "Why, God-damn you, Clete. Your wife's pretty but not that pretty. I wouldn't give her a nod if she tagged me on the street." He walked out, letting the door slam.

On the way to his car he slowed his gait. He was thinking of Cletus' funny little defense of his home, and he nearly went back, confident that he could retrieve the situation by loud bullying apologies, good humor, clappings on the back, and false apologies. Before the evening was over he could make Cletus a friend of his, perceiving that the bond would be Cletus' own certainty of having wronged him, a Phelps, but he did not go back. When he thought of himself, as a Phelps, he said out loud, "The conceited little bastard," and he got into his car and drove away.

His self-esteem was intact but he did not feel good. He wanted a celebration now more than before but he could think of no one to help him but Dorothy Wickham. He wanted to stifle his failure at the Hollands' by driving somewhere very fast and drinking ten bottles of beer when he got there. If he did it alone, it would mean nothing. He had to have a companion, and, he discovered with some surprise, the sex of the companion did not matter. A witness was required. He wanted someone to watch him enjoy the gaiety he was determined (now, after what had happened) to contrive because the gaiety would be more real if someone besides himself would remember it later. It would then be, in a small scope, history, instead of memoir. If Dorothy Wickham came with him, his behavior would be prescribed and he would be under certain pressures that he did not particularly want but she was the only one in the whole town left for him to call.

He stood in the phone booth in the hotel lobby waiting for her to answer, deciding on his manner for the evening. When she spoke, he explained suavely his invitation, a new car, a porch overlooking the water, the steaks, the beer.

She did not know, quite, whether she would like to come or not.

Usually a girl said that she was or was not *able* to come. When she consulted her preferences so openly, a rebuke was implied. Walter recognized it. She was still cool because he had pinched her. He said coarsely, "You don't know, huh? Any your folks know?"

There was a silence.

"All right, I'll come," she said.

When she slid into the seat of the car beside him, he reached down and pinched her lightly on the thigh.

"If you're going to do that, I'll get out," she said angrily.

"No. You won't," he said with a cold smile.

While he was driving out to the lake he told her the story of Cletus Holland and he made it seem very funny. In this way he got rid of it and he was able to devote his evening to the celebration.

· XV ·

IT WAS ABOUT this time that he began to go into people's houses. If someone had proposed to him that he was trying to find new friends, to taste, and a little, timidly, to share their companionship and the rich quiet domesticity of their homes, he would have hooted with scornful laughter. Nothing in his upbringing had left room for such weak excursions. He had been reared to consider only certain acts, certain emotions as permissible. There was quite a large number of these but even so the number was limited. Any not contained in his memory of precept and example were not supposed to exist. They were not part of a man, especially not part of a Phelps.

It was, however, about this time that he began to go into people's houses. He did not have any available knowledge of the necessity but it was necessary nonetheless to deceive himself in order to go at all. It seemed to him that he was deceiving not himself, never himself (he was not such a fool), but rather others, the insurance company he no longer worked for and the people who were inside the houses. He took a great deal of pleasure in the neatness of his duplicity, laughing and chuckling to himself.

He got up a list of "prospects" out of the telephone book. After his morning coffee and orange juice he would leave the hotel with his black portfolio in his hand. As the town clock struck nine, he would be sitting in his car scanning his list of possible calls. Having made his decision arbitrarily because the name reminded him of something pleasant or because he was curious about the part of town the prospect lived in, he would start the car and drive solemnly through the streets, lifting his hand in salute to other men who thought he was going to work just as they were.

The name he had picked for the first call of the day was Fred J. Echols on Tiffin Street. As soon as he had driven a little way down Tiffin Street, he knew from its number that the Echols house would be at the "wrong" end, two or three doors from the D. T. & I. railroad tracks. Plaster fell down in those houses every so often because they were shaken by trains. The house was an old frame structure whose clapboard siding had settled into long curves, painted a gray with yellow trim years before and now flaked and worn. Two huge maple trees shaded it and under them the grass grew thin as fern in long tufts overlapping one another like waves. A bed of flag lilies lay by the front steps, unpruned, untended, without any flowers. The shades of the front room were drawn and the screen door looked into a dark house. Walter guessed immediately, "Old people. Poor people," and when he knocked, he doubled his first and banged it hard against the frame of the screen door so they could hear him.

A big old woman answered the knock, scowling to make her eyes accommodate the light and the newcomer standing in it, bringing the smell of the house with her. She wore a spotted bungalow apron and a pair of men's house slippers with elastic sides. When she spoke, she said, "Hello," in a low voice and he knew she was not deaf.

"Is Fred here?" he asked.

"Fred ain't to home," the old woman answered. "What'd ye want with him?" She cocked her head first on one side, then on the other, trying to get him into focus.

"I had a message for him," Walter said. It was at this point that he usually started to giggle silently, sometimes hard enough to shake him a little.

"Wait a minute," the old woman said to herself, and then more loudly to Walter, "I can't see a thing without my glasses." She turned away from the door and Walter heard her massive step go through the house. "You might's well come in and set down while I hunt 'em up," she called.

Walter went in. He had been right. They were a poor old couple. An army cot with a sleazy blue silk cover stood against the wall. A round red pillow, smooth, with an Indian head painted on the front, the kind of thing you win on a paddle wheel at a county fair, leaned against the wall in the center of the couch. At one end was a bed pillow with no case, a pad of blue and white striped ticking with a hollow in it where the old woman's head had lain. There were two rickety wicker chairs held together with binder twine. A sewing machine, all folded up, served as a table, and on its top was a litter of scissors, spools of thread, a small monkey wrench, a piece of beeswax, old-fashioned round black pillboxes, a darning egg, a clam shell, a bottle of some kind of red medicine half gone, and rising from all this was a flower pot wrapped around with green crinkled paper tied on with a red ribbon. On the wall in a dusty frame of gilt was a big tinted photograph of a man with a short brown beard. He had pale faded blue eyes, as if he had forgiven everybody everything, and he wore no necktie. The stud in his collar shone out a brilliant yellow, the one detail that held the eye.

Walter sat down in one of the rockers gingerly. He heard the old woman rattling things and bumping around in the kitchen. She came back into the room. "I can't seem to locate 'em. *You* don't see 'em, do you?"

Almost at once Walter saw them on the floor near the head of the army cot. She must have pushed them up on her forehead, and, as she napped, they had fallen off. He picked them up and gave them to her.

She put them on and her old soft face relaxed. "Now if I can find a pencil . . . ," she said, rummaging in the mess on top of the sewing machine.

"It isn't that kind of message, Mrs. Echols," Walter said. "I just had something to tell him for his own good." He had known it the minute he had seen the house. They couldn't afford insurance. He wanted to laugh out loud. It was curious—he thought he cared nothing for the people but he liked their homes, even the terrible smell, the dirt, and the mess.

She threw up her head and looked at him with suspicion. Her eye lit on his portfolio, leaning against the rocker of the chair, for the first time.

"You ain't a lawyer, are you? Fred ain't in any trouble?"

Walter shook his head while she was speaking.

"Well, they ain't no use trying to sell him anything because he ain't got any money." She was evidently used to this because she stated it as a plain fact without giving it any emotional coloring.

Walter sat back comfortably in the rocker. "And why haven't you got any money, Mrs. Echols?"

She was old. She must be going on eighty, Walter thought, because she did not seem to hear the question as rude. She sat down in the other chair and began to rock back and forth. "Well, Fred ain't had any work since way along last year. Not any steady work, that is. He goes out every day and treads from door to door and sometimes but not very often he gets some grass to cut or some rugs to beat or something. About a dollar, dollar and a half a week, say. And if somebody wants him to hoe in the garden, he gets to bring home something. Brought home a basket of fresh peas yesterday. But no real work. Fred's a carpenter by trade and, time was, he was a good provider but, now, say, if it wasn't for our son, I don't know what we'd do. He works over to Jackson. He's been working right along and he sends us five or six dollars a week and with what Fred makes ..."

Walter interrupted the endless flow of reminiscence that, now, old, was her only real occupation, "visiting." "How old is he?"

"Fred's seventy-nine. Oh, he's failing but he can still step off down the street like a younger man."

"You like him, don't you?"

She almost stopped rocking. It was something she had not thought of in a long time. *"Like* him? Like *Fred?* Say, who are you, young man?" She laughed and laughed, shaking all over, repeating to herself in a warm, guttural voice like a hen with her chicks under her, "Do I like Fred? . . . Do I like Fred?" She took off her glasses and rubbed her eyes with one hand. "Who are you? What do you want?"

"I thought I'd sell Fred some life insurance but if he hasn't got any money ..."

"But why would you ask me if I liked him?" She was still smiling.

"I don't know. You do, though, don't you?"

"Yes." She nodded her head and stared at Walter without seeing him as if she were still deciding. "Yes. I guess I do." She leaned forward lifting her chin to get ready to say something daring. "You know, when you get to be my age, it's kind of hard to tell." Then she screamed with laughter, a high thin scream.

Walter waited until she stopped laughing. "It's kind of hard, huh?"

"Why, sure," she gasped. "You know how it is. No, you don't either. You're just a boy."

"I'm twenty-four."

"That's what I say." She sighed deeply twice. "Well, I'll tell you. You get so used to a man, living with him as long as I have Fred, you know his walk, his step around the house, you know what he likes to eat, you know him breathing at night, why, when it comes right down to it, you ain't two people any more. That's a fact, you ain't two people any more."

"You never fight that way." Walter was looking for an opening through which he could leave.

"That's right," she said dully. The effort of the talk and laughter seemed to have tired her. She was sitting quite still, not rocking, breathing heavily.

Walter stood up. "I'm sorry to have bothered you, Mrs. Echols."

"You going?"

"Yes, I think I'd better."

"What was it you were selling?"

"Life insurance."

"We couldn't afford it. We ain't got the money, like I told you." She smiled suddenly in remembrance, her lips lifted above the bright pink gums of her false teeth. "But, Lordy heavens, I ain't laughed so much . . ." She began to wheeze and cough and chuckle. She bent forward with her hands on the wilting arms of the rocker, ready to boost herself up to her feet.

"Don't get up, Mrs. Echols."

With a grunt, she was up. "You come again sometime. We'll have another visit," she said.

"Good-by," he said. He went out and before he was much away from the house, he heard the squeak of the army cot as she lay down again.

This was one kind of home he visited. A few people slammed the door on him as soon as they learned what he said he wanted. When he did get in, he let the women talk for half or three-quarters of an hour. Then he begged their pardons and left their houses. Only sometime later after he had gone would they remember in a puzzled way that he had not tried very hard to sell them any insurance. The recollection frightened some and they would worry about it; the others forgot him at once.

A name on Walter's list said Carl Herzog, 213 Elm Street. It was near St. Peter's German Catholic Church. Herzog, a factory foreman, was a "Hill Dutchman." Walter stopped his car in front of the house and got out. The house was the usual white clapboard with an open gable facing the street and a hip roof over a little front porch at the side. The blinds were drawn in the parlor to keep out the sun. There were no toys on the sidewalk or bare spots on the lawn. The house had been newly painted with red trim. There was a brick-bordered bed of flowers, none blooming, set exactly under the parlor window. A small circular bed of crimson peonies lay at one corner of the lawn surrounded by a low wire fence, and the grass was evenly cut. As he went up the front walk Walter could see two or three neat rows of sweet corn in Carl's garden at the back. The Hill Germans were all like that, neat and hard-working. He tried to remember who Carl Herzog was.

[173]

He knocked on the screen door. He could see no one in the living room as he peered through the screen. He noticed a doll with a big dirty blue silk hoop skirt that covered the telephone. It sat on a small stand with the phone book hanging beside it. He thought it queer because a house like this would ordinarily have a wall telephone.

"Hi-ya, buster. What's new?" he heard a woman's coarse voice say. "I been watching you in the mirror. Come on in."

Walter went in. He saw an oval mirror on the wall.

"In here."

She was in the small front parlor with the blinds drawn. She was about thirty years old. She had a gaunt face with high cheekbones and thick lips. It was a face that would be beautiful from some angles and ugly from others. From the look of her mouth she had daubed it with lipstick while he was coming up the front walk. Although it was eleven o'clock in the morning, she wore eye shadow and mascara and there was a bright flush of rouge on either cheek. She lay stretched out on a chaise longue and he suspected from her carefully maintained immobility that she had arranged a pose, had even tucked her dingy blue satin house-coat along her thigh and calf to take his eye when he came in. Her feet were bare and she wore satin mules with dirty fur at the instep. The house-coat was open, opened, he thought, and he could see her swelling breasts almost to the nipples. She lay back with her hands behind her head and a cigarette in a corner of her mouth.

She looked so much like a "bad girl" in a movie that he had a hard time keeping his face straight. He did not think she was a "bad girl," at least not the kind she was pretending to be merely because she was a foreman's wife and St. Peter's red brick church was only a few doors away. This was not the kind of wickedness that grew in his home town. He was sure of that.

"Park yer carcass," she said, without changing her pose. "What's on yer mind?" She kept her voice down in her throat.

"Are you Mrs. Herzog?"

"So what?"

"Is your husband home?"

She pursed her shiny crimson lips and shook her head gloomily.

If he had been sitting in darkness, eating from a sack of popcorn and watching all this on a screen, Walter would have divined at once that her husband was a brute; that he himself (Clark Gable) had been pining for this moment; and adultery would be about to pop. In the Elm Street daylight, the convention did not hold. There was a wrapper from a candy bar on the floor beside the chaise longue and the corner of a confession magazine stuck out from under it. She looked foolish.

He wanted to laugh. If he had had the confidence, he would have pretended to be Clark Gable, picked her up off the chaise longue, called her "Honey," and carried her into the bedroom but he feared what he would have to do there would be done with so much awkwardness that she would think him innocent and virginal. He feared to have anyone think him innocent and virginal.

He could not make up his mind about her. She might not be play-acting at all, but he could hear the shouts of children outdoors and the hum of a truck in second and he could not really convince himself she was a whore. At the last moment she would refuse, laughing at first and, when he pressed her, bridling into outraged anger. He knew she was lazy because she was trying to fulfill her wishes with second-rate materials, idling in a homemade imitation paradise, but, as he looked down the curve of her leg, he reflected that at least she was trying and she did have a beautiful leg.

"What did you want with him?" she asked, brushing a cube of ash from the blue satin.

"I wanted to discuss his life-insurance program with him," he said. There was no interior laughter at the silly phrase. The situation was too exciting for him to feel a joke even if he made it himself.

"Discuss it with me. He gives me the paycheck." She said this coldly, inflating the statement with her sullenness to make it seem to mean more than it did. "Whaddaya mean, program?"

"How much insurance does he carry?"

"He don't carry any."

"Don't you think he ought to? Suppose he was *taken?*" The modulation of false emotion in his voice was habitual. He hardly knew he was making it.

"I'd get along." There was a slow smile. She lifted one bare knee and settled her heel on the cushion. "Don't you think I could get along, big boy?"

"I don't doubt you could find a job, Mrs. Herzog," Walter said. He could not keep his glances from the soft white calf.

"Say, what's your name? Mine's Mimi."

"I'm Walter Phelps."

"Oh." She looked him up and down. "Yeah." A look of real envy collapsed into her smile. "You live in the big house there on Maumee, don't you?"

"I used to. Until last year."

"Why, say, that's right. Your old man was killed. He and your mother, too. *I* remember." Her normal voice was a thin soprano. "It was in an auto accident, wasn't it? Gee, that's too bad." She had come out of her pose and was behaving naturally. She noticed it herself while she was speaking and Walter saw it trouble her. She stopped talking and glanced at him to see if he had caught her. "So you're not living in the big house any more, huh, Walter? You had trouble, huh? Your old man, he didn't have any insurance, huh?" She had covered the opening again.

"It didn't do any good."

"So you're a poor boy now. Peddling insurance. Well, I'll be God-damned." She laughed in her throat, putting out her cigarette in a standing ashtray. "But you're a nice-looking poor boy just the same."

Walter grinned. "What are you trying to say?"

The possibility that all the flummery of the cheap props and the movie-acting backed by a serious intention made her seem to him superior. Since he felt clumsy and she had stripped the Phelps off him in a few sentences, he tried to be naïve, making the best of the pose because he knew no other although he despised himself for knowing only one. He had heard of women like this in the monstrous legends of his peers but he had not expected to meet one here, in his home town, where it was not conceivable that he should not be able to meet any situation easily.

"You're a big boy, too."

"What do you mean, Mrs. Herzog?"

She flung herself irritably around on the chaise longue. It was hard to play opposite green actors who would not pick up their cues. "*Mi*mi, for Christ's sake."

"OK, Mimi," Walter said. He wanted to string this out to get time to make up his mind. There was no repugnance, only this anxiety.

"Look, you're a big boy. You went to college. I read about it in the paper. Can't you tell what's on my mind?"

"Yes, but ..."

It always happened in a dark place and it was the man who was the hero. And if she was going to be sarcastic and bully him, he wouldn't be ready although there were some men, to hear them tell it, who were always ready, who could take it anywhere they found it, bright or dark, but he was unready, and he had always believed that something took care that you were inevitably ready at this crisis. The roughness and the

[176]

"You're damn right. And it was free and I don't ask you for two dollars or a present or a God-damn thing. . . ."

"Am I supposed to give you a present?"

She slapped his face so hard he almost lost his balance. There was a second when they both stood gaping at each other. His hand went to his cheek and she ducked around the corner of the bed to see what he would do. He rubbed his cheek.

"I didn't mean to hit you that hard, Walter. Honest, I didn't."

"It's OK. I've got to be going."

"I'm not a whore."

"All right."

"I'm not a call girl."

"I didn't say you were."

"I just put out to my friends, and any time you want it you come back."

"All right." He started to go. He turned back. "Thanks a lot."

She went into her pose, leaning against the bedpost with her weight on one foot. She held up one palm and waggled the fingers up and down, calling pertly, "Come back soon."

He went through the house and out the front door. No one was watching him from the adjacent front yards or porches. He got into his car and drove away.

All he could think about was the husband's face so meek in the doorway. The fear he had suffered at the coming of his footsteps and the apparition of this soft obedient man who had been bringing the fear was like a dream, something that did not happen except behind his eyelids and at night. He knew he would remember the weak politeness of that "Hi," the trick of the whipped child or the painful hoopla somersault of the little dog, all his life. Over his lunch, staring at the sweat on the bottle of beer in front of him, when he had remembered it enough and could use some judgment, he knew he had seen a man made less by the repetition of insult. He wondered how he would look at Carl Herzog the next time he saw him and how Carl Herzog would look at him. Was there so much patience crowded into him that he would smile and accept him as one of the family or was there, especially if he had drunk a few beers, still a vent for his first corrupted hate?

After he had eaten his lunch and gone back to his room at the hotel to take a shower, he saw his thick legs and soft torso, wet and soapy, and he began to think of the woman. Movies always ended short of the bedroom and he had a curious respect for her. She had absorbed a style from the movies, crude and foolish though it was, and she had used it as far as it would go but she had gone unfurnished with any borrowed gesture into her bed and taken him with her. And now, although it was not what it was cracked up to be, since nothing actual could have borne the weight of dream and forethought he had given it, and during the scene he had not played the heroic part he had intended, he had done it. He was an initiate. It would make a tale to tell other males after he had revised it suitably. He was, he thought, fully a man now. Mystery was gone. He soaped and scrubbed pleasantly and after he had dried himself he lay down naked on his bed and read the morning paper.

· XVI ·

IN FRONT OF HIM was a kind of shed under a maple tree. From a limb of the maple hung a length of chain with an old auto tire at the end of it. The shed was somebody's house—there were no addresses here. It was one room, covered with torn tar paper, and beside the open door there was one window. It had a broken light stuffed with a wad of cloth and filthy lace curtains at either side. In front of the shed the ground was bare as children will make it bare, and spying around the corner of the house he saw the faces of two children, bright-eyed, wild as mice. He got out of the car and jumped the ditch. The children ran away into the weeds behind the house.

Behind the thicket of dock and pigweed stood a row of poplars planted years before by the promoters because they grew quickly. A breeze was blowing past him through the poplars. It threw up the silver undersides of their leaves, quivering almost brightly enough to flash in the sun. He stopped at the edge of the ditch with the trees in his eye. He was not watching them for any reason, merely receiving the image of this gray-green flickering movement, and he wondered, paused this way, "Why am I here?" There had been no purpose in coming here. He did not hope to sell insurance. In the past two or three months occasionally someone had offered to buy a policy and he had whipped out his rate-book and deliberately talked them out of it. He used the portfolio that contained the rate-book to get an entry into people's houses, the portfolio and the statement that he was an insurance salesman, and relying on the old deference Americans have for salesmen, he usually got in. He had never asked himself clearly why he wanted to sit listening in the dank parlors or kitchens he visited. He knew only that if he went a day without doing it, he was uncomfortable. Out here it was impossible, it had always been impossible that anyone would have enough money to buy insurance, and he rarely called at houses where a sale was impossible; it was not part of the subtle game he was playing with himself. Why, then, was he here, even to perpetrate his little joke? He stood slouched before the little shanty, his portfolio hanging in front of him from both his hands, staring blankly at the steady tremor of the poplar leaves as people stare at running water. Something in him gave a sanction to all his absurd pretending. It was enough that it was all right to continue; he did not question himself any further. He remembered the children's faces. He straightened up and started for the door of the shanty.

Drooping askew on scraps of leather for hinges, there was a screen door. The screen was rusted out so badly that bits of it fell off as he knocked. Nobody came. Nobody answered. At the threshold he caught a heavy damp smell of stale food, kerosene, and used clothing like the smell of an old farmhouse. He waited a moment, unwilling to go away. His eyes relaxed from the sunlight and he began to see what was inside: a kerosene stove with three burners, two white iron beds with the paint chipped off and the bedclothes in a mess, some homemade shelves with rows of cans and bottles on them, and, by the door, a listing wooden table with a blue worn oilcloth cover. As his eyes went over the room again he saw that what he had taken for a moil of bedclothes on one of the beds was a man. He lay without motion and if he breathed he did not show it, an old man with a bald head and a grayish unshaven face. He lay flat and rigid with long sloping hands and huge wristbones shining like studs outside the sheet. Walter spoke. "Good morning." There was no answer, no movement, but he did not think the old man was asleep.

He opened the door and stepped inside. It was dirtier and more odorous than he had expected. He tiptoed over to the bed and stood at the foot, looking down at the man. His eyes were closed, drawn shut, his eyelids like the lids of a snake. There were two spurts of brownish hair growing out of his nostrils and the flabby purses of his jowls were spread over the soft scraggy flesh of his neck. The vein showed in his eyelids and along his temple. His mouth looked stiffly shut and, slowly—it was hard to see—he breathed. A fly walked from the crown of his head to the tip of his nose, stopped, rubbed its feet, and walked again into the thickets of his eyebrows and down into the lashes. It ran lightly half across his eye and Walter thought he must be dying. At last the eyes opened slowly, blue. The fly twinkled up his forehead and the old man did not move. He looked at Walter.

[183]

"Good morning, sir," Walter said.

The muscles on the left side of the old man's face trembled and set themselves tense. The left side of his mouth opened a little showing a brown tooth. But he did not speak and Walter knew he was paralyzed. He noticed then the smooth dirtied whiteness and softness of his idle hands.

The fly ran down his brow and Walter bent over to brush it away. Suddenly he felt a whack on his thigh. He heard the screen door slam. He turned around. A little girl with tangled hair was just swinging a barrel stave. He caught it before it hit him again. She jerked it through his hand, leaving some slivers in his palm. She stood with her bare feet together and the stave ready.

"You stop. That's what we do and you can't do what we do because this ain't your house," she said, bobbing her head for emphasis.

"What is it you do?"

Her face broke into a grin of delight and she ran over to a crock with a plate over the top that sat on the table. "I always catch 'em here," she said. The top of the plate was thick with flies. She made a quick grab and caught one in her hand.

"What's in the crock?" he asked.

"The mush."

"What mush?"

"*The* mush, silly. Don't you eat mush?" She was standing again with her feet close together in a lithe childlike pose, holding the fly in one hand and apparently petting it with the other.

"There," she said. "This is what we do." Tiptoe, slyly, she went to the side of the bed and, stealthily avoiding the old man's steady gaze, she put the wingless fly on his forehead. It crawled round and round and she danced up and down noiselessly, hugging herself, and stifling her laughter with one hand over her mouth.

"What do you do that for?" Walter asked.

"Fun." She froze and lifted one foot high in front of her in some private experiment with balance. "Look! He always looks that way. Sometimes he makes a noise."

The old man was rolling his eyes desperately upward as if he were trying to see the fly, as if, seeing it, he could still catch it.

"Who is he?"

"Grandpa. Look!" She pointed at the old man again, giggling and jumping up and down.

"Why do you want to torment him?"

"Fun," she said, still entranced by the fly. "He's funny. He's awful funny."

"Where's your mother?"

"Down to the Welfare. Today's the day they give out flour."

"Where's your father?"

There was a half-voiced gasp from the bed. Walter went over, brushed the fly off to the floor, and stepped on it.

"Damn you, you killed my fly," the little girl said. She flew at him and started to pummel him and kick him with her bare feet. Walter took her wrists. She tried to bite and she kept kicking him.

"You'll just hurt your feet. Come on, now. Quiet down. I'll give you a nickel if you'll be quiet."

She dropped her hands and faced him with attentive grace. "Where is it?" she said threateningly.

He took a nickel out of his vest pocket and gave it to her. She whirled around and ran to a little boy who had come in and was standing silently by the door. "Look what I got! Look what I got!" She danced around him with the nickel flat in her hand.

"Candy?" the boy said without moving from his place. He was about five years old. He wore nothing but a once-washed feed sack with a hole cut out for his head and two for his arms. The faded emblem of a flour company was on his chest.

The girl stopped dancing at once and hit him on the top of his head with her fist. "No. Not for you." She dragged one foot after her in a glide and began hopping again. "For ME! For ME!"

"If I give you another nickel, can he have one?"

"Why?" she asked suspiciously.

"So he can have some candy, too."

"You gonna give me another nickel. Then I have two nickels. Then you gonna give him one?"

"Yes."

"Just one?"

"Yes." He reached into his pocket for a dime and gave it to her. "That's a dime. Two nickels."

"I know, silly."

He seized her hand and pried the fingers open. "Now give me that nickel. Come on." At last she released it. He went over to the door where the little boy stood leaning, scratching his back up and down against the doorpost, and gave it to him. The boy turned it over and over, held it up between his thumb and forefinger against his eye as if it were transparent, flipped it into the air and caught it, and held it on the flat of his hand close to his face studying it.

"What's the matter? Haven't you ever had a nickel?"

The little boy looked up solemnly and said, "Never."

"Where's your father? Say, what's your name, anyway? How old are you?" he asked the girl.

"Who wants to know?" she said, swinging one arm violently.

"I gave you a dime. Tell me."

"My name's Annie. His is Don."

"Don what?"

"Don Carson. His middle finger's short. Don!" she bawled at him. "C'mere."

The little boy came forward obediently.

"Show him the finger."

He stuck out his right hand proudly. His middle finger was about an inch long, unjointed, with a complete and dirty nail.

"Where's your father?"

"In jail."

"What for?"

"He's sick." She started to dance away, holding her dress away from her thin little thighs with one hand. She said coolly over her shoulder in a mocking knowing voice, "We never use the word 'drunk' in front of the children. That's what Ma told Mrs. Jaeger. I hid in the weeds."

"Your father's in jail for being drunk?"

"Sure. Every time he gets his Welfare check." She moved a backless chair in front of one of the shelves and climbed up on it, poking among the bottles, sacks, and cans. "See? Here's one he forgot." She giggled. "No, he didn't. I hid it. Me and Don're going to try it." She climbed down and handed him a little oblong bottle with square corners. On a yellow label printed in blue were the words *Jamaica Ginger (Alcohol 98%).* "That's what he drinks," she said.

He shook the little bottle. The bubbles came up in it, winked, and were gone. He did not know exactly what to say. What was there to tell a child? "What does he do it for?"

She skipped over and jounced up and down on the edge of the old man's bed. The old man opened his eyes and stared at her, trying, it seemed, to scowl. She put her head back smiling, and looked at him out of her half-shut eyes, cocking her head on one side. "You look funny. Fur all over you. Don! Do this."

The little boy paddled over to the bed.

"Do like me. Go on. Put your head back," she said in a bossy tone, grabbing his head and forcing it back. "Now look at him out of your eyes. There. Don't he look funny? See the fur?"

"Uh-huh," the little boy said and kept his head back, surveying the whole room.

"I know why Pa drinks. He's trying to burn his God-damn guts out," she said seriously.

"What does your father do?"

"Nothing. Plays with me and Donnie when he's out of jail."

"I mean, what's his trade? Where does he work?"

She looked surprised. "Golly, I don't know."

"Hasn't he ever worked?"

"I don't know."

"How long have you lived here?"

"Always. We're too God-damn poor to live anywheres else."

"Your mother says," Walter finished.

"Uh-huh," she said. She rolled herself backward and forward against the old man's shins.

"Don't do that. You'll hurt him."

"Aw, he can't feel anything. Ma said he couldn't. He can't feel a thing."

"He's your grandpa?"

"Uh-huh. Say, did you ever see a yellow butterfly?"

"I think so."

She got down on her hands and knees and reached under the bed. The little boy mimicked her, feeling aimlessly around. She slapped his head and he stood up resignedly. At last she pulled out a big leather-bound book, folio size, with *Animate Creation* stamped in gold on the cover. She sat on the floor and began to leaf through it.

"Where did you get it?"

She nodded her head toward the old man. "It's his'n. Ma said there used to be more of 'em but they sold 'em. This is mine. I hide it." She found the pages she was looking for. "Get down here and look."

The book lay open and on one page there were seven or eight moths and butterflies, their wings nicked and dingy, but some of them still keeping their rich colors. Delicately she picked up a little yellow butterfly with spots on its wings, the kind that hovers around cabbage plants. She turned it over and held it up, her eyes fixed on it, her mouth open with her breath coming gently out.

"It's pretty, isn't it?" Walter said lamely.

With it still in her gaze, she said, "I go like butterflies. I go up and down and around flying just like they do. All blue I am. All blue like this one." She picked up another. Then, ashamed perhaps that she had shown this feeling or afraid he would laugh, she looked at him boldly. "I catch 'em with my hands."

"With your hands? How?"

"Just like this." She made a quick swipe through the air.

"How do you kill them?"

"Oh, pins. I stick pins right between their eyes. They're mine," she said defensively as if she had heard this was cruel. "All butterflies are mine. I used to talk with 'em——" Here she imitated a grown-up careless nonchalance. "But lately I kind of got out of the habit." She looked at him, running her glance from his hair to his shoes, not appraisingly but more as if she did not want to forget him. "I like you. What's your name?"

"Walter."

"Don't like it. Do you like it, Don?"

"Never," the little boy said, squinting up at Walter.

"He always says that. Grandpa used to say it when he could talk. You ask him anything, he'd say, 'Never.' He's a nasty old guy."

Walter took out his pocketbook, pulled out a corner of a ten, shoved it back, and took out a twenty-dollar bill. "Annie," he said, "I've got to be going and I want to make you a present, you and Don. Here."

Suddenly she was shy. She put her hands behind her and rubbed one cheek on her shoulder. "That's a twenty-dollar bill."

"Yes. Take it. It's yours."

"All of it?" Her eyes opened wide.

"That's right."

"Gimme a quarter instead. Ma'll take a twenty-dollar bill away from me."

Walter thought this over but since the gift had more to do with him, helped him more than it did her although he could not quite think why, he said, "No. You keep it."

"All right," she said soberly. She turned a leaf of the big book and fitted it carefully in. "There. It's the next page after the butterflies." She took up the book, holding it close to her chest, turned around on her knees before the bed, and then she did an odd thing. She straightened her skirt with one hand and fluffed out her bobbed hair meticulously as if this were a ritual, bent over and shoved the book inch by inch under the bed to lie behind old paper bags and a torn rubber overshoe. She stood up and dusted off her hands.

"So long, Annie."

She stared up at him and then at his portfolio that he had left standing against the table leg. "What you got in that black bag?"

"Nothing."

"I bet you got money."

"Oh, no, I haven't."

"You're a liar," she said smoothly. "Do you go everywhere? You going to Mrs. Jaeger's?"

"No. Why?"

"Ma never told me about you, Walter."

"I'll come and see you again, Annie."

"I'm going to keep that twenty-dollar bill forever. Good-by." She turned away at once, pulled a feather from the pillow where her grandfather's head lay, and began to tickle his eyelids. Once she started to look around but when she saw Walter was still there she jerked her head back shyly.

"Good-by, Don."

The little boy said nothing and slid one foot out along the floor until he nearly lost his balance.

"Say good-by to him, you little bastard," Annie snapped, her face still hidden.

" 'By, Walter," the boy said.

"So long," Walter said. He went out and slammed the door.

He drove slowly northward through the town into the "paved district" where the stores were. After stopping at a red light, he speeded up a little, went past his hotel a couple of blocks, and stopped in front of the jail.

The jail was a square hulk of yellow pressed brick. The sheriff and his wife lived in one side of the building, and there were curtains at the windows on that side. On the other side the windows were barred. There was a small wooden front porch painted gray and on it the sheriff sat with his feet on the rail. He was a big man, six feet four or five inches tall, and they said he weighed an even three hundred.

Walter went up the steps of the porch. "Nice day, Charlie."

The sheriff started from his doze, spat over the rail, and squinted his eyes. "Why—Phelps, Walter Phelps. Come on up and seddown."

Walter sat down on the top step. He did not have the American's usual fear, distaste, or hatred of cops because he had grown up considering that policemen and civic officials were in some obscure way retainers of his family's. Now that his family was dispersed and its power declined, he suffered some embarrassment in front of the sheriff. He did not know how much he could safely ask.

[189]

"What're you doing now, Walter? Somebody said you quit the bank. I never could see that staying cooped up all the time, even with all that money. Tain't a hell of a lot of satisfaction running money through your fingers when it ain't yours." He laughed loudly and spat over the railing. "Somebody said you were selling insurance."

"You don't want any, do you, Charlie?"

"Nope. I'll go for my hide and tallow."

For the sheriff, the conversation was better than sitting alone and Walter could not see that it was going to go in his direction of its own momentum. He did not nor did any of the men he had ever seen know how to do a spontaneous kindness without looking foolish, yet he did not try to devise any oblique approach. Some inherited standard of behavior stirred him and he brought the matter out bluntly.

"Say, Charlie, I want to get a man out of jail."

The sheriff's face stiffened a trifle. One man less meant a smaller allowance for the food his wife gave the prisoners. He spat first and then said, "What for?"

"Turns out he's a friend of mine." That seemed a safe way to put it.

"There'll be people to see."

"Oh, hell, Charlie, I don't want to monkey around. I'll give you the money for the fine and costs and you fix it." Fearing that the offer might be interpreted as a devious attempt at bribery in some way, he went on quickly. "You see the judge or whoever it is."

"Hmm," the sheriff said. Walter discerned from his tone that he was willing to do it, that he thought it was a silly irregular proceeding but Walter did not recognize the sheriff's habitual deference to the Phelps name which had forced his consent although there was no longer any reason to defer to a Phelps.

"You see him every day. Just tell him. I'll pay."

"Damned if that ain't what your old man'd have done," the sheriff said laughing. He looked suspiciously down at Walter.

"I've got the money."

The sheriff grunted, rocked back on the hind legs of his chair, and let his feet down with a thud. "All right. Who is he? We only got three in there."

"I don't know his name."

"Friend of yours, hey? Well, what's he look like?"

"I don't know."

"Well, good God Almighty, how in . . ."

"He drinks Jamaica ginger."

"Oh, Benny Carson from up off the Boom, huh? What in hell you want to get him out for? He'll be right back in."

"I want to get him out."

"You got the cash? Fine was twenty-five dollars and seven-fifty costs." Walter discovered that Charlie Givens was aware that his father had died poor.

"Come on in while I get the keys."

The office was a little coop with a roll-top desk and a swivel chair in front of it. A wooden bench ran along one wall. There was a calendar over the desk with a naked girl on it. The sheriff reached into a desk drawer and took out a wire ring with some big keys on it.

"Thirty-two dollars and a half, was it?" Walter said, laying the money on the desk.

The sheriff fumbled with a pad of paper in his thick fingers. "Wait a minute and I'll give you a receipt."

"If I get the man, I don't need a receipt."

The sheriff did not answer. He bent over, sighing, and wrote out a receipt for the money and gave it to Walter. To be finical about his records was a sign that he was a competent public officer and he wanted Walter to see the sign.

He thrust a key into the lock of the door that opened into the cell block, a heavy screen of flat strap iron, made years before in Haynes's blacksmith shop. He opened it and bawled, "Benny! Hey, Benny!" He looked around at Walter. "Now you'll get a chance to see what your friend looks like."

There were cells only on one side of the corridor and it was a little dark. A serious-looking man of about thirty-five came walking out. He had dark hair and eyes and he was clean-shaven. His shirt and trousers did not look dirty. His shoes were old and the soles were loose.

"Yer a free man, Benny. He just paid your fine."

The man looked at Walter without any question on his face. The whites of his eyes were clear and his skin was a smooth dark tan. He did not look drunk or like a drunkard. He did not recognize Walter and as Walter had nothing to say, he said, "Much obliged" without smiling and walked out of the office and down the jail steps.

"God, he's hung-over," the sheriff said.

He did not look hung-over. He looked more like a plumber or an electrician who had finished repairing something inside the jail and was now going away again. He did not seem disposed to be friendly.

WALTER'S GRANDMOTHER had called him up on the telephone to tell him to come to dinner with her. He had promised submissively. He had not seen her in several months (she had reprimanded him severely for this).

Since the big Phelps house had been sold, she had moved into one very much like it as a paying guest, bringing with her only a few "sticks" of furniture and the two black japanned boxes crammed with prophecy. The town was full of spinsters, young and old, because most of the men went away when they were young to work in big cities. This Miss Baker, his grandmother's hostess, had dutifully served and outlived her parents and stayed on in her big brick house, a plump placid woman who kept a brindle tomcat and a maid to whom she always spoke sharply. As Walter walked down State Street under the arch of maple trees he looked scowling at the lace curtains of the houses he passed, certain that behind some of them, old women sat watching the street, ready to see him and comment later to a maid, a tomcat, or a sister, and he knew what they would say about Todd Phelps's son.

He pulled an old-fashioned enamel handle on the heavy paneled door and deep in the house he could hear the bell swinging back and forth, tinkling. Miss Baker's maid let him in and seated him in the parlor while she went upstairs to his grandmother's room. The parlor had a high ceiling and the windows ran from it to the floor but they were shrouded in lace curtains starched stiff as tin, overlaid with dusty peach-colored velvet drapes, and the maple trees grew so close to the house that the room was dark and dank. There were two gilt chairs and the sofa was cherrywood upholstered in black haircloth. He could remember a visit to this parlor when he was a little boy. Nothing had changed. Rubber plants seemed to live forever. It was not comfortable but it had all been expensive once. A clock set in a frame of greenish marble clotted with gold ornaments struck five with a hasty beat. Interrupting it, a tall grandfather's clock in the hall began its brassy strokes. Farther away in the house he could hear two others and at last they were all dominated by the massive bong-bong-bong of the town clock. His grandmother had set his visit at five. She wanted to talk to him.

The maid returned and said, "Mrs. Phelps wants you to come up."

He stood up.

"It's the third door on your right on the second floor."

He marched up a long staircase without making a sound on the thick carpet. The corridor was dark as night but he found the right door by feeling along the wall. He knocked, then opened it. At first he thought there was a man in her room. A loud orotund voice was speaking, but as soon as he moved around the door he saw a fine cabinet radio. His grandmother was seated in an armchair with her feet crossed on a bench that stood before her dressing table. She was listening intently with her cheek on one fist. She had not heard him come in. Probably the maid had put her ear to the door, heard the radio, and guessed that she was in. She certainly did not seem to expect him.

He stood still a moment looking at her. She had not aged. He had seen very little of her since the funeral and he expected her to show more lines or creases in her face or some pallor underlying them, a sign at least of what had happened to her, but he could not see a one. He started to walk toward her. The movement caught her eye. Without smiling, she pointed to a seat in the big chintz-covered chair opposite hers. He sat down with his hat on his knee and waited. She was staring a little to the right of him, her face quiet and her eyes half closed but shining. After a moment it was clear to him that she was not going to stop listening to the radio. He began to listen also. It was a soap opera.

The situation seemed to depend on whether a little boy, Robby, who spoke in a nasty shrill well-bred voice, would be able to recognize his father, Martin. He had just done a long stretch in the State Penitentiary for a crime that his wife, Lorna, a clear, rich, contralto, believed to her soul he had been wrongly convicted of. Grandma was present also, and Walter decided at once that Grandma's job was supplying minor complications in the plot, for hers was not the comfortable voice that suggests biscuits in the oven and snow beating around a warm house. Grandma was a bitch, "ailing," she said in a high cracked whine. She seemed to be certain for she said it again and again in different ingenious ways that little Robby would never recognize his Daddy. By a steady attrition she forced a sigh that whistled around the mike and a low-voiced tearful admission out of Lorna that Martin's hair had turned white, she knew, she couldn't deny it, why pretend? She had seen him every visiting day and Martin was gray as a badger and his face was "gant" and Robby had been such a little tyke when he was arrested. . . . A heavy knocking was followed by a piercing squeak and little Robby put Grandma's nose out of joint by screaming, "Daddy! Daddy! Dads!" The chill air of his grandmother's bedroom was filled with twitterings and throaty chucklings of joy, and a rich baritone soothed them all—Daddy was home again.

[193]

His own grandmother had relaxed, smiling, then she stiffened, waiting for the hook that would pull her back to the program the next day, the seed of catastrophe that would blossom tomorrow. It came. Old Grandma said, "Martin, where air you going to get the money to pay a lawyer to prove yer innocent—*if* you are." A pipe organ began a dreamy strain. His grandmother sighed and switched off the radio.

She remained quiet for a moment, her eyes shut, smiling in memory of her pleasure. Abruptly she sat upright, wide awake, put her feet on the floor and said in a brisk scolding tone, "Well, it's about time you came to see me. The idea! It's been three months since . . ."

"I know, Grandma," Walter interrupted. "Where'd you get the radio?"

She looked fondly at the cabinet. "They wanted a hundred and seventy-five dollars for it but I beat them down to a hundred and seventy." She turned her bright piercing gaze at him. "My tool-and-die stock paid a dividend, of all things. And I was thinking what I could buy myself as a consolation."

"Consolation? For what?"

Slurring it over as if it were the least interesting part of what she had to say, she said, "For your father's death. I couldn't think and I *couldn't* think what to buy and all of a sudden it came over me, 'Why don't you buy your own radio? Then you won't have to go traipsing up and down stairs forty times a day.' And I wouldn't have to be fighting with Eula Baker all the time. She hasn't lifted a skillet in twenty-five years and all she wants to listen to are the recipes and the home-making programs. So I bought this one—they said it was solid walnut but as soon as I got it home, I took my nail scissors and pried up one of the corners. Just as I thought, veneer."

"Is the food good here?"

"When Eula stays out of the kitchen, it is. Now you take today, Eula's up in Lansing for the D.A.R. convention." She lowered her voice and spoke more rapidly to show that gossip was coming. "You know she only made the D.A.R. twelve years ago. She couldn't find that ancestor. It was somewhere in Maryland, no, Delaware, and she hired a genealogist and she even went down there and hung onto his coattails while he hunted through the records and at last they found the proof. Now she's county historian and covered with mosquito bites."

"Why? Does she . . ."

"She's taken the dates off every headstone in Hamilton County, Clinton, Tecumseh, Bean Creek, Raisin Valley, and even those little cemeteries you see on a hill out in the country. They're just alive with mosquitoes. What's that stuff?"

He followed her thought nimbly. "Citronella?"

She nodded. "Lotion. Covered with it all the time. All she went up to Lansing for was to snoop around and see if somebody wouldn't mention her for High Grand Muckymuck or whatever they call it." She paused and looked out of the window vaguely, drawing her brows into a faint scowl. She sighed once or twice and stared at Walter blankly as if she didn't quite know him. Then she smiled quickly. Memory had occurred. "I pay twelve dollars a week here. The food ought to be good, don't you think?"

"Twelve a week isn't so much nowadays."

"Your grandfather paid two," she said scornfully. "And they did his washing. I have to send mine out."

Walter grinned. "That was back when eggs were three cents a dozen and the butcher gave you calves' liver free for the cat, wasn't it?"

She did not acknowledge that she had heard anything. "Twelve a week's scandalous." Doing with an abstract air one of the things that are rude to a guest but profoundly convinced that the rudeness will pass unnoticed because it is done openly and without embarrassment, she turned on the radio again. A blare of band music shook the machine. She winced sourly and turned it off. "I forgot that one comes on at this time."

As he watched and listened, Walter was glad he had come. Her chatter made him, as it always did, friends with his past, and, since he was so clearly a part, even an embodiment of it, her vitality renewed his pride in his family. It did not occur to him that he had few ties with Eula Baker or her Revolutionary ancestor, or few with his grandmother. He could never be wholly frank with her unless he was angry. Yet, to sit with her in this cold sunlit room made it seem as if nothing had changed for him, even though the room was in a different house and the radio was new.

He was dimly pleased somehow, although he did not try his thoughts on it, to see that she had "failed" a little. The past year had made some changes. She had never lost the thread of a conversation before and it was incredible that she could give her serious attention to the banalities of the radio soap operas. Physically she did not seem to alter. As he had done ever since he first heard of such a thing as hair-dye, he cocked his head to see if the late sunlight shining on her hair revealed any of the oily off-tints that would prove she was touching it up, but her hair was still a miraculous smooth black. It seemed out of the question to think it would ever go gray. In his mind there was a weak half-noticed wish, a mere quick velleity, that it would. Propriety demanded it. Why, now, she should grow old, get white hair, collapse into senility, he did not ask himself. Instead, he said to tease her, "Do you want me to go now, Grandma?"

"Go?" she said, jerking herself upright. "Go? Why? You just came. Eri's coming."

He threw up his head and immediately let it sink again to hide his alertness. "He is?" he said politely.

"Yes. I thought I'd have you both over for dinner. We don't get together often enough. You're all I've got left, you know," she said, smoothing the skirt over her knee, watching her hands smooth it.

They were going to get after him about something. To appeal to him as one of the remaining kin to huddle near her as if to receive her love or to assuage her loneliness was preposterously sentimental in his grandmother. It was almost a symptom of decay that she could find it in herself to make such a plea. She was a tough old girl and it was hard for her not to be candid. Very likely Eri had told her not to say anything until he arrived, and she with her love of plotting had concurred. She would be candid enough later when she had Eri by her side.

As if it were a shadow his uncle cast before him, a picture of Eri grew in Walter's mind, not a snapshot with the details unemphasized, a blank face merely lighted, but a portrait with all the features given their meaning. Take the haircut (his hair was the color of Walter's, a dark chestnut, but on Eri, graying). He could tell by looking at him that he made the barber cut the sides as short as he could without using the clippers. Only farmers let them clip the sides. He was careful because of women. Like an old second baseman, arm tired, legs giving out, who turns up one last time for spring training, Eri did not want them to spot the gray. The pomade was for the women also; they liked a man neat. He would not be wearing his glasses. They would be deep in an inside pocket, safe in one of those leather-covered metal cases that snap shut, and Eri would frown at him, trying to strip away the aura of astigmatic fuzz that clung to him, because women liked a young man with all his faculties, and Eri used his glasses only when he signed things or drove alone at night. College boys wore shirts with buttoned-down collars; so did Eri. Although he would exhale the mist from the day's first drink, he would be plump and clear-eyed. This was his afternoon nap—to refresh him for the evening's woman. He would not have a potbelly, for, although he ate well, he exercised with spring dumbbells and a rowing machine. He did not want to look funny with his clothes off.

[196]

His face would show, as it always did, pride, severity, contempt, chiefly in the muscles around his mouth, and this expression was not a bait for women. It was, like his dark suits and the brown shoes he made his houseman wear until they assumed a proper modest color, a statement that his life was important and the manner of his living it was nobody's damned business. It was the way his face looked all the time (unless he was too drunk and even then some muscular automatism usually conserved it). This complacent steadiness of mien masked a covert paradoxical self-gratulation on his idleness and a latent determination to maintain it. Eri was intelligent enough to perceive deliberate waste but it would be only an amusement privately enjoyed for him to dream of the great things he could do if he would. Actually he was careful never to lift a finger because he wished to be the one man in the town who defied its values by drinking, lechery, and waste of time. It made him feel important to be the only one who dared, who had persisted for so long a time. Others cracked up, took cures, lost money, and, in the end, reformed or died. Not he. He had the stamina for waste. He could touch pitch and keep his linen clean. Except for his youthful collars, he dressed, moved, and frowned like a judge and it was all a ruse to invite criticism so he could scorn it.

His grandmother had been surreptitiously spinning the locator button of the radio, getting abrupt squawks of music and voices. *"Jed's Mother-in-Law* don't come on for ten minutes yet," she said as if to herself. She turned to him and said in a voice like a pounce, "What about that Wickham girl?"

"What about her?" he said.

"You've been dragging your wings around her."

"Are you having me tailed, Grandma?"

"Tailed? What's that?"

"Have you hired a detective to follow me around and . . ."

"Don't be a fool. You have, though, haven't you?" she said with childish triumph in her voice.

"I've seen her a few times, yes."

"What are you up to?" she asked sternly. "Are you going to marry her? Foolish question. You don't want to get married now, do you?"

"No."

She was sitting on the edge of her chair, her fists on her knees. "She pretty?" She stood up and began to pace the floor, grinding her beads in one hand, bright, angry, and familiar. "Oh, you're such a fool. Hanging around here going to seed." She stopped, glaring at him. "I wish I was a young fellow like you. I'd show you a thing or two."

"Well, you're not," he said bluntly.

She glanced over her shoulder with a look almost of terror. "No. No, I'm not." She sat down heavily. "I'm an old woman and I want to boss you around, you and everybody else, because . . ." She paused and giggled. She said in a warm intimate voice, "You know, I nearly talked myself into a fright. When you get's old's I am, you think there's somebody behind you saying, 'Hurry!' and I know who 'tis." She reached out and turned the radio button unthinkingly. A soprano shriek made her jump and she flipped it off. Her face changed. She was solemn. "It's death, that's what."

Walter burst out laughing.

His uncle Eri entered the room. "What's so funny?" he said. He laid a straw sailor hat on the bed and began to mop his face with a handkerchief.

"Oh, here you are," Mrs. Phelps said brightly. "Walter was just making fun of me." She smiled at Walter, obviously expecting some humorous explanation.

Walter said nothing. It was the time to watch and be silent. They were going to try to make him do something important or Eri would not have been there at all. There was a pause.

Eri put his handkerchief back in his breast pocket and sat down in an old bar rocker, leaning backward with his legs crossed. "How's the insurance business, Walter?" he said.

"I'm not selling it any more."

"Somebody—I can't recall who it was—said you called on him and he was ready to take out a little more and you talked him out of it," Eri said in an even colorless voice as if what he was saying had no importance whatever.

"You bought a car," his grandmother accused him.

"Why, yes. My tool-and-die stock started paying off the same as yours," Walter said. He wondered why these inquisitions had to be conducted civilly. It was more of a strain.

His grandmother caught her son's eye, and she edged forward until she was sitting on the edge of her chair again. She put her chin on her hand and watched as intensely as if there were a surgical operation going on before her.

"I didn't know Todd left you any stock," Eri said, pretending that the information had been welcome.

"Some," Walter said.

"So *that's* why he quit work, Eri. Just as soon's the stock paid a dividend, he quit his job," his grandmother said. The piece had fitted into the puzzle.

"I don't like to intrude into your affairs, Walter, but I wonder if you would tell us your plans," Eri said, looking at his nephew for the first time. He smiled.

"Why?" Walter said.

"We're the only relations you've got left. We have your best interests at heart. Why wouldn't we? Maybe we can help you," she said, throwing out her hand.

"How?" Walter asked.

"I don't think there are any grounds for the intense suspicion you seem to be harboring," Eri said. He smiled again. It was a little longer than a flicker.

"When Grandma said you were coming to dinner too, I knew right away the two of you were going to try to make me do something. What is it? Stop the charm, Eri, and you quit pretending, Grandma. Come clean. What do you want me to do?"

He saw his grandmother put her hand over her mouth to hide a snicker. Eri glanced up at her in annoyance. "Todd," she said. "You even look like him." She scowled, doubled up her fist, and brandished it. " 'Come clean. What do you want me to do?' Just exactly what Todd would have said. Isn't that right, Eri?"

Eri looked at her coldly. She made a sheepish face and pretended to cower back in her chair. "You're a young man, Walter. You had a chance at an excellent education, and, to do you justice, you made the most of it. I always thought Phi Betes were grinds but I think you could have made it if you had applied yourself, not that I think you should have gone quite that far, as I say, but the capability was there."

"Why, thank you very much, Uncle Eri," Walter said, looking straight at him.

"Your grandmother and I were thinking that it might be wise if you took some thought for your career. It's true you won't have the financial backing you were led to expect but that is because of circumstances over which you have no control. However . . ."

"Are you a member of the Rotary Club, Eri?" Walter asked.

". . . you are young. Your health is good. *And* you have a certain income."

"What do you want me to do, both of you? Name it. Quit this monkeying around. Do you want me to get a paying job or what? And if you do, why?"

[199]

They were three idle people. It was very funny that they should sit here arguing with such cold fierceness in the dusk of a summer's day, two of them trying, so far as he could tell, to prod him out of the soft condition they lived in so comfortably. Age excused his grandmother, although, to do *her* justice, she would have worked if there had been any job she knew how to do. If Eri were to be condoned at all, it would have to be on his own strange moral grounds, his gloomy persistent defiance of civic piety in a community that did not know what he was doing and would not care if it did. None of them produced anything. (This was Marx, remembered from Economics 51.) He supposed they were therefore theoretically useless, certainly useless in Russia. There they would be buried by soldiers in long overcoats on some vast steppe, but this was Hamilton County; chicken was frying downstairs—he could smell it; the two of them would argue, fail, and presently they would all go down to dinner. He did not think of his own idleness or why he had prolonged it so far.

Eri was answering his question with a spate of florid clichés, ". . . undeniable that your father was not in the best of odors immediately following his death, so you can hardly be blamed. You were bearing the brunt of your father's deficiencies. However that may be, the fact remains that any career worthy of your efforts in this town is not open to you. Now it is not as if it were still necessary for you to remain here to keep up the estate. . . ."

His grandmother jumped up. "Oh, Eri, keep *still*. You jaw and jaw and you don't say anything." Eri sat back in the rocking chair, his plump face bland and composed. To emphasize his withdrawal he took a cigarette from a silver case. "We think you ought to get out of town. Eri thinks you ought to get a *job* out of town, Lord knows why, he never did a tap in his life. . . ."

"The discipline. Work is discipline," Eri murmured through a little cloud of smoke. Walter stared at him in admiration. Eri was impregnable. Nothing could touch him.

". . . and I just want to see you go. I've told you before. I don't care if you get a job or not. Only *go*. You've only got one life. Look at Todd, killed in his prime. You may break your neck on my front steps tonight— and you will, too, if Eula don't get them fixed." She was striding irritably around in the little enclosure made by their chairs. "There's more to you than you've ever used before and you'll never get a chance to use it here. I don't care what you do. Just get out of this rut. Go anywhere. . . ."

"China, Grandma?" Walter said.

She leaned over, putting her hands on the arms of his chair. He could smell the lozenges she used to sweeten her breath. He was startled to see a twinge of real anguish wring her face. "Don't sneer at me. Please don't sneer. There hasn't been anything for a man to do in this town since your grandfather's time except to repeat himself like a clock. Just pile up money. If you went somewhere else, you could . . ."—she was running down—". . . do big things. There are things to do, adventures. There must be things you could do. . . ." What were they? Her eyes held a look of panic. Had she been prey to rumors? Was this poor town a sample of it all? She had traveled very little; the terrible "perhaps" stifled her. She straightened up and walked slowly back to her chair and sat down.

For a second or two Walter shared the elixir of his grandmother's enthusiasm. If there were a plot to send him away, hers was a part she could play sincerely. He could travel; he had enough money. He wanted to walk down Prince's Street, admire the graceful heels and elbows of the little dancers of Pnom-Penh, eat at Foyot's, and be accosted by a beautiful Eurasian in the Bubbling Well Road. All these were possible, but later. He was reserving them as a housewife saves her "good" silver for a great occasion. There was plenty of time just as there was plenty of time for him to begin a good and noble life, for he had never doubted that germs of goodness and nobility lay within him. He would place his talents at the disposal of humanity or the nation (not the town; it was too small) at any time it pleased him to make the exertion. When he had read of such men as Raleigh, Lee, Roger Williams, or Father Damien, he had felt an instant kinship—they had done exactly as he would have done, would do but later. He was "officially," so to speak, a good man. How else could he recognize weakness and flabbiness, stupidity in others? But at the moment his affairs were entangled somehow. Some things (what things?) needed clarifying and he could not very well go on to this splendid career until he was ready.

Eri was relaxed, occasionally blowing a long plume of smoke out of his mouth. He did not believe anything his mother had said. She was an old lady well into her declining years, and he could not permit himself to be offended by remarks that were little more than the maunderings of senility. He was wiser than she if only because he was still so robust, so young. All this loose talk about gigantic, romantic, distant deeds was claptrap. For he knew, oh, he knew the dainty, the minute ecstasies of repetition. His house was quiet; his clothes were sober; his days seemed like one another, but at night, in the quiet, in the darkness, he knew how sumptuously each delicate titillation could be varied, and what to do if they smiled, blandishments for the proud, and if they cried, whether to turn them out or gently to console them. This knowledge was valuable because it was so intricate and so hardly come by, but his mother and Todd's big lout could scarcely be expected to see that and he certainly did not propose to explain it to them. "I agree with your grandmother," he said.

"If I don't go, what?" Walter said.

"I think you'll regret it," Eri said.

"Of course he'll regret it," his grandmother said.

"You'll see that I do, is that it?"

Eri smiled suavely. "Hardly. How could we . . ."

At the foot of the stairs a brass Chinese dinner gong was beaten harshly. The fried chicken was done.

Out of its echoes came Eri's quiet voice, "For your own good, and with that thought in mind, we decided to ask you to come and . . ."

"I'm going to stay right here in town," Walter said.

Eri rose and settled his tie between a thumb and forefinger. He was seriously angry.

Walter was surprised to see tears running down his grandmother's face. Perhaps the occasion had meant more to her than he had surmised. He stood aside and she passed out of the room dabbing at her eyes with a handkerchief. Eri preceded him.

The long dark chute of the stairs was before him. Going primly down behind his agitated kinfolk, he asked himself why he couldn't go? What was keeping him? Black against the darkness, he could see his grandmother's coiffure dipping and rising as she blew her nose and wiped her eyes. Eri had urged him to go merely because he could not bear a rival, but she had been honest. At least she was not trying to get rid of him for reasons of her own. She was thinking of him, quite possibly with some odd affection. He could accept this but he could not return it. Some faint dislike or resentment prevented him. With a start that made him almost miss a step, he perceived that he was requiting her for an insult to his father. When he had first arrived, she had said something disparaging, he could not recall just what, but the anger with which he heard it had remained, a foolish anger, but it was real. That was why he had been vaguely pleased to see that she had "failed."

As the hallway, paved with big squares of black and white tile, spread itself out before him after the narrow stricture of the stairs, he recognized that he was staying, idle, in the town because he was doing something for his father. His father was dead, and, he faced it easily, rotten. What could now be done for him? Why should his own idle figure be a suitable memorial? It was idiotic. He did not believe in ghosts, but, with a prickling in his spine, he admitted there had been some purpose? command? that was only now obtruding and he had been obeying it faithfully since the death. His idleness was filial, and, as the brightness of the dining room burst upon his eyes, he knew that idleness was not going to be enough.

⌒ PART FIVE ⌒

· XVIII ·

ONCE A MONTH the patients went to the clinic of the sanitarium to be given reports on their X-rays and brief examinations. As they left they took a bottle with a rubber and enamel stopper with them which was to be filled and returned the next day for urinalysis. Nearly everyone was nervous until he had gotten his report, and afterward the unlucky ones were often in despair. Eddie had seen women crying over luncheon, eating steadily—they did not dare not to—but with tears streaming down their faces.

Eddie and a young man named George Brice had been through the clinic the first thing after breakfast and they were standing on the porch of their cottage talking and looking off at the mountains. Eddie's first report had been good, and he had discussed it from every angle. Brice's had read, "No change." This was regarded as a good report also. Anything was good that showed no decline. Brice was heavy, tall, smooth-fleshed. He weighed two hundred and ten pounds. He had been playing tackle for Fordham the fall before and somebody had thrown a block on him in the third game. He had coughed as he stood up and one of his team-mates had pointed at the ground. He had coughed up about a pint of blood. He had refused to leave the game, and when the coach had forced him to go to a doctor and the doctor had told him he had tuberculosis, he said, "Well, I'll just finish the season before I go to bed." This was not courage and it had nothing to do with loyalty to the old team. Brice was having a very good time and he hated to stop as long as he did not feel ill. Brice always had a very good time. He had bought half a dozen chocolate bars on his way up from the clinic and he was eating his second one, talking with his mouth full. Eddie liked him because he did not take his condition seriously. He regarded the sanitarium as a resort hotel, and after he had come to know Brice, this attitude cheered Eddie a great deal because his first acquaintances had speculated about the nature of death all day long, and one of them had actually died.

"Here comes Harold. High-tailing it up here to write his mother," Brice said.

The walking pace set by the staff was two and a half miles an hour and Harold Breadon was hurrying up the path to the cottage as fast as he could within that limit.

"Look what they gave him to piss in," Brice said. Breadon was carrying a big brown bottle about eighteen inches high, the kind seen on druggists' shelves. "Hi, Harold," Brice called in a fake warm friendly voice. "How'd you come out?"

"They said there was definite improvement. They could see it very plainly and Forman changed the prognosis. He said only two more months, maybe," Breadon said. He was flushed with excitement at the good news.

"Uh-huh. 'Maybe.' " Brice said cynically. Then, the old friend, the kind avuncular tone, "Care for some chocolate, Harold? Full of calories and you know what calories mean. Glorious health."

"Why, thanks, George." Breadon took a chocolate bar and unwrapped it.

"These got nuts in 'em," Brice said. "Say, where'd you get the big brown bottle, Harold?"

"Clinic. Why?"

"You got yours, Eddie?"

Eddie lifted his, clear glass with the enamel stopper, holding about a pint. Brice held up one like it.

"Hmm, that's curious, Harold. Very strange," Brice said judicially. "You don't know why they gave you the brown one, huh?"

"Why, no. They just told me to take it."

"Uh-*huh*. Just told you to take it, eh?" In a different voice, less ominous, eager for information, bright and again friendly, Brice said, "Say, Harold, how old a woman is your mother? I remember her so well from her last visit. Your mother's a fine woman, Harold, and you're one lucky guy to have a mother like her. I'd place her right around forty, forty-one years old."

Eddie watched Brice, expecting him to wink or make some sign as he gave out this nonsensical pious chatter, but Brice stood with one foot on the porch rail, munching chocolate, red hair, fat face, and his eyes on Breadon.

Breadon almost colored with pleasure. "Oh, you've got her 'way too young, George. I'll admit she doesn't look her age but she was fifty-two last March."

Brice raised both arms in a massive gesture of surprise. "Fifty-two!" He turned to Eddie. "Would you believe it? Fifty-two years old? That little woman? Eddie, you can't believe it."

"I've never seen her," Eddie said.

"That's right. She was here before you came, but I swear I've never seen a younger-looking woman. You're her sole support, aren't you, Harold? Only child?"

Baffled by the extravagant praise of his mother, Breadon seemed relieved that it was going to lead to something else although he obviously did not know what. "Yes. I'm all she's got."

"And it must be *very* hard on her, you getting TB this way. It's terrible." Brice shook his head because it was so terrible. In a dead colorless voice, he said, "Want some more chocolate, Harold? Go ahead. I got lots." He held out another chocolate bar.

"Oh, I don't want to eat up all your candy, George," Breadon said.

"Shucks, I'm rich. When this is gone, I'll just buy more. I can't let it alone. You know that. Go ahead. Take it."

"Well, if you insist," Breadon said. "I think I'll sit down." He sat down in one of the porch chairs, crossed his legs, and undid the candy wrapper.

"Never stand when you can sit. Never sit when you can lie down," Brice quoted from a staff lecture. "Good old Harold. Ha! Ha!" The laugh was so deliberate and bogus that even Harold glanced up through his spectacles, but Brice went on at once, "Good chocolate, ain't it, Harold?"

"I'll say."

"What's your mother doing now that you're not there to support her? Living with relatives?"

The smile lifted the whole of Harold's long weak face. "I *am* supporting her."

"Hell, you can't keep books here."

"No, but you see, here's how it is. I've been bookkeeper at the coal company four years the eleventh of next month. I was assistant for a year before that and I wasn't absent or tardy any of the time, so when I notified Mr. Gillingwater I was sick, he said my paycheck would continue right through the course of my illness so that's what Mamma's living on."

"Why, say, Harold, that's fine. Old Gillingwater must be a pretty shrewd judge of human nature, yes, sir, a pretty shrewd ... I suppose you carry quite a lot of insurance?"

"Say, what is all this, George?"

Brice began to walk up and down, chewing and sucking. He stopped short and threw out his hand abruptly. "See there? You finished all that chocolate bar."

"I don't follow you. What's the chocolate bar got to do ..."

Jerking his head and showing his teeth, Brice shouted, "You like chocolate bars, doncha? Eat 'em all the time, doncha?" He softened, stood erect, and spoke quietly, almost endearingly, "You're fond of sweet things, aren't you, Harold? Like candy, chewing gum, lots of sugar on the cereal, two spoons in the coffee. Isn't that right?"

Harold acted as if he had only now discovered how wrong this was. "Yes. I guess I've got a sweet tooth," he said guiltily.

"Of course you have. Of *course* you have. That's why I was asking about your insurance."

"But what's a sweet tooth got to do with life insurance?"

"I was just thinking of your mother, pal."

Harold stood up. "Look. You tell me what you're talking about, George Brice."

Offhand, Brice said over his shoulder, "They didn't tell you up there, huh?"

"Up where?"

"Clinic," he said, licking his fingers one by one.

"What do you mean? Forman said my X-ray was good. He said I was a lot better. I gained three pounds this month. I ...."

Brice looked at the floor, tritely pulling his lower lip, held up his hand three inches in front of Harold's face to silence him. Brice glanced swiftly at Eddie and back again. "Eddie, I think this is the best way, don't you? Give me your frank opinion. We both want to do what's best for old Harold, don't we?"

"I guess so," Eddie said. All he was doing was waiting for Brice finally to pull the joke.

Brice nodded in gratitude. He had folded his arms and was stroking his chin, holding one elbow in the other palm. He looked up sharply at Harold. "They didn't tell you what that big brown bottle's for, huh?"

"This?" Harold bent down and picked up the bottle they had given him at the clinic.

Brice shut his eyes and nodded.

"It's for urinalysis, isn't it? They just gave it to me. I thought that was what it was for."

Brice shut his eyes again and shook his head. He sighed, took a step forward, and put his arm around Harold's shoulders. "This is where it's tough, boy. This is the clutch. You've got to face it squarely and I know you will." He patted Harold's shoulder. He went on sadly, "You're playing both ends against the middle now."

"How? What do you mean? Good God, George, say it right out. Don't beat around the bush this way."

"Cursing won't help, Harold. Courage will." He patted Harold's shoulder and stepped back away from him. "They give out those big brown bottles when they think you've got sugar diabetes."

The tension in Harold's face vanished and he looked as if he were going to cry. "Oh, no," he said.

Brice pursed his lips and wagged his chin up and down solemnly. "They want a big sample, see?"

As if Brice could heal him, Harold began to talk rapidly and anxiously, "But George, I feel fine. Honest, I do. I'm feeling better every day. I haven't noticed any more trouble. I . . . ."

"You don't notice sugar but it's there just the same," Brice said coldly. Then he smiled, moving his head cheerily as he spoke. "I'm sorry, Harold. I hated to tell you but sometimes a fellow's got to take the responsibility and I had to take mine. That's the reason I spoke about your mother. I know how much you value her. I know how much you love her. It's not easy to take that long subway ride at the close of day and eat and help Mother with the dishes and put on that green eyeshade and plug away at those correspondence-school courses, but you did it. You did it for her. You wanted to be an executive *but* you were smart. A little bit of each week's pay went into the insurance, didn't it? So now your mother won't have to worry. Uh, how much were you carrying, son?"

Perhaps Brice had overdone it because Harold stiffened suddenly and said, very loudly for him, "I don't believe it. I don't believe a damn word of it."

"Oh, yuh don't, eh?" Brice roared. He snatched his own bottle off the railing and held it out. "Have I got a bottle like that? Has Eddie got a bottle like that? *No,* you God-damn jughead. *You've* got the big brown bottle." He walked away disgustedly, muttering, "Don't believe a word of it, huh? Try to do a guy a favor and see what happens." He reached the end of the porch and turned, watching Harold standing foolishly with the bottle dangling from his hand. "I suppose you want *them* to tell you, huh?"

Harold sat down hard with the bottle between his feet. He did not answer for a moment. He tried to spit through the neck of the bottle. At last he said, "No. I believe you."

"Don't take it so hard, boy. It may not be fatal."

Harold had looked up and was staring out at the mountains across the valley. He did not seem to hear Brice speaking at all. "I was valedictorian of my class at Stuyvesant," he said as if he could hardly believe it any longer. He jumped up, knocking over the bottle, ran off the porch and down the path. Before he had got down the steps Eddie and Brice saw the tears running down his face.

Brice began to giggle. "He's gone to call her on the phone. She'll be up here tonight." He laughed, rocking back and forth, shouting "Ho! Ho! Ho!" until it echoed through the trees. Eddie laughed with him briefly.

"None of that stuff was true, was it?" Eddie asked.

"Christ, no," Brice said, choking and shaking his head. "They—they just ran out of little bottles, that's all."

Eddie ran down the path after Breadon. He found him in the telephone booth at the post office, shouting at the New York operator. Eddie pulled him away from the phone and told him it was a joke.

"He was just having some fun. You know Brice," he said.

"That's a terrible thing to do. That's a terrible thing to do. You're sure he's lying?"

"I told you."

"What a terrible thing to do!" The return of Breadon's pride, now that he had been permitted to continue to live, made him tremble. He stared blindly out of the door of the post office, rubbing one arm up and down, and shivering.

Eddie watched him briefly. Now that Breadon was safe he was no longer pathetic and Eddie had never been friendly with him. He went out of the post office and climbed the path to his cottage.

Eddie went up the stairs to the second floor and down the corridor to his dressing room. He took off his clothes and got into a pair of flannel pajamas. He pulled on a blue woolen sweater. From the top of his bureau he took a novel in one hand and balanced a pack of cigarettes on an ashtray in the other. He kicked open the door to the porch, tossed the book onto the high white iron bed, and got in. He opened the book.

Immediately the door opened on the other side of the porch. Kopfers, his porch-mate, came out and began to pace up and down the space between their beds, swinging his head on the turns like a caged animal. He was a lean, sallow man, a Swiss, he always said, who had a nose like a meat-chopper. By profession he was a "mechanical dentist" and in his room he kept a little table that was littered with chunks of red rubber, plastic, instruments, odd staring teeth, and a spirit lamp. He had cured at Davos first. The Swiss doctors had done a phrenicectomy for one lung and he had been given a pneumothorax here and he was supposed to rest a great deal but he could not because he had something wrong with his thyroid that would not let him. He ate twice as much as any of the other patients—Eddie had seen him pour the whole serving dish of boiled potatoes on his plate in a heap—and he seldom came out on the porch except for a change of path. He was excitable. The other men in the cottage knew it and they treated him soothingly on all serious matters except when they were bored and wanted to tease him into a display of anger.

He had made three or four circuits of his little space without taking any notice of Eddie when he stopped with a stamp of his foot. "I heard him. I heard him," he said accusingly.

Eddie shut the book and looked around impatiently. He was tired of Kopfers as a porch-mate. He knew by heart which boards creaked under Kopfers' foot. On cool nights Kopfers stuck his head in a woolen stocking cap and put himself into a pair of outsize pajamas, tied the legs around his ankles, and patiently stuffed the legs full of wadded newspaper instead of spending twelve dollars for an electric blanket. All night the paper would rattle loudly every time he moved. They said Kopfers was well off, too. "Heard who?" he said. "Brice?"

Kopfers was off again, wagging his head in satisfaction. "I shall report him this time. He is unfit for the company of decent people. He is heartless and he is too loud about it. Heartlessness I can endure but that loudmouth . . ." He spat on the porch.

"Hey, cut that out, Kopfers. They give you a paper bag for that," Eddie said.

"Ah, these diseases!" Kopfers flung up his hands in disgust. "I have had trouble with Brice before. You had not yet arrived. It was at the beginning of the summer."

Eddie picked up the book and tried to find his place again. Kopfers suffered under injustices all the time and Eddie excused his own rudeness by thinking that it was the thyroid that always made him want to talk too much about them.

Kopfers was not deterred. "I reported him to Forman. That was a mistake. Forman is a mere physician. He has no power. I should have gone to the Head where the power resides. Strieder laughed at me. He is a friend of Brice's." Kopfers surprisingly sat down on the side of Eddie's bed. "Burcham!"

"What?" Eddie said without looking up.

"Do you know what I did then? Do you know what I did?"

"What?"

"I called him out."

Eddie heard the archaic phrase, one that he would not have thought Kopfers knew. He looked up. "You what?"

"I called him out."

"You mean you challenged him to a duel? What for?"

"It was an insult. *Lieber Gott,* you can understand that, can't you? He insulted me. My honor demanded satisfaction." He went on in a loud voice, striding up and down again, but Eddie did not hear him. He was thinking of the big white-pillared houses of the Mississippi Delta and how, in books, it was always handsome young men in white ruffled shirts who came out with such wonderful polished phrases about their honor. It seemed strange and somehow regrettable that probably his only chance in life to hear them said should come in a TB sanitarium and that this jumping-jack Kopfers should be the author. He had not suspected Kopfers of honor.

"What did he do to you?"

"He insulted me, I told you. My home and my profession." Although he was in full stride across the porch, Kopfers threw out his chest.

"But what did he say?"

Sullenly, Kopfers said, slowing down his steps, "It is not necessary to repeat it. I have two Luger pistols I bought once in Mannheim. I could find no one in this pigsty to act for me so I presented myself to him with the pistols, loaded, and I told him to come with me up the mountain and we would shoot it out."

Eddie suppressed a smile as he thought of Kopfers "presenting himself" to George Brice with the long strands of curly hair hanging in his wild eyes as they were now. "What did George say?"

Kopfers whirled around. "Oh, you call him George, eh?"

"Look, Kopfers. I like him. I think he's all right. What did he say?"

Kopfers shrugged hopelessly and looked down at his hands. "Oh, he insulted me again. I went to strike him and he caught my arm." Kopfers stopped as if he were exhausted, staggered backward until he felt his thighs strike the edge of his own bed, and sat down heavily. He seemed depressed and he spoke quietly. The lids of his eyes relaxed from their usual stare and because he now seemed normal, Eddie, watching him, realized that he had always believed Kopfers to be almost insane. Kopfers sighed and went on in a low earnest voice. "He picked me up in his arms like a baby although the lifting of heavy weights is expressly forbidden in pulmonary tuberculosis. I could not even struggle. He carried me upstairs here and laid me down on my bed and kissed me. Then he laughed."

Somehow this caper of Brice's made Eddie feel wretched.

"You have heard him laugh. You heard him today." Kopfers was silent a moment and licked his lips. "That poor Breadon." He stood up and went into his dressing room. He came out again at once. His long hair was parted in the middle and he was brushing it vigorously away from the part with a pair of military brushes. He always gave twenty-five of the double strokes and Eddie counted silently with him. He finished, and with a brush in each hand, he said, "I shall now go report George Brice to the Head of the sanitarium and demand his expulsion." He clapped the brushes together and went into his room. In a moment Eddie saw him go down the path. As a sign of the importance of his mission, he had put on a gray Homburg hat.

Kopfers was funny. The intention, the hat, the long steps made with the turned-out feet were all funny, and, as he picked up the book, Eddie expected to laugh or at least to chuckle. By all the gauges of his past, in all former situations, Kopfers would be comic, but here, now, he found himself remembering what Kopfers said. He did not wish to remain, or rather he was not, whether he wished it or not, remaining a spectator to the manner of Kopfers' actions. The humor had leaked away.

Through the trees he saw the long suave outline of the mountain against the sky. The mountain always irritated him. It was so calm, and, watching the changing of its shadows, he felt an obligation to think. No one likes to be obliged to think when no problem quivering for solution demands it.

As he lay staring out from his porch, with his finger holding the place in his book, he admitted shamefacedly that there was a problem or some shadowy question to answer of a kind he had formerly avoided, and if he screwed his attention tightly to the book, the problem would go away. He opened the book and began to read again.

He was startled to hear the click of a door-latch and Kopfers walked slowly out on the porch. He could not have had time to make his complaint to the Head. He had come back for some reason. Eddie looked up and saw him gloomy and lugubrious in a cheap brown tweed suit with the coat tightly buttoned, the trousers baggy, and the Homburg set straight

[213]

on his head. He was standing there watching Eddie, evidently trying to make up his mind to speak.

"What did he say?" Eddie asked.

"Nothing. I have not seen him." He paused, reached up with both hands and took off his hat. He had jammed it on so hard that the sweatband had left a reddish weal across his forehead. He was holding the hat flat against his chest. It was an attitude of supplication although Eddie was sure he did not mean it to be. "I have come to ask you to go with me," Kopfers said.

"Me? What for?"

"To ask for Brice's dismissal."

"I haven't got anything against Brice. I told you."

Kopfers looked down at the hat. "Come anyway."

"But why?"

"If I go alone, they will laugh at me," he said, looking up defiantly.

"No, they won't."

Soiled by the laughter of others, Kopfers looked at Eddie, a smooth face, large, soft eyes with the great comic blade of nose between them. "Yes. They will." And Eddie knew it was true. Although he would never laugh at Kopfers again, others would until he had demeaned himself before them. "They will laugh, I promise you. Come. Get up. Put on your clothes," he said with his usual energy. He came toward the bed to pull down the covers.

Eddie jerked them up taut and said, "Lay off, Kopfers."

"You are a friend of Brice's," he accused.

"He hasn't done anything to me and I'm not going to help you get him bounced."

"You're a fool, a fool, a fool," Kopfers shouted furiously. He threw the hat to the floor and stalked into his dressing room. Eddie heard the whirring of a little lathe that Kopfers had bolted to his table. He turned it with a foot treadle. Kopfers was consuming the injustice by working on a plate of false teeth. A breeze rolled the gray hat around the floor a little but Eddie let it lie.

He reached for his book once more. In it like gifts were compressed Italy, love, and war. In fact, the book contained life, which he would, as soon as his X-rays permitted, get up and begin to live. This time positively; no more putting off; no delay. Gradually, but he did not yet know by what light, it grew clear to him that what had occupied his time, that long string of days begun in the obscurities of childhood, had been a habit he had acquired for no reason that he knew. He had worn black stockings as a boy because his mother had put them on him and she had put them on him because she saw other boys wearing them. He had gone to church first because he was taken, and then for a while until the inertia wore off because other people did. And looking back, forgetting the fury of his anticipations and how many of them had been fulfilled, he seemed to have learned nothing in college. He had accepted everything with a prodigious meekness, performed the obvious, and he had done it partly because you are like that if you come from a small town but more because he was waiting for his life to begin. The beginning, he had numbly believed, would come to him as a gift. Someone would start it for him or chance would thrust him into it. He had hurried through situations and friendships because they were, somehow, not authentic, never looking once at things except to use them and shortening many meetings because the people lacked the distinction and the style of those in books.

And now, as if he were being rebuked, the image of Brice, red-faced, vociferous, deceitful, and a memory of Kopfers with the fancy hat pressed to his chest, funny, but when he should have laughed at this moment of mute supplication, no laughter, in its place a disturbing sadness, these two swam in his head merging like twice-exposed films, separating to be clear and shouting silently to him some message he could not catch, at last with a shudder he realized that this was his life, here, of all places, sick, of all conditions, and these were two living men. He could not hasten away, shrug off, be free of what the two of them had done that day. It had touched him and suppress it though he could try to do in favor of this splendid Italy, he was concerned. He was irritated that an eccentric like Kopfers should add the last push to conviction but he could see Brice as a bad man, not one to denounce exactly, yet wicked in a manner he could not yet discern.

Apart from the wickedness (and he could actually use the word "wicked" in thinking about Brice, a word that hitherto had aroused echoes of organ music, the stained-glass Christ, bland and injured, whose robe cast bluish reflections on his sleeve, and people dressed in their best crowing in the lobby of the church afterward), he liked Brice. He had vitality. He was in revolt against the disease and before his gibes all the pale fat patients lying in their beds waiting for improvement, for the slight greenish luminous haziness in the X-ray to clear, felt they were wasting their time. He made jokes.

Jokes were benign here; jokes were healing; it was a good thing for the poor patients to have a laugh for themselves, wasn't it? Then why was Brice such a bad man? Eddie knew. The moment of conviction had come when Kopfers had looked at him with such sad eyes, Kopfers, who would undoubtedly die, and perhaps quite suddenly unless he could lie down more than he did.

It was, however, an emotional certainty that he ought to explain. There was an obligation to explain it now that he admitted that Brice, Kopfers, and everybody were not passengers on a train that would soon, magically, arrive at the station where he, Eddie Burcham, would begin his real life. (He wondered at his carelessness in doing the things he had done, in allowing the things to happen to him that had, since as he knew now they were parts of the only life he would ever have.) So he set himself to explain slowly as if it were a fifth-grade arithmetic problem.

Breadon was sick. He would not be there if he weren't. What Brice had done to Harold, a soft excitable youth, was to upset him, harrow him, make him send for his mother, who was probably, as Brice predicted, already on the train for the sanitarium. It would take Harold a week to get over his terror and the wasted week would show in the next X-ray and for the worse. As a joke, of course. Brice did not intend any of his performances to be taken seriously. Each was presented with a wreath of laughter, Brice the vital interlocutor, gauging all his gibes and cracks to the temper of his audience, shrewdly making every speech humiliate his victim in the one place he could stand it least: his pride? No, maybe just his knowledge that he was alive, and Brice would stand there smiling and damage it, hurt it, stain it.

George wanted other people to die. It was absurd but now that he had said it to himself it became valid because it was simple and he hastened to find the reasons before his friendship for Brice, now a little faded, would make them seem unjust. George would not shoot anyone for a joke. He was only willing to attack their last security, hands off, with words. Since he was always ready to laugh at anything, even the jokes of others, it might be that he did not know his own jokes always kept the same goal. Perhaps his bustling disobedience of the rules, skulking down to the beer-joints in the town after the lights were out, all his defiant acts might mean that he was saying, "Look, I'm all right. There's nothing the matter with me," because he feared there was, that death was not a joke which was the property of the doctors to foist on someone or jerk away as they pleased. And did he want others to share the fear he was hiding so adroitly? Maybe that was it. Eddie watched a heap of cumulus clouds dissipate themselves above the mountain. Below, on the ground floor of the cottage, he could hear the booming of Brice's laughter as he told someone else about Harold

[216]

and the big brown bottle. No, it was even simpler than that. He did not even feel horror at once.

Brice wanted other people to die because their deaths would leave him still living. These other deaths would be a proof of his own strength, the simplest, the least obscure. Before he had time to make any judgment of his discovery, slipping in through the gate of his mind came the notion, with a sardonically gleeful cast to it as if a part of himself were bent on showing him that he was no better than anyone else, "You want other people to die, too, for the same reason." It was true. All he could say to lighten it was that he did not try to hurry them, like Brice. Perhaps everyone had the same wish because they were afraid.

Fear seized each one in a different way—some cringed openly; some were silent, enduring it with dignity; others joked, like Brice, to hide it, but they all suffered it. In the effort to cast it out or merely to live with it, they mistook the nature of their struggle. There was no daily pain. The silent action of their blood was not visible any more than were the bacteria. Perhaps because they lived in a Christian country they felt the need of drama, and with a deep pretense, too deep ever to explain it to them, they made the struggle personal, straining to find adequate enemies, and at last coming to wait and hope for the death of their new friends, the acquaintances they had made here. He himself recalled the furtive satisfaction he had enjoyed when he had gone down to the railroad station to meet someone arriving and at the far end of the platform, not hidden, but out of the normal range of attention, sat three pine boxes. He knew, all the patients knew, they contained coffins and in the coffins were men and women they had eaten with, walked with, nodded to or known. The weak ones, his inferiors, the dead.

He got out of bed and stood up. He ought to do something about this. For amusement the patients were encouraged to give talks or put on slowly paced theatricals in the evening. He could not remember any play and few gave speeches except doctors who were patients and they always lectured on the disease to a crowded house. He had a disease to lecture on also. Should he make arrangements with the staff and have them set a date for his accusation? For what could he say except an accusation? He could see himself, awkward, diffident, in his best blue suit, not knowing how to begin. He would falter and stumble through his little speech and they would laugh at him. And after he had explained it all, supposing he were able to communicate it as clearly as he saw it now, would they feel any shame? Would they stop wishing for the death of others? Could they stop? He doubted it. He did not think he could stop it himself. It seemed

[217]

to be, now that he thought of it, one of the very conditions of humanity.

If he could not persuade himself or others, perhaps he could atone for his own part of it in some way. He would have to settle his remorse in his mind and out of it let some sort of kindness spring, and, as he would so far as he could see always wish for the death of others secretly and show it in a hundred little ways, so must the kindness to them be continual. Because the wish was for an absolute, the last finality, he could never make any reserve to his kindness. (He did not ask himself what he meant by kindness.) He flipped a cigarette away and looked out over the valley softened by the blue fall haze. It was a good place to make a resolution. He would continue, then.

· XIX ·

WALTER WAS ONE of those people who are awake when they open their eyes. He did not flounder between day and night for an hour or until he was spoken to, confused among the monstrous labors of his receding dream and what the morning had for him to do. He jumped out of bed alert, the day lying before him as endless as an egg and, for all he knew, as full, but once on his feet he knew his leap had sprung only from habit and he would walk slowly into the bathtroom and loll in the tub before breakfast until the ends of his fingers shrank and he had identified all the boyhood scars on his bare shins.

Before he dressed he often struck poses before the glass in the bathroom door, chest thrown out, belly sucked in, and one tense arm behind him like the photographs of Charles Atlas. Fifteen minutes a day with some spring contraption and he too could bulge with muscle and defend his sweetheart against insults in the street. Was it worth it?

He dressed as carefully as if he had an appointment, recombing his wet hair after he had mussed it pulling on his undershirt. He came to be able to spend a full half-minute selecting a necktie. All his shirts were white, in the tradition of the financier, and they took him no time.

On his way through the lobby he would buy a morning paper at the cigar stand and take it into the coffee shop to read over his breakfast of orange juice, toast, and coffee. He read the newspaper conscientiously in the way people do who have nothing else to do, prisoners, invalids, the old. He did better than that: he tried to make a picture of the real world, the events masked by the formal news accounts. He was not optimistic (and he savored this as a rude betrayal of the standards of the City Club).

He did not believe "conditions" were getting any better. War would come eventually in Europe, perhaps a revolution here. Others would suffer and die in terror (and in his leisure he could imagine the sufferings and the deaths), but not he. Or, if it were necessary, he could do it laughing haughtily at his enemies because he had the strength. Nothing could beat him down. He was intelligent enough to suspect that his chances, anyone's chances, were better to be beaten down than to be lifted up and honored, yet he could suffer, if that were how things were going to turn out, and he would not care. Others could suffer and he would not care. (The suffering he envisioned was violent and bloody. That it could be quiet or that he, in these meticulous imaginings, might also be suffering, waiting as he was in darkness, was too improbable to suggest itself.) He was strong. It was something in his blood, he knew that.

After he had finished breakfast he would return to his room, sometimes stalking past the day clerk without speaking, for, with no special interest in horse racing, he had decided that friendship with him was impossible. He would usually find the maid cleaning and airing the room. She was a vague tired woman of fifty who wore a cloth around her head and had cut slits in the toes of her shoes to ease her corns. Early in his stay she had bent his ear on two successive mornings with the story of her sister's millennial goiter, "bigger than them summer squashes," and now he always said, "Good morning," kindly but nothing else.

The rest of the morning he listened to music or read. At first he had waited until the maid had finished her chores but now he would change chairs or lift his feet up out of her way without embarrassment. He had brought all his family's records to the hotel. His father had once heard Caruso as Rhadames and the performance had fixed his taste chiefly on Italian opera, although he had admitted *Carmen, Faust,* a few waltzes of the elder Strauss, and, oddly, some music from *The Pirates of Penzance* and *The Mikado*. Walter had not added to the collection. He would play these over and over with the volume of the machine turned down low, and the music did not make him think of Vienna or a stage with a singer on it. If he was reminded of anything at all, it was a darkness, a gloom open to light with long lace curtains at one side. The place that contained the darkness was the library of the big Phelps house where the old cabinet phonograph stood deep in one corner and a long blue streamer of cigar smoke rose from the wing chair where his father sat listening. Walter smoked a cigar also, occasionally taking it from the side of his mouth to whistle an aria, and he thought he liked music.

While he was listening, he would sit in a heavy overstuffed chair by the window and clean his fingernails. He had a little kit. When his nails were long, he would clip them with a patent clipper and save the tags. The nails clean, he pushed the cuticle down until the faint half-moon showed. He would snap the tags between his thumb and forefinger at some target, a rose in the dirty window drapes or the wastebasket across the room. He grew to be quite accurate.

Or he would go to the closet and bring out one of his four pairs of shoes to clean and polish. He had a cigar box filled with brushes, cans of polish, brown and black, saddle soap, rags for cleaning, flannel for polishing. He shined a pair every morning.

Sometimes he would turn the shoes over and find tiny bits of grit or little pebbles embedded in the leather of the heel. Fascinated, he would remove them one by one with a nail file as if they were gems, preserving them in a small heap on a piece of newspaper. The Cardinal of Bogotá had the largest emerald in the world. He constructed a gentlemanly expedition to steal it. Pretend to be an agent for Baldwin Locomotives, with letters of credit, two heavy trunks filled with old magazines, and introductions to present to the President and the Minister of Public Works. A Catholic, he would say. Could the Minister . . . the Cardinal? *Naturalmente, señor.* And under the tall ceilings of the palace he would meet a greasy fat man in severe red robe and biretta; or did he wear a little red skullcap around the house? And kneeling over the thick archepiscopal hand he would come off his knees with a small .22 automatic in his palm. Surprise at the towering effrontery? The necessity to prod with the barrel? The hurried passage down several corridors to a room with a little casket and at last the fabulous green stone. Thanks, pal. He would take the little pinch of recovered pebbles and sift them into the wastebasket, a good job done.

He kept books on a table beside his bed. A few were in leather bindings. He had brought these from the big house before it was sold. Others he had bought, mainly novels and biographies. He had received good grades in his literary courses in college and he had a quick memory for the facts of authors' lives. Uneducated people hearing his rare talk of these subjects sometimes thought he was "literary" but they were wrong. He was merely young enough to go through the ceaseless round of comparisons a young man makes, who, having tried nothing, is all potential, and there is no immodesty in seeing how much he is like the hero in a book, where he fails or even where he is superior. Walter, lying on his bed scratching the red fur of his chest, smoking a long cigar, thoughtfully wetting his thumb before turning the page, made all the comparisons. If he seemed to be stronger, tougher, braver than the hero, he was pleased. If not, he remembered it was only a fiction or the biographer was very likely partial. Either way, he felt that he had improved the time. It had been a scholarly interlude, pleasurable, and, in the way he had been taught to think of culture, vaguely therapeutic. Mingled with this was the aristocratic assurance that, by his countenance of them for a whole morning, he had encouraged the arts.

Occasionally he would pull out a drawer of his bureau, lift aside a stack of shirts, and take out one of the books of pornography. Twenty minutes after the funeral he had taken them out of the house and hidden them in a barrel in the garage. When he came to live at the hotel, he had hidden them again. He read them through soberly and studied the pictures. They did not excite him and force anything to his mind except the moment he had discovered them in his father's bookcase. He was willing to believe they had some meaning for his father, and when he knew his father better he would find out what it was. Meanwhile he held them in his hands and examined them ceremonially every few days.

When the town clock struck twelve he snapped his book shut. He got up, washed his hands, combed his hair again, put on his coat and went down to lunch, his first big meal of the day. Usually he ate in the coffee shop bent over a magazine, no longer quite aware that he was avoiding people's eyes, but sometimes he would vary his choice and eat in another restaurant, lunchroom, or even a drugstore. He was getting fat. He did not mind it. (His father had had a corporation. His father had liked good food.) After lunch, he returned to his room, stripped off his coat and shirt, and lay down for a long nap.

On awakening, he took a walk. There were people who should see him, into whose gaze he ought to intrude, strong, well dressed, circumspectly pursuing what to them would be his mysterious business. Beneath the excuse that he wished to preserve his health through exercise in the fresh air, he wanted them to know Todd Phelps's son was still a resident. If he met any of his former friends, he was civil. He answered questions politely, looking a little over their shoulders, but he asked none himself.

"What are you doing now, Walter?" they would say.

"Living at the hotel," he would answer.

The questioner would wait to hear him elaborate and all Walter might do would be to move his eyes from the street traffic to the man or woman in front of him.

"Oh," the questioner would say. "Be seeing you."

During each little meeting, Walter smiled contemptuously without

[221]

knowing it. The smile acknowledged their reluctant ignorance of what he was "doing," and stressed his refusal to tell them anything.

He was sure he knew what they wanted, why they stopped him at all. They were looking to him for help. In small towns there is a common public delusion of innocence and simplicity and it is one of the bulwarks of the republic. Individual citizens may have divined the complexity of their own sins and they hide the knowledge out of shame because they think it is peculiar. They see many societies devoted to good works, Chambers of Commerce, Lions, Boosters, Exchange and Kiwanis clubs. Because so many good works have been done and the public will to do them is so strong, they believe the community to be virtuous. The group is good, unlike their private selves. From this premise they concluded that if the group is good, its members are good also. Only they themselves are aberrant, strange, and wicked. They know how strenuous virtue is (a life, in fact) ; they cannot change to it because of the press of business. Since they accept the illusion of innocence and simplicity as truth, they feel it would be an endless task to poison the benign air in which they live because so many breathe it. All that remains is to find out the shortcomings of others to keep from being alone. Old women watch behind curtains. Men receive as balm the slanders dropped carelessly in the street. A known drunkard is a confrere; accounts of trials are welcomed. It is the loneliness they cannot endure and Walter suspected each was trying to catch him betraying himself so he could become under these disguises their friend. He could no longer believe in the frank sunlit friendships of his boyhood. They would not appear in his life again. And he could not accept these mean associations in which all affection would be hidden that were proffered him in the street because of his devotion to his father. He was better alone until he found out what he had to do.

Yet, as his walks grew longer, he went nearly every afternoon to the playing field to watch the high-school football team practice, standing quietly on the sidelines, the brim of his hat blown up by the wind. He had never played high-school football—that particular obeisance to custom had not been necessary because he was a boxer and could knock anyone down who said he was yellow.

When the coach saw that he intended to be there every day, not to offer his advice but to have it so obviously ready that it could not be ignored, the coach began to talk to him (he knew who he was, of course), and gradually the coach came to use him as a sort of assistant. In the middle of the season, Walter bought a sweatshirt and a baseball cap. As soon as he saw him in this outfit, the coach, instead of being bothered by him, felt ashamed not to accept the full help of such a loyal alumnus, and he let Walter coach the second string. This was agreeable to Walter. He had always liked the beautiful fall days, and when they practiced in the rain he seemed to be hardening himself for some obscure trial in his future. The school furnished him a pair of old football shoes to make his costume complete, and every Saturday afternoon he sat on the bench beside the coach, the indispensable ear for the coach's whoops and rages. He was very faithful in his football "work." He turned up every day because it refreshed him to see so many people putting out so much muscle to do something so simple. (Of course, they were very young.) Perhaps, later, after this waiting was over, he also could find something he could strain after as devoutly as the football boys. He could accept them as friends, say "Hi!" to them on the street and buy them cokes in the drugstore, because they were too young to be involved in his trouble, but when they asked him to stand next to the coach in the team picture, he refused.

After practice, for the walk back to the hotel, he put on a topcoat over the sweatshirt, stuffed the baseball cap and the cleated shoes in his pockets, and returned the same unexceptionable young man he had gone out. He stripped down in his room, and he would often shadowbox in his bare feet before the mirror of the bathroom door. He danced around on his toes, flicking out his left. He settled his left foot to lay in right crosses, hooks, and uppercuts until the breath came in snorts from his nose. He pretended no opponent—it was just exercise. When he had worked up a sweat, he took a quick shower and dressed, usually changing into a clean white shirt in deference to his hope that the evening would turn up something exciting. He was hungry.

He had a choice of two restaurants that could offer him the right menu for his last meal. He would make his choice of the two before he left his room so that no one would see him display any hesitation elsewhere. At the cigar counter in the lobby he would gravely buy an evening paper and six cigars.

He walked into any restaurant erect with his newspaper under his arm, staring at the guests, even his acquaintances, as if he were invisible. He took a back table. He ordered the biggest and most tender steak the house afforded and with it two bottles of beer or a pint of domestic Burgundy. He grew very tired of steak every night but he continued to order it because it was the richest dish on the menu. It was an assertion of the simplest kind like all his public acts. He ate and read the paper without lifting his eyes except to give an occasional formal stare around the room. He talked to so few people and so briefly that he heard no gossip of himself and he began to think he was almost anonymous in the town. This gratified him because he knew no Phelps could be anonymous in this town, concealed, yes, but not anonymous.

By the time he had finished dinner, paid, and left the restaurant, it was nearly dark. The street was a gorgeous alley of red and blue neon lights. It was then, his face mottled by their reflections, that he came nearest to sadness, an emotion that a few steps changed into one of two angers, either his familiar hatred for the people of the town or a short obstreperous rebellion against the tedium he labored in. Neither lasted very long, for it was dispelled by his curiosity before the garish posters at the box office.

There were two movies. One ran to Westerns and horror pictures; the other showed B's and sometimes A's. Each changed its program three times a week; thus, he might, if he could endure it, find six evenings out of every week occupied. His endurance grew less and less. There was a sign hanging in front of an insurance office across from the hotel. The autumn winds made it swing. When it swung it squeaked. When he discovered its dreadful monotony, he nearly always went to the movie but he became jaded. Even epics could not dazzle him and he was pleased only if there were a beautifully photographed woman to look at.

He did not pay another call on Mimi Herzog because he was ashamed to meet her husband again. He did not telephone any of the girls he once had known in high school or college. They were in a limbo of his own making along with his other friends. He saw Dorothy Wickham once a week (and for the meeting it took him as long to dress as it did her). He was not anxious to appear as a suitor and he did not wish to give her parents any reason to make hints. As the fall passed, he came to use the word "beautiful" when he talked to himself about her, and he often sat staring at her across the room without saying much of anything, or he would talk a great deal about trivialities, give long accounts of books he was reading, myriads of details of meals he had ordered and the deficiencies of the restaurants, perhaps a minutely reported campaign against a local laundry —he had gone there three times, once in the rain, and at last had seen the manager, who turned out to be a little bastard he had known in the sixth grade of the Central School and, his eyes bright with triumph after a half hour of preliminaries, Walter would tell how he recovered the lost shirt, white, costing originally $2.75. Only half aware of this long babble (the reasons for it, he would regret he was not on the sofa beside her making time but his loneliness forced him to keep talking even when he could see how bored she was. He could hardly explain to her why his life was so

[224]

petty since he himself was merely waiting for the causes to be vouchsafed him but he could not help trying to inflate the pettiness, to give it some dim color of adventure.

After the movie or his rare date, he had to return to his room. Two or three times he bought a bottle of whisky, at first a little thrilled because he had always heard drinking alone was dangerous, but he stopped it because of the stupidity of the thing after he found himself seated in an armchair facing the mirror in the bathroom door and conducting a serious argument with his reflection at one o'clock one morning. He usually lay in bed reading until his eyes ached, starting up at a late key rattling or a footfall in the corridor. Sometimes he would get out of bed in his pajamas and stand barefooted before the window with his hands on his hips, staring down into the dark street, spotting a late walker, thinking, "He sees my light. He wonders what goes on up here"; and the belief that his one light in the wall of darkness had impinged however briefly on someone's journey home consoled him.

On none of the hundred days like this, picking at the heels of his shoes or shutting out the squeaking of the sign, did he have more than an inkling of his wretchedness. It was his duty to wait. There was something his father wanted him to do.

· XX ·

IT WAS NOT MUCH of a discovery but it was something. The day clerk wore a toupee. Walter had never seen him when he had looked at him before. He had tried not to talk to him and when he bought cigars, magazines, and newspapers, he was already pulling away, paying him at arm's length, but on this wet fall Sunday evening, his boredom was stifling. He dawdled over the purchase of his evening's cigars long enough for the clerk to change from a mere equiphonic purveyor of tobacco into a man. The toupee was brown; its hairs were shiny; and the part was almost white like living scalp. ("Must wash it," Walter thought.) It had probably cost quite a lot of money because it blended unobtrusively with the loop of surviving hair around his skull. The clerk seemed gray only at the temples.

Once the toupee had been detected, the clerk's face withered almost visibly into its true age. Instead of a youngish man trying to get a stake by playing the horses, the clerk was just an old sport. What Walter had taken for hope was habit, sclerotic and monotonous. Now that he could see him as an old man, he became quaint and tolerable, perhaps worth listening to. He listened.

"... only harness plugs, but people don't remember them any more. *Dan Patch*, 1:55. *The Harvester*, 1:58¾. Every big horse used to have a cigar named after him. I seen cases full of 'em. It was an honor to own a horse that had his face on every cigar band in the gutter. But now? They're all gone. The sport of the kings is dying."

He wondered if the clerk had a little wooden pedestal for the toupee to rest on at night. "Yes, sir?" the clerk said to someone else, and Walter moved away from the counter.

He went to stand beside a potted fern looking out the front window. It was raining hard and in an hour it would very likely turn to sleet or snow but now the pavements were wet and shining in the headlights of cars. He stood with his feet apart, leaning back a little from the weight of his folded arms, unblinking, almost hypnotized.

"Got a match?" a man said to the left of him.

Without ceasing to stare out into the street, he stuck his left hand into his coat pocket, pulled out a book of matches, and held them out.

"Much obliged." He heard the scratch of the match, the puffs of the draw, and a cloud of blue cigar smoke passed in front of him.

"Nice night for ducks," the man said.

Ordinarily Walter's first impulse would have been to rebuff him for being a stranger and voluble, but now, thinking of the day past and the evening ahead of him, he felt a queer gratitude that anyone should want to know him and he responded to it diffidently. He turned, smiled, and said, "Yes, it is."

The man was the kind who wears a white muffler inside his suit coat. The suit was blue serge. The hat was a dingy fawn color with a half-inch ribbon and the face was plump, clean-shaven—he could smell the traces of shaving lotion—and the eyes were masked by hexagonal rimless spectacles. He was teetering back and forth on his toes.

"I seen this movie last week in Hammond, Indiana. It's good but I'll be darned if I want to see it twice," the man said.

"Who you with?" Walter asked.

"Empire Shoes. I call on Egan's and Walter Haley here." He turned to face Walter, beginning a fake sociable laugh that bulged his jowls. He laid his hand on Walter's arm. "Now don't ask me how's business because there ain't any. No, sir. Not a bit. They're going barefooted." He stopped the laugh and became serious. "I don't know what they think they're doing down at Washington. . . ." He looked around over his shoulder. "Couple of chairs over there. Let's sit down." They sat down with a standing ashtray between them. The salesman held his cigar over the ashtray, looking at it with a scowl, and flicked the ash off with his little finger. "It's my opinion, my considered opinion, that we're in for a long, hard pull if not revolution." This was evidently one of his prize openings for he stopped and looked squarely at Walter to confirm or deny.

"Suits me," Walter said.

He saw the eyes behind the spectacles quickly assess his tie, shirt, and suit and the salesman said, "You work in a factory?" in a chill offhand voice.

"No. I was thinking of a monarchy."

"A *what?*"

"Having a king. The best people of this country have got to do something to protect themselves from these Reds." Walter said this seriously, giving his voice an emotional color of fanatical earnestness. "Washington's full of 'em. New York's full of 'em. We've got to . . ."

"Now, wait a minute. Whoa. I'm radical but I'm not's radical as all that. I've voted Republican ever since Harding but I couldn't stand a king. That ain't in favor of our institutions. Why, a king could cut your God-damn head off."

"There's a lot of heads that ought to be cut off, maybe."

"No. No. I couldn't stand that. No. I'd arrest these Reds, give 'em a fair trial in the courts and throw 'em in jail just like they've always done in this country. Do you mean a kingdom with lords and dukes, and . . ."

"Sure. Why not? They nearly had it that way at the beginning."

The man gave his head two vigorous shakes. "Nope. Won't do. That's foreign." He leaned back in his chair. "All I want is to see some business where a man can make a little money, have a little home and sit back and enjoy life. This God-damn Roosevelt—you married?"

"No."

"You don't know when you're well off," he said in a sly confidential change of tone. Then he resumed pompously, "I believe in the home, our American home. It's a great place, yes, sir, a great place." He lurched forward and struck his fist into the soft plush of the armchair. "But I want to see it so you can have a home, have some comfort, have some peace and quiet. I want to make enough money so I can satisfy the demands of that home and not piddle around, *piddle* around, PIDDLE around week after week. . . ." He spoke very quietly. "You see, I've got an extravagant wife. Spends every nickel I can claw in. Never satisfied."

"What do you give her the money for?"

The salesman laughed sarcastically. "You're not married." He pulled his voice down into a violent hoarse whisper, "I gave that woman thirty-five dollars one day last week, Friday, it was. I just got in off the road, came in tired, worn out, and she was waiting for me, always Johnny-on-the-spot, and I gave her thirty-five dollars. I expected it would go for the home, household expenses, and what in hell does she do? Goes right downtown the next morning and blows it on some yellow rag she calls a hostess gown. A hostess gown. I said to her, I said, 'By Christ, you go on spending money this way and you'll be lucky if you got a roof to be a hostess under.' That night we had to eat out. There wasn't a damn bit of food in the house."

"Why don't you divorce her?"

The salesman shook his head, sighing. "I couldn't stand the publicity."

Walter snorted in spite of himself. He pulled out his handkerchief quickly and wiped his nose as if he had been taken by a sudden sneeze.

"It's a fact. I couldn't," the salesman said. "Mr. Vinson, our sales manager, is moral. No liquor, no smoking in the office. I'd lose my job if I divorced her and God knows what I'd do then." The tight skin on his face loosened and he sank upon himself weakly like a doll with the sawdust running out.

"Looks to me like you're stuck, doesn't it?" Walter said briskly.

The plump little man perked up ready for a denial. He thought better of it and relaxed, saying merely, "No. I get along." He was looking out of the window. He stopped talking to Walter and began to talk to himself. "So she thinks she's got the whip hand over me, huh? Thinks she can tell me what to do." He turned in his chair to face Walter until he was nearly crouching on the floor. He was trying obviously to be reasonable, to rid himself of his anger, but it sounded more like a plea. "It was just after I went to work for Empire seven years ago. She started to accuse me of—oh, you know what a traveling man's wife would accuse him of."

"So you *did* start to chase women just to show her."

"I never chased a woman in my life. I always go to a house."

"Oh."

"A man's got to get some pleasure out of life, hasn't he? Honestly, don't you think a man owes it to himself to—well, get what he can before the Grim Reaper . . ."

"It's only two blocks from here. North, on the other side of the street. It's an old house three stories high and there's a front porch with big square pillars and a balcony. Ask for Lide," Walter said.

"Oh, you know all about it!" he said in a loud, fraternal, kidding tone.

"I've never been in the place. Everybody in town knows all about it." He was not offended by the imputation that he should know all about Lide Carter's house, rather by the salesman's manner. As he was saying he had never been there, it occurred to him that it would be a way to get through the evening. The house had been a mysterious landmark all his life and as a boy he had been able to recognize all the girls. He could see his mother drawing away from them coolly in the downtown stores, heavy, buxom, painted women, who had fixed the image of "whore" forever in his mind. He could not recognize them in the street now. Undoubtedly Lide had a new string of girls.

"Don't get sore. I just thought a good-looking, well-set-up young fellow like you would be sure to know the girls, that's all. Don't take offense. I didn't mean anything. I get so damned nervous about my wife I don't know what I'm saying . . ."

"As a matter of fact, I was thinking of going down there this evening. If you want to come along . . ." He said it coolly because he knew it would puzzle the man.

"Say, I've got a bottle of whisky upstairs. Let's go up and have a drink first."

"All right."

They passed between two rows of other guests, the salesman almost tiptoeing as if his intention would be discovered and denounced by all the old women knitting in the chairs if he walked naturally.

In the room, the salesman drew open a drawer of his bureau and lifted out a bottle cradled in a clean shirt. He went into the bathroom and came back with the water glass. He handed the bottle and glass to Walter. "Help yourself."

Walter poured out two fingers of whisky into the glass, and the salesman lifted the bottle. "Good hunting," he said.

Walter swallowed about half his drink. It was bad whisky and he had a hard time to keep from coughing. The salesman drank two little sips, rubbing the mouth of the bottle with the palm of his hand between them. They had nothing to say to each other.

The salesman went into the bathroom again and returned with a hand towel around his neck, squirting hair tonic on his head, and massaging his scalp with the other hand. He set the bottle of tonic down and dug at his scalp with both hands. He bent his knees, thrusting his stomach out, and combed his hair carefully before the bureau mirror. "Y'ever use this stuff? Keeps your hair from falling out."

He spoke ingratiatingly, as if the fall of a single hair at this time or presently would be a serious matter, as if each hair made a loud clank when it hit. Walter said, "My hair doesn't fall out."

Tightening the knot of his tie, settling the handkerchief that stuck peekaboo out of his breast pocket, pulling the cuffs of his shirt down, and brushing the coat sleeves off with one hand, he said with intense curiosity, "It *don't?* You're lucky. Mine comes out all the time." Before he finished speaking he was digging at his nails with a pocket file. He put one hand out in front of him and cocked his head on one side to squint at his nails. At last, neat and scented, he stepped over to the mirror again. He lifted his chin and tried a stern expression, probably, Walter thought, the one that made him look like an executive. He held it a few seconds without the least self-consciousness and let his face relax again. He came over to Walter, who was leaning against the wall watching, thrust out his hand, and said, "Samlich's the name. Carl Samlich."

"Mine's Walter Phelps."

His hand was shaken vigorously and Samlich said, "Hodda ya do?" twice. He opened the door and drew back to let Walter precede him. The rank rich fumes of the hair tonic were wafted out from under his hatbrim all along the hall.

They walked stiff-legged down the dark Sunday street. The sleet had come and the sidewalks were slippery. The wind blew loudly through the bare trees and the limbs clattered together like poles. Samlich turned up his coat collar and ducked his head against the wind and anyone's recognition. Walter was more relaxed. He did not think about what he was going to do. He made no plans because Samlich was setting the tone and it was fun to watch him.

At the corner of Lide's lot, an old ornamental iron fence began. Walter had heard that it had been made on old Fred Burke's order for Lide at the Lake Shore carshops before he himself was born. As he opened the gate, he became excited. He had visited brothels before, to wait for friends, but Lide Carter's was the archetype. He did not quite know what he expected except vice and shame and here these would be rank, vivid, and obviously depraved.

There was a well-shined brass bellpull beside the heavy door.

"You pull this?" Samlich said.

"Naw. You kick out the windows and jump in," Walter said.

Samlich did not seem to be irritated by this. He gave the handle a pull and immediately folded the collar of his overcoat down and patted it nervously. He took off his hat and ran his palm over his wet and reeking hair. As the door opened he was wiping his face with a handkerchief. He was sweating, as cold as it was.

Lide answered her own front door because she never let drunks in the house. She flung it open wide and stared up and down with an affronted air as if she were a matron whose honest home had been mistaken by libertines.

Even in the bad light, Walter saw that Samlich was quivering. He had taken a humble, almost cringing posture and he said with a weak cordiality, "Why, good evening."

"Come on in. Don't keep me standing here with the door open," Lide ordered.

They walked in. They were in a narrow hall. Three doors were set in the walls, white doors, and they all were closed. At the foot of the stairs on a small dark table under a mirror stood a lamp with a lace shade on it. Lide stood beside the table sizing them up and Walter looked at her reflection in the mirror. Her hair was dyed a bright red. From the roots of her hair down into the depths of her massive décolletage the powder lay like dust and the rouge on her cheeks was bright and startling like a clown's. She was wearing some kind of green satin wrapper with flounces, and since her corsets had long ago begun to gouge and hurt her, she looked like a tub with a cloth over it.

She was saying, ". . . Sunday night. I ain't got but four girls."

Samlich arched his back in eagerness and cried in a high twitter, "Four? Four little darlings? Why, that's wonderful. Isn't that wonderful?" He spun around, asking Walter.

Walter grinned at Lide and looked back at Samlich. "Sure," he said.

Lide swept across the hall and opened one of the doors. "You can wait here. I'll call 'em."

The first thing Walter noticed were the heavy blue velvet curtains covering the windows. They were very old and the nap was worn off in patches but they let no light through them to the outside. He knew because he had often skulked around the house with Eddie Burcham when they were thirteen or fourteen years old. He felt that he was doing Eddie a friendly office to find out what kept the light in. The rest of the room was furnished in gnarled old oak furniture. A carved table with a marble inset stood under a dusty crystal chandelier. On the table were two ashtrays, dimestore ashtrays, and Walter was disappointed. He had grown up with the legend that Milo Gold Tip cigarettes were always at the elbow of the gentlemen guests at Lide Carter's. There were two battered divans facing each other from opposite walls. They were littered with all kinds of cushions; some were circular, covered with silk, exactly like his grandmother's; one was covered with petit-point, another with crochet work. There was a square hard pad of buckskin with a fringe around the edges, and there was one with the head of an Indian maiden painted on it in bold colors, bearing the inscription, *Happy Days at Petoskey, Mich*. The room smelled powerfully of sandalwood incense and somewhere in the house a radio was playing.

Samlich had taken off his coat and hat and was sitting on the edge of one of the divans, smoking. His white muffler was still inside his collar. "This is a nice place, isn't it?" He inhaled, shutting his eyes. "Smells good, don't it?" He couldn't sit still. He got up and stood for a moment, running his tongue over his lips and tapping his foot. He was smiling and through his glasses his eyes glittered. "Oh," he exclaimed, throwing his head backward. "I hope they're pretty." There was something female in the warmth and sweetness of his antipication. He seemed to be stifling in the scented air and he could hardly talk, as if his tongue were swollen.

"You're not a virgin, are you?" Walter asked. No man should behave this way in front of another, Walter thought.

As he had at the door, Samlich took the remark with a sickly forbearance. He smiled. "No. I'm not. I told you I wasn't. Back at the hotel." He went walking up and down breathing deeply. If there had been a vase of roses in the room, he would have buried his face in them.

The door opened and three young women came into the room. One was blond, two were brunette, all three wore kimonos of different colors, and, except for the high brassy color of the blonde's hair, they looked like any three young women in kimonos. None of them were pretty but one of the brunettes had a face that Walter thought attractive. The blond said, "Hello, boys," as she walked in. They were followed by Lide Carter. The three of them lined up with Lide standing in front and to one side of them like a lecturer.

"Here you are, boys. I said, four. There's three. One's busy. This is Miss Higgins. Miss De Flore. Miss Calman. Step right up and take your pick and it's five dollars before you go upstairs." Lide stood there tapping her foot. She did not want any hesitation. She liked a quick turnover. She always made the girls stand in a row.

Samlich was overcome with shyness but his actions were as brutally critical as those of a judge at a stock show. He gazed at the blond Miss Higgins with one hand up to his mouth. He stood hardly two feet away from her. She was smiling unembarrassed. Samlich stepped sideways to stare at Miss De Flore. She looked him straight in the eye. As he was

[232]

stepping sideways again, Lide bawled impatiently, "OK. Show him what you got, girls." With a single movement they opened their kimonos and held them wide, giggling. Samlich fell back a step and looked around nervously at Walter. He began to tremble and a large drop of sweat rolled down his cheek.

"See anything you like, son?" Lide said.

"Certainly," his voice squeaked in a falsetto. He swallowed. "Yes. I like them all."

"Fifteen dollars and you take 'em all," Lide said. She was beginning to be amused and the girls were swaying and their ribs and bellies worked convulsively with the laughter they were holding in.

"Oh, I couldn't afford that. I'd love to but I couldn't afford it." He was peering at them, bending and straightening, twitching and shaking, as if he feared something he saw might be counterfeit or vanishable.

"Come on. Come on," Lide said with sudden harshness. The girls stopped laughing to themselves and wrapped the kimonos around them neatly.

Samlich had inspected the blond carefully. He slid up to her drawing one foot after him. Miss Higgins? Would you——" he gulped. "Would you like to have me?"

"OK," the blond said. "Let's see the five bucks first."

"What? Oh. Yes. The five . . ." Samlich had pulled his wallet out of his hip pocket and clumsily dropped it. Money, credit cards, photographs, and snips of paper spattered on the floor. Samlich knelt and raked them together, muttering anxiously, "Just a minute now. Be right with you."

Lide Carter sighed and looked over at Walter. She seemed to be quite friendly. "You going upstairs?"

Walter shook his head. "No. I'll wait."

Lide nodded peremptorily to one of the brunettes, Miss Calman. The rest of the people left the room, Samlich already running his hands eagerly up and down Miss Higgins' back. At the door Lide gave a last monitory glance. The door was shut. Miss Calman sat down immediately beside Walter on the divan, leaned herself against him, and said brightly, "You sure you don't want some nice loving, honey?" As she spoke her hand slid up his thigh.

Miss Calman was chewing gum and her breath was peppermint. Walter looked into her face without answering. What signs were there? Was this the frightful mien? She had a small crescent-shaped scar under one eye nearly obscured by face powder. "No," he said. He pushed her hand away from him. "I'm just waiting for him."

[233]

"I know a wonderful place to wait. It'd be nice and warm in bed." She shuddered luxuriously and wrinkled her nose.

"Have you ever been beaten up?" he said seriously.

She jerked herself away from him and spoke as a human being, "Say, we don't go in for that kind of stuff here."

"I don't want to beat you up. You've got a scar under your eye. I just wondered."

"I did that falling off a motor bike one time. It was up by Port Huron. We hit a stone in the road and bango! off I went." She stood up and said in a cool normal voice, "Sure you don't want to go upstairs?"

"No. I'm just waiting. If you have anything to do, go ahead."

"OK." She went out of the room.

Except for the faint music of the radio, the house was quiet. The wind whirred loudly through the telephone wires outside and he could hear bits of sleet strike the window. There was nothing to do at all. The room was impersonal, like a doctor's waiting room without the magazines. It was not a place to be idle in and if anyone came into the room, he did not stay long. Walter stood up. There was a door at the end of the divan opposite him that led into the next room. He knew that he would be cussed out good and plenty if he found Lide Carter in the room but he turned the knob and pushed. It had not been opened for some time. It stuck and then opened.

Miss De Flore and Miss Calman were playing Chinese checkers. They were sitting in two ratty old wicker chairs with the checkerboard on their knees. They stopped playing and stared when he came in.

"Jump quick. It's a rape," Miss De Flore said.

"What's the idea, big boy?" Miss Calman said.

"I just wondered where the radio was," Walter said.

"There it is," Miss Calman said, pointing. On a cheap dressing table stood a small radio.

"So get out, huh?" Walter said.

"You better not let old Lide find you in here," Miss De Flore said.

Walter looked around the room. It was about twelve feet square with one heavily curtained window. An army cot ran along one wall covered with a tattered silk cover. There were four chairs and the dressing table, littered with powder, cosmetics, combs stuck full of hair, and brushes. Two or three shiny photographs of men were stuck in the edge of the mirror. The room was hot.

"Is this where you wait for trade?" Walter asked.

"I mean it, big boy. You better get out," Miss Calman said.

[234]

"This is where the doorbell rings," Miss De Flore said. "There over the door."

Above the door that led into the hall a graceful bell was set on a curlicue of iron with a wire attached that ran into the wall. It was an old hand-hammered bell, and, as he looked at it, Walter tried to recall whose house this had been long ago before Lide Carter took it. A doctor had owned it, he recalled, a man he had never seen, who had been a major in the U. S. Army Medical Corps in the Civil War. He had kept a pair of fine roan horses. His grandmother once had told a joke about the major. It had something to do with the war and the major had said, "Union by first intention had failed." All the grownups had laughed and he had gathered that a pun was involved, some medical term, but he did not know what it was nor could he remember the major's name.

"The bell rings and you paint your faces and get set for the little act, is that it?" Walter said.

"Look," Miss Calman said. "You'll catch hell if you don't get out of here."

"What do you care? It'll be me catching it."

"Aw, let him alone, Bella. It's your play."

The two girls seemed to forget him. They moved the little colored balls around the board, swearing occasionally, and squealing like children when they made a good play. Walter sat down on a chair to watch them. They paid no more attention to him.

Miss Calman had slid off her high-heeled pumps and she wriggled her toes as they played. Her kimono had fallen open and Walter could see her large breasts. She had rouged the nipples. She chewed her gum vigorously and scratched herself along the ribs under the arms. She had a good figure and she did not know she was being watched.

"Oh, damn it to hell," Miss De Flore wailed. "You always beat me." She tipped the board over and all the little balls fell on the floor and rolled around.

"Now pick 'em up. Go on, pick 'em up." Miss Calman grabbed a lock of Miss De Flore's hair and yanked it.

"I will. I will. You think you're so damned smart." She got down on her hands and knees, grumbling and reaching for the little balls.

Miss Calman let one leg hang over the arm of her chair and she looked at Walter sitting somewhat primly on his own. It was a calm appraising look, made with confidence because she had seen many men in circumstances unique and revealing. She seemed to wonder what kind of man, not what kind of customer he was.

[235]

"You've got a nice little friend there," she said. "I was afraid he wasn't going to be able to contain himself until he got upstairs," she said with sarcastic nicety.

"I don't know the guy," Walter said.

"Why are you waiting for him if you don't know him?"

"Something to do."

"You live here in town. I've seen you."

Somehow it seemed to be a compliment. Walter did not know quite what to say. He had never made social conversation with a working whore before. "Oh, I'm around," he said finally.

"Find 'em all yet?" she called to Miss De Flore, who had her head under the army cot. There was a muffled answer.

Miss Calman held her arms above her head, stretching and yawning. "Oh, I hate Sundays. Sunday's the longest damn day in the week."

"You from Port Huron?" Walter asked because he thought he ought to say something.

"Who wants to know?"

"I just asked."

"I'm from Troy, New York." She spoke in a loud voice, "And in this caw-nah, lad-eez and gempmen, we have *Jake Kilrain!*" She clapped loudly. "That's his home town. He fought John L. Sullivan down in Mississippi and got his can beat right off. He's some sort of cousin of mine."

"That was a long time ago, wasn't it?"

"Scarcely a man is now alive," she said. "My brother, he thought we had one good one, maybe we'd have another, so he tried it awhile but . . ." She whistled and pointed her thumb at the floor.

"You come from a sporting family, don't you?" Walter said.

She merely looked at him with cigarette smoke drifting out of her nostrils. Then she got up and picked a nail file off the dressing table and started to file her nails.

"Did you go through high school?" Walter asked.

She looked up, surprised. "What's that got to do with the price of eggs?"

". . . the eighteenth of April, seventy-five.

Scarcely a man is now alive.

Who remembers the famous day and year," Walter said. "I learned that in high school. I thought maybe you did."

"I got bounced out in the eleventh grade," she said.

"Oh," Walter said.

Miss Calman was tapping one thumbnail with the file. "You want to

[236]

know what for, don't you? Well, you're right. And now you want to know how I got into this racket, don't you? I'll tell you. I was betrayed."

Miss De Flore, reading a love magazine, shrieked with laughter. Miss Calman kept her face straight. She did not even look at Miss De Flore, who subsided into chuckles, staring with determination at the open magazine.

"Yeah?" Walter said. They were having some fun with him. Well, he had asked for it.

"I'll tell you how you can tell a guy that's green. There's one sure way. He always wants to know how you started, and the answer he wants to hear is that somebody cracked you over the head with a blackjack and you woke up in a hook-shop. Well, there's one thing you can put in your memory book, big boy: I never saw a blackjack in my life."

Her statement of what he had intended to say was accurate enough to be embarrassing. He did not like to be called "green." He said, "Miss Calman?"

She looked up at him, her nail file poised. "Yeah?"

"Want to go upstairs?"

"We ask our customers not to pick over the merchandise," she said.

"Do you want to go upstairs?"

"Bella's very good," Miss De Flore said in a high mincing voice.

"You shut your head," Miss Calman said to Miss De Flore, who ducked her head back into her magazine, giggling. "What you been doing, buster, playing eeny-meeny-miney-mo all this time to make up your mind?" She stood up stretching and yawned and Walter was sure she knew as well as he did the gibe that had decided him.

Walter got out a five-dollar bill.

She took it and laid it on the dressing table. "I want that there when I come back, see?" she said to Miss De Flore, who made no sign of hearing.

She took a fresh towel off a pile on the dressing table. Bending, she looked in the little mirror, ran a comb through her bobbed hair, and powdered herself here and there. She stood erect, drew her kimono around her with great niceness, and said in her professional, joking, patronizing voice, "Well, all aboard for a big ride."

Walter followed her out of the little hot room and up the stairs.

In half an hour he came down again, the girl behind him, whistling.

"You come again. Ask for Bella," she said. She gave him a card. It was very high-toned. Engraved in severe script was *Miss Lydia Carter*. Beneath the name it said, *Divertissements* and in one corner, *Bella*. Walter knew where the *Divertissements* came from. It was the Frenchman. He remembered him, a dapper little man with a mustache. Everybody in town had pointed him out because he was French and because he actually wore button shoes with cloth tops. He had been Lide's husband for a while a long time ago.

"I think I'll wait for that other guy, or has he gone?"

"Who? Hot-rocks? I'll ask Mabel." She stuck her head into the little dressing room, and in a moment leaned out again. "Still at it. You can wait in there." She pointed at the door of the scented waiting room.

"You come on in and wait with me," he said.

"Not allowed," she said.

"I'll go back into the dressing room then."

"Aw, honest, you can't. Lide'd raise hell if she caught you, and I'd get myself in trouble. You wait in there. He can't last much longer," she said.

"All right. Good night," he said.

She smiled, the first time he had seen her do it. "Good night. Come back again," she said. She went into the dressing room.

He yawned and looked at his watch. He heard a clatter down the stairs and Samlich burst into the room; hat and coat on, not quite looking at Walter. "Come on," he said gruffly. "Let's get out of here."

They left the house. The storm had gone and the trees were sheathed in ice. It was like a fairyland. They stumped along stiff-legged over the slippery walks. At last Samlich said, "I didn't think you'd wait."

"I did, though."

"By God, I won't be able to get out of town tomorrow if the roads are like this."

· XXI ·

WITH HAT AND COAT ON, a tricorn hat and a coat of Persian lamb, Mrs. Wickham stood before one of the living room windows running a finger over the sill. The straight lines of the coat hid her dumpy figure. Her age showed only in the forward set of her head and in her bowed legs; she had begun to walk on the sides of her feet like many women past fifty. She turned and held her finger up in the light of the single floor lamp. There was no dust on it. Company was coming and she was a good housekeeper. A fleeting complacency obscured her anxiety for a moment, then it returned and she plumped out a cushion on the sofa and, glancing nervously around the room, went into the kitchen.

Beside the sink stood an unopened bottle of Scotch whisky. She took a corkscrew from a drawer, laid it beside the bottle, and patted it. She opened the icebox door. Standing in front of the milk on the top shelf were two bottles of soda water. There were a dozen eggs and some bacon in case they wanted anything to eat later in the evening. She wandered back into the living room. She examined the ashtrays again to be sure they were clean and empty. She tore the cellophane and foil off two packages of cigarettes and pushed a single cigarette a little way out of each package invitingly.

He shaved every morning but her husband's beard was black and heavy. At dinner she had stared at it until, as she intended, he ran his hand over his chin. Nothing was said. (They had been married thirty-one years.) At the moment he was upstairs in the bathroom shaving. As they were going to the movies so as to leave Dorothy alone with her company, Walter Phelps, it was unlikely that Walter would see her husband for more than five minutes but now that he was, as she put it, on the downgrade, she was worried about money and she insisted on having all the details of her daughter's hospitality to young men strictly attended to. The smoothness of her husband's chin was equally as important as the clean sill, the whisky, or the soft lighting. She wanted to have "things" make a nice impression. If anyone had been so rude as to point out that the house was a trap and her daughter, bait, she would have been outraged.

Since they had been poor at the beginning of their own marriage and she had had to do all her own work while pretending not to, she had been terrified of poverty. It kept her awake nights, and the poverty that now frightened her was a state in which she could not keep a maid or have her hair done every week, a miserable life when they could not turn in their old car for a new one every year and Fred would have to liquidate some of his life insurance or annuity holdings. She had regarded the depression as temporary and at first, because Fred was a salaried man and at her persuasion had never played the stock market, she ventured to think they might skin through the year or two years of bad times. When he was told he would have to sell his house, move to another town, and take less money, she knew they had been overtaken like so many of their friends. Now she lived with a fear that made her muscles tense most of the time that something else would happen to them.

The first blow had been bad enough. It had been lightened only by the fact that Dorothy was in her senior year at college and the long drain of their children's education was nearly at an end. Now, for Dorothy's sake and her own, it was clearly her duty to get Dorothy married off. Although she herself would never have dreamed of taking a drink when she was her daughter's age, the young people all did it now and she saw no harm in taking a cocktail or two before dinner although she stopped what had hardened into a custom when her husband had developed this stomach condition. (There was something a little shameful in admitting he had ulcers. So many people said they came from boozing and Fred had never done that.) They had not had a bottle of liquor in the house for years but she wanted to be sure that Dorothy would be able to seem as well off as the other girls in the town, and this was why she had told Fred to buy the whisky.

Her husband's status as manager of the fence company carried with it, as perquisites, invitations to join the Country and the City clubs, and for her, the best bridge club. They had joined. With assiduous subtlety, the most adroit she could conceive but obvious enough to the mothers of sons only or to childless women, she had inquired about the eligible young men. They were few. Young men, she was told, usually went elsewhere, to a city. She heard Walter Phelps's name mentioned often, sometimes with pity, oftener with scorn, yet, as a woman who was shrewd enough where her interests lay though dull and ignorant everywhere else, she could detect the envy in the statements, the rankling, wasting envy of the small town, and she concluded erroneously that young Phelps could not be as poor as they made out. The old lady was living with Miss Baker, wasn't she? And the Phelps brother, the bachelor, the awful one who drank and chased women, he had his own housekeeper, house, and a Packard car, didn't he? She had observed without knowing it that second generations of rich families were often queer, eccentric, and she believed it was a whim of Walter's that made him live at the hotel. She wanted to believe this because, as a newcomer, she resented the patronizing gifts of information made to her by the old inhabitants and she wanted to prove that she was more astute than they on their own ground. She had caught only glimpses of Walter on his other visits and she wanted to wait around until he came, sitting with her hat and coat on and her purse in her lap as signs that she was at the point of leaving. She did not care whether he was handsome or not, well mannered or not, or even well dressed. She was looking for money. It would excuse every other flaw and she was sure she could tell if he had it. It made little beckoning gestures.

She was not aware of her own ruthless single-mindedness. She honestly believed that she wanted a respectable hard-working young man who would make her daughter a kind, gentle, and generous husband but she had warped all her other, lesser desires to lie along her chief one, money, and if a suitor had the marks of wealth, she would be able without any disingenuousness to endow him with good looks, fine manners, even a nice taste in clothes, as well as the less important qualities of honesty, indus-, try, and kindness. She was really looking for a son-in-law who would not only reflect credit on her as the mother of his wife but who could, now that she had accustomed herself to the possibility of catastrophe invading the snugness of her life, lend the old folks money or, why not, give them some if another blow should strike. So she sat with her ankles crossed genteelly, a ripple of worry about the decorations of her house disturbing her mind, her face disintegrating from an earlier firm-faced prettiness under its mask of powder, her figure gone but hidden under a corset and a dress too youthful for her, blankly waiting. Presently her husband came down the stairs and sat down across the room to wait with her.

"She dressed?" Mrs. Wickham said.

"I don't know. I didn't go in her room."

"I hope she has sense enough to wear that yellow dress. Have you ever seen Walter?"

"Only in a bad light. At night. He looks all right."

"This is eleven times," she said smugly.

"I doubt if he'll propose tonight, Eunice," he said jocosely.

She ignored his remark as in bad taste. "Didn't Dorothy say he sells insurance?"

"He did. I don't know if he still does. I can't handle any more, though, now."

Forestalled, she lied to keep from admitting it: "I wasn't thinking of that. They say he lost all his money."

"Well, he can work. I did."

"How long does it take an insurance salesman to get up big accounts?"

"Oh, my God, let the girl have some fun. Don't be pushing her into the arms of every fellow she meets."

Coldly Mrs. Wickham replied, "Do you know how much it costs a month for Dorothy to live at home? You don't keep the accounts. I do. You'd just as soon let her tear around for two or three years. I want to see her well married. Is that anything to be ashamed of?"

It was useless to argue. They had been over the same ground before in other places with other young men in view ever since Dorothy had gone to college. It was hard for him to realize that his little girl had grown up. He did not mind, he liked to have her at home no matter what it cost. He cut the tip off a cigar neatly, raised his eyes expectantly to his wife's face, saw that she was watching him primed to say "Not in here," and he put the cigar in his vest pocket ready to light when he left the house.

Upstairs before a triptych of mirrors on her dressing table, Dorothy Wickham, in a white silk slip, carefully applied a scarlet lipstick to her mouth. She had already bathed. She had done her nails and brushed her hair two hundred strokes. She had pressed the yellow wool dress in the late afternoon and it hung from a wire hanger that was hooked over the top of an open closet door. It had been a part of the etiquette she had learned in her college sorority always to keep a man waiting and she did not intend to slip into the dress until she heard the front doorbell ring. Meanwhile there was nothing to occupy her except to purse her lips and color them.

She had not been expressly instructed in the role she was to play this evening but she knew all about it because her mother never really talked about anything else, by hints, comparisons, allusions, and every feint she could think of. Little by little the ideal had been set before her, the girl who married well.

Her mother was just beginning to emerge for her as a person. The protective cloud in which there were gifts and comfort, the very climate in which she, a child, had lived was dissipating, and this person had faults that could be recognized and judged like those of everyone else. This discovery seemed vaguely treacherous. It seemed to her still a little daring to criticize her mother even silently when even a small open disagreement brought such voluble reprimands as well as the menacing gestures of authority, neither of which she could disregard. When her mother stated, "You can just as well love a rich man as a poor one," love seemed to suffer. In college she had seen too many students working their way through, waiting on table, living in cellars, working night shifts in factories, to share her mother's fear of poverty. They were cheerful, and, one of her chief criteria, they had a good time. Although it would be heresy and she never dared say it because she would be nagged about it for weeks, she had just as soon marry any man if she loved him.

It never crossed her mind that she was ill equipped for marriage. Although her mother could set an excellent dinner on the table when the servant was away, she had never been taught to cook. Kitchen work would roughen those beautiful white hands. It was true they were beautiful. As she had them posed, they looked like the hands in a lotion ad, twisted into rigid grace. Her mother had, she could remember, made all her dresses when she was a little girl but she herself could hardly sew a button on tight. Just once her mother had referred in a mysterious bitterness to her "wifely duties" and hurried on to speak of wholesome things, and she had gathered that it meant going to bed with one's husband, in this case, Daddy, which seemed a funny idea because all they did when they went to bed was talk, or rather, her mother talked. She could hear her through the wall every night. She knew it for a reference to sex. She was twenty-three years old. She had been elaborately kissed by several young men on sofas, in doorways, and in the back seats of cars, yet she did not actually know the details of intercourse. She assumed placidly that her mother would tell her about it when the time came, that it was a very simple business of renouncing yourself physically to the man you loved. You lay still; something wonderful happened to you but you must be careful or you would have a baby.

She had heard and repeated the dozens of dirty jokes that circulate in a sorority but she did not know the meaning of the words that brought the laughter and her embarrassment at her own ignorance kept her from asking anyone. She had never seen a naked man, and, since she was eleven years old and had been caught doing it by her mother, she had never looked carefully at herself. She did not perceive any inconsistency in her ambivalent sentiments toward sex as a turmoil to be shunned because it was dirty and imprudent, and a deeply attractive goal about which she was growing more and more curious.

She heard the doorbell ring, and, glancing at her wrist watch, she gave herself five minutes. She examined her face in the triple mirror and brushed her hair away from her face again. As she stood up she congratulated herself on her figure with the familiar mingling of pride and shame, and, getting into her dress, she began to think about Walter Phelps.

She liked him well enough. She had liked all the young men she knew well enough. They seemed to expect to kiss her, and after the proper maneuvers of delicate hesitation she let them. In her way she was as hardened as a courtesan as long as it was only kissing. She had never been able to rave about men as she had heard girls do in college, throwing themselves on a bed after a date, babbling and screaming with delight, apparently. She hoped soberly that she would find someone she could rave about in that way. Walter was not the man. His distinction was the pinch he had given her on the thigh. It had made her wary but otherwise he appeared to be little different from the others. She would permit him to talk to her, to sit beside her, to take her to the movies or to dinner, and, if he wished, to kiss her, and she would respond adroitly and muss up the hair on the back of his neck. Further than this she had no plans for Walter Phelps.

She knew her mother had, though, and she knew she would probably fall in with them. Her mother had implied that it was time, now that the preliminaries of the acquaintance were past, for her to find out "how he was doing" in the insurance business, and it was no less than her duty to ascertain how much of the Phelps fortune was left. (Slyly, she did not tell her mother that Walter no longer sold insurance.) She knew very well that if there was what her mother considered *enough* money in the control of Walter Phelps, the hints would become more frequent and abrasive.

She decided as she was going downstairs that her first glance would tell her whether she could ever marry him or not. If he looked handsome in any way, carried himself well, made a gesture like a movie star, or even said something clever, she would consider it.

When she entered the living room, everyone rose and she noticed with a shade of annoyance that her mother had turned out all the lights except the floor lamp across the room from the sofa. For the first time in her life she sensed that her mother did not care what she did as long as marriage lay at the end of it. She suddenly felt lonely, surrounded as she was by father, mother, and prospective husband.

The first glance at Walter, while she murmured, "Hello," showed him a big grinning young man with glasses in a neatly pressed blue suit and black shoes brilliantly shined. She did not think she could stand marrying him, no matter how much money he had, yet she knew that she would obediently try to find out how much.

The Wickhams left. The young people at the door bade them good-by very cordially. They were both embarrassed at the obviousness of the ruse to leave them alone together and they were uneasy because neither of them knew what the other expected to be the nature of the struggle in the field so plainly left prepared.

They walked back into the living room. She sat down and settled her dress over her knees meticulously. He sat down staring baldly, certain it would disconcert her, not that she minded if he looked at her legs—she knew they were well shaped and as long as he did not try to touch, stares were flattery but they were both aware that convention demanded somewhat fruitlessly that he ignore them, and the annoying embarrassment she tried to hide rose from her effort to follow rules that no longer had any meaning, an effort she thought ludicrous.

At last after what seemed a long time to her, he lifted his gaze to her face, grinning.

Desperately, hardly thinking of what she was saying, she flung out quite loudly, "Well, what have you been doing?"

"Well," he said loudly, mocking her, "I had a sirloin steak and French fried potatoes and then I went upstairs to my room and took a bath and shaved and . . ."

"I don't mean that. I mean . . ."

"Nothing." Although he said it merely to make conversation difficult, merely to kid her, once it was out he was ashamed that he had nothing fascinating to tell.

"Oh, Daddy just got some Scotch. Have a drink?" she said brightly. "Sit still. I'll get it." She jumped up and ran out.

He followed her and in the clean tiled kitchen he took the bottle away from her, removed the lead foil and pulled the cork while she got out the ice and soda, all this in silence, portentously, as if the whisky were to be some aphrodisiacal philter.

He poured out two strong drinks and they went back into the living room. He sat in his chair again, she on the sofa. He lifted his glass. "Prosit!" he said. He had learned the word from the Hill Germans.

She said eagerly, "What does that mean?"

"Oh, good luck, good health. It's German." They drank.

"Well, what have *you* been doing?" he said.

She lacked the aplomb to bait him back. She tried to think of a literal answer, finding that she had so little to say that could possibly interest him in the routine emptiness of her life, its vast blank reaches so feebly illumined, and she almost choked with fear that her mother might be right. Any kind of existence rather than once she had to sum up with "Oh, nothing much."

"Oh, come on. You've had your hair done this week. Who did you see at the beauty parlor? What did you read under the drier?"

She was not yet angry because this kind of talk was customary from young men, this or an insulting extravagance of compliment. She received the compliments in a manner both irritated and naïve: she would methodically discount each one and call the givers liars to herself. She could ask wearily why she should be somehow forced to sit and listen to such stuff, yet she made the meek conventional reply because she was afraid of candor. She did not know where it might lead and she was not quite ready to follow it anywhere at all. "Oh, you know what beauty parlors are like."

"How the hell would I? I don't hang out in them."

"Yes, but . . ."

"Come on, tell me about them. No man knows anything about them."

Miserably she told. Perhaps he wanted to find out but she doubted it. She stifled her disgust that a man and woman could not be provided with a different way to meet from this banal fencing, and she began to wonder how she could turn the conversation to his finances.

He knew he was acting like a fool, and the stamp of his particular foolishness, a stamp becoming helplessly more familiar though not more welcome, was to play the boor, to seize the occasion to insult people or hurt them or make them feel cheap and for an end he could not foresee except that there was a brief vengeful satisfaction in what he did. Why the casting of these scornful trivia toward a beautiful girl should satisfy him when he was nearly willing to be tender and, but for the workings of his family pride, frank, he did not want to ascertain very strongly. He preferred to be whipsawed between the compulsion and his desire because he was afraid to find out what compelled him, what beside this obscure duty to his father.

Some men secretly expect catastrophe. Seeking it, they push themselves into danger, let quarrels rise to violence, or, if they are passive, unlike Walter, they await it wondering if they could endure the accidents that strike others when the accidents strike them as they will surely do and few recognize in these impenetrable hoped-for agonies the images of death, casting the shadow of its constancy backward over their lives to taint and shorten them. Nor could Walter discern these images. The stagnancy he lived in seemed merely and vaguely dangerous yet ordained upon him as a son and inescapable save by the exits of insult and hatred for the whole town. This girl, beautiful, desirable, was a part of the town and would have to suffer what he inflicted, if nothing more than these clownish sneers and twinges.

". . . would that be possible?" she was asking.

He had not heard the beginning of her question. To hide his inattention, he said, "Hmm. Say it again."

"If something went wrong with the drier, could a woman get a big enough shock to kill her? If her hair was wet?"

"I doubt it."

"I thought she was wrong. She said her sister was a beauty operator, too, in Kansas City and one day there was a woman under the drier, and all at once it made a buzzing noise and threw out a lot of blue sparks, and the woman slumped down in the chair. Before they could get her out, she was dead."

"I don't believe that could happen. Not very often anyway."

"Well, anyhow, she said the insurance company was suing her sister. They seem to think it's her fault the machine went wrong. Would it be?"

"What?"

"Her fault."

"I don't know."

She knew that her next question would be crucial for her mother's purposes. More than ever she felt a repugnance toward asking it, toward her mother, toward the whole crowding set of imperatives that made it necessary to slight her honesty and sense of decency, yet the question came out with a pretended innocence, "Don't you have to study these things? I thought you'd know all about it."

"What do you mean, study?" he asked in a coarse voice.

"I thought all insurance men had to study, oh, claims, statistics—*you* know."

"Maybe they do."

"Don't you know?"

"I'm not an insurance man. You know that. I told you," he said lightly. He believed her to be more like her mother than she was, steeped in convention, although he did not suspect the intent of her questions. It had not occurred to him that he was particularly "eligible" or even a "bachelor."

Although he had flaunted his idleness before her often enough, it was too strange for her to believe that he had quit his job, left what she took for his "career." The idleness must be a sort of vacation. Doctors did not stop being doctors, lawyers, lawyers. It was incredible.

"What do you mean?"

"I quit. I told you all about it. I got tired of it so I quit."

"I know you told me but—what are you going to do? What are you doing now?"

"Settin' here lookin' at you," he said with a rustic accent.

"No. I mean . . ."

"Nothing. I don't work. I just hang around on street corners and pass remarks at decent women. I'm the kind they tell you to look out for."

"But you've got an income."

"Peanuts," he said. He had never told her how much his income was. It had never occurred to him. Phelpses did not talk about money except in business and this was not business.

If, as people said, he had no money, she did not see how he would dare to loaf around. Now that she had started to play her mother's game, she was wrapped up in it, and she felt a twinge of disgust, not genuine disgust, not her own, but as if she were feeling for her mother. "But you're looking for work, aren't you?"

"Nope," he said, grinning. He was determined to make her face a wrong fact—that he was almost penniless.

"Jobs are pretty hard to get now. Daddy says they turn away a hundred or more every day up at the factory."

"I'm not even looking."

"But ..."

"What do I live on, eh? That's what you want to know, isn't it? Because if I'm broke, you won't see me any more, eh?"

She was genuinely fearful. Doubtful though it was, she thought he had read her mind or, worse, that she had been inept and let him see what she was after. And to be caught doing something cheap that she had not wanted to do at all, doing it only out of obedience, or filial love or what was it? made her seem weak and despicable to herself. "Let's get another drink." She stood up and started for the kitchen.

He followed her, nagging triumphantly. He wanted to present himself in as bad a light as he could and it took no special percipience for him to choose poverty. He knew his own kind. Nothing would make him acceptable, no sort of handsomeness, no birth or blood, no courtesy if his cuffs were frayed and he had no money to buy new shirts. Poor, he was loathsome. Rich, a wonder. He was determined that she should find him attractive, just the male, not the Phelps, nor the college man, nor any of these things, merely himself and naked if he could arrange it.

". . . and yesterday I sold my typewriter. Tomorrow let's see, I've got a calfskin bag. But before long, I'll run out and I won't have anything to sell. It'll be the middle of the winter then and I can go live at the jail. You know they'll put you up at the jail if you haven't any place to go."

She was making the drinks. She looked up sullenly. "I don't believe you. You're joking."

He looked at her soberly and shook his head.

Holding a bottle of soda water in her hand, she scanned his face to see if she could see a lie.

"I mean it. I'm just about broke," he said laughing as if he were trying to soften a painful subject.

She handed him a drink and took a sip of her own thoughtfully. Now that she believed him, she felt a rush of sympathy she mistook for affection. This light-heartedness seemed to be bravery before a catastrophe that, despite her hatred of her mother's wise saws, was real, for how could you live without money, especially now? She could see him thinner, shabby, living perhaps in one of those dreadful little huts made out of piano boxes and tar paper on the edge of town. The people sat there huddled around little wood fires, heating things in coffee cans like tramps. She wondered if she could smuggle—for the means would have to be secret—food and even money to him.

"Do you want me to go now?" he said smugly.

"Don't be absurd."

"That sounds good now. Fine talk. Fine talk. But wait till I call you again. See what answer I get."

"You can call me any time you like and I'll go out with you." Saying this brought her nearer to a decision.

"Uh-huh," he said scornfully.

The kitchen was too bright a place to kiss her. Otherwise he had constructed the scene very well. He had brought her to think he was fairly repulsive because he was penniless—he had seen the sympathy soften her face. When he kissed her now, she would be assenting to an act that violated mildly all her social and moral upbringing. Sometime he would come drunk and unshaven. He took a swallow of his drink, set it down, seized her in his arms and kissed her, forcing her mouth open.

She endured it passively and when he stopped she slipped out of his embrace and walked into the living room. He took this for a further invitation but she was really looking for a place to sit down where she could talk to him. She had decided to tell him all about her mother. They would be candid, open, frank with each other from now on, without compromise or skulking. She was deeply excited.

They sat down beside each other on the sofa. He bent her sideways and kissed her again. At last she sat up, touching her hair with one hand.

"Get away. I want to talk to you," she said. It was a new voice to him, lower in pitch, without her usual nervous tension as if what she was saying were a kind of joke she knew would not be funny.

A little surprised, he picked his drink up off the floor and lay back against the cushions. "Well?"

"I mean that about your calling me up any time . . ."

"I will."

Frankness did not come easily and she tried to find a beginning. "Do you know why I told you about that woman who got the electric shock?"

"No."

"It was so I could get you to talk about the insurance business. I thought you still meant to sell insurance and I thought if I could remember an accident, and when you asked about the beauty parlor, I was lucky because . . ."

He stuck out his tongue and gabbled meaninglessly to mock her.

"I'm not making very good sense, am I?" she said.

He shook his head, smiling, and said, as if he were telling a child to speak slowly, "Now what is it you're trying to say?"

For several years she had foreseen a break with her mother. In looking forward to it, hoping for it, searching for and concocting opportunities to use later, she had always thought it would come in some moment of tense drama. Her mother would be aghast and penitent immediately while she herself (putting on her gloves) would smile, shake her head, and go. It was not happening that way at all. Instead of the clear finality of leave-taking, with herself right and her mother wrong and everything settled, here she was fumbling around talking until she felt guilty—she was betraying her mother somehow.

She knew that once she had made the statement of the hatred she actually felt, some tie would be snapped between her and her mother. She could see that she would be gentle and considerate of her wishes for the next few days and the reason would be that she had wronged her mother. She was an ungrateful child. But she could not stop talking. A certain momentum had been started and he might think she was crazy, no, not crazy but stupid if she stopped and was silent now that she had begun. It was hard to be laughed at before you had even begun what you wanted to say. Looking down in her lap, she saw that her dress had ridden up over her knees again. She pulled it down automatically and began again. She was breathing quickly. She felt she was drawing on her bravery as if she were in danger and at the same time it all seemed absurd.

"My mother wanted me to find out how much money you've got." Was this her life? Did she have to make everything cheap in order to live honestly, endure this young man's clowning which she could endure only because she believed his life was equally imprisoned and he was shut behind his own peculiar barrier? (He was making his eyebrows crawl up and down over his squinting, grinning, eyes, muttering, "Ah-*haaa!*" in a falsetto satire of a villain in a melodrama.) Wouldn't he ever stop? Must her sincerity be either buried or laughed at?

"Aren't you going to say anything?" she said.

"What is there to say when you see it all?"

It was not enough that he should say he understood. To make her defiance real, it was necessary for her to insult her mother. She had to say it now at the very least (and she could foresee that she would also have to say it all over again to her mother when she found the chance and the strength). "My mother," she began (the phrase "My mother" put some distance between her and Mother) "thinks I ought to marry you, not because she likes you or cares if I like you but because she thinks you are rich. She has heard that your father lost his fortune in the crash. She knows insurance men don't make money until they've been at it a long time. So, she suspects the rumors are wrong—you must have some money left. If you have, she wants me to marry you, but only if you have."

She waited, but all he said was, "That's just what I said."

"You don't want to marry me, do you?" she said as if she were sure he didn't.

"Certainly not."

"I wish you'd be serious."

"Why? What the hell's serious about this? You don't want to marry me."

"I don't want to marry anybody now."

"*Pre*-cisely," he said. He grabbed her, kissed her, tickled her ribs and patted her bottom.

She pushed him away. What was it that he knew? Why was he so sure of himself? Perhaps it was because he was male.

"The curious thing is, your mother's right."

"You mean I ought to marry you?" she said contemptuously.

He held both hands in front of him to push her away. "Hold it, sister. Take it easy. Don't crowd me."

Now at last angry, she jumped up and started walking up and down. "Oh, I wish you'd stop acting like a fool."

"*As* I say, your mother's suspicions are right. I've got some money."

"You lied to me then? All this stuff tonight about . . ."

With a false meekness, he collapsed against a cushion, smiling weakly. "Sympathy. I wanted your sympathy."

"I wish you'd go home," she said coldly. She had never said this to any of her callers before and she expected it to work like magic.

He did not move. He said, "*But* it's not enough money. I told you two or three months ago. So your mother's right and wrong all at once."

"What do you mean?" she said.

"I get about three hundred dollars a month from some stock I own.

Three hundred dollars is plenty for me but not for two people, not the way I want to live. Your mother wouldn't think I was a good catch. That isn't money enough."

"Why did you lie to me?"

"And I haven't got more than two or three hundred in the bank."

"Why did you lie to me?"

It irritated him to hear her so serious because everything she said seemed to be melodramatic, a quotation from a play or a novel, and since he believed she was setting a trap for him (and he had already forgiven her for doing it) he did not want to put up with these seeming-earnest appeals. If she made enough of them, she would come to believe them herself and then she would be really angry if he joked about the situation. He liked a light tone. He wished she could say something witty.

"To keep in practice," he said at last.

She had never tried to define the honesty, candor, and decency she was trying so hard to establish. They had lain shining in the comments and criticisms of other people, but she was quite certain that any of these excellent qualities could be possessed and exercised if you merely took them up like tennis or embroidery. Honesty was only not-lying; candor was not-concealing; and decency was being not-mean. If she were told that she would have to work to show any one of them, she would feel cheated because virtue was easy. Up to now she had neglected it certainly but now she needed it, and when, as willing and well intentioned as she felt herself to be, she was met with sarcasm and laughter, she was sure she was abused and defrauded. She could not side with her mother but someone had changed the colors of the virtues since she first had heard of them in Sunday school and let them lie as they always had, good but remote.

Still doubtful, thinking that patience was forced on her by Walter's obtuseness and not by the nature of what she wanted to do, she made herself calmer and tried again, "I'm trying to be honest with you, Walter." She could not keep a shade of feminine reproach out of her voice.

"You mean you haven't been honest before?"

"No."

"Then why are you giving me hell for lying to you?"

She did not answer him. She said, "When I was sixteen years old, my mother used to come into my room when I was dressing. She walked around me looking me over and I thought she was complimenting me but now I can see she would have looked at a horse she was going to sell the same way. 'You'll never have to wear a corset, my dear, if you just watch your weight.' Or, 'You've got your grandmother's legs, Dorothy, she could hold a blotter between her knees and one between her calves.' I thought she was doing me a favor, 'trying to get me ready for a good husband,' she said. But it was only pride then, and now there's fear in it, too. The depression terrifies her, and if I marry rich she thinks she can beg off my husband if anything happens. You see, I want to talk about this because I'm a little scared to think this way at all. I couldn't tell another girl because all the girls I know think their mothers are fine women and they think the way mine does. I wouldn't worry Daddy with it and you are the one person I know best here." She paused. Walter uncrossed his legs and crossed them the other way.

"I'm breaking with my mother. Do you see that?"

Walter did not say anything.

"You know how you remember your childhood? I have got to forget mine because then she seemed to be really kind and generous. I remember going to my first parties and how she would talk while she was brushing my hair beforehand. And we went to a place in New Jersey one summer and we used to swim in the ocean and she was very kind then. The sun shone every day." She paused, recalling the ocean with the sun on it. "Now I am talking about it I can see she loved me then and I can see she even loves me now. Everything has been done with the best intentions, and maybe there is a lot of selfishness in love. If someone asked her if she loved me, she would throw up her head and sniff and get mad that anyone could even ask the question. Of course she loves me but it stifles me and shuts me up and I have got to throw it away and keep just a pleasant relationship with her from now on. Out of gratitude if nothing else. I wouldn't want to hurt her." At last she stopped, and although she had been looking at him all the time, she saw him now and she felt a tenderness, an affection for him because he had been there to listen.

He sat staring at the cigarette in his hand, motionless, letting the ash lengthen, a pose that committed him neither to sympathy nor to neglect. Hardly anyone, certainly not a girl had ever talked to him before with so little reticence. As a Phelps he was barred without knowing it from taking the problems of women seriously yet she had been earnest enough, awkward enough (and the second guaranteed the first) to convince him for a moment that she was only a human being in trouble, and he thought if he did not feel the dim, implacable weight of his obligations, a weight he surmised was growing heavier, more dominant, he would have liked to help her.

Instead he pretended to keep back a yawn, stood up, said, "Don't do anything rash. Remember she's your mother," bade her good night, and rode back to his hotel.

· XXII ·

HE WAS SITTING in his hotel room in the easy chair. He had bought a tapestried footstool. His feet and crossed legs were resting on that. He had not been out of his room for two days, and he was wearing his pajamas and an expensive foulard dressing gown his mother had bought for him in New York while he was in college. He was not drinking at the moment, although the maid had taken out an empty whisky bottle, a dozen empty beer bottles when she had cleaned the room in the morning, and there was a bottle of whisky with the seal unbroken standing on the bureau. He was not reading, not asleep, not looking out of the window. He was engaged in an act of obscure defiance.

It gave him no pleasure to sit this way yet he felt the weight of a vague, increasingly familiar obligation that made him do it. He had gone through all the reasons he could think of the day before and rejected each one as feeble or unsatisfactory. He knew that no one in the town was sitting like this, immobile, idle without excuse, in the middle of the afternoon, unless it was a few very old people. And in no town across the country, Maine to California, was there another young man twenty-five years old who sat like this from choice. Some poor, some unemployed, yes, but they would do it desperately or because they were numb from hunger, rebuffs, or disappointment. Yet the intimation that he was unique was not what kept him in his chair.

He was denying himself the luxury of self-approval and the admiration of other people because he had another goal. He did not know quite what it was although to sit in his chair staring at his feet in crumpled leather slippers was one of the ways of achieving it. "I'll show 'em," he said to himself but he could not quite tell what it was he was going to show to whom.

There was a loud banging on his door, not a staff banging, no maid would dare. He did not move at first. Somebody was using his fists. He heard talk and laughter. He had callers but he could not think who they might be. Nobody paid any attention to him any more. He opened the door.

Bracey James put his hands on his chest and pushed him back, shouting, "Hi, you old wet smack!" He had time to see that it was Bracey and smell the liquor on his breath but it did not act like Bracey.

He stuck one leg behind him as a prop and pushed Bracey backward. "Don't you push me, you son-of-a-bitch," he said. He did not really mind being pushed. He did not know why he returned the shove except that it was for the same reason he had been sitting stretched out in his chair a few moments ago. It proved something. It defied, not Bracey whom he had not seen in three years, but somebody.

He saw another man in the hall who was giggling softly and saying, "Go on. Push him, Brace. Give him a big push." This second man had a long mild shiny red face and the tips of his teeth showed beneath his lower lip. He was older, about forty.

Bracey was now pounding him on the chest with the tips of his fingers, shouting, "Walter, you old bastard, you old poop, you old wet smack!"

Because he was bigger than Bracey and demonstrating his vague defiance, he grabbed him by the collar, gave a big jerk, and threw him into his easy chair halfway across the room. The older man picked up a black satchel and stepped deftly inside the room, shutting the door after him.

"What the hell is this?" Walter said. The voice was louder and coarser than his normal one.

"Aw, we came to visit you, Walter, old kiddy, old boy. Come on, gimme the grip. Old fraternity brothers, Red. Watch." Bracey stood up with one hand outstretched, a big V of space between his third and fourth fingers. Walter stood watching him. "Come on, Walter. Show Red how we used to shake hands back in college days. Come on."

"Shake hands like that all the time, huh?" Red said. He had sat down on the bed still wearing his hat and ragged overcoat. Little pools of water were forming around his feet from the melting snow he had brought in on his shoes.

Walter seized Bracey's hand and shook it. Bracey wilted limply to one side. "Ow! You don't have to break me up." He straightened up and said reproachfully, "You're not very glad to see us."

"Said you'd be glad to get drunk. Put the show on the road, he said. Old college pal. That's not it, huh?" Red asked.

"Who the hell's this guy?" Walter said, lifting his thumb at Red.

"Who, Red? He's my buddy. Red Carey. We're in business. Business partners. Show him, Red."

Red bent down and lifted the black satchel to the bed beside him. He snapped it open. It was bulging, packed tight. Walter could see two bottles of gin without labels and a bright shiny egg-beater. Red took up the egg-beater, removed his hat, and held it over his forearm courteously. The egg-beater was in his other hand. "Modom," he said seriously, "This god-damn egg-beater does the work of three. It is soundly made of stainless steel as you can easily see, cannot rust or show wear, it has nine blades in place of the customary three, and if you'll gimme an egg, I'll show you a light standing froth in a jiffy, fifty-three cents." He threw his hat into the corner of the room, gave a leap upward, grinding the handle of the egg-beater, and pointing its spinning blades at Walter, he made a grinding noise, "Rah-o, rah-o, rah-o!" He capered and danced around the room and stopped in front of Walter. "You know what we do, Walter? Some-times, not often but sometimes, we get a dame that keeps chickens. So a bowl. So an egg. I whip it up for her, a nice creamy froth. Sure enough, the product *satisfies*," he shouted. He clutched his overcoat collar to his throat with one hand and threw out the other, open, pushing something delicately away, a tragedian. "It shows what you get to know. You get to know things. A lot of things, bud. Some good, some bad. Some are handy. Some you don't know what to do with and you stay up nights trying to find out. Like this: what does a dame do with one beaten egg, huh? Asked yourself that lately? A cake? It don't bake no cake, no pie, no Parker house rolls. One lonely egg, see, in a nice creamy froth. She likes to see the wheels go round but when they stop, there's the egg all beat up. It makes her think. So *I* say," he stood erect, sassy, a thumb in his armpit, "I work this out. It takes time but I work this out. So I say, 'Lady, if you'll bring me a salt-shake I'll show you a trick.' So she brings me a salt-shake and I salt the egg, hold up the bowl, and let it slip into my mouth. For *eating*. Five eggs one day I got."

"I can't do it yet," Bracey said. "He gets a couple eggs every day. Neat, eh?"

"Who wants to eat raw eggs?" Walter said.

The older man, who seemed to be limp most of the time, who sat or stood caved in as if he were exhausted, sprang upright like a soldier at at-tention. "His father sent him, huh?" he asked in a husky voice. "Didn't his old man send him, Brace?"

"Send me where?" Walter interposed.

Now it was scorn, overdone, the lip lifted too high, the eyes too narrow. "Ta cah-lidge," Red said. As if he were begging for food, he scuttled over to Walter with one hand out, "Honest, Walter, he sent you, didn't he? He's a rich man, ain't he?"

"He's dead."

Without feeling or inflection, Red made a perfunctory acknowledgment, "Sorry tuh hear it," and then resumed at his cringing, pleading flippancy, "He was a rich man, wasn't he? He had lots of money? Didn't he have a bank account?"

"He had a bank," Walter said grimly, intending to turn Red's meaning, to suggest sympathy for his father.

But Red spun around on one heel, throwing his arms out. "Ah, what the hell we talking about?" he said, and collapsed face down on the bed with his eyes shut.

Bracey was sitting in the armchair with his legs crossed, and his feet in battered four-buckle arctics, the interested spectator. "Well, Walter, nice to see you. What're you doing now?"

This was Bracey's old manner, the way he used to talk in college except that there was a little difference. There was an undertone, not exactly of sarcasm or contempt; rather it seemed as if the manner were no longer natural. It was a feat of memory, like that of single women who keep a voice for children.

"Nothing," Walter answered.

"Yeah? I tried that for a while. Say, there's a bottle of steam. Right there. Right there all the time and I never saw it." He got up and started to feel of the bottle. "You expecting us, pal? You all ready to start? Can I draw the cork for you?"

"Go ahead." Walter had decided to let them have the "party" because he was confused. At first he had resented the interruption of his ceremonial idleness but now he had come to see that he might as well call it off. He considered for a moment, giving them his permission, suave, cordial, go ahead, boys, and then not drinking himself, remaining quiet and superior, but it occurred to him that these were not the people he wanted to impress. It would do no good. They would say he was crazy and ignore him, at least he thought they would as soon as they got good and drunk. He had never seen this Red Carey in his life and Bracey James had become somebody else from the nosy little campus politician he had known in college, a man who wore a derby and a Chesterfield overcoat to class with gray gloves and a camel's-hair scarf neatly crossed over his chest, who installed an extension telephone in his room at the fraternity during the campus elections, who never drank because there was the Hi-Y vote to consider. These clamps had come off. Bracey was someone else and he liked him better, what he had seen, but the new man was still a stranger, and, as such, somehow irrelevant. And he was glad to see someone.

"There's a glass in the bathroom," Walter said.

Bracey looked up, bright, quizzical, a new expression. "There is?" he said as if he had just heard of bathroom glasses in hotels. "You use it." Then he remembered and Walter could see it cross his face. "That is, if you don't mind Red and me drinking out of the bottle."

"You're damn right I mind you drinking out of the bottle." He picked up the telephone and asked room service to send up some ice and three glasses.

"Class. I knew it," Red said. He was sitting up. He yawned and ran both forefingers in his ears and waggled them up and down.

"Well, Jesus, Red, I told you I'd get us a warm place. Don't bitch about it now we're here."

"You punks don't have to stay here if it don't suit you," Walter said.

"Ah, yes we do. Ah, yes we do. You try throwing us out, big boy. See how far you get." Red sat down again with his hands in his lap and it looked as if he were talking to something he was holding in them. "I talk back now. Don't I talk back good?" he said in a soft voice.

"What's the matter with him, he nuts?" Walter asked.

Red stood up, hands at his side, palms outward. "I live a beauty-ful life."

"He believes it," Bracey said. "He really thinks he does."

The ice and glasses came then. They were brought up by a little fat colored man in a dirty uniform. "Little party, Mr. Phelps? Yes, *suh*. Thank you, *suh*." Walter had often talked to him in the lobby of the hotel and he had not employed a Southern accent or an old field hand's gestures as he was doing now, walking backward, bowing and grinning, murmuring, "Yes, *suh*, yes *suh*." Walter gave him a quarter and said, "Get out of here."

"Yes, *suh*," the bellboy said and shut the door after him.

"I'll make the first drink," Walter said. "After that, you can go hand over hand." He made the drinks and handed them round.

"*À votre santé, m'sieu*," Red said gracefully and drank.

Walter could recognize it as a very good French accent. He was a little surprised but he said nothing.

"Red is one of these guys that didn't get home from the war. He stayed in France. He got back just in time to join the Bonus Army," Bracey said.

"France, eh?" Walter said. France was a country he intended to live in someday as soon as this queer little chore was finished.

"Yes, sir." Red smacked his lips. "Great country, France." He was leaning back in a chair with an ankle on the other knee. He was still wearing torn rubbers and Walter could see the livid shank of his leg in the gap between his sock and the cuff of his trousers. It was a thin leg. "I never had opportunity to visit France until the late war. I came to love it. . . ."

"Tell him about your shoe store in Brest," Bracey said.

Red turned fiercely. "Shut up." He lifted his head again, smiling, and resumed in his light, confident tone, "And with the end of the hostilities, I felt"—he drained his glass and sat looking fondly at it, empty, turning it in his hand—"that in spite of the ravages of war, there were circumstances favorable to my financial improvement." He leaned back pompously. "And . . ."

Bracey had been watching Red. He did not seem to like the false front, the rich man's air, he was putting on. Bracey interrupted him. "He got shot through the shoulder near Metz. They put him in the hospital and he stays three days and scrams out of there AWOL. He hitches a ride on a truck to Brest. . . ."

Red had made himself another drink and was crouching in his chair listening attentively, straining forward as if he had never heard the story before. "Naw. It was to the railroad. I came into Brest on one of those *huit hommes, quarante chevaux*. First the truck, then the train." Walter marked again his easy accurate French. He spoke exactly like old Professor Salomon.

"OK. The truck, the railroad, what the hell. So the first night he's there, he's going along a line of warehouses near the docks. There's a hole in one of 'em and the guard's away someplace up in the line. He ducks in through the hole and he smells leather. The place is full of shoes. He loads up with four, five pairs and takes them and hides them, regular army shoes, brand-new. And the next night he gets four, five more pair. . . ."

Red broke in tensely, "This warehouse—at the corner, a loose plank, see? I put it back every night so they wouldn't see the hole in the daytime. Pat the dirt around it. Lay two empty bottles over the dirt. Careful not to break down the weeds. I kept it hid good." He did not see Walter. In his light eyes lay the image of the source of the only wealth he ever had. "And for one pair of those shoes I get a Frenchman. I give him just one pair and he lets me live in his house a week, sleep there, eat there, drink there. . . ."

"And that's where he ran his store. A racket, huh?"

"I had four thousand francs cash." He looked up and out the window, where it had begun to snow. "Jee-zuss. Think of that." Then he resumed his erect chatty pose. "But it was easy to see that this arrangement

[259]

couldn't last indefinitely. Half the male population of Brest was walking around in Government Issue, purchased from me. It was only a question of time before discovery would take place. So I left."

"Where'd you go then?" Walter asked.

Nodding, his lips pursed, speaking as if his little journey were the most natural thing in the world, implying that he made it in a first-class railroad carriage or by private automobile, a Panhard or a Rolls, perhaps, he said, "Paris, of course."

"What did you do in Paris?"

A childlike smile brightened his face. "The Armistice hit as soon as I got there. I put my uniform back on. They gave everything away free. It lasted a long time. I was *un soldat Américain*. I got the best in the house."

"My father was in Paris then," Walter said.

"He was? Was your old man in the war?" Bracey asked.

"Yes. He was a captain."

"I bet he was. I bet he had one of them Sam Browne belts on, too. I bet you he did," Red said.

"So what?" Walter asked.

He saw Red watching him. Something had happened to Red, he could not tell what. It had made him smile, say things and put expressions on his face at odd times when ordinarily he would have expected something else. Now none of the sarcasm of Red's remark showed in his face. It was shaped into a calm kindly expression as if the two of them had made some compact or other, a plan of mutual action, and were about to go ahead with it. There was nothing irritating in Red's expression and he did not expect him to answer his sharp question.

"I had an uncle with a Sam Browne belt. One time I was at his house when I was a kid and I put it on. Only I got it upside down. I had the strap between my legs like a God-damn jock strap," Bracey said.

"That must have been comical," Walter said coldly. If Red was impervious because he looked so kind, Bracey could pay somehow for the crack about his father, just because it had been voiced, because it had stirred the air in the room. He had to get even with somebody. If he had been sober, he would have hated anybody who slighted or insulted his father but he would not have done anything about it necessarily unless the insult had been large, bitter, and direct, especially if the offender had never known his father, if he had been a stranger like Red. Now, having drunk a third of a bottle of whisky, somebody had to pay for even the lightest slur. The whisky was nearly gone. He picked up the bottle and held it against the light of the window. It was too dark outside to see anything. He got up

[260]

and turned on the light. "It's gone," he said. "Get one of those bottles of gin in your bag," he said to Bracey.

He saw Red look at Bracey blandly. He saw their eyes meet. It was a protest against setting out their own liquor but Bracey ignored the look, fended off its intentions by the brusqueness of his movements as he stepped over to the bag and took out the bottle of gin. It was clear that Bracey was now in the company of an older friend than Red. He was being guided by an older protocol and Red was alone. He pulled the cork and set the bottle on the table. No one asked for sugar or lemons or anything. They all drank it straight or with a little plain water.

"He said you just got back from France in time to join the Bonus Army," Walter said. "What'd you do in France all that time?"

"Tell him about the laundry," Bracey said.

"All right." Red hunched his chair toward Walter. "I worked in a laundry in Paris. It was a little laundry."

"Show him the hands, Red."

"You have to get up close to see," he said, opening his hands and holding them out to show the palms. They were full of a myriad of tiny cracks and creases that almost obliterated the major lines of heart, head, and life. "Hot water done that. My hands were just like anybody else until I worked in the *blanchisserie*. You put 'em in water ten hours a day and those cracks come in 'em."

"Hmm," said Walter, glancing at his own hands. "Work in the laundry all those years?"

"I wished I had. They were nice people," Red said. He did not seem to be evading Walter's question; he was recalling a pleasant memory.

"No, he didn't work in the laundry all those years. He was runner for a cat-house," Bracey said.

"That's true. I was. So help me Christ, I was. It wasn't so good. They didn't have any place for me to sleep but a damn broom closet and there wasn't any window in it. I waxed the floors mornings. Wax floors every day, the French do. And you have to leave a design on the floor in wax, but, boy, how it stunk up my bedroom, that stuff."

"Free nookie, though, he says," Bracey said.

"Yes. It was free. But you get tired of that."

"Oh-oh. Oh-oh. Not me."

"Yes, you do. You just get to liking a girl when she gets sick and has to go away to England."

"I should have thought it was a beauty-ful life for you, Red," Walter said with a bogus joviality. "What made you give it up?"

[261]

"I ain't French. I got homesick."

"Did you have a home?"

Red looked at Walter, rubbing his hand up and down his thigh. "You want to kid me, huh, Walter? You want to keep kidding me, huh? What for? Where's it get you?" He looked straight at Walter's eyes. "Yeah. I had a home once."

"You had a wife and kid, didn't you tell me?" Bracey said. He took a drink of gin out of the bottle.

"You bet. In 1917 I had a wife and a little girl. I was a horse wrangler at Eaton's dude farm at Wolf, Wyoming, then. I never liked *her* much but my little girl was cute. By the time the war come, my wife was setting the little girl against me some and I knew she would more later. So I join up to be a soldier boy and my wife took the kid and went to live with her people at Buffalo. Not Buffalo, New York. Buffalo, Wyoming. I tried to join the calvary but they made me walk to the war."

"All horse wranglers get ruptured," Bracey said. "He told me."

Red looked at Bracey and he looked back at Walter, smiling. "It took me a long time to get to Buffalo. When I got there, my wife was dead and her people was dead and my little girl was grown up and living with her aunt. She played on the high-school basketball team. She didn't know me, of course." He stood up. "I talked to her. She knew I was her daddy all right. And I got her to give me the money she had saved up and I took the train down to Cheyenne."

"Took your daughter's money she had saved up, eh?" Walter said.

"Nice guy, Red is. I told you," Bracey said. He had thrown his legs over the arm of the chair and was flapping them up and down. The buckles on the arctics clinked.

Red looked at them both in turn. He saw they were ganging up on him. He was a stranger to them both, now. He still smiled and he said in a conciliating tone, "Yes. I'm a nice fellow, Brace. What good was I to her? All she knew was that I was her father and I was a bum. She was a nice kid. It wasn't hard to get her to give me the money. Her aunt didn't know she did it but I knew her aunt would find out later and then my kid would know I was a bum for sure. She wouldn't ever wonder if she passed up something not knowing me. Now hoddaya like that, Walter?"

The tension of Walter's anger had been mounting. He was faced by two strangers. They did not count for anything. What he had at first welcomed, even named in his head as they were entering, as "normal human contact," a healthful thing that he wished to have at least to sample because he was in doubt of the course of idleness he was pursuing, not able

[262   ]

to assign any meaning to it and wishing to counteract it if only that an atmosphere of gregariousness might throw it into some focus where he could examine it critically, now all this had become distasteful. His father had been made fun of and he himself was being cajoled into sympathizing with a bum he thought was a clever liar.

In spite of the light shed down through the pressed-glass shades on the chandelier, the room seemed dark. The walls of the room had faded and he seemed to be standing alone in this dark place, blown upon by winds and surrounded by strangers who were hardening into enemies, people who did not count, who had interrupted him in what he wanted to do (whatever it was), to whom any demonstration he might make would be incomprehensible because they were strangers turning into enemies. He knew the mythic signs of his own drunkenness, however, and he merely grinned at Red.

"You never told me that, Red. I never heard that. Holding out on me, pal?" Bracey looked up from his swinging feet. "Jeeze, look at it snow."

They all looked toward the windows. Down before the panes floated the big feathery flakes of a heavy snow.

"Know where we spent last night? Odd Fellows Hall, Monroe, Mich. It's a good dodge. Red thought it up. We asked the head Odd Fellow if we could. No heat but there are rugs on the floor. Say, Walter, I think I'll take a bath." Bracey swung his feet to get up out of his chair, watching Walter to see if he would say no.

Walter said nothing. Bracey started to take off his coat very slowly, deliberately singing a fraternity song under his breath.

"It's gonna be a rough night, Walter," Red said.

"The Odd Fellows have a nice hall here," Walter said.

"You mean we can't roll up on your floor?"

Bracey, who was fiddling with the knot in his tie, pulled it tight again and centered it in the opening of his collar.

"No," Walter said.

"Why, say, fellow, that's kind of tough. You're a brother to Bracey, ain't you? Didn't he say you and him was brothers? I didn't hardly think you'd toss us out into the snow tonight. We just hit town. We kind of thought you might let us sleep here, just on the floor, see, as long as we didn't disturb you any," Red said.

They had come only to sponge off him. Red was watching him. Bracey was standing with his coat in his hands, undecided whether to leave it off or put it back on.

"No. You get out. Now."

"A brother, hey?" Red turned his head in scorn. "What kind of a brother is that?" He looked back at Walter with a faint wheedling smile. "We wouldn't hurt anything. You got lots of room."

"What the hell, Walter, what the hell, why not?" Bracey said.

"I don't want you around, that's all. Beat it."

"A rich guy. 'My old man's got a bank. My old man's an officer.' The fucking brass," Red said.

Walter hit him, and with a sudden horror, felt how easily and lightly he went down, the soldier, the launderer, the pimp, the horse wrangler, the father. He was watching Red's body scrambling to get up when he was hit on the side of the head with something. He remembered afterward his astonishment that Bracey would have the guts to hit him at all, much less with a bottle. He did not fall from the blow. He stood shaking his head in surprise. He felt a soft blow in the pit of his stomach and he dimly saw Red in front of him again. Then it became a dark melee with only the heavy sounds of breathing and the squeak and crash of furniture.

· XXIII ·

CHARLIE RANK'S TRAVELER'S REST was a tourist camp on the edge of town, the good, the western edge, where a long street full of homes ran straight into the country. On one side of the road a red filling station sat under a big elm tree and across the road were nine little two-room houses, each with a double bed, a bathroom, and an electric hot plate with two burners. The nine little houses were arranged in the shape of a U, four on each side with one at the bottom. Charlie had sold his farm in '29 and, holding onto his money until '32, he had built the camp. To supply work for the carpenters and masons gave him a virtuous feeling then but he did not really believe there was anything wrong with the United States. You could sow wheat and it would come up and you could thresh it and sell it, couldn't you? A sow would have a litter if you brought her to a boar, wouldn't she?

He set his price at two dollars a night because he expected a spate of tourists. The tourists did not appear and he figured he was charging too much. He cut the price to a dollar and a half, then a dollar. Only a few people ever stayed there and Charlie took to buying little bottles of vanilla extract at the filling station under the big elm and letting young couples from the town rent a cabin for an hour or two for two dollars. In this way he was able to buy a great many little bottles of vanilla, and he could sit before the stove of his own house next door to the camp, rocking and talking to himself, without feeling any of the shame and disappointment. When Walter Phelps drove out to his place three days before Christmas and asked if he could live there, Charlie said he was real pleased, especially after he got the name straight.

By the time Walter had moved his clothes, the record-player with its albums of records, his radio, and his books into the main room of the cabin, there was not much space left. He brought in the easy chair and the footstool and jammed them into the corner by the bed. His clothes bulged in the little bureau and on wire hangers behind a flimsy curtain on the other wall. The place seemed snug but it was cold.

"Isn't there any heat in these cabins?" he asked.

"Why, I got one of them electric heaters, I loan 'em when they come out, but . . . no, they ain't any real heat." He turned toward the door. "I'll go git you that heater. It'll warm it up some. You just plug it in and . . ." He shut the door.

The place was quiet. There were no trees left standing to rake through the wind; they had all been cut down long ago. Occasionally there was a hum, crescendo, and a car passed by. Walter stood in the room watching the smoke of his own breathing. This was his home now and there was not room to swing a cat. His throat tightened inside. The word "home" had caused it. He did not know why he had thought of it. Before, he had been merely "staying at the hotel" and he had not pretended that it had been any more than a transient warren for him to hole up in. Maybe this little cabin suggested a home because it was a separate building and maybe his throat seemed to close because he was alone in it. He drew a big breath and blew it out in a rolling cloud of gray mist that hung briefly before him in the chill air, then dissolved.

It would take about three days before "they" began to talk about him. *You know where that Walter Phelps is living now? Isn't that a terrible place, a tourist camp. Right in the dead of winter? What do you suppose he does with himself?—not that I want you to tell me. Todd Phelps's boy is staying in a tourist camp out on the edge of town across from the Big Elm gas station, what do you think of that?* He could imagine the smirks on the faces, the triumph in the voices speaking across dinner tables, the sneers going up in steam in the street. They would talk. Well, he would live there anyhow. He wanted to see the day's newspaper.

He went out of the cabin, got into his car, and drove into town. He bought an electric heater, a big one with a shiny copper reflector. From a street huckster shivering on a corner, he bought a Christmas wreath of holly with a bow of cheap scarlet ribbon attached to it. He bought the afternoon's *Telegraph* in a cigar store and he went to sit in his car to read it. He turned first to the "News in Brief" and found the story under the heading HOTEL BRAWL: *Walter Phelps, 25, Carl Johnson, 25, and Norbert Carey, 39, paid fines of $50 and costs of $16.25 apiece in Justice Rowe's court this morning following a week-end spent in the County Jail after their arrest Saturday night. They were charged with disorderly conduct in the St. Charles Hotel. Proctor Sample, the hotel manager, said they staged a fist fight in Phelps' room and broke several articles of furniture.*

He had given his own name because it was natural to do so. It was only after Bracey James had said that his name was Carl Johnson that it occurred to him this was an occasion when an alias might help him but he knew immediately that an alias was useless because he knew the arresting policemen and they knew him. Red Carey had answered to his right name with a curious disdain of the consequences as if nothing could stain him any longer. Walter had paid their fines, the costs, and the bill presented by the hotel manager and had left the court without speaking to them.

He laid the paper on the seat beside him. The streets were full of hurrying Christmas shoppers, their arms full of packages, pushing through the slush on the sidewalks. Idly he watched them pass. He did not see anyone he knew. He slid under the wheel of his car and got out. He returned to the cigar store, bought six nickel cigars, and went into the telephone booth at the back of the store. He called Dorothy Wickham's number.

She answered and he said, "Hello, Dorothy, am I going to see you tonight?"

"Yes, you are." Her answer was immodestly loud and prompt and it made him laugh. It was as if she had been trying to see him.

He was on his way out, he had got as far as the popcorn machine when the big idea struck him. If "they" thought they had seen anything in the newspaper item, he would show them now. Already he could feel the shame "they" would expect to cling to him which he would reject and hurl away. Boy, how he would show them! Erect, his chest thrown out, he thrust his way through the crowd on the sidewalk.

He was turning into the jewelry store when he met Mrs. Bill Reynolds coming out, her arms full of small parcels, and her nose red from the cold. As well as he knew her, he scorned to speak first, and he set his face in a grin which was to answer her greeting. She said nothing. She looked squarely at him, recognizing him and suppressing the recognition by stiffening her cheeks, and passed him by. He had a flash of terror and he gave a loud coarse laugh to hide it. He wanted her to hear his laugh, and he

[266]

turned around to see if she had, as if there would be some sign, the lobes of her ears flash on like a light. She walked on without looking back and he felt a weak triumph as if he had scared away a little animal of some sort.

He entered the jewelry store and bought a lady's wrist watch, set with a few diamond splinters, for forty dollars. It was laid in a red composition leather box, wrapped in Christmas paper and tied up with ribbon in which were entangled two dark green leaves and a berry of false holly. The sale had been made. The clerk was trying to edge away to make the next one. Walter kept him, however, by staring blankly into his eyes trying to remember, to boost his memory over the little fence of immediate bitterness the snub had raised. The bed was ready, the season's gift for bait, what else? At last the image of a bottle of bourbon whisky wrapped in dirty shirts in a suitcase appeared to him. Now all was ready. The whisky was in his baggage at Traveler's Rest.

The town clock on the City Hall struck five. It had begun to snow. The faces of the shoppers were pallid in the lights from the stores. His confidence in the opportunity the coming evening would give him to degrade himself and to defy those who exclaimed over it was waning until he reached his car. Once started, he jabbed the accelerator, drove recklessly over the slick streets until he reached the edge of town. There he opened her up to fifty miles an hour, sliding like a black bug over the ice, skidding into the yard of the Rest and throwing up a feather of snow until he stopped.

There was a light in his cabin. He found old Charlie seated in his armchair chafing his hands before an electric heater.

Nodding, he looked up. "I brung you that there heater. Heats it up good, don't it?"

Walter, standing, could see his breath on the cold air. The old man was like a dog, there, sidling in his speech, rubbing up against his leg. "Yes. It's fine. I bought another one, though. It's going to be cold tonight."

Charlie's eyes opened wide. "Yes. Well. Mebbe." He boosted himself out of the chair. "If you want anything, come on over to the house. I'm always there."

"OK."

The old man went out slowly and crossed the yard, wide between the legs, with little mincing steps for fear of slipping. Walter could see him dark against the snow.

Walter opened one of his suitcases, pawed in it until he found the bottle of bourbon and a glass he had taken from the hotel stuffed with three pairs

[267]

of socks. He set the bottle and the glass on the little bureau and brought in another glass from the bathroom. They were speckled from the hard water. He shined them up with the tail of a clean shirt. In a place like this, he thought, there will be thumbtacks stuck in the wall and he found one holding up a calendar. He fastened the holly wreath he had bought to the outside panel of his door. He was not making his own little festival. It was done in mockery of those who were. She would notice it as she came in, a pathetic attempt at a little Christmas cheer. Women liked that kind of thing and, because she liked it, she would attribute the liking to him and so be confused later, when his arrangements, his little plot, quite beyond her expectation, would be consummated.

He went back inside the cabin and pulled down the bedclothes a little, trying the sheets between his thumb and finger. They were like gauze but they were clean, good enough.

He remembered he had eaten nothing but it was not worth while to drive back into town just to eat. He opened the bourbon and took three swigs straight. He plugged in the new electric heater, set his alarm clock for seven-thirty, and lay down on the bed. He went to sleep almost at once.

At seven-thirty, awakened by the bell without having consciously heard it, he stood up, stretched, and yawned. He did not think he had dreamed anything. He bathed, shaved, and brushed his teeth. He combed his wet hair carefully and put on clean clothes. He straightened the bed covers, emptied the ashtray, and opened the front door so the room, the home, could air for a moment. The two heaters crackled in the draft of cold air. He looked the place over. There was hardly space to turn around, what with the bed, the chair, the bureau, the heaters, and his other baggage, but it was clean. He had not had time to mess it up. He turned out the light, and making a leg, like Chaplin in an old comedy, he swept his arm down in front of him, bowing, showing his teeth, and saying in a light false voice, "Yes. This is where I live. My home." He made little beckonings with both hands. "Come in. Come on. Further. A little more. There, now. It's not so bad, is it?" He gave his loud rough laugh. He went out, locked the door behind him, and started into town to pick up Dorothy Wickham.

He drove sedately to her house. Now was the time to be smooth and civil. *It was true the weather was cold but it looked like a white Christmas. All one's childhood Christmases had snow on them, didn't they?* That was the stuff. Curry the old sharp sentiments that were always lying doggo in these people, ready to be roused with kindness, a pat on the head. Break their God-damn hearts.

He parked his car and went up the front walk. The Wickhams, though their child was grown, still kept to the custom and a Christmas tree glittered in their front window. Calm in the living room behind the tree sat her parents. He paused to look at them. Mr. Wickham read the evening paper. Mrs. Wickham had a workbasket in her lap and was sewing on something, mending socks probably. In how many houses in the town, the state, the whole Union, was this placid scene repeated, blurred a little with differences, but the smug and quiet two the same, Papa reading, Mama sewing?

Hiding the door knocker was a holly wreath like his own. He gave it a wanton jerk and threw it into the shrubbery beside the low steps. He knocked at the door. Almost immediately the door opened and Dorothy rushed out with her coat and hat on.

"Come on," she said as she passed him. She ran down the front walk with careful little steps and got into the car. He followed.

Before he pushed the starter, he said facetiously, "Good evening, Miss Wickham."

She only glanced at him. She was breathing hard. She was angry or moved or something. It was probably anger. In the movies he had seen angry women look at someone and look away, as she had. He started the car and drove slowly away.

She said nothing for several blocks. She lit a cigarette and said, "Where are we going?" He could tell she had decided not to talk about her anger then.

"Oh, haven't you heard?" he asked with bogus courtesy.

"Heard what?"

"Why, I thought we'd go out to my house. I thought you'd have heard about it by now. Don't you read the paper?"

"What are you talking about?" She said this in a cool voice. It was not a request for information. It was a demand that he acknowledge that she was mistress of the situation by virtue of the emotion which still burned even if it had been visibly suppressed. She did not intend to give him, at least, not now, the usual feminine deference. He was rather pleased at this signal of determination, for he had expected that his asking about the newspaper story of his arrest would release a flood of sympathy for him. He liked her at the moment. The light on the plump curve of her cheek and her eyes black in the dimness made her seem very lovely.

During his glances at her he wished to be sincere and open with her, to say something that would show his honest affection. She was a good girl. He wanted to tell her so, but it had been so long since he had behaved without some sort of dissimulation to anyone that he was afraid he would

[269]

be too awkward. As a friend acting with affection or a lover genuinely loving, he had no sophistication.

As he had not answered her question, she asked another, "Where are we going? What house are you talking about?"

They were nearly at the town limits. He pushed the car's speed up for a last straight dash and wheeled it skidding into the courtyard of Traveler's Rest. Old Charlie kept one bulb burning bleakly at the top of a little pole with his sign beneath it. Walter shut off the motor. "Here we are. This is my home, now."

They got out of the car. It was a close night, no moon, and out here on the edge of the empty fields the wind blew the snow hard at them. He unlocked the door and switched on the light. She stepped in. She did not seem to be surprised at the small crowded room. She took off her hat and her fur coat. She kicked off her rubbers and swept them into the corner with one foot.

He waited for a moment, discouraged beforehand by her coolness and the brusque alacrity of her movements. Something had happened, or she had come to some decision that gave her confidence, but, absorbed in his own plans, he did not try to divine what it was. She sank down in his armchair and thrust her feet out on the footstool. "Give me a drink," she said. "I see you've got it ready." All he could do was to grin. She was taking the play away from him. Perhaps his plan would fail. The whisky would unstring her, though, give her enough of it. He went to the door, filled two glasses with the fresh snow, and melted it with whisky. He gave her one of the drinks. He switched on his radio and found some soft music. He plugged in the two heaters which cracked and groaned as the copper reflectors expanded. Alcohol, music, and presently heat, all with a bed so near that its hint was plain. He sat down on a rickety cane-bottom chair. Already half her drink was gone and she was staring vacantly ahead of her.

It was awkward, but he had to make her talk. He said, "Well?"

"I had a fight with my family tonight. About you."

"So they *did* read the paper," he said.

"I'm twenty-three years old."

"Big girl now."

"What's the matter with you, Walter? Why . . ."

" . . . don't I act right?" He made it a statement.

"Yes. Why do you make it so hard for anyone—well, to go out with you, let alone be friends."

"We're friends, aren't we?"

"Give me another drink."

He made another drink and handed it to her.

"What did they have to say? Tell you you have to think of your reputation? Boy, they'd sweat if they knew where you were now, squatting in a trailer camp." He stuck out his open hand sentimentally. "But it's home. The only one I've got."

She did not smile. He could not swing her attention away from herself. She was serious and he submitted to it. "What happened?" he asked in a normal voice.

"I guess I hate my mother."

"Don't hate your poor old mother. She wants the best for you," he said.

He was merely an ear. All she needed was a listener now and he was it. He perceived this and made up his mind to recede into the pattern of the fly-blown wallpaper and leave her alone, talking.

"Mother always reads the paper first. It comes about four o'clock and she has it all read by the time Daddy gets home. The whole thing started at the dinner table. She put on her nasty voice, 'Nice friends Dorothy has, I *must* say.' Can't you hear her? Dad had to ask what she meant. 'Didn't you see the paper?' And she repeated the whole story as if she had memorized it. Dad said 'Hmm,' and that was all. She could see he wasn't going to explode or anything so she turned to me"—she moved her whole trunk without twisting her waist—"like that, formally, and she said, 'I forbid you to see Walter Phelps again.' I said, 'I've got a date with him tonight.' Then it started. I felt sorry for my father, that was all."

He sat tilted back in his chair against the wall, with his drink in his hands, listening. The wind howled around the cabin and the cheap lace curtains stirred at the windows. The room was getting hot.

"I'd leave home if I had something to do," she said.

He shrugged. "Take up social work. No, I mean it. I'm serious."

She smiled suddenly. "After what I told her, I'll hardly dare go home tonight." .

He knew all about it suddenly. She had come out here willing to go to bed with him that she might insult her mother. He was to be merely the instrument of her anger. He wondered why it had taken him so long to see this. He let his chair down with a bang and got up, saying casually over his shoulder, "Big bed right there." He went to the little bureau and took the red case out of it, wrapped in its Christmas paper. "Merry Christmas," he said and handed it to her. He wanted her to feel that his effort at generosity was pathetic—it was really an ugly little watch and he doubted if it would keep time—and coming just after the long angry memorial of her quarrel with her mother, this ungainly affection would be touching, he hoped. Somebody loved her. He watched her face as she unwrapped the parcel.

The paper rustled a little in her hands. She did not give little cries or exclaim. Her face remained sober as she opened the box. She looked up at him and said, "This is very kind of you, Walter," and he knew that the particular moment was a failure, but only as he had planned it. He had wanted the gift of the silly little watch to melt her, make tears come to her eyes, and all he had done was to give spur to this half-suspected intention of hers.

"I wanted you to have it," he said, his belly heaving to suppress his laughter at this solemn fatuousness.

Briskly she said, "And I'm going to repay you." She lifted her feet off the footstool gracefully and stood up. "I'm going to give you something you've wanted for a long, long time." She chuckled. He had never heard her do it before. "Make me another drink and I'll tell you what it is." She handed him her glass.

He made the drink and gave it to her. She talked, all the time walking back and forth in the small clear space. "I decided tonight. Aren't you curious? I've always wanted to do something handsome for somebody and it might as well be you. It will be a lot of fun." She clucked and rubbed her hands together, took the drink and put it down in three gulps. "There. Don't you want to know what it is?"

He nodded.

"Me," she said. Bowing her head she began to unbutton her dress at the top. As he did not answer, she glanced up at him without lifting her head. "What's the matter? Frighten you?"

He shook his head.

Although he had half expected her answer, the overwhelming reciprocation for his little gift, the culmination of his autumn's hopes, he found himself mutely nodding and shaking his head like a moron. Her coarse ease seemed habitual and a fierce suspicion dried up all his plans. Perhaps she was not what he had thought; perhaps he had entered a room that had always been there but he had never visited; perhaps there were other men, here or elsewhere, for whom she had done the same kindness and undressed before. It was a good joke on him to bring her out here to beg for her maidenhead, to fill the evening with a long dishonest whine of solicitation, and then have her do him out of the chance. He was about to speak, to throw something nasty at her to prove that she had not deceived him when he saw her hands shaking as she pulled her dress over her head. Her hands shook and her knees shook.

She was innocent. This boldness she had taught herself, conning it over, every speech and gesture, practicing in front of the mirror perhaps and whispering the words, hoping they would cover her fear, relying on the phrase and movement fixed beforehand to carry her past it. He could see this clearly and when she threw her dress over the chair, she went to sit on the bed. At first she sat with her hands spread on the bed at each side of her, then she clasped them over her knee but the trembling went on; she could not stop it.

"I don't know what I'm shaking for. It's not cold in here," she said in a timid voice. Her brazenness seemed to be exhausted. She had practiced only so much of it. She stood up.

She was wearing a black transparent slip and underneath it she was naked. Walter went over to her, kissed her, and ran his hand over her body. She stood tense as if she might suddenly leap into the air.

"Take it off," he said.

"My beautiful slip that I've been saving for a year now?" she said.

"Take it off."

"Let me go." He released her and she took off the slip. Embarrassed or ardent, he could not tell, she thrust herself against him. He could smell some heavy perfume. She was quiet in his arms a moment and then she stepped away, saying contemptuously, "All set?" It was another practiced speech.

"Why not?"

"Turn out the light."

"No."

She whirled around, apparently furious. "Turn it out, I said."

"You're very beautiful. I want to look at you." There was that much truth he could safely say.

She gave a sniff, walked over to the bed, picking up a cigarette and a book of matches on the way, and lay down with her knees up, crossed. "You turn out the light," she said coldly. She lit the cigarette, swinging one bare foot up and down.

He flipped the wall switch, and, what he had forgotten, the room was filled with a rich copper glow from the heaters, like the lights of hell. His shadow climbed the wall and spattered out black on the ceiling. He could see a long orange thigh and calf clearly. The rest of her was dark.

This was the time he had waited for and he found he had forgotten to prepare the insult. He had decided when he reached this point to refuse to go on, to say at this moment something brutal that would leave her chilled, ashamed, and degraded so that she would hate him and, most important, tell everybody how she hated him, but he had forgotten to make up anything to say. He stood there foolishly behind the glow of the heaters with the sweat prickling his face, listening to the wind. As if the darkness were a light that exposed him, he saw himself as he knew he was, a bad young man at the bottom of the world, for here was as good a bottom as any. To be idle he had rejected any number of good and useful things to do. And when he stirred at all, it was to annoy someone or hurt him or laugh at him. By permitting the fight in his hotel room, he had given his friend James and Carey perhaps the last push of discouragement. And, as soon as he could find the words, what he was about to say to this girl, an innocent girl, a beauty, too, could frighten her at such times for the rest of her life, make her a spinster or a timid miserable wife. He knew that his life in recent months had been led deliberately and he ought to be ashamed of it but he was not ashamed because there was this obscure filial reason for it. He was sick of the effort it cost him to achieve this concentration on himself, the willful debasement of being always unkind, but it had a purpose and wretchedly he hoped that if he could discover it precisely, he might somehow be justified.

All at once a scene appeared in his mind, full and bright, like a vision. In a little wooden pavilion, painted white like the old bandstand in South Park, he was shaking hands with a lot of people, all of whom he could nearly recognize. He had done nothing special, given no gifts, helped nobody, rescued none helpless, made no benefits to the community. They were merely shaking hands with him, each with a smiling face, decent, kindly faces because he was a friend, a spontaneous demonstration. Soon he had been greeted by all of them and they went away, in sunlight, some waving back at him. He skipped down the steps of the pavilion. There was a hill in front of him, sandy, warm, and dry. He climbed it slowly, taking pleasure in the pull of his back and leg muscles. At the top, lying naked in a clump of light grasses, Dorothy was asleep with her arm thrown up over her eyes. He lay down beside her, waked her with a gentle touch, and pulled her to him. The sea was at the foot of the hill, calm, a heavy blue in the sunshine, and when he lifted himself up to see it, he saw the long green grass stems against the sky and, raising himself further, the water. That was all. Nothing like it had ever happened to him before, in dream or reverie, and it seemed to him that if he had not been withheld from hoping in this mysterious way, he might have hoped for that. But, considering what he had to do, it was foolish to wish for it. And he was probably a little drunk.

He licked his lips and stepped over to the foot of the bed. She lay with one arm over her eyes. She took it away and stretched out one leg. "Please hurry," she said.

"Nothing's going to happen," he said.

"What are you talking about?" she said, turning her head to look at him with a stirring of distrust.

"Get up and get dressed. Nothing's going to happen." He watched her throw herself upright, the glow striking her cheeks, shoulders, breasts, and belly. He was seeing it all from far away, like looking through the big end of a telescope. She was no longer any concern of his personally. She was a "carrier" now who, because he wanted her to, would go out and infect a great number of people.

His private laughter began again. "I will now make a prepared statement. Nothing is going to happen. Get on your clothes."

It was an economy of movement and he seemed to have time to appreciate it. He saw her slide one leg over the edge of the bed and she was, it seemed, slowly, without the least effort, taking a graceful stride toward him. He could tell exactly what she was going to do. She slapped his face, lacerating his cheek against his teeth. She stood in front of him. The shadow of her arm obliterated her face; he felt the pain of the next slap and her face reappeared stiff with anger. It was quickly covered with shadow, then the burst of pain again. She stood there panting. In the dim light, he could see the skin of her ribs shine and grow dull as she breathed in and out. She seemed ready to slap him again but she did not. Maybe the blood he could feel running down his chin stopped her, startled at a rage she had never loosed before. They were very solemn, he sensed, like two dolls facing each other, fixed, and he thought, "I'd better make certain of this." He slapped her face but not very hard. Then he came out of it and could bustle.

"Come on. Put your clothes on," he said. He went over to the wall and flipped the light on. She would hate that.

She did not cry. She sat on the footstool pulling on one stocking. She snapped the garter round her leg and reached for the other stocking. She started to slip it on but she let her foot down.

"You dirty bastard," she said.

He was sitting in the chair nonchalantly tilted back against the wall. "No," he said in a reasonable, placable voice. "That's one thing I'm not: a bastard. And I wouldn't talk that way if I were you. You're a nice girl."

She tossed her head up, flinging the hair out of her eyes. "I'm better than the whores down at Lide Carter's."

"All right now. Stop talking like that. Get dressed," he said sharply.

[275]

Now it was his play to be grindingly tedious. He laughed. It was intended for a rich chuckle. "Boredom, first, wasn't it? I'm not much but I'm about all there is around here. Then a kind of jealousy you didn't know you had. You heard about my professional friend, and a very nice girl she is, too. And thirdly," he said pompously, ticking it off on his finger, "you were really going to show Mamma a thing or two. Not that you would tell her what you did this evening but from now on you would have had something you had put over on her, wouldn't you?"

She was putting on her coat. She looked up. The starch was gone out of her now. She said, "Will you take me home now?"

He leaned forward. The two front legs of the chair bumped on the floor. "Yes. I'll take you home."

"There's blood on your face."

He rubbed his hand over his chin and mouth and looked at it. Some flakes of dried blood lay on his palm. He picked at his chin with a fingernail, peeping at the disgust he saw in her face. He wiped it with a handkerchief. "There. All off?"

"No. There's a lot more." It was a touch of pride. She would remember this little evening.

He went into the little bathroom and scrubbed his face with a damp washrag. When she saw his face clean, she opened the door and a blast of wind flung it back.

As they started for the car, he saw a man bent against the wind, holding his hat, scuttling away from his cabin. Knowing beforehand it was old Charlie, the proprietor, he ran over to him, sliding the last few feet, and grabbed his arm. "What the hell are you doing here?" he shouted. "Looking in my window, huh?"

Still hanging on to the brim of his hat, shouting against the wind, one hand up in supplication, he cried, "Honest . . . honest . . ."

"Honest, what?"

Charlie leaned toward him to shout in his ear. "Honest, I ain't never done that before. I didn't see nothing. You didn't do nothing. Honest, I'm not that kind of a fellow, honest, I ain't."

He looked at the old man shivering with fear and cold in the darkness. Perhaps, as he said, nothing had happened, nothing at all. Certainly it had not seemed real. It was a kind of farce like everything now except, he remembered suddenly, there was a purpose behind it. He did not feel like doing what you were supposed to do to such men. The old man's loneliness was as much a part of him as the stubble that masked the flabby outline of his chin. He patted old Charlie on the shoulder, knowing that Dorothy could not see him through the darkness and whirling snow. "That's all right," he shouted.

She was sitting in the car.

"Peeping Tom," he said. He started the car and turned back toward town. Before the headlights the snow blew across the road in long veils like water flowing white across the road. "Interesting evening, wasn't it, Dorothy?"

He took her home. When he stopped in front of her house, she said, "Don't get out." There were tears running down her face.

"OK."

She opened the door, slid out, and walked slowly up her front walk. She stopped to wipe her eyes and blow her nose before she went in. He drove away and went down to Lide Carter's.

· XXIV ·

MRS. PAUL IVERSON had never become really a practiced hostess. She stood before the red pressed-brick fireplace of the Country Club, sensible of the warmth from the stick of burning applewood, her mind on the stretch, anxious about a hundred details. Two little grooves in her forehead were the anxiety; the lift of her soft rouged cheeks were the hospitality, ready for anyone who should come so soon. She wished to appear serene at this time of crisis like those women she had seen at the Monday Club in Toledo who stood calm beside the visiting lecturer, not at all crippled by his greatness, introducing him, vouchsafing smiles precisely graduated to the social rank of the women who appeared before them, above all, calm, not flustered, yet there was this trouble with the punch going on in the kitchen at this very moment, something about a bottle of curaçao which was unprocurable, and a part of her anxiety strained through the doors behind her to be with the cateresses, plump German women off the Hill, who were pouring and sipping and trying the mixture. As she looked straight before her through the French doors and the porch windows beyond, she could see the violence of the snowstorm. The swaying trees and the clouds of white like smoke made her fear that perhaps none of her guests could make it—they might get their cars stuck in the drifts or run them off the road. Or worse, they might look out as she was looking and, weighing their warm safe houses, her importance socially, and the pleasures she might offer against the howling weather, they might decide to stay at home.

[277]

She wanted a big cheerful party. A minor annoyance was a pain that lay in her lower spine and when she moved ran fiercely down the outside of her left thigh. Dr. Bowes, the osteopath, had called it lumbago and yesterday he had hurt her frightfully when he cracked what he called her "sacroiliac" back into place. If she stood with her knees bent, it did not pain her so much. She tried to catch her image or some part of it in the glass of the French doors opposite to see if she would dare, wearing high heels, to stand with her knees bent. Would it show? Would she look peculiar? She could not tell. She straightened up with a gasp and bent her knees again at once. She was safe in that posture until the first guest came.

She worried for a moment about the tone of the party. If she had dared have her way, she would not have served any liquor at all. She had seen enough drunkenness in the past ten years and she had never learned to drink well herself. All she had to do was to take two cocktails and the next day her head pounded and her eyes felt as if they were crossed. Her husband had suggested she go to a doctor about it. Maybe he could give her something to make her hold her liquor and she had been about to protest when she realized he was being facetious. She had come to admit that he was more intelligent than she and that certainly was one of the signs—she could never tell when he was joking. She did not want people to get too drunk and make love and quarrel, yet, if she had let the invitations read *Tea* and had actually served tea instead of letting them read *Tea* and serving punch as she was doing, everyone would say the party was dull and old Mrs. Carroll Smith would make some cutting remark the next time she saw her. She was afraid of old Mrs. Smith, the wife of the president of the *other*, not the Phelps, bank. Mrs. Smith was from the East and was supposed to be adept in foreign subtleties unpracticed here. If the men would stay, if there were only some way to make them stay with the women instead of all congregating together in a herd, it would be much nicer, but she knew what would happen. There would be a few minutes, half an hour at most, while the guests were arriving when there would be a general mingling. As soon as everyone had gauged the kind of party it was by noting the guests—was it merely the Iverson group of friends or was it the society of the whole town?—the men would drift to one end of the room and the golf pro, always a guest ex officio, would start a conversation about golf, the greens, the caddies, next year's tournaments. Slowly the sport would be exhausted and the men would talk business. With a thrill of horror at her disloyalty she thought how she hated the plump red beefy faces thrown back in laughter, and the rings of backs that always were turned to her, at the women's end of the room, like a row of elephants' behinds.

She had always wondered why it was that men and women could not converse together. She had read explanations of this in women's magazines but she did not wholly trust them. They were too clever and biting and they laid the blame on the women. It seemed odd to her that a woman should have nothing to say that might interest a man about, oh, the government or travel or business or, well, anything except running the house, but the rare times she had tried to insinuate herself into men's talk they had listened with hardly courteous impatience until she finished, thrown her a remark of the kind she would use to stop a child's gabble, and picked up where they left off. Perhaps in other countries like France or elsewhere in America it was not like that. She did not know. She had not traveled much except to go to Detroit and Toledo to shop and to the northern part of the state every summer so that Paul could fish.

She would be glad, however, to let the men flock by themselves if only the party went smoothly. Was it time to light the candles on the table? She glanced at her wrist watch. It was five minutes to five. She walked over to the table, automatically glancing at the plates of salted nuts and suffering a twinge of annoyance that she had allowed herself to be so penurious—there were too many peanuts showing and not enough cashews, almonds, and pecans. The plate of chocolate bonbons suddenly looked silly. She tried the crispness of the potato chips lying in turbulent waves around a dish of cream cheese and found them satisfactory. She would have liked to go out into the kitchen to supervise the last touches the cateresses were lavishing on the platters of hors d'ocuvres but she restrained herself because she wanted to act as if she were used to having many servants—all she had was one girl who cooked, did the housework, and the light laundry. She picked up a book of matches from a wood-and-copper tray laden with packages of cigarettes, opened, and a neat row of blue match books with *Paul and Olive* written across them in gold script. She struck a match and lit the candles, each with its sprig of holly tied with a red ribbon, worrying dimly whether the wax would run down on the tablecloth or not. The guests should be driving up any minute now but she could see no one approaching because the road was hidden in the gusts of snow. She went back to her post before the fire. She wished she could sit down for a minute, her feet hurt so, but she did not wish to be found not standing.

Mrs. Ludwig, the chief cateress, came in with little steps carrying the full punch bowl, ice and all. Mrs. Iverson went to the table and took a little in a glass to taste. It was, she thought, too strong and there was something in it that made her mouth seem furry. She said, "It's very good, Mrs. Ludwig."

"They's lots more in the kitchen. One of the girls says that stuff, that other stuff we couldn't get . . ."

"The curaçao?"

"That's it. She says it was made out of lemons or oranges so we just stuck the juice of half a dozen lemons in it. Give it some of the taste anyhow."

"That was a good idea," Mrs. Iverson said. Ordinarily she would have used smart instead of good but that seemed flippant and she had a vague fear of flippancy before hired help.

Three glasses of that and old Ferry Culver would begin to tell about his early days in the lumber camps around Saginaw. Aside from the usual profanity, *god-damn* and *hell* (Mr. Culver never used *son-of-a-bitch* or any of the others before women) and the tedium of his lifetime reminiscences, he was not offensive. Phil Buxton and George Ammadinger would spill—they always spilled something when they were drinking but they never said much, and if George drank enough he would go to sleep somewhere. Reese Curtis had ulcers and he might not drink at all if his wife persuaded him sufficiently, or, if he did, he would take one or two and go home right away. Earl Osgood would sing but usually he did it in the bar. She had never heard him sing in this big room in all the years she had been coming to parties here. "Flow Gently, Sweet Afton" and "Marching Through Georgia" sung in the bar would not disturb anyone.

It was the younger men she feared, the men of thirty-one or -two, who had not yet discovered that you live all your life in a town, see the same people nearly every day, and it isn't smart to be nasty to anyone. They had been brought up on this dreadful prohibition liquor and they drank like fishes. Some of them, like Wilbur Ball and Ham Brady would be drunk when they came and their wives, too, and there was no telling what they would do. Last Christmas Ham Brady had fed Ernestine Cutter martini cocktails for a straight hour and had taken her out into the cloakroom and charged people twenty-five cents to go in and look at her appendix scar, and she was only nineteen, a sophomore at Smith. And Wilbur Ball had drunk himself sullen at one of the summer dances last year, and after going around with his face like a thundercloud all evening he had paid the orchestra leader five dollars to stop the music and give a roll of drums so he could make an announcement. Everyone had quit dancing and Wilbur had said, "I wish to state that Rita Yaeger has been sleeping with Dick Fellowes for over a year and . . ." Dick had run up to Wilbur but Wilbur knocked him down and Fred Yaeger had run up, too, and Wilbur had knocked him down, and then Wilbur had turned to the orchestra who were all grinning and said, "Play," and people were helping Dick and Fred to the washroom and, oh, it was terrible. What he had said was true but there was no need to broadcast it that way. These young men were strangers. She was afraid of them and if anything like that happened tonight, she would just die of mortification.

Paul read too much. Maybe that was it. The doctors here and at Ford's in Detroit had said there was nothing organically wrong. But after the crash when they didn't feel they could go anywhere or do anything, Paul had begun to sit at home every evening and read, not only magazines and newspapers but books. He started using her library card and she used to look at the books mornings when he was at the plant. They were all about politics and Europe and economics. He never talked to her about them. He just sat every night and read until twelve o'clock. He had had to get his glasses changed. He had become gloomy and morose and lately he was getting irritable. Nothing suited him and frankly their sex life was no longer happy because he didn't seem to want to do anything much any more. He did not go out evenings except once or twice a month and she had driven the Ford up past the factory and she had seen him—his office was on the ground floor—working away at his desk. The only conventions he went to, he had taken her along so she knew it was not another woman.

As soon as she discovered that, she began to be frightened. If he had been chasing after other women, it would have been an insult to her and a problem for her to solve, but nothing, she knew now, for her to fear. People had mentioned to her the psychological shock of the market crash, and well she could remember the day Paul had come home and said that the seventy-six-thousand dollar paper profit had vanished. That evening he had got drunk but he had seemed all right the next day, and later she had even heard him laugh about it. She hesitated to ask him about affairs at the plant because he made it a point early in their marriage never to discuss business affairs, but at the bridge club and the D.A.R. she talked with other women and she could certainly read the papers. There was no business much in the country and she wondered if that might be the reason. She tried to concoct subtleties but none of them led her anywhere near the subject so one evening she asked him point-blank how things were going at the factory. He had looked up over his book, just a glance, without any movement of his face, and said, "Better than last year. We're getting some orders," and he had turned back to his book with such deliberation that his reluctance to say any more was obvious.

[281]

She persuaded him to take out one more insurance policy, just a small one, because he would be enraged if she asked him to go to a doctor for an examination merely because she was worried. She called on the insurance examiner to ask him to be thorough and to send her a special report. It came and it said her husband was in good health and again she was baffled.

The worst thing had happened last October. In the middle of the night she had been wakened by a little noise, a creak of the floor or a door hinge squeaking. At such times she always clutched Paul but he was not there, not in bed, and she sat up in alarm. It was a beautiful calm moonlit night. She saw him by the window, just standing there, and when she asked him what on earth he was doing, he answered her in a soft quiet voice without turning around, "Just looking at the trees." It was like hearing someone speak who was insane. Although she knew she would see only the elm in the back yard and the maples across the way, she craned her neck to see if there was anything strange there but there was not, only the trees. She felt her throat tighten and a chill go down her spine and she took refuge from the terror in anger and ordered him to come back to bed. He came quite docilely and neither of them had ever spoken of it again. Someone had been burning leaves and the night air held the smoke and whenever she thought of the incident now she seemed to get the odor of burning leaves. She had read a poem in a magazine which connected smoke with the autumn of the year and the autumn of the year with the autumn of life and this poem made her feel very badly because Paul was only fifty-two and she was forty-seven and this was not the way she wanted it to begin to end with him reading and standing awake by windows in the night.

People always spoke enviously of the money her mother had left her. They said *she* didn't have to worry, but only Paul and she knew that the money was in a joint bank account nearly exhausted. Last month she had drawn out fifty dollars and had given a dinner party in desperation. Perhaps he would enjoy being sociable—it was the last thing she could think of. It had gone off very well. Paul had worn his tuxedo and had shown himself willing to mix cocktails. He had been civil. He had told a few jokes and for a while during the evening she had completely forgotten him but the next evening she found him with a paper knife cutting the pages of some book he had sent away for and she thought nothing had been accomplished. He had seemed to enjoy himself at the moment and with a comforting flash it occurred to her it might have been the liquor. He never drank when the two of them were alone and he rarely served anything when guests dropped in for the evening but once he had drunk quite a lot.

She remembered terrifying evenings when they had driven on dark aimless journeys at sixty miles an hour. Now, exhausted by her worried conjectures, she wanted him to drink again, not entirely—and she was almost shrewd enough to perceive it—that she wanted to heal him of his melancholy although she honestly wished she could change him back, but more that she would be more comfortable if she knew what was wrong, and if he took to drinking she would know and she could deal with it. This was her chief reason for giving the Christmas party.

The first guests were the Shorts, Tom and Marty. Tom had gone to the university with Paul and had inherited his father's clothing store shortly afterward. Mrs. Iverson greeted them cordially. They were old friends. They reported that they had seen Paul at Ferry Culver's drinking Tom-and-Jerries. He would be out as soon as he got his car started. The motor was cold and he needed a push.

The next guests were Wilbur Ball and his wife and a guest who was staying with them, a rather pretty girl who was wearing too much make-up. As she had foreseen, they were already a little drunk. Wilbur began to slap Tom Short on the back and shout at him in a parody of the kind of greeting his elders usually gave. It was accurate enough to be recognizable. Mrs. Iverson began to feel a little breathless and very watchful. They made the place seem already full and she found herself listening for tears, a shouted insult, or the splintering of furniture. They were the sort of people who left her nothing to talk about but the weather and she watched them nervously over Tom's shoulder all the time she was talking to the Shorts. They were drinking the punch very quickly, making little jeers about it, and when Mrs. Ludwig brought in the trays of hors d'oeuvres, she saw Wilbur Ball take three, one after the other, just hogging them down.

She saw old Mrs. Carroll Smith stamping her feet on the porch. She was wearing her old sealskin which she never changed, year after year, and Mrs. Iverson felt a tingling in her knees. Mrs. Smith was not the acknowledged dowager of the town: she was the vice-dowager, serving in place of Mrs. Henry Phelps, who never went out any more, at least to parties. She hastened toward her as she came in, eaten with anxiety. She took the sealskin coat, held Mrs. Smith's hand while she stood on one foot to take off her fur-lined boots, babbling about the happiness of the season and the unpropitious weather. At last Mrs. Smith was ready. Touching the gold chain around her neck, she stared baldly at the decorations, mere holly wreaths and a few scattered sprays of cypress. She scrutinized the serving table, spotting the bonbons at once and saying in a loud murmur, "Candy? How queer." Mrs. Iverson at last wooed her over to a chair before the fire. "I see you have omitted mistletoe, Dora. It's not Christmas without mistletoe," Mrs. Smith said oracularly. The very instant she heard judgment, Mrs. Iverson felt better. The party was not, she remembered, something only for this old girl's approval—it was for Paul. She said bravely, "I didn't want any," and she turned to look toward the door where Paul was coming in, his gloves dirty and long streaks of snow on his overcoat. She watched him take off his coat and hat. He showed no anger because his car had not started. He went into the washroom and she lost sight of him because the guests were now coming in droves and she had to greet them cordially (although she had seen all of them within the last day or two) with a cordiality that meant high falsetto shrieks and handshakes that made the soft hanging flesh of her arms ripple. She had to keep an eye on the punch bowl without seeming to, on the nuts, the cigarettes, and the trays of hors d'oeuvres. Also she kept scanning the crowd like a swimmer boosting himself up to peer over the crest of a wave to watch Wilbur Ball, Ham Brady, and the other younger people for trouble. All the time she felt she should be with Paul, trying to make him happy. She couldn't see him anywhere and this made her worry.

All at once a wave of quiet passed from the doorway the full length of the room. She was so busy watching the hushed guests, the turns and stares, that she was late to turn herself and stare at the source. Just inside the door, removing his overcoat and helping the girl remove hers, stood young Walter Phelps, grinning. With him was this girl who at first seemed really quite good-looking, a marvelous figure, and, to tell the truth, in those first few seconds Mrs. Iverson did not think she looked a bit worse than any of the other young women. She was flustered but she remembered immediately that she had not invited Walter Phelps and as she focused her thoughts, she remembered why—he was a Phelps, to be sure, but he was no good. He was drunk all the time; he hung around that "bad house" all the time; he had been expelled from the hotel after some drunken brawl, and only the night before last he had taken Dorothy Wickham out and insulted her frightfully, Marty Short had telephoned her about it.

Talk began again in a loud hum as Walter and the girl started to come toward her. Panic took her. Jumbled memories of famous hostesses and their famous replies wiggled crazily through her head, and she sensed that she could make her everlasting reputation in the town if she could only think of something crushing to say to him but her lack of practice as a hostess stifled her ingenuity, and the expression on Walter's face, the sneering grin so like his father's, kept her silent with a flush of deep red creeping up her neck and underneath the rouge. She had seen Todd Phelps too many times humble people by his monstrous insults, each tossed out with this sneering grin, to even think of turning away his son.

Walter escorted the girl to her and with an inclination something like a bow, he said courteously enough, with all his teeth showing, "Mrs. Iverson, this is Miss Bella Calman. She's staying in town."

And Mrs. Iverson could only push a smile up her face and shake hands. The group of people around them watched, silent, fascinated, while outward in circles ran the tense whispers, some angry, some snorting and giggling.

Walter turned with false obsequiousness to old Mrs. Smith, seated on the divan. He said, "Mrs. Smith, this is Miss Calman"—here he stood erect with his eyes jerking from side to side over the crowd and said loudly out of the grin—"whom I took the liberty of bringing."

Mrs. Smith looked the girl up and down over the top of her glasses, admitted her to the town's society, and said, "Home from college, my dear?"

From the back of the room Mrs. Iverson heard the raucous voice of Wilbur Ball. "Home from college, hell. That's Bella from Lide Carter's."

The girl, who had been standing there so graceful, so demure, suddenly tossed her head back and bawled, "You musta been there or you wouldn't know, bud."

The older men roared with laughter. With the laughter, mingled, were gasps and angry explanations, and loud altercations burst out between wives and their husbands. Walter Phelps turned his head brightly from one group to another, grinning. Mrs. Smith tried to scuttle away from her place on the divan and he assisted her lurches out of the soft cushions by putting his hand under her elbow. Furious at his betrayal of her authority, she pulled her arm away and fell face down on the divan. Like a man at a zoo, Walter pointed her out to the Calman girl and they both laughed and clapped their hands. Standing beside them, Mrs. Iverson was so distraught and ashamed that she allowed herself an unusual candor of motion. She was openly chafing her hands and rocking from side to side as she turned her head this way and that looking for her husband. She wanted him now, badly. The ghastly situation was far beyond her powers.

She saw the crowd part in front of her. With an air of great, almost dedicated authority, Wilbur Ball came forward, his face grim. He was quite drunk. He was a fighter and Mrs. Iverson knew there would be further trouble. Wilbur was probably sore because the girl had made him the butt of the older men's laughter and Mrs. Iverson began to paw at Walter's sleeve and whimper, "Now don't. Now don't," over and over without knowing what she was saying. Her nose had started to run in the excitement. Beads of sweat were dribbling down her face and she kept smoothing Walter's sleeve and watching Wilbur Ball come toward them, with this terrible slowness, begging people's pardon on the way.

At last he reached the rug between the hearth and the divan. Without a word he let fly a long swing at Walter, who caught it neatly on the palm of his left hand, and, looking around as if to free his sleeve from Mrs. Iverson's attentions, he struck out with his right hand and hit Wilbur Ball on the chin. He seemed to fly through the air. He hit the back of the divan. It held him. He sat there a second with staring eyes and then slowly crumpled over on one side.

The next thing she noticed was Walter still grinning and delicately dusting off his hands. "Anyone else?" he said, looking casually over the assemblage. He smiled at Bella Calman, who was standing a little behind him, and asked, "Enjoying yourself, honey?" Mrs. Iverson was uttering little gasps of shock. Her feet did not hurt. She felt no pain in her back, and she had forgotten the heavy shame of her embarrassment. She was now afraid that Walter would wreck the place and that someone, even she herself, might be seriously hurt. Two men were lifting Wilbur off the divan.

Apparently no one wanted to approach Walter until at last Ferry Culver bustled through the crowd. Walter welcomed him with a wave of his hand and began, "Miss Calman, this is . . ."

Ferry Culver interrupted him, "See here, Walter. This is no way to act, forcing yourself into a party you weren't invited to and bringing a woman like this . . ."

Walter whirled something around on the end of his watch chain. Although she was still dreadfully agitated she remembered she had seen the same action before and in the same place. She had watched Todd Phelps stand on this hearth rug twirling the medals he had won for boxing in college on the end of his watch chain. The resemblance gave Mrs. Iverson a curious sensation, as if the son had resurrected the father. She shuddered for she had loathed Todd and now she hated Walter for spoiling the party.

Walter said, "Woman? Miss Calman is about the same age as your grand-daughter, I believe."

"But she's not the kind to bring into the presence of ladies. . . ."

"What does she do they don't do? She looks just like them. Old Biddy Smith thought she was a college girl."

"I haven't come here to argue with . . ."

"All right, Mr. Culver. Go away," Walter said in a reasonable tone.

Fuming, clenching and unclenching his hands, having at last reached a tension appropriate to the occasion, Ferry Culver shouted, "By God, you can't do this, young man!"

As if Mr. Culver were denying him a simple, obvious right, Walter said deferentially, "But I am doing it, Mr. Culver. It can't be too offensive to you. You were down at Lide Carter's last Tuesday night and I don't think you were there on business. You even asked to see Miss Calman, didn't you?"

The girl was relaxed, amused, her hands on her hips, with one foot stuck out to the side, cocked on its heel. "That's right," she said.

"Now it's possible you wanted to go over her furniture but . . ."

Different people laughed this time. Older men who knew exactly the size of Ferry Culver's bank account; men who owed him nothing; younger professional men, the doctors, lawyers, and dentists.

Culver turned abruptly away and started for the cloakroom, followed, as if a spell had been broken, by all the men whose wives were dominant and their wives. As the crowd thinned out, Mrs. Iverson saw her husband, Paul, sitting on the table beside the platter of hors d'oeuvres, laughing as she had never seen him laugh. She charged toward him, miserable, exhausted by the appalling strangeness of the last few minutes, and she ran her head into his chest blindly, almost upsetting him before he had time to prepare an embrace for her.

Walter watched the party break up from his station on the hearth rug while Mrs. Iverson sobbed on her husband's shoulder. As the first paroxysm brought her a little relief, she looked around at him, her face swollen and splotched by the washing away of rouge and powder. In a shrieking, strangled voice, she cried, "Go away, can't you?" and collapsed again on her husband, sobbing, "Paul, make them go away. Make them go away." Paul Iverson stopped patting her shoulder and left her with her back turned, facing the windows, busy with her handkerchief.

He walked rapidly toward Walter. "Now, God-damn it, get out."

He saw Walter's grin fade and a sober, tense, almost desperate expression come over his face. "All right," he said. "Come on, Bella."

Iverson followed them, talking loudly and angrily, hustling Walter along by the arm. When they reached the cloakroom, he followed them in. Iverson's face was gloomy and he took Walter's hand and shook it. "It was swell. It was swell," he muttered to Walter, looking at him with a grave thankfulness. With no change in his expression, he shouted, "AND STAY OUT!"

Walter looked at Bella and shrugged his shoulders. They put on their hats and coats. As they went out Iverson was still comforting his wife in front of the fire. Neither looked up.

⌐ PART SIX ⌐

· XXV ·

EDDIE MADE HIS DECISION to leave the sanitarium suddenly. He had gone to the library to return a book and to kill time for half an hour before his monthly appointment at the clinic, and he found himself involved in a long conversation about Thomas Mann with the librarian. A clock was before him on the wall. The librarian was stimulated by the discussion and it was not necessary to say much. He could lean on the desk either actually or apparently weighing all she said and never look at her, watching rather the hands of the clock or, himself warm and protected, the little whirlpools of snow blowing under the spruce trees beyond the window, or the roof of the dining hall, white and puffed along the edges like some fabulous pastry.

"It is only here that we feel Time," the librarian had begun.

"Explain," Eddie said.

Outside (the librarian stressed the word as if it were a strange place, fully as distant as Russia or Atlantis) one is never conscious of Time. One's life is a succession of days in hope or memory and it is divided by the events that fill it. A normal life is full enough, varied enough to permit only seldom a reckoning of the time they take, thus a love affair may remain in one's memory, freshly, vividly, with more immediacy than a year in a dull office.

"A love affair might take a year," Eddie said.

The librarian was a New Yorker. She had an intellectual confidence that allowed her to say anything. "I meant a single sexual encounter," she said.

"I see," Eddie said. The librarian was thirty years old. She wore horn-rimmed spectacles she often gestured with as if to prove she did not need them.

Here (and she gave the word an intimate warmth as if she were speaking of a place as well loved and forgivable as home) it is different—one is totally idle. Far from sticking up sharply in this idleness, events blur. Their succession becomes confused and it is hard to remember whether something happened yesterday or a week ago. Did he agree?

"The last part's true, anyhow," Eddie said.

She tapped the little thick red copy of *The Magic Mountain* which she always called *Der Zauberberg*. It was a very popular book in the sanitarium. Those who could not understand Frau Chauchat's French or cared little for the philosophical ideas of Western culture read it eagerly as a guide to life in a Swiss sanitarium, to learn, so to speak, how the other half lived. The librarian had studied it assiduously and now she was explaining what Mann had been trying to say.

That (whatever it was) was the first shock Ziemmsen gave Castorp and it was the dreamlike quality of its passage rather than the events that filled it that Castorp was to discover later to be Time's essence. Idle, one could feel Time, the librarian said, as if Time were a rare plush. In the world, one suffered merely the event. But, of course, Mann could only describe the phenomenon; he had not experienced it. It had been his wife who had been ill at Davos. He had gone there to be with her and to comfort her. It was she who had told him about Time and he had made up the structure of the novel from what she said, a very intelligent woman.

The librarian had a large store of knowledge about famous lungers and she could rattle off the tuberculous incidents in the lives of Keats, Andrew Jackson, Laurence Sterne, Simon Bolivar as glibly and passionately as if she were linked to them by greatness instead of disease. Because he did not often have the opportunity for intellectual conversation on the plane on which the librarian wished to conduct it, she made Eddie a little nervous, her pale eyes trying to hold his own, and her pale face earnestly mobile, with a dark red swoop of hair drawn into a knot at the back of her neck. She had been there five years, they said, well enough to go back to her job in the city but somehow paralyzed, unable to leave, not frankly lazy like the two old happy shoemakers who played cribbage all day long, but afraid that she no longer had the resilience to withstand the massive insult of another breakdown if the city were too much for her.

"I'll have to think that over," Eddie said politely, pulling himself briskly erect to show that the conversation was finished. "Oh. Merry Christmas," he turned back to say, and he went up to the clinic.

The doctors at the clinic were adept at giving their reports. The high professional standards of the sanitarium demanded that they inflict the exact truth, and long practice had taught them to deliver this truth in low monotonous voices without haste or stress, like voices uttered by a machine or an idol, remote and unconcerned. It was not that the doctors minded the responsibility; it was more that they did not wish to seem responsible because if they betrayed the least sympathy they could not avoid the excitement of the pleas and imprecations that the patients would throw at them since their reports were, in the nature of the disease, oftener bad than good. They merely wished to avoid more work.

Eddie heard the doctors say, alternating in bland antiphony, that he was not making much progress. There was still some fever, especially in the evening. He had gained no weight in three months. The healing of the infected areas was not very marked in the X-ray. There was a pause, during which one doctor blew on his glasses and shined them with a scrap of surgical gauze which he then threw into the wastebasket, and the other shifted papers about on a desk. The pause was for any questions the patient desired to ask. Eddie asked none. He thanked them and went out.

Leaving the office he felt a light slap on his ankle. He looked down. His shoestring was untied. Just outside the door in the corridor he got down on one knee to tie the shoestring. While he was making the knot he heard one of the doctors, the older, the more reliable, say, "Burcham's going to be a chronic." The doctors did not know he was within earshot; the floor of the corridor was carpeted with thick coco matting. The statement had been made so casually that Eddie knew it must be true. The younger doctor had replied, "Yes. Looks like it."

He wanted to go back to the doctor's office and ask them, "What do you mean by 'chronic'?" It would trap them if he asked that. He had been eavesdropping, and it would be unkind to make them resume their dull, muted, clinical manner after they thought they had got rid of him. He had come to take hope as a narcotic, a dangerous but thrilling indulgence, and from now on, certain that the habit was fixed, he recognized that the amount of the dose was determined by the margin of uncertainty. He did not want to learn the meaning of *chronic* as the doctor had used it.

The sanitarium was one of the oldest in the world. It had been doing its work for half a century. In that time, the authorities had learned, as the wardens of prisons learn, that no man can keep to a regimen all the time. The steady observance of the rules depressed the patients finally. They grew worse. Some relaxed secretly, drinking or indulging in clandestine love affairs, but often shame or remorse seized them and they grew worse also. The need for some public mitigation of this exhausting regularity was admitted, and the authorities made it known unofficially. Whisky was bought and engagements were made weeks ahead of time. Although he had not made a date with any of the women patients, Eddie had bought a modest pint of whisky and he had looked forward to Christmas with a cheerful enthusiasm.

His enthusiasm had stopped and the meticulous plans for all these parties seemed a little silly. His point of view had shifted and all at once he knew why. He was thinking of the holidays as if he were an outsider, contemptuously. If he were thinking in this way, it must mean that he already considered himself to be an outsider. He wanted to go home.

He turned away from the window and walked quickly out of the building and up the icy path toward his cottage. He went out on his porch and lay down in his clothes with a blanket over him. He ran his hand over his forehead and felt of his cheeks. They were hot and he probably had a little fever. He did not want to know how much and he lay still, his stomach fluttering. This was shock. This was what happened to you when you were genuinely surprised.

He stared at the familiar pattern of boards in the ceiling, wondering a little at the firmness of his decision to go home. "Decision" seemed to be the wrong word. Suddenly, like a change of weather, without volition, his return was inevitable. Why home? What was home?

He did not particularly want to see his mother. The long trailing grief over his father's death and her bitter astonishment that she should be so troublously visited again by the illness of a son had at last turned a random resentment into a belief in the malignity of the world. Her letters showed it. She was without luck. Everyone picked on her. If he went to live with her, she would hound him night and day with a querulous kindness that he could not entirely reject because she was his mother. It was offered with a passion she was certain was love; if he grew restive under it or showed the least complaint, she would call it ingratitude and really tear the house down. At home he would be comfortable but he would pay for it.

What then? He could not tell yet whether he would be strong enough to take back his newspaper job. It was possible but hardly probable. As soon as they learned that he could infect anyone in the office, the editors might not want to hire him again. If they did, they would spare him, treat him as an invalid. He would get no interesting assignments and he would never be promoted, a kind of pensioner. He could not picture himself, gray, bent, in a green celluloid eyeshade and long black cloth sleeve-guards, setting type or writing up the short ads.

Why tell anyone? Why not go back, take up the job, and see what happened? Perhaps the disease would never trouble him again—such things had happened. The staff did not like to admit it because it was their policy to be realistic and realism was on their side, yet there had been unusual cures, even a miracle or two. There was the case of Tommy Keegan, one lung gone, the other going, total weight seventy-five pounds. The physician on rounds had looked at Tommy's chart, glanced at the frightful emaciation of his face and wrists, and said, realistically, "Tommy, you better send for Father Sullivan." Accompanying the doctor had been a student nurse, assisting him for the first time. For some reason, very likely the wish to live which he mistook, he fell in love with her, and, for a stranger reason, she fell in love with Tommy. Without giving him any chance to live at all, with the whole staff visiting him every day to watch incredulously, Tommy got better. He did not "fight" to live or do anything dramatic. They had let him see the student nurse every day and he got better. Only a few months ago he had left the sanitarium after seven years, a round-faced, jolly little man who was going to repair radios for a living, and, with the simplicity of a fairy tale, Mrs. Keegan went with him. What about that? Of course, there was no one he himself was in love with and he doubted candidly if his appetite for life was great enough to work any miracle.

What was most likely to happen was that he would work four or five months, lose weight, run a few degrees of fever every day, and have to go to a hospital again. Not quite so likely but an eventuality that occurred oftener than any miracle was his death. He could not honestly tell himself that the courthouse run on a small-town newspaper was so fascinating, so valuable a work that it was worth a chance that had such desperate possibilities lurking in it. And, more important, if he told no one, he might infect someone. It would be a dirty trick. With the awkwardness of a man handling a new tool, for his "kindness" was still new and deliberate, he decided against it.

Here the trees were pine and spruce and oak. At home they were maple, and fall was scarlet, not green and brown. At home people spoke to you carelessly, sometimes asking how you were without especially caring, just as a politeness. Here people asked how you were with almost fawning eagerness because they wanted to know—if you were better, they were immediately miserable, and when they made the required congratulation, it

[293]

took all their stamina to conceal the jealousy and sadness that tore at them. They could not be friends, and at home he had a few, people he could take for granted like old Walter, who was going straight to hell, his mother said. He wanted to see him as he wanted to live again in a house where he knew his way in the dark, to be in the midst of a climate where there were no surprises. Home was better because there was an ease in it. There pine trees grew properly in graveyards. That seemed to be all there was to it. Familiarity was safety, even health.

With the faint glad shouts of the other men in his cottage dressing to go to lunch, this rare holiday exuberance, he fell asleep. When he woke, the mountainside was in a bluish shadow. He could hear the footsteps of someone just leaving his dressing room. In the hall George Brice said, "He's still asleep. He's curing, the bastard."

Another voice said, "Oh, let him alone, George. He'll wake up pretty soon."

"Pretty may not be soon enough. This Scotch won't last forever."

"Come on. Let him alone. . . ." The voices faded and he heard footsteps on the stairs.

He had slept through lunch and the Christmas party they had counted on so long had begun without him. He jumped out of bed and shuffled quickly into his dressing room. The pint of whisky was hidden, safe, on a shelf in his closet. He brought it out and let it stand shining on top of the bureau while he dressed. He heard a woman's laughter downstairs.

The sitting room, which usually had the depressing impersonal air of a hotel lobby, was now specially clean. Festoons of red and green paper drooped from the corners of the room to the central chandelier. A fire made of red paper, an electric fan, and an electric light fluttered in the fireplace and in the corner stood a Christmas tree—one had been supplied to every cottage. It was not very lavishly decorated. No one had remembered to buy decorations when they went into the village except Spruille. He was a bank cashier, about forty years old, who was always taking cold baths and scrubbing himself with a rough towel. He had three children and he could remember things like that. A few tinsel ropes and half a dozen colored balls relieved the heavy green of the tree. The room was full of its odor.

The wicker table in the center of the room had been cleared of its out-of-date magazines and laden with bottles of soda water and a big dish of ice cubes. The private bottles of whisky belonging to the three men in the room sat there also. Every time a drink was made, the owner used his own bottle. The only guests were Brice, two other men, and a lean angular woman, one of the oldest patients although she was about thirty-five, Velma Baker. She was sitting on the sofa with Brice and she was giggling.

Eddie came in carrying his bottle by the neck. He made himself a drink. He gave them a toast and sat down, waiting for conversation to be resumed. He did not think Velma Baker attractive and he resented her early arrival although at any other time he would have felt sorry for her. She was going to die. They had told her. She believed it, and he had believed what he had heard, and she carried a desperate nervous jollity with her.

"... so he says to me, 'What's a lesion?' Can you feature it? 'What's a lesion?'" Brice was saying. "Now what can you say to a drip like that? I said, 'Carl, a lesion's a little hard ball. You know about gallstones, don't you? Sure. Well, a lesion's a little hard ball like a gallstone only it forms in your lungs.'"

Velma Baker shrieked with laughter.

"Downtown the kids play marbles with 'em. They're perfectly round. Gallstones sometimes got corners on 'em, irregularities. But the action of the lungs makes lesions round. The kids go to the clinics and get sackfuls of 'em every day after the operations. The doctors save 'em."

Velma Baker was laughing helplessly, gasping out "George" in two well-defined syllables, *Jaw-urge,* panting and laughing and pressing her sides. She had both lungs collapsed and exertion made her breathless. The other two men had not heard the story before and they laughed also. Brice sat leaning forward watching Velma laugh as if he were watching a machine at work. Suddenly he set his drink on the floor, jerked Velma up standing, and slapped her face.

"Cut it out," he said. Her laughter subsided in chokes and giggles.

She sank down. "I know. Thanks, George." She began to giggle again and George sliced away from her viciously with his hand flat as if he were going to hit her. "Shut up, I said."

"All right."

"Tell you stories, huh?" he said disgustedly. Then, remembering his audience, he leaned forward and began to explain. "Velma's got paroxysmal auricular tachycardia. It's a heart condition. . . ."

"I'll say," one of the other men said.

"The meat heart, not the love heart," Brice said.

In mock protest, Velma said, "Oh, Jaw-urge."

"Both lungs down, see? The mediastinum's two inches out of line."

"Three inches," Velma said proudly.

"The last time I saw your plate, it was two inches."

"It's three now. I'm taking fifteen hundred C.C."

"Golly. Fifteen hundred?" George was impressed.

"What's the mediastinum?" one of the men asked. He said it in a warm cozy voice that was intended to flatter Velma by showing an interest in her interior. He had his eye on her. He knew her reputation. A married woman, too.

"It's the partition between the lungs," Brice said scornfully. "It's three inches out of line and it pushes the heart over. Get her laughing and her pulse'll go two hundred or better. Any excitement."

"That's right. Thank you for the help, George," Velma said, coyly because she was the center of attention, a spectacle Eddie found repulsive.

The man who was eying Velma was Davidson, a graduate student of history, who wished to be in love. He had been a patient only three months, and, timid, he could not yet express himself with the sophistication peculiar to the place. Since he saw no vivid historical implications in his life among these people, he gratefully refused to think at all and whenever he talked, especially to women, he used expressions he had heard other men using without ever inquiring whether they were appropriate or not. He wore a dull red necktie every day and steel-rimmed spectacles. There was a scurf of dust and ravelings on a volume of von Ranke lying on his bureau.

The other man was Hank Riebel, an automobile salesman. He could talk like the ads. With a straight face, necessarily, since he believed what he said and considered his business manner of speaking as a cultural acquisition, he could say such things as, "In our new 1935 model, you will thrill to the surge of power released when you lightly press the accelerator." He had learned how to do this (studying the printed ads at night) because he wanted to buy a little farm where he could raise his children in open sunlight, an ambition he never put into words. He could see the children playing, casting dark shadows, a wind blowing their dresses. Now, sick, he was terrified and he hung around George Brice because George did not seem to have any fear and Riebel hoped without thinking about it that he might absorb the fearlessness or learn how to make it if he kept close enough to the source.

To Eddie, it did not seem to be much of a party the first hour or so. They talked of nothing but tuberculosis and they talked about that every day. Brice was the impresario, striding up and down the room with a drink in his hand, joking, ridiculing hopes, wishes, anticipations, running the conversation on one track.

In one of the inexplicable lulls Davidson stood up, and straining after nonchalance so hard that his jaw quivered, he said, "I guess I'll sit over here," and he crossed the room trembling to sit beside Velma on the sofa. Brice swaggered over and humiliated him and Davidson could not say anything. He tried to detach himself from his surroundings, sat mutely in a huddle, wretchedly conscious that the moments when Velma might welcome him were passing.

She became drunk. Eddie could tell because she sat with her head in her hands staring at the opposite wall. Soon she would begin to talk about death in a disjointed, maudlin way, full of scorn for everyone else since they were going to live or at least expected to. Sometimes she seemed to portray death as an exclusive luxury cruise that any others who were present were not rich enough to afford. At other times she merely protested softly, whimpering. The sun had gone down. Nobody switched on the lights. The artificial fire in the grate cast a reddish glow .

Eddie was bored. At last he stood up and announced, "I'm going home tomorrow."

Brice stopped his pacing. For once he seemed frank. He could take no attitude but envy and Eddie could sense this envy and the others' beating around him like a swarm of flies. "They tell you?" was all Brice said.

"No. I'm withdrawing."

It was like a sigh. They all relaxed. Brice said, "Oh." Eddie was not, then, cured.

"What you going home for?" Brice asked. "You know what they say about people who go home to cure."

"Yes."

"There was a fellow here last year. He was nuts about this occupational therapy. Made the best baskets you ever saw. Made 'em out of switches, willow switches, clothesbaskets, market baskets, God knows what all. He made Velma a little basket out of sweet grass. You still got it, haven't you?" Brice looked at her.

She was still staring at the wall with her chin in her hands.

"Velma!" Brice said sharply.

She turned her gaunt rouged face toward him with dignity.

"Cut that stuff out. This is Christmas."

"Go to hell," she said.

Brice shrugged. He took up his march up and down the room. "This guy had the idea he could go home and make baskets in bed and pay his way, see? Lie there in the bosom of his family weaving baskets. So he went." Brice walked the length of the room without saying any more. It was a cue for a question.

Riebel took it. "What happened to him, George?"

"Lasted just ninety days."

"I'm not in bed," Eddie said.

"OK. I'll give you six months," Brice said promptly. "I mean it. Curing at home is bad business. You're an ambulant patient, sure. So you amble around to see all your friends. You won't rest. You'll have visitors. . . ."

"I may even get a job," Eddie said.

Brice looked steadily at Eddie for three seconds. "You really are going home, aren't you?"

"That's what I said."

Brice swung away from him and began to tell a long story about a former patient, a refrigerator salesman who said he was an Eagle Scout, who chased after the nurses and went for an automobile ride and came down with miliary right afterward and died and a little woman he had never said anything about, a little woman with a bird on her hat, his wife, came up to get the body.

He had not quite finished when several people, men and women, came stamping up on the porch with their arms full of packages. They paused outside to take off their boots and galoshes, then they threw the door open and came in. They put the packages on the wicker table and the mantel. They were full of food and drink, whisky, gin, a lone bottle of brandy, boxes of candy, salted nuts, and Christmas cookies. There were five men and five women, some of them married but not to each other. There was a good deal of miscellaneous shouting and screaming until they got their coats off and the first drinks made.

As soon as there was a little quiet, Brice, still in the center of the floor, pointed at Eddie and shouted, "*He's* going home tomorrow!" There was perfect silence until one man with a longer memory, abler than the rest, less damaged by his sojourn, raised his glass and said, "Good luck."

"*But* he's just withdrawing," Brice said.

The sullen envious looks vanished. The women said, "O-o-o-h," in long-drawn-out voices. Now he was merely a fool. They needed no bonds with him. He would carry no hopes with him when he left, their agent, doing what they would all like to do. Loud talk rose up about their own affairs.

Eddie sensed the force of his dismissal from the group, and he felt already like a visiting observer. He took his drink and withdrew to a chair in the corner to watch. The scene might be worth remembering, he was trying to persuade himself, but his resentment of the way they had treated him burst through his effort to be calm. More slowly came this new scrupulousness, the effort to be kind. It had not been very decent of him, he reflected, to say he was leaving the sanitarium. It started too many thoughts. It might have spoiled the party for some of them.

He looked around the room. Velma Baker sat with her knees apart, her head and hands hanging down, and God knows what images of mortality mowing and grimacing behind her broad uncomely forehead. They all knew each other's behavior so well and he could see that Velma had endured her gloomy peep show nearly long enough. Soon, with bright fevered eyes, she would offer herself to the nearest man with an almost religious insistence. It might have been one of the unregarded instincts. She reached for the act of life as a talisman, perhaps, to ward away this death inhabiting her and certain, inevitable. On the other hand it might have been only a trick she had learned because she was slab-sided and ugly. Who could refuse a dying woman?

Davidson had roused himself and was entreating her in the only mode he knew, that of a lecturer, with broad solemn gestures. She paid no attention. The decision she always made when she was drunk was a private matter. Davidson would be startled when at last she raised her head and said, "Let's go upstairs," but before he touched the first step he would be chagrined to learn that his awkward blandishments had been worthless. Something else, something that she contained, had turned the trick.

A man named Bill Matters who had been drinking enthusiastically all the afternoon thrust himself up out of a chair with a set face, walked out, and went to sleep on the floor of one of the dressing rooms. The air had filled with cigarette smoke. The group had broken up into couples. Brice had taken Bill Matters' girl, a newcomer, very pretty, from the Polish section of Cleveland, and had gone to sit halfway up the stairs. Eddie sat diffidently in his corner taking a little drink every half hour. Someone had brought a portable record-player and one couple were dancing stiffly to the music, laughing hilariously. Someone was always making a drink, or taking a handful of nuts, and sooner or later each couple tried to dance.

By eleven o'clock they forgot to play the records. In the dim wavering light from the fireplace Eddie could see one couple embracing in a corner and another pair wriggling on the sofa. People talked in low voices, tittered, and were silent. Eddie wanted to go to bed but he was afraid it would seem a kind of insulting condescension. He had drunk the whole pint of whisky but it had only made him sleepy. At last he got up to go to bed. For some reason he thought he ought to go on tiptoe. When he turned into the hall, he saw Brice and the Polish girl sitting on the bottom step. In a lubberly disgust at her scruples, Brice whispered hoarsely, "Why of *course* I'm going to marry you."

[299]

When he saw that Eddie wished to pass and go up the stairs, he gave him a bloodshot glance of annoyance and slid to one side without speaking. Eddie said, "Merry Christmas," but Brice had already renewed his vehement persuasions.

In darkness on the top step sat Velma Baker and Davidson. She was going on about death.

"You don't know what it's like. Nobody knows what it's like to be dead."

Davidson whispered fatuously, "I'll take care of you, darling."

Velma answered in a kindly whine, "You won't need to. I'll be dead and gone."

Velma was against the wall and Davidson had both arms around her as if she might escape. Guiltily Eddie wanted to laugh as he stepped past them. Evidently Davidson had made the grade and was finally in love. "Merry Christmas," Eddie said. There was no answer. He felt his way down the hall and went to bed. It was very cold in bed in spite of the electric blanket. The wind howled through the trees. Eddie lay with two pillows diagonally across his face with only his nose out, and his nose was greased to keep the steam from his nostrils from congealing and freezing to the sheet. He was already a long way from the people downstairs. His imminent departure gave him a kind of health, and he asked himself if it would be unkind or presumptuous to pity them.

· XXVI ·

THERE WAS A SLOW vague recession of some brutal force he had dodged or escaped; a loud sound dwindled into silence; and the darkness of the avoided conflict brightened as if a cloud had lifted. He lay by a roadside, weak but restless among tufts of dock, milkweed, and thistles. He tried to get up, thinking it was time to be on his way. Then he saw the pale oblongs of the row of windows, and Walter knew he had waked up. It had been only a bad dream. He scratched a match, shaded the flame with his hand, and looked at his father's watch. It was ten minutes to three. They would be coming for him soon.

He sat up and reached for his clothes. Gasping, sighing, and snoring, thirty-nine other men lay in the two rows of cots, all asleep except maybe Ziglia, all defenseless but protected against the chill and the dew of the spring night, any little animals, rats or moles, sudden storms, safe from everything but themselves. He wondered what they dreamed about. If he himself, that is to say, a strong normal man, bearing no special affliction, could be harrowed by a fear which only now had left him, did they dream worse? Did the weak-headed have a stronger terror to cope with? Or was the night only a darker day filled with the monotony of the same, not always unpleasant delusions? What were the dreams of the alcoholic, who, now confined, could drink no more; of the man who thought he was Rudolph Valentino—was he Valentino in the night-time, casting hotter glances, gliding in a more voluptuous tango because all the skeptical eyes were shut; of the sober gray-eyed man who was perfectly all right except that he could not resist a temptation to feel little girls; of the sad man who did his work but never spoke; and Ziglia?

Holding one shoe, listening, he heard Ziglia sobbing. It sounded like a woman. It went on all night, every night, like the echo of an unbearable grief. He set the shoe quietly on the floor and tiptoed down to Ziglia's bed. He bent down to peer at him but he could see nothing. He put out his hand and touched Ziglia's cheek. It came away wet with tears. He wanted to wake the little Italian and tell him everything was all right but perhaps it was not all right for him to wake up in the ward. You could not tell about these people. The dream with its grief and tears might be better than to be waked and find himself here in the dark.

Walter went back to his cot and put on his shoes. He was ready. They could come any time. He stood up and walked to the door with the utmost care so as not to wake anybody. When the door opened, he would be standing there and nothing would need to be said. Nobody would be disturbed. Every night while he was waiting this way (for he had gotten into the habit of waking a little before three) he would listen to the breathing, the long sighs and the twisting in bed and he would wish there was something he could do for them to give them some ease but there was nothing and he knew it. They were not within his help. When you got to know them, most of them were really very gentle and you excused the rare shouts of terror and the occasional breaking of a chair. Nothing they did seemed comic any more and he could almost say they were his friends.

The lock clicked and the door opened. The keeper stuck his head in and listened. Walter waited. The keeper straightened up, beckoned, and stood aside to let Walter pass; then he locked the door. They were in a brick-and-cement corridor with the lights in little steel cages in the ceiling.

"Listen at him," the keeper said. "Come right th'ough the door. He's a sure-enough snorer, that little dago."

"Thanks for getting me up, B. F."

"They be along in a minute," the keeper said. He sat down behind a little table in a chair cocked back against the wall and began to read a frowsy copy of *Love Story Magazine.*

Walter went down the corridor and out through the dark reception room. He sat down on the front steps of his building, B building. The moon was down but every star in the sky was shining. In a few minutes the wind that came before dawn would blow and stir the little newly planted elm trees. It was the only time of day he was alone. He had about four minutes. He yawned, shook his head, and looked at the stars. Mars was the pinkish one. He lined up the North Star from the handle of the Dipper, tasting the residue of the pride he had felt years ago when he became a First-Class Scout. He was absorbed in the memory of the merit badges he had won, the bright little emblems his mother had sewed on his sleeve, when he heard them coming and saw them, shadows. There were three or four with Theo walking a little ahead. He stood up and called, "Morning, Theo."

"Hi, Walter," Theo said, without stopping.

They walked down the gravel paths two by two, some of them whistling, some kicking at tufts of wet grass. They stopped at C, D, and F buildings to pick up the rest of the crew. They went through the empty dining hall to the kitchen, where all the food was prepared. Jimmy, the other baker, arrived first every morning, and he had put on a big pot of coffee. The men got into white coveralls, waiting for the coffee to boil. Theo brought a can of cream, a sack of sugar, and a handful of spoons. The coffee boiled. They each had a cup, sleepy, without talking much. Then they went to work.

Because he was big and could handle it, Theo, the master baker, had given Walter a job on the mixer. It was a big metal tub, now fresh and clean, with four rotary blades. Each batch of flour, yeast, salt, sugar, and water was weighed up by Theo, and dumped into the mixer by one of the other workers. The mixer was turned on. Theo would stand and watch it a minute or two as if he did not trust its operation. (He was an old-time baker who had once done this with his hands.) He would go away to superintend the making of some pies and cakes and return before the batch was finished. When it looked to be the proper consistency, he switched off the blades, and Walter, after dipping his fingers into a can of cottonseed oil and rubbing it on his hands and wrists to keep the dough from sticking, would lift up a mass of dough about as big as a bushel basket, turn, and jam it into the hopper of the separator. The separator pushed the dough through a nozzle the thickness of a loaf. A blade timed by a neat train of little gears descended and a dough-loaf was cut off, slid out on the lip of the machine, and tumbled down on a conveyor. Theo's assistant slapped the loaves into pans and they were wheeled off to the ovens in trays.

Walter liked the work. No one bothered him, and after his job had been explained, no one ordered him around. It made him seem useful, for the thousand loaves a day were eaten by people who were still human beings with hunger coming three times a day even if they were crazy, neurotic, alcoholic, or whatever. (They were the first group of people he had ever thought of as "human beings"—all others gave him reasons to like or hate them, and even these would also in time.) Also there was enough noise so that he did not have to talk to anyone—he merely shouted. And the work itself was intermittent. While Theo was weighing up a batch, he could help himself to another cup of coffee and, if they were out of the oven, to half a pie, hot, apple or peach or custard. The bakers did not mind.

It had taken him two months to catch enough of a doctor's eye to prove to him that he was trustworthy. The doctor made the rounds every morning about ten, alone, wearing a white coat. The asylum was overcrowded and he walked rapidly through the ward looking to the right and left as if his head were on a swivel. If everything stood as usual, he did not stop at all and the ward took about twenty seconds of his time. Walter had contrived to stop him one morning for a short exchange of questions and answers. The next day he had gone to work in the bakery. The doctor had remembered him—he had seen his dossier when he was entered. His name, Phelps, seemed to be known, and there had been, it turned out, a slight mistake made by the staff when Walter had been admitted to the Reception Building. He had been ticketed an alcoholic and they had given him the routine treatment, hydrotherapy, a session in the tubs. If, the doctor explained, they had known the circumstances, why (he smiled), it wouldn't have happened.

"If you knew the circumstances, you wouldn't have admitted me at all," Walter said. It had been pleasant to talk to a well, sane human being who did not exert his authority. That made him forget himself, as he perceived he had done, for the doctor's face assumed its stolid professional glare, and their proper relationship, the narrow, not-quite-human relationship of doctor and patient, asserted itself. Every patient believed himself to be unjustly held.

By ten-thirty in the morning the day's baking was done and he was returned to the ward by the day keeper. Lunch made a break and then the hard part of the day began. The evenings were not so bad because he went to bed at seven, as soon as he came back from dinner, but the afternoons were empty. There was a battered radio but it was almost impossible to hear a radio program all the way through because someone else was always turning the dial and a protest might bring on tears, a fit, or a fight. The magazines, although he read them all, were not to his taste—they were Westerns, adventures, loves. He was never sleepy enough to wear out the time sleeping. Sometimes he talked. At first he had talked quite a lot. There were a couple of harmless megalomaniacs in the ward who were egged on to talk by the other patients, but the tales of their millions, their mistresses, and their awful power soon palled on him. One was General Grant, an old slobbery man who chewed Copenhagen snuff, only he was Grant, the President, with the war forgotten, a curious choice. The other, a younger man with blue eyes and light hair, was sometimes Wallace Reid but oftener Rudolph Valentino. He had a tweed cap for his Reid act and he narrowed his eyes for the Italian and gabbled incessantly about "babes," stopping only to do a few awkward tango steps he recalled from his hero's movies. The injustices the others had suffered, their life stories and their hopes, were pallid beside General Grant's and Valentino's but after a few days Walter felt a certain disgust as if he were laughing at the earnestness of children, and after those first few days he merely asked them politely how they were.

All he had to look forward to in the afternoon was four hours flat on his back staring at the ceiling unless the keeper decided they should go for a walk, two by two, down the gravel paths, nudging each other and laughing high shrill beckoning laughs if they saw a ward of women exercising. If the guard was a good one he ignored the laughter. If he was a bad one he snarled and ran along the line striking the persistent gigglers with his fist. The patients, even the feeble-minded and the low-grade morons, had a different manner for each kind of guard like animals wary of danger. After half a mile of walking around the grounds, they were led back to the building and shut up again. Some days they did not go out at all.

To adapt himself to the asylum, to make some sort of endurable life for himself, he found he went through various stages attempting all the time killers he could find. After the radio turned out to be no good, and the reading (and he could not think of anyone "outside" whom he could ask to send him books), he discovered that he was standing up most of his free time. He was surprised to learn that he knew exactly how many paces it took him to get from one end of the ward to the other. He had not noticed how much he was on his feet or what had occupied his mind while he was walking up and down. Once he became self-conscious, he tried to be reasonable.

He was there, shut away for society's good, because he drank too much; because he had insulted people; because he had caused disturbances, public disturbances, for which he had been jailed. That was what they said. He had certainly done all those things and that made them right but only in their perception of him as a nuisance—he did not think he deserved to be put in this place.

Looking back from this island to the mainland of his life, all his offensive acts seemed silly, although the occasions for the acts arose naturally enough. People who were idle often drank, and the drink, because it made a commotion in the body, skull, and stomach, was a spurious activity. But why had he been idle when, as he admitted, there was much for a young man to do, much that he intended to do, only he was sidetracked somehow? If Mrs. Iverson complained that he had ruined her Christmas party, he could answer that his tomfoolery was no greater than the practical jokes of three or four other young men he could name. If men came to sponge off you, tried to move into your hotel room, was it natural to resent it or not? And if you told them to go and they refused, was it wrong to toss them out? Especially if in the course of the refusal they insulted your family, your own father?

There was the source of it all. He had been impelled by something he took for granted so deeply even when he was making himself hated (and he had wanted to make himself hated), it seemed to be the performance of so obvious a duty, that he could hardly question it, and the duty was one he owed vaguely, inexplicably, to his father. Any other defense he made of his behavior was poppycock.

It was impossible to owe a duty to his father. His old man was dead. And nothing from his Sunday mornings in the church basement in his boyhood had made him believe that Father was peeping at him from behind a cloud up in the sky, exhorting him. He had read about Sir Oliver Lodge and seen photos of ectoplasmic shapes in the Sunday papers but he was sure there were no ghosts. Nor were all these stupid acts a complicated memorial ceremony for his father. Still there was a duty somehow, and he owed it to this man, his father.

What then? What was a father? To answer, he intended to make himself think dryly and accurately and he had begun with a sentence, "A father is a man who is a parent," but this was interrupted by a memory of green leaves and grass, much greener than any he saw now, and in the midst of all the green, heroic, breath-taking, there was his father hitting Mr. Burcham, but he was old enough to cool the vision by his criticism—a father was not necessarily a man who could pitch a hard right cross. There was more to it than that. A father was head of the house, the tent, the cave. All right, his father was certainly that. He hunted while the squaw did all the work. Not quite accurate, for his mother always had a hired girl and his grandmother did all the mending but the hunting was true enough. A father ruled his children, cared for them and helped them, and growing from his father's crumpled dress-shirt front as keenly and bitterly as if it had been a dagger, the scene in the upstairs room of his fraternity came back to him, the time his father drove him away, betrayed him (he felt) when he came to receive his first drink of whisky from his hands, but immediately he could see that it was nothing to fret about. He wondered that he had even remembered it at all. His old man had been taking his ease with friends; he had been drunk; he had merely forgotten the promise, a natural thing to do since the promise had been made four or five years before. What else was there? A father begat you. You didn't ask for it, however.

He never got any further than this. The burden of the duty remained, however, heavy, fatiguing, mysterious, one he would be glad to get rid of.

By the time it was full spring, he entered the last phase, one of resignation. He was the fully experienced patient, there, but no longer puzzled about why he was there, no longer trying the solace of amusements. He stopped standing up, he stopped walking, he began to lie on his bed like the others in the afternoon. He recalled the fervor of his earlier thoughts about his father with amusement as if they were the youthful indiscretions of an old man. Slowly, without any shock, almost as if he had known it all along, he realized that there was no term to his commitment. He knew his uncle Eri had known this when he talked him into it.

He might be in this asylum until he was an old man, like the old buzzard from A building who had ground parole and spent all his time near the visitors' entrance, dressed in the wintertime in a blue double-breasted suit with a linen handkerchief trailing out of his breast pocket, and in summer wearing neatly creased white flannels. He talked to himself about his misfortune, the loss of his former wealth as a coal merchant (and Walter learned from a keeper that the loss was real), and if a visitor stepped past him on his way to see someone else, the old man would raise his voice and gently try to inveigle the visitor into listening for a moment. If he had a listener, he would preen the ends of his mustache, puff out his chest, and a faraway look came into his eyes as if beyond the window he could see the old rich heaps of anthracite and Pocahontas in his coalyard. A visitor gave him this chance for a little journey backward in time. Without alarm Walter could see the old man as a model of what he himself might become.

He was not alarmed because his stay in the asylum was outside of time. It did not count, and it did not count because he had never imagined anything like this happening to him. It was not part of his idea of himself, and because of this he would not grow any older. Presently, someday, it would end and he could take up his life again where he left it off. This was not a conscious argument he gave himself. It was a secret assumption and he never used it as a consolation. All he had to do was wait. He came to know the contours of the shoe soles of the man who lay across from him. He observed the wear, watched the sole grow thin, and for several days in April he waited until he could say, "Charlie, you've got a hole in your shoe." He had speculated on the precise day for over a week.

No one visited him and he received no letters except two from Eddie Burcham, who had come back to town from the sanitarium. He had received few letters from Eddie before. They had seldom been separated long enough to write letters. People did not express themselves very well on paper, he knew that, but unless he was mistaken Eddie had changed. The disease had made him gloomy, and he made it a point to abhor gloomy people. He could hear his father, snarling, "He's a God-damn grouch." Neither Eddie's letters nor his own answers intentionally revealed anything about their real feelings. They wrote in a high facetious style with polysyllables every time they could insert them, but just the same Eddie seemed depressed. He did not say how his TB was or if he was working. He did say he would get over to the nut-cracker someday to see old Walter, that was all.

He read Eddie's letters nine or ten times until he caught himself doing it. Then he threw them away. He did not expect Eddie to visit him, and he did not miss his company particularly. If he missed anyone, it was Bella Calman, the harlot.

One day, Peanuts, a good keeper, put his head in the door and said, "Walter? Visitor."

Several patients looked up, some enviously, the others curiously. They kept track of other people's visitors as well as their own. They knew this was his first.

Peanuts unlocked the door to the Reception Room and whistled for another keeper to take over because he had to go back to sit outside the ward. Walter looked around at the crowd of people, women mostly, mothers or sisters, who were sitting on the benches and wicker chairs. He did not recognize anyone. His new guard was Kidney-foot, a hillbilly, who gave down on one foot a little when he walked. He was young, strong, and, oddly for a hillbilly, a nice guy. The hillbillies were the only guards in D, where they kept the violents. They liked to beat up the violents, and at first Walter could excuse them because they were poor ignorant Tennesseeans who had been lured up north by labor agents and then laid off from their jobs and left to starve for all anyone cared. Many became cops in Detroit and beat up Negroes, others guards in prisons and asylums. Now he had changed. He no longer made any excuses for them. If they were heels, they were heels. If they were nice guys, they were nice guys. He took them one at a time like the other patients. "Hi, Kidney," he said. "Who is it for me?"

"Yonnuh he is," Kidney-foot nodded toward the door. Beyond the screen, he saw Eddie and with his first glance he saw that the back of Eddie's neck was thinner.

"You want outside with him?" Kidney asked. "Go awn. I'll sit on the steps."

They opened the front door and Walter noticed gratefully the courtesy with which old Kidney removed himself and sat on the steps.

"Hi, boy," Walter said.

"What do you say, Walter?" Eddie said, looking him over quickly, seeking any change. Walter saw for the first time that friends or lovers are dead while they are apart. They shook hands diffidently.

"What can you do? Do we have to go inside?"

"We can walk up and down here. Not too far. I've got to make him look good," Walter said loudly enough for the guard to hear. Kidney winked at him over the cigarette he was rolling.

Eddie kept looking at him. He said, "Well, how is it?"

"It's all right. I work in the bakery."

Eddie walked a few feet away from him, at one side, probably so he could look at him without seeming to stare and perhaps embarrassing him. Walter knew what Eddie suspected. He was waiting for a sign of madness or degeneracy. He chuckled. "Your mother get you all primed?"

"Crazy through liquor is what she said."

Walter bent his knees, waggled his head until his lips flopped, and shook his limp hands up and down from the wrists. "Gimme a drink, pal," he said hoarsely. "I gotta have it. Gimme it, gimme it."

"Nuts," Eddie said.

"That's what you expected, wasn't it?"

"Yes, I guess I did. What are you in here for, then?"

"I got drunk too often. That part's true. But I'm not an alcoholic. I'm not crazy. I'm my uncle's nephew, that's all."

"What's Eri got to do with it?"

[308]

"I was in his way. So he and Grandma shoved me in here."

"They commit you?"

"No. I signed the papers but they would have if I hadn't." He stopped. It was the first time he had thought of Eri in a long time. "I can't figure him out really. There's something—the bastard—" Then he was ashamed. Eddie was the one person in the world who had known him when he was invincible, a boy, and he was ashamed to make any admissions like this in front of him even though they were no longer boys. Eddie himself had been laid out, conquered, and with something of the old boyish rivalry, like a taunt, he asked, "How are *you?*"

Eddie did not seem to hear the taunt in it. He merely answered the question. "Oh, I've still got one lung collapsed. I wrote you about that. Toward evening I get a little fever, not much. I'm still an active case."

"Are you working?"

"No. I haven't tried. I might infect somebody. I just lie around. Read. Listen to the radio."

"Hell, come on over here. That's all I do. What'd you come home for? I thought you went away to get cured."

"I got sick of it. I wanted to come home."

Thus they talked, severe, formal, with the formality of old friends who must, because they are intimate, let their feelings be surmised or guessed at. Eddie sensed this. Neither wanted to confess to the injury the past year had done him. Each needed to seem whole and to present his disease or his residence in an insane asylum as a course accepted deliberately as if it were his whim to have fever or to live with the mad. It was not honest, Eddie decided. He wanted to tear it down, and, as he talked, scuffing the pebbles on the gravel path, feeling the bright sun on the back of his neck, he thought perhaps he could discern the reason he wanted to break down this formal, friendly pretense. He was carrying death in him. One could say without stretching the truth too far that he had come home to die. (And as he thought of it, he thought again, uneasily, "Have I decided or am I helpless?") Time would tell—he no longer had anything to do with it. (Or had he?) It could go either way but if he were to die, if it grew bad enough for him to see the approach of death, he wanted a friend, someone he could talk to. His mother was alien now. Walter would do. Let them return to the old way of talking, nights lying in the grass, or by the riverbank in the spring.

"I guess it was the light here and the trees," Eddie said. "I thought about them a lot lying up in the mountains. People, not so much. You, maybe."

Walter was embarrassed for him. He should not talk that way. He said nothing.

"Have you ever noticed the sunlight in this part of the country? There have never been any painters here. I guess they all go to New Mexico. It's clear most of the time but sometimes in the spring and fall, I think 'aqueous' is the word, watery. And there are the trees in the front yards. As far as I could tell, that's what I missed. That's home. Funny, isn't it?"

Humoring him, Walter said, "Uh-huh."

"It was strange to me there. Spruce trees, pine. They were everywhere and they always surprised me when I saw them at night against the sky. I know how maples look, any way you take them. I didn't want that little jump of surprise when I looked at a tree. So I came home. You see, don't you?"

Walter thought he understood but he could not come right out and say so. He said, "Uh-huh," again, and then asked, "You feel all right? Is there any pain?"

"No. There's no pain. The fever's a nuisance. You can't read much with fever because your eyes get tired. The trees are full of purple martins in the evening. They all come in a flock and light. I listen to them. It's familiar. It's what I remember."

"What do the doctors say?"

"Oh, they're sore. I should have stayed up there, they say. As soon as she heard them, Mother got sore, too. She's afraid I'm going to die on her. I'm here and it's the worst thing I can do."

"Are you going to die?" Death did not seem to be sacred, and he was not superstitious, but somehow you did not talk about it, especially your own.

"No. I don't think so. You see why I came, don't you?"

At lot had happened to Eddie. It had made him simpler, less scornful, but by some parochial standard Walter still kept, it was indecent to speak with Eddie's frankness—he could not tell why. There was no reason for it but as soon as you recognized the style, only the style of speaking, you felt habitually that it was indecent. Yet he knew better. It was the right way for friends to speak to each other, if friendship meant anything, but he writhed as he had done on his first visit to dancing school at the thought of speaking the same way. He wanted to but he could not force it out.

"Why do you want someone to know?" Walter asked. "What difference does it make?"

"You don't, one doesn't live alone, you know."

"I do."

Eddie grinned and turned his thumb toward a double file of men out for their walk.

"I'm alone just the same," Walter said with a tinge of pride.

"No, you're not. You depend on someone. I have had to give up my mother because intellectually my perception that she is a fool is stronger than my filial affection. Not give her up, exactly. I see her every day and let her nag at me but she's no longer a mystery to me. Her anger doesn't frighten me any more, and what makes her happy doesn't make me happy. I don't depend on her. You say you work in the bakery, huh?" he finished briskly.

"Yes. They wake me up at three in the morning and we do a thousand loaves." He never thought he would take any pride in the work he did here. You could adapt yourself to anything. You were living all the time. And to pretend that you could take time out, not have it count, as he was pretending his stay in this asylum did not count, was a mistake. He almost blushed.

"How long are you going to be here?"

Walter shrugged. "I'm not an alcoholic if I don't drink and I haven't had a drink since Christmas. Whenever they get around to letting me out."

Eddie left the path and sat down with his back against one of the little elm trees. "Let's stop walking. Come on, sit down." Walter sat down on the curb. He picked a flat blade of grass, laid it between his thumbs, and blew a harsh long squeak.

"I don't know how long they'll keep me."

"Why don't you get a lawyer and find out if you can get sprung legally?"

"It hadn't occurred to me," Walter said. Nearly all the other patients talked about getting lawyers. Some even got them, shady-looking gents with gold teeth or men who were too cheerful. Walter had heard them planning, the patients talking so hopefully, the lawyers flawlessly confident, and the patients were still there. It had seemed useless, a resource, in fact, only of those who were weak in the head. He had never thought of doing the same, and when he thought of it now, the image of Horse Egan appeared in his mind. He knew Eri would stop Horse from doing anything. In a curious way, Horse was the only permissible lawyer—the family had always had him. He shook his head. "Besides, I don't know any lawyer I could trust."

"What the hell were you doing when they put you in here? What gave them their excuse? Everybody's got a different story. I heard you got fired from the bank because you went into Cunningham's Drug Store with the

[311]

day's checks in a leather sack, and you laid your Dad's Luger on a table and sat down and counted the checks right there."

Although he knew he was the subject of rumor, Walter was a little shocked at the lie that was being told about him. He grinned, shamefaced and proud. "They say that? No, I never did that."

"They say you used to go down to Lide Carter's and beat up all the girls every Saturday night."

The first shock dissipated, he saw himself now the hero of a legend. In homes, over the green-felt tables of the City Club, in high-school locker rooms, at cigar counters, "they" would be talking about him now and for a long time, "a bastard, a son-of-a-bitch," but historical. He felt that it was right "they" should hold him in this hateful awe. "No, I never hit any of them. I spent a lot of time there but there wasn't any trouble."

"But what for?"

"Wenching is one of the recreations of a gentleman, isn't it?"

"Not when you live in the house. I heard all about the Iversons' Christmas party. What was the idea of lugging that tart out to the Country Club? Just to get Ferry Culver's goat? They haven't stopped kidding him yet. They say it's the funniest thing that's happened since . . ."

"Who says so?" Walter interrupted suddenly, almost angrily.

"Oh, I stopped in one day down at the *Telegraph* office just to see how the boys were doing. They told me."

"Everybody thinks it's funny, huh?"

"Yes. Why? Weren't you trying to be funny?"

He had not been trying to be funny. If he had intended the guests to remember anything, it was that he had insulted them. They could recall it as humorous if they first remembered it was insulting. A wish to confide in Eddie surged up in him. He almost began to tell him that all he had done he had done deliberately. He had wanted to outrage the town, to insult it, humiliate it. He nearly began to speak but he stopped himself for he knew that, after he had explained all this, he could not tell why. Eddie would ask him and he could not answer. He said in his snarling, guttural voice, "Nah, I wasn't trying to be funny."

"You sound just like your old man."

"Hey, Walter! Time's up." Kidney-foot had come up on the grass behind them and was standing politely ten feet away. Walter jumped to his feet with far too much energy. He looked at the keeper, then at Eddie as if he had been asleep. He had just realized that he missed his father terribly.

Eddie was saying, ". . swell to see you. I'll come again if this doesn't send my fever up too high. I'll know by six o'clock."

"Sure, sure," Walter mumbled. His father was dead. Of course, he would miss him. It was quite natural. Eddie's face took on more clarity of outline. The old apathy came back. "Sure, boy. Come any time. I'm always home," he said. "Take care of yourself."

Eddie said, "So long," and walked away down the lawn toward the carpark. Walter leaned against the tree with one hand, watching him. Kidney came up beside him. "Friend of yours, Walter?"

"Yes. Nice guy. I grew up with him."

Eddie was turning toward the car-park. He stepped off the low curb down onto the gravel. He staggered, put his hands to his face quickly, took them down, and stood turning his head slowly to the right and left. He took a step and clapped one hand to his face, his eye, the left eye, again. He walked very cautiously to his car and got into it. After a moment, they saw the car start, and Eddie drove away at fifteen miles an hour.

"Must've got a bug in his eye," Kidney said. They walked back across the lawn and into the building. It had been nice to see Eddie, a nice change for the afternoon.

· XXVII ·

MRS. BURCHAM STOOD in the corridor listening. The door was thick but she did not dare stand too close to it because the cleaning woman might open it suddenly and find her there. Mrs. Burcham could hear the indistinct burble of her voice asking him to get out of bed and into a chair while she changed the bed. Faintly she could hear the rustle and flop of the bedclothes. The sound of the vacuum cleaner began and Mrs. Burcham relaxed and walked, no longer on tiptoe, down the corridor and into her own bedroom. The discovery would not be made today.

Ever since Mr. Burcham had died, she had talked to herself a little. She made a joke of it. She sat down limply on the bed where she could just catch the image of her face in the glass on her dressing table. "I never thought I'd live this kind of life," she said. Because it was a joke to talk to herself she always smiled when she did it. Now it was only a muscular smile, an habitual grimace. The life she was living was monstrous. She could not think about it for more than a few seconds at a time—she would review in her memory the first time she had entered his room (the room of her son, although she had ceased to think of him as that and treated him as a fate, a punishment for a mass of sins and crimes she never had committed) and the shock that came to her in the growing darkness when she saw

[313]

the little blue flame of the alcohol lamp. (It had looked rather cute, blue and wavering. There had once been a woman in town who had made ornamental powder-puff boxes and on them with little tools like a dentist's she would mold roses and forget-me-nots out of colored sealing wax and she had had a little alcohol lamp in which to heat the wax and the finished boxes had been cute. She had owned one herself, forget-me-nots, until just recently when she had thrown it in the trash barrel.) And she had said to him—how warm her voice had been, how natural her curiosity—"Why, what are you doing, darling?" He had jerked his hand down, startled, sworn, blown the lamp out, told her to sit down, and then had answered her. She could never think beyond the answer.

Or she could recall the journey, the long, long, journey up the marble steps of the Mechanics Bank Building, three flights, all cold, all marble, with dirty curved brass plates in the corners of the steps to prevent dust from lodging there and the steps themselves littered with blobs of chewing gum, the dust itself, cigarette butts, and long wavering wisps of hair and ravelings, and as she reached the third floor, the smell of that office piercing through the other odors, would she ever forget it? What could she say? The waiting room full of dingy magazines she had never seen, and a woman sitting there holding a rag up to her eye with blood and pus seeping through and as she watched, choking, swallowing, yet knowing she must stay, the stain on the rag grew. And to have the doctor know her name, bowing in a dirty white coat, "Good evening. Mrs. Burcham, is it?" enveloping her in the fume of his bad breath. And lastly, how easy it was, the whole matter. It was illegal. She could go to prison, but it was easy. She could say to herself (with the smile), "I skulked back through the streets like an old alley cat." But she could not remember the skulking. It was too horrible, people sitting on their front porches staring at her as if the little package had a light in it. The imprint of her public return was somewhere in her mind but it was not on call—only the shame and fear it had engendered.

And yet, peeping into her mirror, smiling her smile and talking, she suffered a treacherous ambivalence of emotion. She was proud of her resilience, she who had been so much an invalid all her life, so delicate in health. She now suffered the jerks and hauls of a strain that no one else in town had undergone. Other women, although she had not heard of them, may have had dope fiends for sons and had the dope fiends tubercular but they were not so fine-grained as she, not by any means. (How Charles used to hold her bare foot in his hand, touching the blue veins, and his large moist eyes looking up asking, always asking how his little girl had been that day? Had the thunder frightened her? Had she been able to eat a little? How he

had worshiped her! And then had died. It was mean of him to die.) A silk thread would not lift the same weight as a coarse hank of rope and yet—she touched her gray hair—the thread was lifting it. No one in the town had ever suffered quite so much, and never to breathe a word of it.

She heard down the corridor the light click of Eddie's door. Mrs. Waters must be finished cleaning the room. She waited until she saw her go past, carrying the vacuum cleaner. She hurried to her son's room at once, hoping that she might forestall—but no, there was the alcohol lamp already burning, the bottle of distilled water beside it, and the box of morphine pills. He was gently disengaging the point of the hypodermic needle, shaking it lightly into the tablespoonful of boiling water that lay balanced on the lamp-rack above the flame. The point of the needle slipped off. Defeated, she stood in the doorway watching. He shook two tablets out of the little box into the spoonful of hot water. He had explained that he could make his dose and sterilize the needle simultaneously. He felt her standing in the doorway and turned around.

"She makes me nervous," he said curtly.

"You said eleven o'clock. It's only ten-thirty," she said, coming forward.

He was trying to slide the hollow housing of the needle point over the nipple of the ampule and he did not answer. He lifted it up carefully. It slid slowly back into the boiling water in the spoon. He tried it again. It fell. He tried a third time, his hand beginning to quiver slightly. It stuck. He tipped the ampule so that the needle pointed upward, and screwed the needle on, touching only its base with his fingers. He worked the plunger and sucked up every drop of the morphine solution into the hypodermic. He gave it a couple of squirts, a few drops each, to see if it was working. Then he looked up at his mother. "Do you want to help me?" he asked. Without waiting for her reply, he blew out the alcohol lamp, shook the spoon once, and laid it in a cardboard shoe-box lined with absorbent cotton.

"Yes. I'll do it," she said. She had learned to do it three weeks before, disgusted yet amazed at what she had come to.

From a roll wrapped in blue paper he took a wisp of cotton. He took out the glass stopper of a bottle of alcohol and doused the cotton until it was wet. He pulled up his pajama sleeve and pinched and pulled his upper arm just below the deltoid muscle. He scrubbed a small area with the soaked cotton and threw it into the wicker wastebasket beside his bed. He pinched the cleaned flesh of his arm up between his fingers. "Right there," he said.

She picked up the hypodermic, held it out from her, and squinted at it as she had seen him do. "There's no bubble in it."

"OK."

She thrust the point of the needle a half-inch into the flesh of his arm where he had it pinched, and shoved the plunger down with her thumb. When the liquid in the ampule was gone, she pulled the needle out. He rubbed the spot hard. "Thanks," he said. The loathsome rite was finished.

He lay down again on the bed, propped himself on his pillows, and lit a cigarette. After the first drag, she spoke as if she had just come into the room at that instant. "It looks as if it was going to be a nice day after all."

He turned his head toward the window and saw the sun was high enough over the house to touch the trees in the side yard. He looked back at her. "Yes. I thought it was going to rain this morning."

"Why, the sun was shining when I got up," she said.

"I mean early this morning. There was fog then."

"Oh." She knew what he had been doing this morning early. He had not been able to sleep. She thought he looked like a pirate with the black silk patch over his eye. It gave him a dashing look, eerie, though, in a way.

He was waiting for her to ask the crucial question, the question she had come to ask. He did not mind her asking but why did she have to approach it circuitously through the weather? He said nothing, looking at her out of his one good eye, smiling.

Awkwardly because he had left the move up to her, she said, "Do you think you'll get up today?"

He had turned and was punching up his pillows. He lifted the front of his pajamas and peered down at his chest. It was spotted with little wisps of cotton like the one on his arm. She had seen the two on his arm also when his sleeve was up. "I don't think so," he said, speaking down into his bosom. It made him look ashamed if he did not refuse, staring right at her face, a bad little boy.

He had lately tried to spare her as much as he could, and he was willing, since he saw that she did not know him at all, to try modest little deceptions to placate her. He was an only son. She must have had hopes for him and he had lain still long enough to know that a disappointment was a disappointment. It would not matter to her finally whether he had gone against her wishes deliberately or without meaning to. He was no good for anything she could understand. He was a burden, and since he did not intend to die, he would go on being a burden for a long time. He could remember his childhood, when he had loved her blindly, as his father had, his beautiful scented mother. It was only fair that he treat her kindly.

"It's such a nice day," she said warmly. "I thought perhaps I could drive you over to Ann Arbor to . . ."

"I don't feel like it, Mother."

You must not excite invalids, she knew that, and she made a strong effort to hide her anger. What could you do with a sick man who would not see a doctor?

"But if he still thinks there's a chance of saving your eye . . . Even if it didn't work the first time . . . it's healed now and . . ."

"Its too big a chance, Mother. Those doctors are not sure enough of themselves. I've just lost the sight of one eye, that's all."

"But these terrible headaches. It might help them."

"Oh, I take morphine for them," he said. He wished she would not nag at him. The morphine was beginning to calm him and he was only bland where he might have been angry.

There was a table beside his bed. It was piled with books and magazines. A half-empty carton of cigarettes, an ashtray of beaten copper, two or three pencils, and a big notebook were scattered among the papers. The week's newspapers, the *Telegraph,* the *New York Times,* and some copies, three weeks old, of the *Manchester Guardian* lay in a neat pile on the far side of the bed. This was where he lived now and the books and papers and the radio were what he lived on. He had no visitors because at the advice of their doctors even his friends hesitated to come to see him.

He was quite cheerful when the pain behind his eye allowed him to be and since he had been home he had come to see his room as a pinnacle from which he could survey the world. By reading, thinking, and listening to what good radio programs he could find, he was preparing himself to resume a place in it. Burcham Stylites, he called himself.

He believed he had made a discovery. It was new to him, although he suspected that the notion had been found and used before. His discovery was this: you could take yourself in hand. That was all. Somewhere, in college probably, he had picked up the conviction that you were controlled entirely—he had waited for things to happen to him. But not any longer, no more waiting for beneficent surprises. He wanted to be a kind, decent, intelligent man. Somewhere (where?) he had lost the common, the local desire to be rich and famous, although he could not have forced himself to admit it yet to anyone because he had talked to so few people seriously in the past year or two that he could not say it simply; it would come out in stammers, hemming and hawing, and almost anyone he knew would be mystified, perhaps contemptuous. He could try to be kind, try to be decent —he did not have to wait on inspiration. With enough effort, a sort of kindness and decency could be achieved at once, and he tried to be kind and decent to his mother, failing sometimes when the pain was bad, but trying again. Intelligence he might have to wait for until he had read and studied and meditated. "Meditate" was a powerful word. No one he knew had ever meditated except possibly some of his college professors although he doubted it. They were puzzled juiceless men. Philosophers did it, historical figures, saints. And he was sure, such was his confidence, that if some man long ago had found the requisite concentration and intensity, he himself could also.

Day after day he tried, lying on the hot bed with only his pajamas on, smoking one cigarette after another, conscious out of all his surroundings only of the change of light as the sun moved, pulling his thoughts back from straying, thinking steadily about the career he would make when he was well, a young man blind in one eye. (The retina had detached itself, been repaired by a kind of spot-welding process, fallen off again, and now he could distinguish only light from dark and occasional fleeting distortions, and he had this headache.) His decision had gone deep enough to make him sure that a half-blind tubercular young man could be of some good in the world. He could read only an hour or so a day. Most of the remaining time he was awake he thought about his reading as best he could.

He did not want any more doctors. He had decided he could cure himself. He wanted a little more time to examine his sureness of this and so he took morphine, for without it he could not think clearly. As soon as he felt that his decision was sound, that a cure was possible, he would test his strength by cutting down his dose of morphine. He often examined himself to see if his delay were merely an excuse for drug-taking given himself by himself in some other guise. He did not honestly think it was. If his mind was any good at all, it should control his body, although he suspected the two were not so separate as people said—the false separation made discussion easy, that was all. Mind was merely the conscious part of the body. If he could train his mind, lying there, healing would take place. He would get well.

He would have been glad to explain all this to his mother but he believed her love for him stood in the way. He had never talked like that to her. She loved him and she would say "yes" to anything he said if he said it often enough to convince her that he was serious but she would not comprehend a word of it. She had no way of grasping what he meant by "kind, decent, intelligent" because she was reasonably sure she was all three already, then why the fuss? He wished she would stop trying to persuade him to go back to the doctor at Ann Arbor who could give him no assurances whatever that he would get the sight of his left eye back again, who said only that another operation was "worth trying."

She began to shift herself, to move around nervously. He had caught on to that when he was about eight years old as a sign of anger. She was angry again and he had caused it. He wished he were acute enough to say exactly the right thing to remove the anger but all he could think of was a lame "I'm sorry, Mother. I know you want me to be operated on again but I'm convinced it won't do any good. I'm just going to be blind in one eye."

"Another operation might stop the headaches."

"Sit down. Sit down on the bed," he said, beckoning to her unobtrusively.

"Florence Nightingale said never to sit on a patient's bed," she said, stepping back a little. She had heard that at the Woman's Club.

"I'll stop taking morphine pretty soon. That's what bothers you, isn't it? I don't blame you. It's bad. And I hate to have you go and get it."

Nothing he could say would sweeten the fact he had refused her. He had been stubborn. He had talked too long. In a fury, his mother cried in a high, strangled voice, "No woman ever had a son like you." She rushed out of the room and he was sorry he had, as he thought, brought her to tears.

He shut his eyes. He was growing tired. He heard her soft footfall on the carpet. He opened his eyes. She was bringing him the mail. The mail was the *Times*.

"Were you asleep?" she asked quietly.

"No, just thinking. Thanks." He took the paper.

"I was just talking to Mrs. Reynolds. She said that Walter Phelps was out."

"She did? When . . ."

"She saw him going into his uncle's house about an hour ago. She was sure it was Walter. Do you think he'll be coming up to see you?"

"Yes. I expect he will."

"Well, I've got to go out this afternoon. If I leave the front door un-latched, do you . . ."

"Oh, I'll hear him. Besides, he'd know which room I'd be in, anyway."

"Well," she said sadly, "I'll go get your lunch."

He had offended her again by having such a friend. She always kept him informed ahead of time of all her movements and she had not mentioned any engagement that afternoon. She was leaving the house to avoid Walter, as if his reputation gave off spores of infection. He would be glad to see Walter. He was very lonely.

THE WORD OF HIS parole had come. He had shaken hands all around with the good keepers and the bad (his hatred and resentment of them having vanished with his freedom) and with his friends, the shut-up drunks and morons who by an astonishing feat of mimicry preserved the demeanor of the sane and sober. They wished him luck and asked him to come and see them. His car stood in front of B building. Carrying a valise of fine calf-skin, he went down the gravel path and got into it. His foot automatically pressed the clutch and he reached for the key. He stopped and sat back in the seat, relaxed. Where was he to go?

Confronted by a choice, he was glad he had one to make. Now, if he were walking, he could turn to the right or the left without being shouted at, and in his car he could take any angle, crossing, or straightaway he pleased. He appreciated this for the first time in his life. His parole was a ticket that admitted him to free will as if it were a show of some kind and he felt it as a show. Although the hot bright days of August and its wither-ing heat were gone and it was now raining in gusts, the colors looked rich, such as they were, and it seemed to him that a pretty girl might pass in front of his car at any moment. He looked around but no girl was in sight, only a doctor and a nurse in a blue cape with scarlet lining. He felt superior to them at once.

He switched the key, pressed the starter, and drew away from the build-ing without knowing just which way he would turn at the front gate. He had been thinking about it for two hours. The law wanted him to go home where it could keep an eye on him once a week. The tool-and-die company, through its vice-president, Merrill Stanley, had withdrawn his income in a nervously friendly letter that covered any reasons for the action under a flood of matey personal questions. His legal obligation to go home seemed unimportant to him because he was sure that the law in his case repre-sented only a crystallization of his uncle's wishes, and in the shock that his liberty had given him, he could say with an almost sacrilegious gusto that his pocketbook was not very important. He stopped his car between the brick posts of the gate that opened on the highway as if here, at the last moment, he would make his decision. He could flee, go away, find work somewhere, and "never be heard of again" (although he did not ask who would never hear of him again), or he could turn the other way and go home. He lit a cigarette, a parting gift from Ziglia, and slumped down in his seat to think some more.

After thirty seconds, he tossed the cigarette away and started the car, staring at his hands with frenzied attention as if the whole matter were to be left to them. Like a somnambulist, pushing the decision away from him numbly, neither thinking nor feeling any compulsion, he turned the car in the direction of his home town. As soon as he had shifted gears and was going along at forty miles an hour, he began to sing. Somehow he had known all along he would go home and that was enough. The reasons, he trusted, would be clear enough whenever he wished to pull them out and look at them. He had let them lie. They had been sleeping in his head for over a year and his confidence that they were just and powerful remained unimpaired. He had acted and he had acted without planning anything. He sang very loudly and waved at other people in cars. After a forty-minute drive, the rain had stopped. He began to see farms and curves and stretches in the road he recognized. Entering the town, he turned up the Hill toward the tool-and-die factory.

As he approached the factory through the mean wet streets of the district, a wretchedness preserved in him since childhood came over him. He had been driving to Detroit with his father and the road led them through bleak vacant lots with smoky factories in the distance, and he who had expected the city to be beautiful had asked his father, a little shamefacedly even then, "Why is everything so ugly here?" His father roused himself from the trance of driving and said, "Ugly? Where?" When he did not answer, his father had not pressed him but he had gathered that the ugliness was of no importance and later he had learned why—the land, all this dirty emptiness, was worth at least a couple of hundred dollars a foot. He was old enough by that time for this to satisfy him but he never entered a manufacturing town without a sinking of the heart, and now he was depressed. Next to the tool-and-die factory, as he expected or remembered, was an open place full of sparse weeds, burdock, thistle, and pigweed. Three big cogwheels, black and rusty, lay in a heap. Near them an old cow was tethered. She stood patiently in the mud, the rope loose around her neck, not trying to graze.

The factory, however, had been recently built, and it had a sterile brightness about it. He got out of the car, went up a short sidewalk across a sparse roped lawn, and entered at the doorway, a semicylindrical niche in the front. The door opened before he touched the handle. An electric eye had seen him coming. He was standing on a long wine-colored rug covered with buff footprints. At his left the receptionist was seated, a girl he had

known in high school. The walls were covered with plywood that he knew
—he had forgotten how he had learned it—was of layers one-sixty-fourth
of an inch thick, yet it looked like solid wood with an intricate grain. The
panels were outlined in shiny chrome and the desk where the girl was sitting surrounded by telephones was a stubby truncated cylinder, covered
with the same papery wood, which went around her waist so that she
looked like a legless freak at the fair.

"Hello, Irma. Is Merrill Stanley around?"

"I'll see," was all she said. She picked up a phone, said a sentence, and
looked up at him. "You can go up."

She seemed disgusted and afraid of him, and she did not look at him
when she spoke.

He went through a smooth door set with a chrome panel for his hand
and down a long curving corridor, constructed for silence. He could hear
no sound although he could feel the vibration of machinery beyond the
wall. The corridor widened and he came upon another receptionist, Stanley's own. She was a woman of forty with all the labored second-rate chic
of the "business" woman afraid of her job. She was dressed in severe black
in what she would have called a "classic" dress. Her hair was neatly bobbed
and neatly combed. The paint, powder, and lipstick on her face were as
carefully applied as a clown's, with a little of the clown's subhuman look.
As easily as he recognized her occupation, Walter divined the reason she
had been hired, to give Stanley's portal an air of mature efficiency and
particularly to remove from any visitor's mind a chance suspicion that
Stanley might cut up with the office girls.

"Won't you sit down?" she said with shopworn politeness. "Mr. Stanley
will see you soon." She had been taught that.

There were three chairs in a row against the wall opposite her desk. They
looked like mahogany. He sat down in one and crossed his legs. In five
minutes he crossed them the other way. There was no window to look out
of. Light came from a fluorescent bar on the ceiling. There were no magazines. By tapping the chair arm with his knuckles, he discovered that the
chair was not mahogany at all. It was steel, painted. The receptionist made
entries in a notebook with a pencil and occasionally typed something softly.

"How long will he be?" Walter asked.

"He will see you soon."

"Is that all you know how to say?"

She flushed but did not look at him. She earned her money.

The waiting wore away the exhilaration of his release from the asylum.
As he sat there he grew more angry at Merrill Stanley for keeping him

waiting than he was for cutting off his income. The one was an insult; there might be some plausible excuse for the other although he doubted it. Where his shoulders touched the wall, he could feel the vibration of the machinery, an unruly structural malaise that the architect had been unable to cure. He looked at his hands, finally, his soft white baker's hands with the smooth pink palms.

"Mr. Stanley will see you, Mr. Phelps," the secretary said. Some secret button had filled with light. He stood up, walked over to Stanley's door, and threw it open.

Stanley was behind his cylindrical stump, bigger than his secretary's, standing and smiling jovially. "Well, when did they let you out?"

Merrill Stanley was ten years older than he. The little gibe assumed an intimacy he would not have liked even in a friend. Stanley grinned on and stood there with his hand stuck out, the hand which he was to take and be drawn with a calculated bonhomie into the chair beside Stanley's own. Walter balked at the edge of the desk with his feet apart. He said, "What the hell were you doing in here, buffing your nails?"

"Oh," he said, as if he barely remembered keeping Walter waiting. "Oh, that. I was on the phone to Detroit. Were you out there all this time? I'm terribly sorry." He leaned back in his chair and clasped his hands behind his head. "Well, how the hell are you? How did they treat you? Christ, I didn't even hear about it until two or three months ago. I was up at the Club and Eri told me about it, said you'd been there quite a while already."

Walter did not want his visit to turn into a social call. "Why did you cut off my income?" he said sharply.

Stanley jerked his belly muscles, pulled himself forward with his elbows on the desk. "We lost a Ford contract and a G-E contract we had been counting on didn't materialize."

"Hmmm," Walter said to himself. "I don't believe that."

Stanley looked up coolly into his eyes. "Sorry, Walter," he said, and Walter knew he had been right to doubt him. If his excuse had been true, he would have protested.

"Eri's behind this, isn't he?"

Stanley looked at him smugly as if he were a beggar or a child, someone without power of any kind. "I wouldn't make accusations if I were you."

Walter lifted his right fist and looked at it, the knuckles whitening. "Do you know how it hurts to get your nose broken, Merrill? It hurts—terribly," he said, softly using the female adverb.

The door opened behind him and Stanley's secretary came into the office. Stanley had pressed a button to summon a witness to the assault, perhaps three or four buttons, a chord of lights, for the witness had been quick. He gave Walter a weak triumphant grin as if he knew the secretary carried a blackjack concealed under her dress.

"I was just talking about how it hurt, Merrill, not whether you could get me arrested for it. I know you could do that but it would hurt first and I don't think she could stop me." All this meant nothing. Merrill Stanley was not the man to hit, anyhow. He walked out of the office.

He got into his car and drove to his uncle's house.

Eri's lawn was beautifully kept. The spiraea bushes were thinned and clipped. And the horse's head of the iron hitching post, a foible of his uncle's, stood at the curb in a fresh coat of black paint. The house was the same as ever: the blinds, upstairs and down, were lowered exactly halfway.

He gave the china handle of the doorbell a twist and regretted immediately that he had not walked straight in. Waiting, he looked around to see if anyone was watching him. There was no one. People did not sit on their porches after Labor Day.

Alec, the houseman, let him in. "Hello, Walter. Come on in. He's just sitting down to lunch. I'll set another place."

"Don't bother, Alec. I'm not staying."

Turning away to hurry to the kitchen, Alec stopped, his brown face settling into the mask he assumed when he did not know what was going on. "Oh. All right, Walter. Mr. Phelps is in the dining room."

He caught sight of his uncle across the living room, through the dining-room door. He was combed and shaven but not dressed, still in a dark red woolen dressing gown and pajamas. He was fatter. He did not even look up at Alec passing through the room, assuming that whoever had been so bold as to call had been successfully turned away. Walter paused, staring at him. The morning's *Free Press* was clipped in a patent newspaper holder and he read it as he ate. At last Eri felt his presence and looked up. The fork did not stop on the way to his mouth. He opened his mouth, took the morsel, laid the fork down, chewing a moment, and at last spoke, without surprise or haste. "Hello, Walter. They didn't notify me."

Walter said nothing. He did not quite know what he was going to do. He pulled out a chair and sat down across from his uncle. Eri gave the newspaper holder a light push. It was on a hinge and it swung off to one side. "Had lunch?" Eri said.

Walter still said nothing. He looked over his uncle's face as if it were a ham or a large fruit, coldly suppressing recognition. Beneath the pink flesh of the double chin Eri's neck was getting stringy. He had nicked his lip shaving. Beneath his eyes lacy, velvety formations adhered like fungi and the eyes themselves looked dirty with a reddish dirt, as if you could shine them on your sleeve and make them clean again, abrupt and cold as the eyes of a pelican. Walter sat with his hands smoothing the sides of the chair. He did not have anything that seemed worth saying. He felt a heaviness, a lethargy, now, when he had expected to be angry.

"You won't mind if I go on eating? I assume you have been paroled." It was a mixed grill, kidneys, sausages, little rolls of bacon, and tomatoes. It looked very good. Walter leaned forward and took one of the sausages in his fingers but before he could withdraw his hand, Eri had jabbed it with his fork. Four little pearls of blood stood up on the back of his hand.

It was, Walter thought, only a childish reflex of Eri's to jab him but it was enough. He stood up and walked around the table. It was hard to hit a man who was sitting down. He seized his uncle by the front of his dressing gown, jerked upward, kicking the chair out from under him, and hit him in the nose, not very hard.

From the first he knew that Eri would not call for Alec. He kept one arm up trying to fend off Walter's light accurate blows and with the other hand he groped beside him on the table. Walter saw, and it astonished him, that Eri was trying to get hold of a small carving knife.

Suddenly, with this, it became a fight, not a punishment. He did not doubt that Eri would try to kill him with the knife, and by bringing a chance of death into this Eri dignified all he had done to him, for if Eri feared his revenge enough to use a knife against it, then he knew his offense had been big. He brought his fist down on his uncle's forearm and shoved him away from the table.

For a squat heavy man nearly fifty years old who knew nothing about fighting, who had taken care to know nothing about it, Eri defended himself well. He gasped steadily. His face was purple with strain but he faced Walter with his awkward hands up and he was bleeding only from the nose. Walter had intended only to cut him up and make him whimper if he could but now he knew he would have to knock him out. If he left him on his feet, Eri would stab him or break a chair over him as he turned to go. They stood in the neat room, wary and silent like strangers.

Walter led three left hands, a little slow each time to give Eri a chance to duck. Then he swung a left hook into Eri's belly, turning all his weight into it. Eri's purplish face was wrung with pain and he collapsed sideways on the floor. Walter got around behind him and hoisted him up against the mantel, where he leaned with one hand on his middle, wheezing and groaning.

Walter set himself. Eri, seeing the blow ready, seeing it start, scowled and his lips made a sneer. As Walter's right hand was shooting forward he saw the sneer. It looked like his father's face and he pulled the blow so it grazed Eri's ear. The face was rigid; it did not change from his father's contemptuous stare, and Walter shouted "Ha!" in surprise and began to chop at the nose and stubborn lips as if he would obliterate them, destroy them finally, turn them back into some primal steaming pulpy mess that had never existed as a man. Under his blows Eri slid down to the floor, Walter stooping and hacking in a frenzy. At last the head swung forward oozing dark red drops down the front of the dressing gown. Walter stepped back panting and stared at the disheveled bloody man propped against the delicate pilaster of the mantel as if he expected the desecration he had finished to crush him somehow or humble him.

Instead, he felt a curious lightness, almost a happiness. He had justified the stupidities and the tedium of his life, he did not know just how. Whom he had beaten down, Eri or his father, or, mysteriously, the two of them at once, and what burden was lifted or what insult avenged was not clear. He knew only that he felt good, freer than before. He was almost grateful to Eri, nearly willing to help him up, take him to the bathroom, and wash off the blood, apologize, shake hands, and make amends some way, but he heard a sigh not from his uncle's throat and he glanced toward the kitchen door. In it, arms folded and legs crossed with one toe pointing into the floor stood Alec, the houseman, motionless, watching him, as he had obviously watched the fight, with interest but no rancor or excitement.

"Don't call a doctor yet," Walter said.

Alec grinned. "Don't worry about a thing, Walter."

And when he glanced back from the front hall, Alec was still in the doorway but he was talking softly to Mr. Phelps, who did not hear him.

Once outside the door, he did not hurry. He walked sedately to his car like a murderer escaping in a movie, glancing up and down the street for witnesses without moving his head. He drove away exulting, thinking, "I've got to tell somebody."

The one he wanted to tell was his grandmother. It had to be someone who knew all about it, who would understand without too much explanation that he had fulfilled his dim filial duty, and in the act of fulfillment he had stopped also the source from which the duty came: the Old Man had been dead but he wouldn't lie down. Until he knocked him down a minute ago. He glanced at the overhanging trees and the wet lawns, still with their summer's green. They were not now, nor would they ever be again, the scene for a heroic occasion. That had been his childhood, a long time ago.

He stopped in front of his grandmother's house. He entered it without knocking and mounted the stairs to her room. The banister was damp and the wet autumnal weather gave the house a musty smell. He could hear the radio in his grandmother's room turned up loud. She would not hear his knock. He opened the door gently. At first he thought the room was empty.

She was sitting on the floor with her feet at one side like a girl. Before her on the carpet were dozens of little curling scraps of paper, her forecasts and prophecies. The black japanned box was beside her. She picked one up, studied it a second or two, and flipped it away from her. Beyond her through the window he could see the soundless dripping from the eaves. He watched her peck in the rubble of scraps, seize, stare, and reject. The giant voices from the radio almost shook the room. Was she deaf now? In the pale light from the window he could see broad gray streaks in her hair and her face had aged and sagged. She was nearly ninety. Kept better than most.

"Grandma," he said at his usual pitch. "Grandma!" he shouted.

She did not hear him. He went over to the radio and turned it down. She heard the silence and looked up.

"You've escaped!" she cried and scrambled stiffly up, hoisting herself by a chair arm. She stumbled through the litter of scraps. "You got away!"

This was like her, to inflate any strange occasion. "Yes. I'm out," he said, grinning.

She clasped him by both arms and put her head against his shoulder. From the sniffs and jerking of her shoulders, he could tell she was sobbing. "All you've gone through," he heard her murmur.

"There, there." He patted her shoulder. "I'm all right." The violence of her sympathy surprised him a little. The years had piled up on her suddenly.

She drew away. Her eyes were the same as ever, bright and avid. "You can stay here." It was a notion of some power to her. She began to pace the floor. She was a little lame, dropping a bit on the off fore, but she ignored it. "She's always after me about my appetite," she muttered. "I'll ask for more. Twice as much." She raised her head triumphantly. "And I can give it to you. She won't know. She's failed lately. Can't see."

"Who, Miss Baker?"

She turned quickly. "Have you seen your wife? Where's *she* going to stay? The lease is up today? Yesterday? No, the lawyer came then. This morning. The lease is up this morning and she has to go, she and Rosemary. . . . "

"Wait a minute, Grandma. I'm Walter. I'm your grandson."

[327]

A spasm of annoyance twinkled over her face. "Of course you're Walter. You've escaped and they're after you and you won't be able to prove your innocence for a long time." She kicked at the pile of scraps with her foot. "I tried to find out. I thought I put it down somewhere but I didn't. Why, of course, you're Walter. You've escaped from State's prison to rescue your wife and daughter."

"You're mixed up, Grandma. I wasn't in prison."

"Where have you been all this time, then? Don't be a fool. They tell about it every day." She flung out her hand toward the radio.

Walter suffered a kind of frantic despair. Nothing was left now, and she was to have been a spectator. He had relied on her approval. She was to have seen him accomplish what he had set out to do and praised him. And now this confusion.

"You can stay here until we hear from her. She can leave Rosemary at her mother's. I can feed you all right. You can sleep in the closet. I guess you'll have to use the bathroom at night. It's down at the end of the hall, or I can get a slop jar." She stopped and smiled. "It's all right. They'll never think of looking for you here."

He started for the door.

"Walter!" There was anguish in her voice. "Don't go out there. They'll find you. They'll arrest you." He could feel her fingers clutching at his back.

He shut the door and ran downstairs. She followed him, shrieking. He shut the front door, ran down the walk, and got into his car. He did not look back but he could hear her thin voice trying to save him, only she no longer knew who he was.

· XXIX ·

WHEN HE SWUNG his car into the driveway beside Eddie's house, he saw the garage doors standing open ahead of him. He drove the car into the garage, got out, and slammed the doors shut. Savoring his guile in hiding his car from the police, whom his uncle would certainly have sent to look for him by now, he tripped over something. It was a large square piece of brown sandstone, four or five inches thick, the cover of the Burchams' cistern. It had been there for twenty years. He had tripped over it when he had scampered through the back yard long ago, a Sioux for Eddie's Custer.

He looked around him, abandoning for a moment his guile and haste.

[328]

There was the row of old raspberry bushes against the back fence; the two clothes posts, thick as tree trunks, with the four-by-six crossarms on which, dangling, he had once tried to chin himself; and clambering over half the porch and most of the back end of the house was the honeysuckle vine Mrs. Burcham could never bring herself to prune. The ease and freedom of his childhood returned like a talisman. And because it was Eddie's back yard, Eddie was all right even if he was not one of the family—he could tell Eddie what had happened and it would be almost as good as telling his grandmother. He felt himself enormously capable, ready for anything, but without strength, weak, almost breathless. He broke into a run across the yard, leaped up the steps to the back porch, and threw open the kitchen door. He plunged through the house expecting to find Eddie or his mother downstairs. Then he heard Eddie call and he ran panting up the stairs to Eddie's room.

Eddie met him at the door in pajamas and bathrobe.

"What have you got that patch on your eye for?" Walter asked abruptly, startled.

Eddie told him about the eye, the headache, and the morphine.

"That's tough, Eddie," Walter said. "I put my car in your garage."

"I heard you. I thought it was Mother. It's stopped raining."

"I know but I just beat up my uncle Eri and I don't want 'em to find me," Walter said, grinning.

Eddie put his feet up on the bed and lay back against the pillows. He lit a cigarette. Walter stood beside the bed. "Did you hurt him?"

"He was out when I left." He straightened himself and it gave Eddie the impression that he threw out his chest. "Take that damn patch off your eye. I want to talk to you."

Eddie scowled at him, opened his mouth to protest, shut it, and jerked the patch away from his eye. Walter was leaning against the bedsprings with his knees, bouncing backward and swaying forward again and again.

"I'm even, now," Walter said. "I got even. It took a long time but I did it."

"Even with who?"

"He was eating lunch when I got there. Doesn't anybody ever get up and get dressed in this town? I sat down with him. I was hungry and I reached for some meat, a sausage, and he jabbed me with a fork. And I got up and hit him but not just because he jabbed me. I hit him for everything and now I'm even. I feel good." The bedsprings made a regular squeak as he leaned against them. A frown as if he were about to ask a question crossed Walter's forehead. "I was going to tell Grandma but my grandmother isn't very well," he finished stiffly, still swaying back and forth. "But I'm all right."

"Sit down, will you?"

As he was speaking, Walter had noticed a tree through the window, a soft maple with the first yellow leaves of fall. "It's the end of summer. What did you say?"

"Sit down. Pull up a chair."

"I'm all right."

"Stop that damn rocking back and forth. You're making my head ache."

"Oh," Walter said, squinting at Eddie as if the room were dark. "I'm sorry, boy." He turned, looking all around the room for something strange, a chair, walked awkwardly to a little straight-back armchair, and dragged it over to the bed. He sat down in it with his knees together, grinning like an obedient pupil in school. "So you're a hophead, huh?"

"Is that all you're going to tell me?" Eddie said gently. "What are you even with?"

"Oh. That. I told you—everything. I won't have to worry any more about—— You see, I was worried there for a long time. I guess it was worry. You said in one of your letters that worry referred only to the future but the future wasn't what bothered me so maybe I wasn't worrying. . . ."

"Look, would you like a drink? There's a bottle in the top drawer of the bureau."

"No. No, thanks. I don't need it. I'm fine."

"What are you going to do now?"

"Lie low until . . ."

"I don't mean today. Are you out on parole?"

"I don't think so. They don't want me back. I talked to the doctor this morning. They're overcrowded. They know I'm not an alcoholic. I never was."

"I know. But what are you going to do?"

"Get a job. Go to work. I've got to."

"Here?"

"Old home town. I was born here. I can get a job here all right."

Eddie looked up at the ceiling. "I can't read much. An hour or so a day. So I just lie here and think." He turned over on his side to face Walter. "Don't stay here. Go somewhere else. You're through with this town."

Walter seemed very tired all at once. He was sitting bent over his elbows on his knees. He did not look up. "What do you mean, I'm through with this town?"

"Have you been up to the cemetery since your folks were buried?"

Walter glanced up in surprise. "No. Why?"

"You never felt any impulse to go out there?"

"No. There's nothing there."

"Where *is* your father, then?"

" 'My father who art in . . .' "

"No. Tell me where you think he is."

"You haven't got religion just because you're sick, have you?"

"You told me when you came in you were even with everything. What does that mean?"

Now that he was calm, Walter could see how excited he had been when he came in. It seemed a long time ago, an indiscretion. He said nothing at first.

"I took the patch off my eye because you wanted to tell me something. What is it? Who are you even with? Your uncle?"

"No. Everybody."

"Who is everybody?"

"Ah, this whole damn town."

"I've been lying here thinking all summer. My mother helped me out and glad to do it. She told me nearly every single thing you've done while I was away. It's probably distorted but I could get the general idea."

"So what?" Walter sat weaving his damp fingers, hardly listening. Although he was certainly free and his elation still cheered him, he was trying to think what to do next and the prospect was gloomy. He could not hide at Eddie's very long: even if she would put up with him, Mrs. Burcham would be sure to blab. A sinister picture of a road-block filled his thoughts—the State Police car crosswise in the highway; the flashlights in his face; the arrest. If he were angry enough his uncle could find him.

Walter stood up. "Where did you say that liquor was?"

"In the top drawer of the bureau. I don't know why I keep it. I can't drink and nobody comes to see me. Assertion of independence, maybe."

Walter had the bottle out. He took a big drink. "Can I stay here till after dark?"

"Sure. Then what?"

"Why, I might go down to Toledo until Eri quiets down. I've got a little money."

"And then come back here, is that it?"

[331]

"I can get a job here."

"If you go, don't stop. You can get a job in New York or Texas or California if you try."

For the first time, Walter considered leaving the town for good. Texas and California were blank green and yellow spaces on a map, for him un-inhabited, far away, and vaguely hostile. Yet, since this morning, he was free. It was possible, as it had been in the asylum, that there were un-known friends in those strange regions waiting for him to discover them. However, he had known the furniture of this room and the vista from its window since his childhood, and if there were no friends here but Eddie, he knew at least the way in which his enemies would try to injure him. He knew the locality and in it there would be nothing strange or unexpected.

"I suppose I could," he said.

"What would your father do if . . ."

Walter threw up his head and said sharply, "I don't know and I don't give a God-damn."

Eddie looked at him blandly, calculatingly. Walter thought he looked as if he were going to hit him, smiled, but dropped the smile. Eddie turned away and looked at the ceiling. "You remember," he began in a soft voice, "when we were going to save up and buy motorcycles and go to California to hunt for gold?"

"We were kids then."

"You said once that your grandmother was always trying to get you to leave town. She can remember the Indians around here when she was a little girl. They weren't much by that time, just garbage collectors, but their fathers shot at the white men and her father's generation shot back."

"Why did you ask me what my father would do if . . ."

"Wait. I'm going to have to take some dope pretty soon and I want to get this off my chest about the Indians and the settlers. The settlers hoped for big things, and a big thing then was a water mill or ten acres of clean ground to plow, and it took all their determination, all the resources of their spirits to beat the Indians and the land sharks and the fever. . . ."

"Clean ground," Walter said contemptuously. "We've got electric lights and cars."

"But they weren't hard to get, not after your grandmother's day. When the Indians were gone and the water was clean and they had a few land laws, there was not much to make people strain, nothing they could put their hearts into. Your family and my family got off the farms as quick as they could. Now a farmer runs some risk. He's fighting the weather and he has to work hard and what he fights is bigger than he is and he knows it. That's why farmers and sailors and airplane pilots have a sort of dignity. But our families, what happened? They thought you farmed to get money. Farming was dirty, slopping hogs was hard work, you get up in the dark to do chores. They could make money easier in town and they thought—not that most of the farmers don't think so even now—that money was ease and safety. Well, they got the ease and safety and what happened? Who has any dignity? Who can you respect all the way around the way you could respect Washington or Lincoln? Who? Horse Egan? Ferry Culver? Bill Reynolds? Your father? My father?"

"Is dignity all a man has got to have, or respect either?"

Eddie looked away from the ceiling at Walter. "It's better than money in the bank, isn't it?"

Remembering his father drunk, his father's dirty pictures, his father's brutality, Walter looked down at his sweating hands and said, "I suppose so."

"We inherit more from our forefathers than they say on the Fourth of July. I think the tremendous effort they made to get set up around here, to get the water mills started, and the farms planted and the towns laid out, I think the effort got into their seed and stayed there, through your grandfather and your father and maybe it's in you and me, the effort to get things. Material things were what they needed then, all kinds of things. And our families are still breaking their necks to get things, useless instead of useful now, but it only takes a part of themselves to do it. The rest withers."

"All right. Are you telling me something? Where do I come in?"

"Your grandmother inherited the old itch to pick up and move on that brought the pioneers here in the first place. She doesn't know why. She's comfortable here and she doesn't want to move, herself, but she likes to feel her life as a show, something intense, and she thinks the moving on ought to be done—she's forgotten why. It's just in her blood. But she's been fairly happy, I think, because she's closer to the old boys."

"Everything looks better a long time ago."

"No. I think I'm right. I don't mean they were more virtuous. They were just stronger. Their lives meant something to themselves and their descendants have been doing the same things they did, getting money, getting things, because it's in their blood. They can't help themselves. But the things, they don't mean as much as they did—they're just signs you've got money. When you had to hack a home out of the woods, you had to think of everything you take for granted now—weather, water, the soil, neighbors for help or company, all those things. Nowadays you buy a house—it's not the same thing. Until you've lived in it, a house doesn't mean anything. To your great-grandfather a house meant a lot before he built the fire on the hearth."

Walter sighed. "Well, maybe you're right."

"None of this means much to you, does it? You can't feel it, can you?"

"It's all true, I guess but—what time will your mother come home? Will she want to put her car in the garage?"

"I'll fix that. Just listen to me. The reason you went around here imitating your father, the reason you *became* your father . . ."

Walter sat up straight in his chair. "What the hell are you talking about?"

"Am I right? Think a minute."

"Eddie, you talk a lot of crap." It was the return of his old arrogance, a resentment that anyone should criticize a Phelps, but he was sorry as soon as he said it because the resentment had been part of the duty he owed to his father and that had been accomplished.

Eddie had shut his eyes. The pain was coming up in his head in long slow waves but he did not want to interrupt the tension of the conversation by taking a shot of morphine.

"You said you were worried about something for a long time, only it wasn't worry because it had nothing to do with the future. What was it?"

"I was getting even for what they said about my father. They hated him."

"Didn't he deserve it?"

"I guess I didn't stop to think."

"Did you love him?"

"I didn't even think of that. He was my father; I was part of him. Everything they said about him, they said about me. I thought he was"— he glanced at Eddie in acknowledgment—"respected, but he wasn't."

"And so you imitated him. You tried to *be* your father and you tried to insult everybody right back. That's what he would have done."

"Yes. That'll do to explain it. The funny thing was, I got tired of doing it. Whatever I didn't inherit from my old man, that part hated it. It was a hell of a chore to be nasty to everyone."

"But you got even this morning. When you hit Eri, you hit the whole town."

"Yes." Walter stood up. "You won't believe this. I don't believe it myself but—you know Father and Eri looked a little bit alike. There was a family resemblance. Ever notice it?"

"You'd know they were brothers."

[334]

"I had Eri propped up against the mantel and I was just ready to lay one last big punch on him, and, I'll hand it to him, he sneered at me. He lifted one lip and it looked just like Father."

"You hit him?"

"I wanted to kill him. I must have hit him a dozen times."

"Because you were hitting your father."

Walter nodded. "It's a hell of a thing."

"Do you see why you've got to leave this town?"

"I don't see that it follows any of this, no. There are people that don't like me here but it doesn't bother me now."

"If your father had lived, what would you have done? Stayed on at the bank. Maybe married that Wickham girl. If you did what was expected, you would have been president of the bank and it would have been easy work. And even if you'd sweated at it, all you would have got out of it would have been more money. But none of this happened. You were left all alone and there was no obvious job for you to do, certainly nothing that would take everything you could put in it. You were an heir, in a small way, but an heir. All you had to do was get through each day, so what do you do to use yourself up? You put on a show in your own private arena. You start monkeying with your relationship with your father. It wasn't conscious but I think it was deliberate. You call it revenge, and just to keep busy you make a damned fool of yourself."

"All right. Hit me again. I can take it."

Eddie rubbed his temples with his forefingers a moment. "You and I are already too old to change this kind of town much. We were born and brought up in it and it has tainted us. And there is nothing in the way we were brought up that suggests to us anything worth doing except to repeat our fathers' lives, that is, to get money because we have inherited our ancestors' fear of the fever, the wolf, and the Indian hiding at the edge of the woods, and we think we can throw money against them all. We are preparing for a catastrophe that can't happen because the wolves and the Indians are gone. And if we make the grade and get all this money, all we'll do is sit on the porch of the Country Club after we retire and feel cheated, wondering what we did with all our time, resenting the hopes we had that told us once there was something big to do."

"I see what you mean."

"But do you agree with it?"

Walter went over to the front window and looked down into the street. A woman was going by carrying an umbrella stiffly over her head although it was not raining. Her face was hidden but Walter recognized her by her gait. It was Mrs. Ormsbee, who had belonged to his mother's bridge club, a widow. She waddled from side to side as she had done for twenty years.

"I guess I had always figured on doing just what Father had done but I always thought, too, that somehow I would amount to something besides that. It would happen."

"That's what they all count on—their luck. They don't try to make anything happen. I would like to make people lead better lives but I don't know how so I keep it personal."

"Better how?"

"Less narrow. Not happier necessarily. Fuller."

"Not here."

"This part of the country is rich and weak and it's made us rich and weak along with it. I know I could join the church or the Communists or Socialists and work my head right off but the upbringing I have had keeps those things from being very real. I can't believe in them. They seem vague and faraway. And I doubt if they would do any good if all of us here believed in them and the reason I doubt and don't do anything about it is the way I have become. I have got far enough to talk but the habits of this town would paralyze me, and you, too."

"I'm going," Walter said. He turned around from the window.

"You know why now?"

"I know why."

"Better wait till dark."

"I know the roads out of here. If they're going to patrol them on my account, they can catch me in the dark, too."

"That's true." Eddie got up off the bed. "So long, boy. Write me a letter."

They shook hands.

"Look, Walter . . ."

"Yes?"

"Do something great."

Walter grinned. "I see what you mean. We've got so it even sounds funny to say it."

"That's right."

"Come on with me. Lam out of here together."

"I couldn't."

"Well, I'll see what I can do. Good-by, Eddie."

Walter went out. Hastily, his hands trembling, Eddie got out his kit and made himself a shot of morphine. He did not hear Walter drive away. Then he lay down.

It had been the biggest effort of his life, and if his will should fail him, a possibility he admitted, it might be the only big effort of his life yet he did not quite believe all he said. It was not necessary for all to leave, an exodus of closed cars, trucks, and pickups was not required. Some kind of full, decent, useful life could be made by anyone anywhere, if he could first conceive of such a life and tried to live it.

But not Walter. He had the coarse strength of his family. He could break new ground, but where it was old and sour the defects of his family would make him rot. As his friend, it had been his duty to send him away, where, as a surrogate, Eddie recognized with a selfish shamefaced pleasure, he could attempt the kind of greatness his own sickness denied him. He had been able to change Walter's flight into a search. Eddie was sure he had been kind and helpful but it came to him suddenly in the empty house with the rain beginning again that he had sent away the only friend he had.

ABOUT THE AUTHOR

ALLAN SEAGER *was born in Adrian, Michigan, February 5, 1906. He moved to Memphis, Tennessee, when he was eleven years old. He lived there until he went to college at the University of Michigan, and, later, to Oxford University. Following that, he was one of the editors of* Vanity Fair *magazine for a year and a half, and is the author of the highly successful first novel,* Equinox. *He has traveled in Europe and South America. At the time of writing, he has a wife and two daughters.*

tr 1-17-49 Pay book